IN HER OWN RITE

In Her Own Rite

ROWAN WILDER

BRONWYN
BOOKS

For Arnica.
Friendships are their own kind of love story. Thank you for the love you pour into everyone around you, including me and this book.

In Her Own Rite can be read as a stand-alone romance, but it was written as part of the Fakari Islands series—a collection of romances that, together, chart a bigger story for the islands. You don't need to read other installments in the series to enjoy this book.

For those who do want to read the bigger story, a quick note on chronology. While this is the first Fakaris book to be published, it's the second in the in-universe timeline. That's intentional! *Worth His Salt*, chronologically the first story in this universe, is scheduled to release in June 2024. There's a preview chapter at the end of this book.

As you read, you might wonder if you're starting in the right place. The answer is yes! (And, for my fellow Star Wars fans, I'm sorry for the déjà vu. I believe it will be worth it!).

THE WINDSWEPT
FAKARI ISLANDS
HALLU
HALLUK HOUSE
NORTH HARBOR
SAROE
THE RING
THE CLIFFS
TEMPLE
MOON LAKE
FIKARIG
COMMON HOUSE
SOUTH HARBOR
WESTEL
OESTER
HALSSEL

FAJJE
THE RUINS
MARIT
KEIST
TOWARDS THE
DISTANT SOUTHERN ISLES

The Fika

and extended family and friends

A *fika* is a Fakari pack unit, usually made up of three to five families, who share pack life together. The names of official members of the *fika* are bolded in the family tree below. Other members of the extended family and community are also shown.

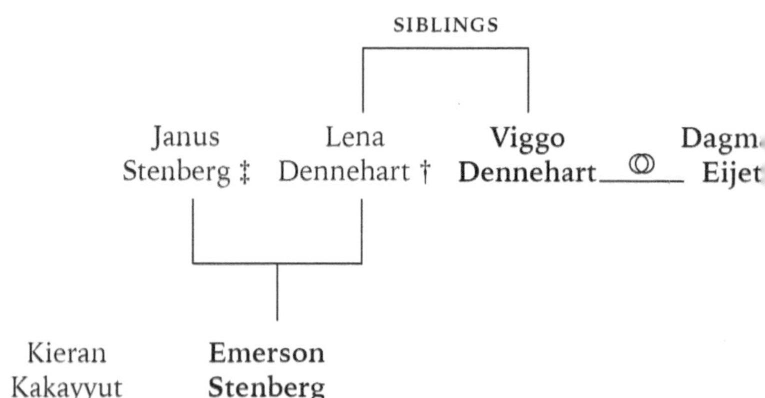

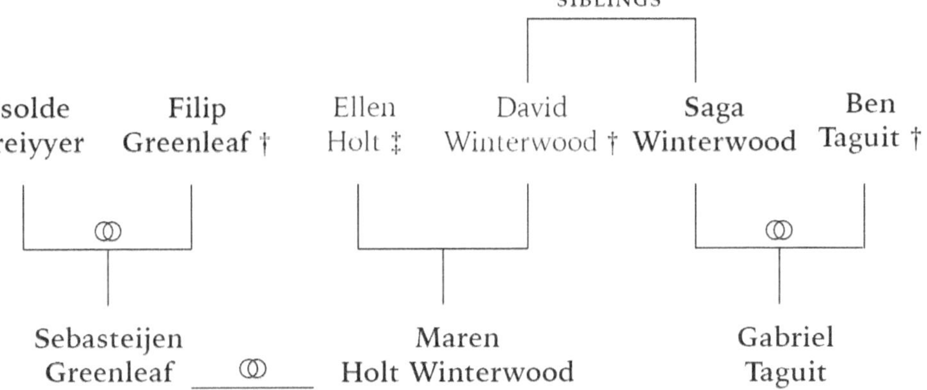

SIBLINGS

Isolde
Freiyyer

Filip
Greenleaf †

Ellen
Holt ‡

David
Winterwood †

Saga
Winterwood

Ben
Taguit †

Sebasteijen
Greenleaf

Maren
Holt Winterwood

Gabriel
Taguit

KEY
† Person is deceased
‡ Person is estranged
⦿ Mates

SENSITIVITY WARNING

In Her Own Rite is a steamy friends-to-lovers shifter romance. Readers should know that it contains elements that may be personally difficult for some, including domestic violence (occurring before the book begins, but shown through memory) and descriptions of physical violence in hand-to-hand combat. There is also explicit sex shown on page—always consensual, and always enjoyed by all!

For a full list of trigger warnings, which will include spoilers, please see **rowanwilder.com/ihor-cw**. If you would like to ask about a specific trigger without risking spoilers, feel free to DM me on Instagram at **@rowanwilderromance**.

1

EMERSON

We're in the water.

It's the start of summer, and even at 8 p.m. the sun is only just starting to make its way down the sky. The lake water is rich and warm, and the surface sparkles with light so bright it's almost blinding. Seb, Kieran, and Gabe are swimming around the shallow end, laughing and jumping at each other while I tread water a little farther from the shore.

I look up at the forest across the lake and notice a gray shadow through the trees. It fades in and out of view, but the shape feels familiar. I start to swim towards it to get a better view, even as my mind realizes: *it's a dream. It's a memory. Come back.*

"Mom," I hear myself say, quietly enough that the guys won't hear. The bottom of the lake drops off as I get to deeper waters. My hair is floating around me, long and golden, and it brushes against my shoulders the same way the weeds do against my feet.

Don't go, my mind says. This is a memory I've dreamed

through a hundred times. I know how it plays out, and still, each time I try to wrestle myself to a different ending. A different story. It never works.

The shadow disappears behind a tree. I swim farther, faster. The guys are far enough behind me that they can't hear me now.

"Mom!" I call out to her. "Mom, come back!"

For a moment I think that she's gone for good, but as I come closer, she emerges from behind the trees slowly, like a mirage. She's wearing the dress I last saw her in, dark blonde hair spilling over her shoulder. She tilts her head, looking at me tenderly.

"Emerson," she whispers. "Oh, baby." She kneels down to crouch by the water's edge, as if to be closer to me.

I know it can't be real. I know she's dead. But Aunt Saga always talks about the spirits of the ancestors staying on the islands, and for a moment I believe—

Something in the air shifts. I look up and see thick, dark clouds gathering ahead where there was sun and clear skies just a moment ago. The shadow of the cloud falls over me, and the water around me grows cool. A low wind rustles over the edge of the water.

"Mom...?" I say. But as I turn to look back at her, it's as though my body already knows.

In the place where she knelt is a wolf, head low, bearing its fangs at me. His sinewy frame and matted fur gives the appearance of something sick, but even the hunger pangs visible in his thin body can't mask its muscle and sheer power.

I know *exactly* what he's capable of.

The air escapes my lungs. I try to swim back, but it's like I can't get enough air. I thrash as the wolf steps to the water's edge, his golden eyes taunting me.

"Help!" I try to call, but the sound comes out like a whisper. The wolf snarls and comes closer, and for a moment I think this is it, and he's going to kill me. But suddenly I feel a pair of strong arms wrap around my waist, pulling me back.

"Hey," says Kieran's voice, low and warm in my ear. "Hey, you're okay. You're okay, I got you."

I gasp and turn to him, climbing onto his body, my legs wrapping around his waist and my arms round his neck. "Kieran," I say, feeling the adrenaline pounding through me. "Kieran, help, get me away—"

"You're okay. You're okay," he says, his voice rich and reassuring. "What happened? I saw you swim out and then you just froze. Did your leg get caught?"

"No, my dad—"

I turn around and point to the clearing in the trees, but it's empty now. I look around and realize the clouds are gone. It's warm and sunny again.

"He's gone, Em. He can't hurt you anymore."

"No. It was real, I swear."

"Okay," he says gently, nodding.

I look up at Kieran's face: broad jaw, for the first time in our lives sporting a brush of stubble. He's a year or two older than me, and his golden skin is glowing with the first hints of this year's tan. His body is so warm. I can practically feel his heartbeat through his skin, soft and steady, bringing me back down to earth.

I meet his eyes, hazel and gold.

"Sorry," I say. "I shouldn't be like this anymore. It's so embarrassing."

"Nah, no worries. When I'm here, you're always safe, okay? I'll always keep you safe."

I look over my shoulder at the trees and the clearing, and for a moment I swear I see a brush of something between the firs. But it wasn't real—it can't be. The only thing that's real is Kieran and his arms around me, holding me together.

MY EYES OPEN SLOWLY, and the first thing I do is look to the window to see the sky. It's cloudy and overcast, *takkagaayu*—thank God. It won't be clear enough for the rite tonight. That means Kieran has at least one more day to prepare. Not that he thinks he needs it.

I turn to look at him, lying beside me in bed. He's in his human form, so I must have slept well last night. When I wake up in a panic, he'll often shift for me, taking the form of a big, fluffy white wolf so I can curl up next to his fur and feel small and safe.

Kieran has the biggest wolf form of anyone I know. His human form is pretty big too: 6'5, his frame broad and muscular from years spent training in the gym every day with Seb. I'm grateful for it, in a way. Knowing he's strong enough to take on the world helps me feel a little safer.

I rest my head close to his, taking in the unique scent of amber, leather, and wood that seems to soak into his skin from hours at the workshop. Most people on the islands have crafts or trades on the side to make ends meet next to their regular jobs. Kieran is one of the only people I know who's been able to turn his trade into a whole career, crafting furniture that sells for a small fortune on the mainland. He started apprenticing just after we finished high school, and finished his training on Keist, one of the smaller islands, around the time I began training to be a healer with Aunt Saga.

The nights he spent on Keist were some of the last we spent apart. We never talk about it. I've never *asked* him to spend the night, and he's never commented on the fact that we've been sleeping platonically side-by-side for years. We're not "sleeping together," regardless of what people like to whisper behind our backs. And he's not pining for me, waiting for me to finally look up at him and take notice. *I wish.*

I scooch closer to him, admiring the way his red-gold eyelashes flutter gently in sleep. My eyes run over his heavy brow, the broad, blunt cheekbones, and a strong jaw that's covered by a thick beard where his teenage stubble once was. The spray of freckles over every part of him the sun touches. I've loved him for years, even before that day in the lake. And to him, I'm just Em. I know because—no matter what we've gone through together—he'd rather go out with half the islands than even *look* at me that way. He's out with a different girl every weekend, staying out as late as three or four in the morning. But no matter what he does with them, he always comes home to me, smelling of soap and a fresh shower so I don't need to scent them on his skin. Small mercies, I guess.

Kier turns in his sleep and rolls onto his side to face me. As his large body moves in our narrow bed, one arm curls under his head, and the other comes to rest between us. I look down at his hand, admiring the strong fingers, the veins running along the backs of his palms, and the thick brush of copper-gold hair running up his muscular arms. I slip my hand beside his, pale and slender in comparison. I wonder how it would feel if he held my hand in his. I wonder how it would feel if he held *me*.

In a moment I imagine his body over mine, caging me in, pressing himself against me. His knee nudging my legs open; his thick fingers finding the crest between my thighs and slipping into me. His mouth on me, tasting me…

At the thought, a ripple of pleasure runs through my body, and I feel the warm hum of desire start between my legs. I swallow and sit up, making myself think of something else. My heat will be coming up soon, and it's already making me run hotter than usual. As soon as I'm turned on, any shifters around me will be able to tell. And if Kieran knew I was getting wet next to him in bed? *Mortifying*.

I stand and turn towards the closet, stripping off my night clothes and pulling on a pair of blue scrubs for my postpartum client checkup today. Smoothing my hair back into a ponytail, I grab my phone from the bedside table, where it sits next to the training salts I set out last night. Then I slip out of the room, heading downstairs before I can wake him. If he's doing the rite in the next few days, he should be getting as much sleep as he can.

I get down to the living room and walk towards the large kitchen, where I see Saga at the counter, making coffee.

"*Morlaa'kut*," she says, smiling at me. Her dark hair, streaked with silver, is pulled back into its signature side braid, and her golden skin crinkles at the eyes as she sees me. She's still in her robe, sage green linen tied at the waist over old flannel pajamas.

"*Morlaa', Aja*," I say. *Morning, Aunt.* She's not my actual aunt, but I love her just as much as my uncle Viggo and his wife, Dagmar, who took me in when I was nine. They're the reason I live in this *fikarig*—the large home shared by the few families that make up a *fika*, or pack—in the first place, along with Saga and her son Gabe, and Seb and his mom, Isolde. Saga's niece Maren first came to the islands last year, and once she and Seb realized they were mates, she moved in permanently.

"Did you sleep well?" Saga asks, reaching for a mug to pour me some coffee.

"Yeah, fine."

"Great. You'll need your rest, with our rounds today and the rite coming up soon."

"You think so? It's been cloudy all week. It could still be a while."

She glances up from the coffee she's pouring and gives me a look. "What are you afraid of? All the elders have done this and lived to tell the tale. He'll be fine."

I chew on the inside of my cheek.

"We've just never done something this big without each other," I say finally. "If he gets hurt, I can't help."

"He's a big man, Emerson. He can take care of himself."

She hands me the hot mug of coffee and gestures for the

kitchen table. I take a seat, curling one leg under me and putting the other up to rest my chin on my knee.

"You weren't nervous for Seb's rite?" I ask.

"Of course, but I had no reason to be. Seb is strong, and he took time to prepare. Kieran has, too."

"But Seb… got hurt," I say carefully. He's walked with a limp since the night of his rite, four years ago now. I can see how Saga looks at him sometimes, watching him with pain in her eyes. He may not be her son by blood, but the people that make up a *fika* become one family. He might as well be.

"Well. We cannot avoid pain. We can only walk through it with courage."

"Is that what you tell yourself?"

"To get through? Yes." She smiles softly, and I can see the sadness in her eyes.

Saga has lost a lot in the last twenty years—a husband, Ben; her brother David; Seb's dad Filip, who lived in this *fika* before he died and was like a brother to her. If it's true that pain makes you stronger, it must be why she's the strongest person I know. And maybe it's part of why I relate to her so much.

I swallow. "Tell me again how it'll go."

"You know how it is, *piu,*" she says. *Loved one.* "You can ask me a hundred times, but it's not going to prepare him, or you, any better."

"I don't care. It'll help me worry less. Tell me, please."

Saga sighs and takes a sip from her mug. "The *reijna,* the wise woman, will know on the morning of the rite that it's time. That's me now, but for my rite, that was still your grandmother."

"And how do you know?"

"The ancestors tell you. I'll feel it in my bones." She raises her mug to me. "You'll see for yourself soon enough."

I shake my head. "No, I'm not anywhere near that yet."

"All healers are sensitive to it. I started to get the feeling when I was about where you are in your training. It wouldn't surprise me if you do, too."

"Maybe." I take a sip of my coffee. "So you know it's the day. And then what?"

"I tell Kieran and the elders. He gets ready with his training pack, and you and I prepare the *kattaka*. That evening, a few hours after the sun sets, we do the ceremony. Then he climbs up to the cliffs alone, so it's just him and the lights in the ring."

"And then he'll fight," I say quietly.

"And then he'll fight."

I swallow. The rite is styled after the founding myth of the Fakari people. The story goes that a hero named Tayyakuk sailed the seas for ten years, searching for a place to call home. He found the islands, but the moon goddess Móra had fallen in love with him and wanted him to stay on the seas so they could be together. She brought storms and disaster, trying to keep him away from our shores. After three nights, he finally reached them and climbed to the cliffs, where he challenged Móra to a battle for the right to call the islands home.

They say she took the form of a wolf and they fought through the night. Finally, as the sun began to rise over the horizon, Móra admitted defeat. And because Tayyakuk won, she gifted him the power of the wolf, and promised to protect the islands as long as his descendants lived here.

Our ancestors built the ring at the edge of the cliff where they fought. Now anyone who wants to assume a parent's seat on pack council needs to climb to the ring and fight for the right to do so, the same way Tayyakuk did. The ancestors take the shape of your greatest fear to make you prove your worth. You either beat whatever form they take, or you outlast them until sunrise.

If you win, you become an elder.

If you lose, the sea awaits below. But that hasn't happened in years.

I take another sip of my coffee, thinking it over. I used to believe it was all myths and legends. *Kattaka* is an herbal drink that makes you hallucinate; it's basically like a bad trip. But that doesn't explain why some people return from the ring covered in cuts and bruises. That doesn't explain why some people don't come back at all, or some—like Seb—carry an injury for the rest of their lives. It can't *all* be in your head.

"What form did the ancestors take for you?" I ask quietly. I can't meet Saga's eyes as I ask this, and look pointedly at my coffee. Her voice comes like a cold wind.

"*Emerson*. You know I can't tell you that. Come now, finish your coffee, and then we'll get going on our morning rounds. Linnea will be waiting." She stands and heads for the stairs to get dressed.

I stay at the table to finish my coffee. As I do, I think of Kieran in that ring. Fighting his demons alone in a way he makes sure I never have to.

2

KIERAN

I wake up hard as a rock, with Emerson sitting on the edge of the bed next to me.

I can smell the scent of her arousal in the air, rich and heady. She gets up to change, moving quietly so she doesn't wake me. She's trying to distract herself, I can tell.

Takkagaayu. I don't know if I can handle having her near me in that state.

I pretend to stay asleep as she slips off the old T-shirt she was sleeping in and steps into a clean pair of scrubs. I keep my eyes closed, willing myself not to take a peek at her as she changes. She's been trying to hide it from me—keeping her distance during the day, and rubbing herself with creams and lotions to mask the scent—but I can tell her heat is coming up and it's already sending me out of my mind.

She ties her hair back and walks back to the bed to grab something from the table beside me. As the scent of her comes nearer, I can feel my inner wolf panting, and almost need to suppress a low groan. It's hard enough to stay away from her the *rest* of the time. Last year when she went into heat, I took a trip to visit my dad on the north island just to keep my distance without going feral for her. This is around this time I usually need to get out of here to preserve my sanity—but since I've started my training, I probably shouldn't leave the island until I complete the rite. And she can't take a well-timed vacation until then either, because she's doing my *kattaka* ceremony. So now my ancestors and her hormones are playing some fucked-up game of chicken and I'm losing my goddamn mind.

Finally, Em slips out of the room to go downstairs. As soon as the door closes behind her, I roll onto my back and look at the ceiling, willing my body to calm down. I try to think about anything else—new orders at work, the gym, my rite coming up —but it's not about my thoughts so much as the scent of her, and the warmth of the sheets she's left behind.

I grip myself to relieve some of the pressure, and resist the urge to stroke myself. I *will not* think about her like that. I never do. At the same time, it feels wrong to think about anyone else. So, instead, I don't get off, and I work out all my aggression in the gym. If Emerson had any idea that *she's* the reason I work out three hours a day, she'd never look me in the eye again.

I turn over and reach for my phone, sitting on her bedside table. Unlocking it, I scroll through the text messages I've gotten since last night. There's one from Caspar, the guy I hired for my woodworking business, letting me know we got a call this morning for a custom dining set. The other is from Sofie, a girl I went out with a few nights ago, asking if I'm free tonight.

I sigh. Another embarrassing habit I've picked up trying to blot my feelings for Em from my mind. I must have gone out with a hundred girls in the last few years, looking for anyone who makes me feel even a hint of what I feel when I'm with her. All those nights end exactly the same: without so much as a kiss, and with me trying to calm my inner wolf down in a freezing cold shower before I slink back to Em's bed just to feel her body near me. Like a wuss.

I should text Sofie back, but I don't know what to say. Instead, I put my phone back on the bedside table, where I see Em's laid out the salts for my training regimen, alongside a glass of water and a note. I pick up the paper.

New salt makeup for rite week!
2g smoked salt, 1g ancient salt, 1g rosemary.
Good luck training today. Don't skip breakfast.
- Em

A smile tugs at my mouth, imagining her preparing these for me before she went to bed last night. Generations of Fakari elders have followed a strict, multi-step salt ritual as part of the training for their rite, since the salts are believed to have special healing and protective properties. But I'm probably the first to have a healer prepare them for me as part of her bedtime routine.

I sit up and sprinkle the salt on my tongue, letting it dissolve before I take the water to swish it down, then pick up my phone and get to work responding to work emails. After about twenty minutes, I finally hear Em and Saga leave the house, and I get up to get dressed. I change out of my flannel pajama pants into gray sweats and a clean gym shirt, sitting folded on a chair in the corner of the room.

Em's room is simple, almost spartan. Her small wooden bed, barely a double, is fitted in plain white cotton sheets. The furniture is all the same stuff that was here when she first moved in. I've asked her before if she wants me to make her a nicer desk—something with enough space for her stuff, maybe a drafting table for painting—but she said no. The only thing in here that betrays any piece of her is the watercolors she's blue-tacked to the wall.

I pull on a sweater and look around at them, admiring the little windows into her world. There's her favorites: purple flowers; the view from the window; a portrait of the gang at the quarry where I first met her. A painting of the aunts—Saga, Dagmar, and Isolde—on a walk through the woods. Maren, laughing in the sun. And then, lying face-up on top of her desk, my favorite: her and me at the quarry on the north island.

I walk over to her desk and look at it again. In the painting I'm in my wolf form, looming large and powerful over her. A protector. She sits in front of me, one knee brought up close to her chest, in her human form as always. Her head leans back against the fur of my chest, and she's gazing happily out at the water. It might as well be us today, but I know this memory—it's us the summer I left for Keist. *That* night, during Fire Week ten years ago.

The painting sits in a dark mahogany frame that I made for her last birthday. I thought she'd love it, and *she* did thank me, but she's never hung it up. Next year I guess I'll get her a bracelet or something.

I clear my throat, putting it out of my mind. Turning back to my pile of clothes on the chair, I tie my hair back into a knot and text the guys to let them know I'm up.

Kieran: looks like today's not the day.
ready to get one more training session in?

Seb: You said that yesterday, dude. You're
ready. Take the day off.

Gabe: Seb's just saying that because he's
tired of you wrestling him into a headlock
every four minutes

Seb: I'm saying that 'cause I'd like to
spend my day off with Maren instead of
your sorry asses.

> Gabe: @Kieran, I'll meet you at the gym in 20

"Woah," Gabe says as I land a punch in the bag he's holding up. "Slow down. Not so hard."

I land another punch with the other fist, and he stumbles back.

"Hey, cool it," he snaps.

"Sorry," I say, using the back of my arm to wipe the sweat from my brow. "Sorry, man. I'm just in my head."

"About the rite?"

"Yeah," I say. Half true.

"Nervous?"

He sets the bag down, signaling a break. Reluctantly, I drop my fists.

"Nah, I'll be fine."

"You're *not* nervous?"

"No, I'm not," I say, and I mean it. I walk to the edge of the boxing ring to grab my towel and water bottle. "I just want to get this over with and get back to my normal training."

I can see him roll his eyes as I take a swig of water. When I take the bottle from my lips, he's still watching me, waiting for me to explain.

"Come on. What should I be nervous about?" I ask. "We've been doing this for hundreds of years. How bad can it be?"

"You're kidding. You saw Seb when he came back."

Reflexively, my jaw tightens. The morning Seb came stumbling back down the cliffs changed everything for me. It's the reason I came back from Keist. It's the reason I practically moved in to Em and Seb's *fika*—or, that's what I try to tell myself. It's why I spend so much of my time trying to keep the rest of us together. Safe.

But Seb isn't me, I want to say. *Seb didn't train as hard as I have.*

And if I'd been in his training pack, he would never have ended up like this. But instead, I swallow and say,

"Well. We'll see what the ancestors have in store for me."

"Any guesses?"

"Nah, man. You know me. I'm not afraid of anything." I give him a wry grin.

"Come on, you can tell me. What have you and Heimig been working through?"

"Seriously, not much," I say. Heimig is the elder assigned to help me with my mental preparation for the rite. "We just sit in his kitchen and he tells me about the glory days. I think all that mental prep is kind of bullshit anyway. Meditation and therapy isn't gonna help you fight a bear into submission."

"So you're preparing for a bear?"

"No. I'm preparing for a fight."

Gabe sighs. "Fine, don't tell me."

"Come on, break's over," I say, setting my water bottle down and stretching my arm for another round. "Get the bag up. Let's go."

3

EMERSON

S aga and I finish our postpartum visit close to eleven, and I consider it a win that there's no spit-up on my shirt.

"I'd like to check in on Anja, too," Saga says as we walk across Linnea's front yard towards my bike. "She had a bad fall last week and I want to see if she needs any help around the house."

"Oh, okay. I'll come with you." We reach the stone wall separating the yard from the main road, and I lean forward to unlock my bike.

"No, why don't you head down to the shop already, and I'll meet you after? Anja's farm is just next door, and it'll be faster for me to get to Moon Lake, anyway."

I feel my mouth twist, but I nod. In wolf form, it only takes five to ten minutes to get to the apothecary from here. With my bike, it's closer to twenty.

It's not that I *can't* shift. It's that I don't want to—*ever*. Saga never pushes me, or makes me feel like I'd be better at my job if I could keep up with her during rounds. But still, I can't help but think that if I were strong enough to do it, I'd be less of a drain to the *fika*, and a better support for the islands.

"Sure, makes sense," I say, keeping my voice light. "Then I'll head down to the shop already and meet you in a bit. Give Anja my best."

Saga gives me a nod and rolls her neck to prepare for the shift. I see her pool her concentration, and then her body folds forward, almost as it's collapsing inwards on itself. In moments, she's taken the form of a large gray wolf, fur streaked here and there with silver just like her braid. The flowy teal shawl she was wearing earlier is still slung around her body, and her stretchy, loose-fitted brown pants are kept in place by her tail, which emerges through a slit at the base of the tailbone.

Saga shifts often enough to accommodate it with her wardrobe in the old way, with loose-fitting clothes. Most of the younger wolves wear clothing with metallic clasps now. A benefit of me never shifting? I can wear things that actually fit.

She dashes off to Anja's house, and I get on my bike to make my way to Moon Lake. It's a misty morning, cool and windy, and the mossy hills are less vibrant than in the spring and summer. The whole islands turn gray in winter, and January is the grayest month of all.

I glance at the sky as I near the forest. Still thick with clouds —no rite tonight, for sure. But still, there's a feeling forming in my gut, heavy as a rock. Maybe Saga's right, and it's the ancestors letting me know it won't be long. I swallow at the thought.

I pass through the woods, heading in the direction of the hot springs and the lake, and finally into the town center. The storefront for Moon Lake Apothecary is close to the outer edge of town, near the woods and the lake for which it's named. I make my way over the cobblestone streets towards her shop, and park my bike outside. Through the window, I can see Maren sitting behind the counter on her laptop, one knee curled under her and the other propped up on her chair.

"Hey girl," she says as I walk through the front door, the bell tinkling behind me. She's wearing a cream Nike sweatshirt today, with bold patterned silk pants and her curly brown hair piled high on top of her head. Maren grew up on the mainland, and you can tell from her clothes, which are way more interesting than anything most of us wear.

"Hey, morning," I say. "I thought you were off today."

"I was supposed to be, but Quinn's helping the guys move some product for the salt business, so Saga asked me to fill in for her."

For a second, I want to ask why they called Quinn in to move boxes when she lives halfway across the island, but I don't bother. I might always be willing to help, but I'm not strong enough to be of much use.

"Anyway," Maren says. "I figured I'd sit here and start on the labels for the new salt scrubs."

She turns her laptop towards me, and I lean over to take a look at her latest design work for Seb's company, Saroan Salts.

"You *just* started this?" I ask, and she nods.

"They're gorgeous." I turn my head to read the labels. "I love the color palette." The original line of salts have deep teal and white labels, but Maren has mocked these up in soft, dreamy pinks and purples, with gold foil setting the logo apart from the background.

"Aw, thanks. I wanted something that felt a little softer for the bath products. I think they're gonna be a huge hit."

"I'm sure."

Maren moves through life like a hurricane. She's had practically a dozen different careers already, and every time she sneezes it's like a new product falls out. Seb's business exploded after she came to the Fakaris, and the whole island is benefitting from their success.

"How were rounds?" she asks me, turning the laptop back towards her.

"Nothing special. I just came back to the shop to put together some new products for this week."

"Cool, I'll help!" She closes her laptop cheerfully.

I press a smile. Normally I love Maren's effervescent personality and tendency to talk—and ask—about literally everything. But not today.

"Oh, it's fine, it won't be anything interesting. Stay here, focus on your work."

"Please, I want to. I haven't seen anybody all morning, and with the weather I don't think anyone's stopping in before Saga gets back. Let me keep you company before I leave to see Seb. Come on, you can teach me!"

"Okay," I say reluctantly. There's no way I'd win a disagreement with Maren, even *if* I knew how to speak up for myself. I head for the curtain separating the storefront from the workshop, and she follows me in.

The scent hits me as soon as we enter. Rose water, cardamom, and shea butter. Along one wall are heavy apothecary cabinets made of deep brown walnut; against the other, a white countertop wraps around half the room, with a large kitchen island in the middle. I see Saga's left out some stainless steel bowls and measuring cups on top, presumably for the healing salves for Kieran's rite.

"What are we making?" Maren asks, picking up a bottle of essential oil from the apothecary cabinet. "Please say it's lip balm. These winters are killing me."

"Not today. I'm making some salves for Kieran, since his rite is coming up. And I want to make some creams for me."

"Ooh, fun!" she says, putting the vial down. "Just for self-care?"

"Uh, yeah. Something scented," I say, reaching for the bergamot, grapefruit, and cedarwood essential oils—the most powerful scent-masking oils we have. I put them next to the clean silver mixing bowls on the island, along with coconut oil and cocoa butter. Then, for Kieran's salve, I walk back to the shelves and take down three large jars of amber liquid.

"What's that?" Maren asks.

"These are almond oil infusions I started on a few weeks ago," I say, bringing them to the table. "Calendula, plantain, and comfrey. If you mix them with beeswax, you make a nice balm that's good for burns and skin irritation."

"You think he'll get *burned* up there?"

"Honestly, I don't know. But we always make it, just in case."

"Damn, this place is crazy. I have no idea why you put yourselves through this. Well. I guess I do." A shadow falls over her face.

"Hey, it's okay," I say, trying to make my voice reassuring. "Kieran would be doing this anyway, even if you and Seb hadn't met."

"Right. But he's doing it *now* because we met, right? So, in a way..."

She shakes her head side-to-side with a guilty expression, as if to say *It's my fault.*

"No, it's just how pack life is. As soon as the younger members of a *fika* start finding their mates, you choose three to do the rite, so we have enough council seats to get our own *fikarig* someday. Seb only did his early because his dad died, and we wanted to make sure we could keep our current *fikarig* if anything happened. If it weren't for that, he'd be the one going into the ring this week, not Kier."

"I guess."

I reach out and put a hand on her arm. "Kieran's not doing it *because* of you. He's doing it *for* all of us. So that, when we have three council seats, we can get our own place one day."

"Alright, alright. Thanks. I just feel guilty 'cause, like, Kieran didn't even want me here to begin with."

I nod. The Fakaris have been isolated from the mainland for generations, and letting Maren in from the States—even when she's half-Fakari—was a big deal. The council was evenly split on the vote, and she was only allowed here because she had living family on the islands. It took Kieran a while to warm up to her, but now they love each other—and bicker—like siblings.

"Yeah, but it's totally different now," I say. "We all love you. And we *want* to get a house together. Think of it this way: with how much Seb and the *fika* elders are arguing, you're doing us a favor. If you weren't here, we wouldn't have thought to move until way later."

"I guess. But still, it's a big deal. And I guess I worry, because of…"

She gestures wordlessly, and I nod.

"None of us saw what happened with Seb coming," I say quietly. "It's not usually like that. It won't be for Kieran. Especially because—" I try to make my voice playful. "This salve is way better than whatever chemical garbage you guys use on the mainland."

She laughs. "Neosporin, probably."

"Yeah, way better than Neasparing. Now come on, I'm gonna show you how to make it. Watch, you'll be ready to start selling these yourself in less than a week."

Maren laughs.

"That was a joke," I add. "Don't get any ideas."

I show her how to strain the oil infusions using a cheesecloth, and together we pour what's left into new, sterile jars. As she writes the date on them, I start to boil some water at the stove on the counter, and get to melting the beeswax in a double boiler.

"What does the bergamot do?" Maren asks, picking up the little essential oil vial.

"Oh, that's not for Kieran's stuff." I keep my gaze on the beeswax as it begins to shine.

"It's for your moisturizer?"

"Mhmm."

"Yeah, I noticed you're wearing more perfume lately."

I feel my face grow warm. Maren is a shifter, but she's new to the islands and isn't familiar with a lot of her own strengths, let alone our culture. Which means she can smell something different about me, but doesn't know how to identify it—and more importantly, not to ask.

"Yeah. I'm going through some stuff. The creams are supposed to help."

"What kind of stuff?"

"Oh, you know. Like an annual thing," I say, hoping she catches my drift.

"Your birthday...?" she asks, like she wasn't here when we celebrated it in the summer.

I give her a look, my cheeks hot. "Come on. Seb or Saga never talked to you about this?"

Maren puts a hand on her hip and cocks an eyebrow. "Uh, I have no idea what you're alluding to, so how would I know?"

"Has anyone ever... did anyone ever talk to you about *heat?*" The last part comes out like a whisper.

Maren's brow knits for a moment, and then her eyes go wide with recognition. "Oh. *Heat.*"

"Yeah, that's... that's what's going on with me. Or, will be soon. I only expect it in a week or two, but I'm already... noticing the effects."

"*Interestingggg,*" Maren says, sitting down on one of the bar stools before the island. "Like what?"

"I'd rather not talk about it."

"Are you, like, horny all the time?"

"Maren!" I say, and it comes out like a little yelp. *Agaayu.* Mainlanders and their openness.

"What? I haven't had, like, true werewolf heat yet or whatever, but I spent 27 years as a normal human woman before I came here. I know how hormones work. Come on, you can talk to me. What's it like?"

My whole face goes red, and I gesture wordlessly for the almond oils we strained earlier. Maren grabs them and walks over, and I measure out one-third cup of each and dump them in.

After a minute, she nudges my arm.

"Come on. It's gonna happen to me, too, right? So why can't I know?"

I swallow.

"Yeah, it's… like what you said," I say finally. "It happens once a year, for about a week. During that time your sex drive is really high. But in the weeks before, the feeling already builds up, like… like an energy, growing in your body. You notice other people more, in a physical way."

My mind flashes to Kieran. His broad shoulders and strong arms. His stupid-hot abs. At the very thought, I feel a rush of desire flood through my body and force myself to focus on the wax in front of me.

"Cool. So is *that* the thing I'm smelling when I'm near you? What is it, like citrus and…" she cocks her head.

"No, that's the cream I made," I say awkwardly. "It's supposed to mask the scent. Anyone who's pack can tell when you're going into heat, so I try to cover it a little."

"Anyone can tell? Isn't that embarrassing?"

"I mean, yeah. But most pack members didn't grow up in America, so they don't ask about your sex life quite so openly." I give her a look, and she laughs.

"But yeah, it's a little weird," I add. "Once you're mated, you and your partner take a vacation during your heat so you're not around other people. Sometimes the unmated women take a solo trip, just to lay low for a few days."

"So why not you? Free vacation, right? You could go to the house on the north island," she says, grinning. We took Maren to the *fika*'s summer house for Fire Week last summer.

I shake my head. "I want to be here for Kieran's rite. And, I guess more than that, I want to be here *after* his rite, in case he gets hurt."

"Good for you," she says, smiling. "You're such a good friend."

Right. Friends.

I look down at the pot before me, where the cacao butter and coconut oil are slowly blending together for my scent-masking cream. I unscrew the bergamot essential oil and add one, two, three drops, then do the same for the grapefruit and cedarwood. As it mixes together, I feel the warmth from the steam on my face and tilt my hand to let another two drops fall in.

This year, I need all the cover I can get.

4

KIERAN

abe and I finish training around one. We've been going easier this week at Seb's insistence, so I can save my strength for the night of my rite. Which blows, because the scent of Em this morning set me off in a bad way, and I need to take the edge off. After the training session, I shower and get dressed, then head to the woodshop to work off the last of my energy.

My workshop is at the heart of town, a few streets over from the forest and Saga's apothecary. When I get there, Caspar's at the scroll saw, cutting something for a dining set. He has his ear protectors on, so I give him a nod and head to the loft to work on some of the new designs. Once I'm upstairs, I set my bag down and put on my own hearing protectors to work in silence.

I pull out the folder of yesterday's sketches. My most recent project is a wedding arch for a mainland couple who's been on my waiting list for over a year. Apparently the brides are both fans of my work, and they're letting me design whatever I want. I spent yesterday on the shape of the arch, and today I start designing the details: grapes carved into the upper arches, half-open pomegranates along the sides. Sparrows and doves carved into the support beams, flying upwards.

I love carving and the physical part of carpentry, but designing is hard for me. Whenever I get stuck, I remind myself what I'm doing this for: saving up so that Em and the rest of the gang can all get our own place. The same reason I'm doing my rite.

I start designing the first dove, and within ten minutes, I'm lost to the world. It's only when Caspar appears next to my desk that I look up.

"Hey, I'm heading out," he says as I remove my ear protectors. "Do you want me to close up shop, or are you staying late?"

"Man, I lost track of time." I look out the window to see a dark sky, then glance at my watch—five-thirty. Em and the others will be heading back to the *fikarig* soon for dinner. "Nah, I'll head out with you. Thanks for checking in."

I pack up my stuff while Caspar makes sure our machinery is unplugged and the power switches are off. Grabbing my jacket, I head downstairs and step onto the street, into the cool night air. He follows and turns off the lights, locking the front door.

"Are you heading to your place?" he asks. "Otherwise we can walk together." His family lives in a *fikarig* not too far from the studio apartment I rent in town.

"Oh, no. I'm eating with Emerson and her *fika* tonight. I'll go see if she's still at the shop. *Aftnu'kut.*"

We wave goodbye and I walk towards the apothecary. The shop lights are off, but I see a glow coming from the curtain separating the storefront from the workshop behind. As I walk through the front door, the bell tinkles behind me.

"Hey. Em?" I call out. I hear nothing in reply, but the smell of whatever she's making back there hits me like a ton of bricks. Citrus, beeswax, something like chamomile…

"Em?" I call again, and walk behind the counter, pulling the curtain to the workshop to the side.

She's alone, standing in front of a row of clean metal tins with her headphones on, carefully pouring some kind of golden mixture into each one. I walk around to come up beside her, not wanting to startle her if she can't hear me. But she's so focused that, even when I move my hand in her peripheral vision, she doesn't look up.

"Em," I say loudly, but she's still pouring.

"Em." I wave again, then reach out to lightly touch her shoulder. Instantly she gasps and nearly drops the jug she's holding. I reach out to steady her hands.

"Sorry, sorry. I didn't mean to scare you." At the look in her eyes and the rapid rise and fall of her chest, I feel my inner wolf grow agitated. She sets the jug down and reaches up to remove her headset.

"*Heij*. Sorry, I didn't hear you. I was in the zone." She smiles apologetically, and my gut twists.

"No worries," I say. "I was just heading back to the *fikarig* and I wanted to see if you needed a ride."

"Is it dinner already?" Her brow furrows as she looks down at her wrist. She's not wearing her watch, and at the realization she looks around, scanning the table. For the first time I look down at what she's making.

"What's all this?"

"Oh, it's for you. For your rite, I mean. I want to make sure we're prepared."

"Em." I grin. "If you think we're gonna need *this* much healing salve, then you have no idea how hard I've been training."

"It's all I can do, you know? To help."

"Hey, relax," I say. "Don't be so worried. I'm gonna be fine."

I wrap my arm around her shoulder in what's meant to be a reassuring hug. But the second I do, something in the air shifts. The smell of whatever she spent all day making was enough to mask her scent until now, but as soon as her body is too close, I can *feel* her, the edge of her heat brimming just under the surface. I drop my arm like I've been burned, and turn my body to look at literally anything else.

"Oh hey, your watch," I say, my voice coming out surprisingly raw. I pick it up from where it was hiding behind a mixing bowl and return it to her open hand without touching this skin.

"Thanks," he says, her voice light. Unaffected. It kills me. "And thanks for stopping by to get me. I'm on my bike today, so I don't need a ride."

Takkagaayu. I don't think I can handle being under her when she's this close to her heat.

Em never shifts—I've only seen it once in my life, on a day I try not to let myself think about. The islands are made for shifters, so Em being functionally human makes for some complicated logistics when getting around. Typically when we're moving as a pack, I let her ride on my back so she can keep up. The rest of the time, she takes her bike. Thank the ancestors she has it with her today, honestly.

She closes up shop as I wait outside. Once Em mounts her blue bike, I remove my clothes and shove them in my bag so I can shift. She looks away as I change, and I hand her my bag to hold onto as we ride out. Then my body snaps forward into my wolf form, and we head for the *fikarig*.

IT'S a full house when we arrive. I shift back and snap on my clothes on the porch, and I can already hear laughter coming from inside the house. After Em locks up her bike and leads me through the front door, we're hit immediately by a wave of light and sound, and the smell of rich, heavy food.

"*Heij, piu,*" Saga says, walking into the hall and spotting Em. "*Et welkommit,* Kieran. Lovely to have you over for dinner." She gives me a barely-perceptible wink, as if I don't basically live here.

"*Takka*," I thank her. It smells like venison and something else —bread? Rosemary? I look over Saga's shoulder at the dining room table, where Gabe is carrying a tray of freshly-baked rolls from the kitchen. I can practically feel my stomach flip with hunger.

"You must be starving after this morning," Saga says. "I'm pretty sure Gabe finished all our leftovers after the workout you gave him today."

"Sounds about right," I say, eyeing the bread.

"You see that, Emerson? He's practically looking through me."

Em hangs up her coat and smiles up at me, and my stupid wolf curls up happily at the sight. Saga gestures towards the table and we follow, walking to the dining room with her coming up behind.

Seb has set the table, and as we enter, his mom, Isolde, comes from the kitchen holding a large pot of stew.

"I guess everyone's here," Maren says.

"No, we're still waiting on Dagmar and Viggo," says Em, taking a seat beside Isolde.

"Oh, they'll be late. Finishing up some business at the common house."

Seb looks up. "Yeah? What's up?"

"Ah, it's nothing," Isolde says. "There's a new petition from some people on the southern isles, seeking asylum. We declined their last request, but they sent another plea."

Saga takes the pot from her and serves herself, then passes it across the table to me.

"The southern isles?" Maren asks. Out of the corner of my eye, I see Em stiffen. I serve myself a large helping of the stew, then pour some into Em's bowl for her.

"Some unincorporated islands, about 200 miles south of here," Isolde says, putting her napkin onto her lap.

"Oh. Are they like us?" Maren asks. "Shifters?"

"...*Iija*," Saga says carefully. *Yes.* "But they're not *pakka*."

Maren looks confused, and I cut in.

"They're shifters, but they're not pack. They don't belong with us."

"Let's talk about something else," Gabe says, glancing at Em. "We're having rosemary venison stew with root vegetables for dinner, and I made rolls from scratch. Enjoy."

The pot makes its way around the rest of the table, and I eye my own plate hungrily.

"So what are they, then, if they're not Fakari?" asks Maren. "I've never even heard of the southern isles before."

"They're politically independent," Seb says.

"They're a *non-entity*," Isolde corrects. "And culturally, they're practically feral."

"They don't approve of any contact with the mainland," Saga adds, her voice gentler than Isolde's. "We were allies of sorts, until Seb's father and your father, Maren, moved to open the Fakaris together in the eighties. Then they broke contact."

Gabe clears his throat. That's not the whole story.

"So how come they want to come here?" Maren asks. "If they don't approve of us."

Gabe shakes his head. "Can we not do this now? I worked hard on this dinner and I want us to enjoy it."

"There's no 'them,' Maren," Isolde says, and I can practically feel the tension coming off of her. "They have no culture. They're just a collection of feral packs on unincorporated territory. *Some* of them want to come here, and I'm sure *some* of them want our heads on pikes. It's not happening."

"Isolde, *kuunalle*," Saga says quietly. *Calm yourself.*

"It's fine, really," says Em.

"It's not fine," I say. "We don't have to talk about this at dinner. We can also enjoy the meal Gabe spent two hours making. Come. *Kututkuk*."

I lift my glass for the toast, signaling the start of the meal.

"*Kututkuk*," they repeat.

I dig into my stew, and *umph,* it's so fucking good. So good that the conversation completely leaves my mind, until—

"Can someone explain to me why you're all being so weird about this?" Maren asks.

"Can we just eat?" I ask. Seb and Gabe may be interested in island politics, but I couldn't care less. But as I feel my inner wolf pace in annoyance, Em gives me a look.

"My dad lives on the southern isles," she says, turning to Maren. "He was sent there after what happened with my mom."

"What?!" Maren's eyes go wide. "I thought your dad was dead."

"He should be," Isolde mutters.

"*Ama!*" Seb snaps. *Mom!*

"He's not dead," Em continues. "He was sent there as punishment."

"He's not allowed back here, *piu*," Saga says gently. "Even if we were to let in the asylum-seekers from the south—"

"We're not letting them in," Isolde says.

"*Nekka*, we're not," Saga agrees. "But even if we did, he still wouldn't be allowed back."

"I'm not worried about that," Em says, but I can hear the tension in her voice. My inner wolf growls at me, wanting me to put an end to this.

"Hang on," Seb says. "I thought we voted on this ages ago. Why are we talking about it now?"

"You're right, it's the same group from the earlier vote," Saga says. "They reached out again, after they heard that…"

"Heard what?"

"After they heard we let someone into the islands."

Seb sets his glass down with force, and Gabe and I give each other a look.

"*Maren?*" he snaps. "We got a new asylum request because of

Maren? Why am I only just hearing about this? I'm on council, too. And this is about my mate."

"This isn't about Maren, it's about opening up the islands," Isolde says firmly. "It's not a new decision. We're just upholding the last decision we already made."

"Why do they want asylum?" Em asks quietly. Everyone ignores her.

"It sounds like a new decision to me," Seb says to his mother. "Otherwise, why are Viggo and Dagmar late? What kind of work is there to do to uphold a decision we already made?"

Out of the corner of my eye, I see Em's posture shift, her shoulders tensing.

"Dude, cool it," I say to Seb, my tone firm. "We're having dinner. Get your wolf in check."

Seb gives me a look and I recognize the beast in his eyes. It's a losing battle—I can see that already.

"I'm a pack elder," he says to his mom, ignoring me. "I'm on council, same as you. I have the *same* rights to information and decision-making. Why am I only hearing about this now?"

"Our laws on letting people in are clear," Isolde says with a sigh, waving her hand. "This isn't worth voting on. It's a non-issue."

"Our laws *were* clear until we had to decide on Maren, and then suddenly they weren't. Now we're seeing the ripple effects. If there's a decision to be made, it should be made by pack council. The *whole* council."

"He's not wrong," says Saga. Isolde gives her a look.

"I completed my rite *four years* ago," Seb continues. "Kieran will be doing his in *days*. We're ready to take on the mantle of pack leadership. I'm tired of being treated like my role on council is advisory. I deserve to have a vote."

"There is no vote," Isolde says.

"I have the same question as Emerson," Maren interjects. "Why do they want asylum?"

The table goes quiet, and I can still feel Seb seething. After a moment, Saga says,

"They say the packs there have fallen into tyranny. The southern isles don't have the same infrastructure or resources we do. Apparently things are getting scarce, and it's putting them under additional strain. There's been an uptick in violent crime."

"We should let them in," Maren says.

"It's not so simple," says Saga.

"No, Maren's right," says Em next to me.

"What?" I say, unable to stop myself. "Are you serious?"

"*Iga'ait*," Saga says with a sigh. *Pups.* "This is not a discussion for dinner."

"We're not pups anymore, Saga," Seb says. "And you're right, it's a discussion for pack council, but I guess we were kept out of that discussion, so we're doing it here. Kieran, you're against?"

"Kieran's not *on* pack council," Isolde says dryly.

"He will be next week."

Em looks down at the table, and I see her shoulders come up, like she's walling herself in.

"I'm shutting this down," I say, putting my hands on the table. "Gabe worked hard for this meal, and *some* of us spent three hours training today. I'm starving and I'm not letting dinner be ruined by council in-fighting. Take that shit to the family room after dinner."

I give Seb a look, and he glowers at me. I take a gulp of my drink as an awkward silence falls at the table.

"So. What else is up this week?" Gabe asks. "Em, how was work?"

"Um, it's good. We, uh, had rounds. And then I taught Maren how to make healing balm."

"That's nice," says Isolde tightly.

I glance at Seb, who's clearly struggling to get his wolf under control. Maren has a hand on his knee and is muttering something to him.

Fuck. That one's on me.

"I'm working on a new wedding arch," I say, trying to make my voice sound easy.

"Tell us," Saga says.

I tell her about what I have in mind, and slowly, the tension eases from the air. Gabe cracks some jokes here and there. After a while I see the tension ease from Em's shoulders, and my own inner wolf is finally able to cool it. But by dessert—Gabe's outdone himself, with brownies rich enough to tranq an elephant —things still feel unsettled, and no one stays long after dinner. Seb leaves for the temple, and Saga and Isolde agree to take a walk together. Gabe, visibly frustrated, asks Em and me to clean up so he gets the chance to clear his head.

"I should probably get to bed, too," Em says as we pile up the last of the dirty dishes. "I've had a long day, and I think I feel a headache coming on."

I nod. It's not a headache. The smell of her heat is getting heavier, and as the hours pass since we were at the apothecary, her little creams are doing less and less to hide it.

"No worries," I say, carrying the plates into the kitchen. "I should let you get some rest. I know my rite will be big for you, too, with my *kattaka* ceremony."

"Oh, yeah. Of course. It'll be good for me to get some real sleep." She starts running the sink, ready to wash the first of the plates as I set the stack down.

"Actually, Sofie had suggested doing something tonight," I say. "So if you need me out of the way…"

"Oh. You're seeing Sofie again?" There's something weird in her voice, and my wolf snarls at me, unhappy.

Stop it, I think. She made her wishes clear. And spending some time apart with her heat coming up will be good for both of us.

"Yeah, maybe. I don't know if she's still free. Here, let me finish up," I say, and gently nudge her out of the way of the sink. "You go get some rest. I hope your headache gets better."

"Are you sure? I don't mind."

"I mind. Let me do this for you."

"Okay," she says softly. Her voice is tender, and I feel something twist in my gut. "Thanks, Kier."

She knows better than to hug me before she heads upstairs.

I text Sofie after I finish cleaning up, and we agree to a drink at the bar across from my place. She's gorgeous, and I try to have a nice time, I really do. I even have every intention of going back to my own place to sleep tonight. But after we say goodbye and I head to my apartment, my wolf won't let me rest. I lie in bed and feel him prowling, snapping at me, demanding that I get up and go to *her*. Em. I close my eyes and try to block it out, but after a few hours, it's clear I'm not winning this fight.

Sullen, I go to the shower and set the water to ice cold. Under the water, I scrub my skin raw until I can't feel the weight of my need for her. And then I slink back to her house and crawl up beside her, pulling her body near me so I can finally, finally rest.

5

EMERSON

I wake up the following morning to see the sunlight streaming into my room, pooling on the floor like honey. The feeling I had in my gut last night has grown heavy, and with a sinking disappointment I realize this is what Saga told me to expect: the knowing in my bones. Tonight is the night for Kieran's rite.

I shift, stretching, and it's only then that I realize I can't move. Kieran is behind me, his body pressed to mine while his arm hangs around my waist. And I can feel something hard pressing against my hip.

Oh my God.

"Kier," I whisper, trying to push his arm off of me so I can get out. But he's too big, and the more I push against it, the more I end up pressing my body backwards onto him.

I feel his erection pulse as my body unintentionally presses against it. At the sensation, a wave of warmth rolls through my body, and I can feel wetness starting to pool between my legs. *Oh God. Oh no.*

"Kieran," I say again, more frantically now as I try to push myself away from him. But at the motion of my body he just groans and pulls me closer, still clearly deep asleep. His face buries into my shoulder and I can feel the heat of his breath and the scratch of his beard against my skin. I let out a low moan, and I feel my breathing grow heavy.

"Kieran, please, wake up," I say, my voice labored. But it's too late. I'm so close to my heat that even the feeling of his body against mine is enough to send me tumbling into desire. As soon as he wakes up, he'll be able to smell it in the air.

God, this is so embarrassing. A blush creeps up my face and neck, and I make myself lie perfectly still, hoping that I can calm down before he wakes up. But a minute later, his erection pulses against me again and my stupid body, betraying me, can't help but react. I let out a gasp and my back arches. My head dips back, falling against him.

Stupid hormonal brain.

I can feel his weight shift behind me as he wakes up. For a second, half-asleep, he pulls me closer, and then he freezes.

He can smell it. He knows.

"Please let me go," I whisper.

Within seconds I'm free and he's pushing himself back against the wall, putting as much space between us as possible. I scramble forward, falling off the bed, clutching the blanket to my body as though it will save me from the humiliation of what's happening.

"Em. *Agaayu*, I'm sorry, I was asleep," he says.

"No, it's okay. It's not you, it's just my stupid body…"

I feel a prickle run over my skin and a warmth blossoming in my stomach.

"I'm so sorry, this is so embarrassing. Please don't look at me," I say, clutching the blanket to me.

"Em," he says. He's breathing heavily too, I realize. Without wanting to, my eyes fall to his sweatpants, where I can see his erection straining against the fabric.

It's huge. *Of course* it is.

"I guess this was bound to happen at some point." I try to laugh and keep my voice light as I turn my back to him, so I can't see the way his body is reacting to mine. "I shouldn't be going into heat for another week or two, but this year I just get... set off more easily than normal. I don't know why. Please don't judge me."

"No, it's okay. This... happens to everyone," he says, his voice husky.

"Don't try to make me feel better, okay? It's fine. I've had to deal with this before, you just haven't been around to see it. I'll be okay. Just get out and I'll see you later today, okay?" I try to keep my voice lighthearted and innocent, to mask the sound of my labored breathing.

"Em," he says. I can hear him climbing out of bed and stepping closer to me, coming up behind me. My body basically hums as he gets close.

"I can help," he said, his voice rough. "It doesn't have to mean anything. We can... we can take the edge off."

His hands brush against my hips, so gentle my mind goes hazy. But then I think of Sofie, or whatever other girl he was out with last night until three in the morning.

It doesn't have to mean anything. How many women has he made this same offer to? How many women has he helped through their heat?

"No," I say, shaking my head firmly. "No, no. Get out and I'll get dressed and I'll see you at the ceremony."

"The ceremony?" His hands fall from my body.

"Yeah," I manage to grind out. "Your rite is tonight. Now get out."

I stand there, fighting to keep every muscle in my body still, as I hear him gather his clothes and walk out of the bedroom to leave me.

6

KIERAN

When I go downstairs, Saga's already in the kitchen with Maren and the guys.

"Kieran," she says cheerfully. "Big day for you. Maybe Emerson already said?"

"Yeah. My rite."

"Ah, good, so her skills are getting stronger," she says, nodding with satisfaction. "I've already told the elders, and Gabriel has made a breakfast with enough protein to last you a week at least."

She gestures to the stove, where a large pan of scrambled eggs and sausage awaits me. Next to that is a jug of thick Fakari yogurt, with honey drizzled on top for flavor. I walk over and start piling the food high onto my plate.

"Nervous?" Seb asks from the kitchen table.

"No," I say, and my voice is still low and rough with sleep. I'm reeling from what just happened with Em, and it comes out gruffer and more aggressive than I mean it to.

"Haven't you heard?" Gabe jokes. "Kier's not afraid of anything."

"Oh, really?" says Seb. "So that time we found a bed of snakes near the quarry and you screamed like a girl, that was performance art?"

"Something wrong with being a girl, Seb?" Maren asks from the doorway, where she's sipping her coffee.

"Abso*lutely* not," he says, as Gabe snorts into his coffee.

I take a seat at the table, digging into my eggs. I can't fucking *believe* I came onto Em like that. What the hell was I thinking? For years we've been careful, keeping the boundaries we needed to to make our friendship safe and dependable—*for her*. And in five minutes I've gone and rubbed my dick all over them.

I groan and run a hand over my face. She's not even in heat yet, and I'm already acting like a feral teenager. Disgusting.

"You good, man?" Gabe asks.

"I'm fine."

Seb takes a sip of his coffee. "Must be that lack of nerves he told us about."

I'm about to reply when I feel a heavy hand slam onto my back, and almost choke on the eggs halfway down my throat. I look up to see Em's uncle Viggo, standing there with a grin on his face. He's in his early fifties, hair an icier shade of blonde than hers, his face tan and weather-worn.

"So, *jenge!*" he says jovially. "The day of your rite is finally here. Never has a stronger man made his way up the mountain."

"Don't encourage him," says Gabe.

"What? This young man has been training since before his father said that he wanted to give up the seat. I don't think I've seen someone this prepared to meet Móra in my lifetime."

"Oh, Kier here is a master at preparation," Seb says, leaning back in his chair. "I'll never forget the Biology presentation where he tried to cover the gaps in his knowledge with Fast and the Furious lore. What was it again, Gabe?"

"The mitochondria is the NOS of the cell," he and Gabe say together, and bust up laughing.

I keep my head low and focus on scarfing down my breakfast as they joke back and forth. After a minute, Saga's hand appears in my periphery with the salt mix for the day of my rite. I take it from her and let the salt dissolve onto my tongue, then wash it down with water. Finally, once the food is done, I stand up.

"I'm taking a walk."

"Don't you need to prepare?" Maren asks, looking up. "What about your day-of ritual?"

"Hey, it's your rite today, man, save your energy," says Gabe.

"Nah, I need to clear my head. I'll be back," I say, and walk out.

THE WALK DOES nothing for me, and I head for Saroe's common house in the mid-afternoon. The *kattaka* ceremony will be just past nine, but before that, it's the guys' job to help prepare me. We go through the five-step ritual to prepare my body for the rite: salt scrub, sauna, cold pool, followed by stretching and hydration. Seb tacks on some meditation—it never works for me, but at least it helps me relax a little after the shame of the morning.

I skip dinner, the usual practice on the day of your rite. After Seb and Gabe have eaten, they return to the common house with my mentor, Heimig, and Ivo, one of the island marshals who I know from the gym. Together, the four of them complete my training pack. They help me loosen up and focus, until it's time to get into my fighting gear. For that, I head into the wooden changing rooms alone.

As a kid, you imagine you'll meet Móra dressed as a Viking, covered in chainmail and heavy breastplates, but no. I pick up the clothing that's folded on the wooden bench: my wool base-layer, and on top of that some synthetic body armor—good against knives, claws, and teeth. That's the only special item. On top of that goes my shirt and a light wool sweater. Seb and Gabe have already packed my rucksack for me: water and a small amount of food, bandages and salve, a hunting knife, and some rope. You can choose to bring bigger weapons, but anything you take into the ring can also be used against you. And besides, I don't need it.

I strap the knife to my thigh and pull on my outer layers, snow pants, and backpack. Just before nine, Seb walks into the changing room.

"Em's here already, with Saga and the *kattaka*," he says, shutting the door behind him.

"Great," I say, lacing up my boots. "I'm ready."

"You know, it's okay to be nervous."

I give him a look. "What is this? Did they send you in here to get me all emotional before I head out?"

"No," he says, crossing his arms. "I came to give you some last-minute advice."

I nod, waiting, but he hesitates. I feel the air grow heavy. The weight of his rite still hangs between us—at least for me.

"Sit," he says finally, and gestures for the wooden bench. I do as I'm told, and he sits next to me, leaning his forearms on his knees.

"Listen, I... I can't tell you how it's gonna be," he says, and I can hear the rattle of nerves in his voice. "But I can tell you not to make my same mistakes, okay?"

"Yeah, sure."

He's silent for a long minute. I can tell whatever he's about to share is as much for him as it is for me, so I wait.

"The body armor isn't made to shift," he says finally. "So don't let your wolf take over if you haven't taken it off. If you rip through it, it's useless. It won't do anything for you, even if you use it to shield yourself."

I nod, trying not to imagine whatever he went through up there—alone, without protection. Without his pack.

"And..." He hesitates, then sits up straight and looks me in the eye. "It's gonna fuck with you, whatever it is. Maybe you won't be surprised like I was. But whatever shape the ancestors take, it's gonna mess with your head. Don't let it shake you. Don't show weakness. And whatever it is, don't give in."

"Okay…" I say again. If I'm honest, I have no idea what to do with this. I can see it means something to him, though, so I nod like it lands.

"Are you ready?" he asks.

"Yeah. Let's roll."

We stand, and I follow him out into the ceremonial hall.

The room is familiar to me—this is where we have all the pack council meetings, and I've been to many to listen in, even if I couldn't vote until now. But it looks different tonight, half-empty and shrouded in darkness. As we near the entryway, I see the healers in the center of the room, gently illuminated by lanterns resting at their feet. The men in my training pack—Seb, Gabriel, Heimig, and Ivo—line up on either side of the entrance, and other men from the council fill in the sides, forming a path that leads me to the healers.

I stand in the entryway, waiting. Once both lines have formed, the men on either side begin to beat their chests and thighs in unison. They stomp their feet, growling and snarling, performing an ancient dance I haven't had to learn, since I wasn't here for Seb's rite. As they begin chanting in Fakari, I walk towards the wise women, the way Heimig instructed earlier today.

Son of Tayyakuk, valiant warrior, the men chant. *It is time for you to prove your worth. It is time to earn your place on the islands.*

I look up at Em. *Agaayu.* She looks so beautiful standing there, waiting for me. The second I see her, I can't look away. Her long blonde hair is loose and wavy, falling around the slight curves of her body. She's wearing the same kind of robe as Saga and Helen, the other healers. It looks strange on her, foreign and overly formal after years of seeing her in mostly loose cotton dresses and oversized sweaters. But it suits her, somehow; the rich color and heavy drape highlight her face—delicate, ethereal. Like an angel, I think.

I walk towards them as the voices of the men grow louder. As I reach them, Em steps between the other healers and me and looks up, her big blue eyes meeting mine. I see her swallow with nerves as she lifts the black stone bowl in her hands up to me to drink.

"Kieran Kakayyut, son of Tayyakuk," she says, and lifts the bowl to my mouth. "May the ancestors guide you and uncover your weakness. May you rise to the fight. May you wrestle into submission the weakness within you and return to us."

She tilts the bowl back, and the *kattaka* spills into my mouth. The taste is bitter, the texture is thick with herbs, like the last dregs of badly-filtered coffee. I choke it down with a cough, and feel it slither down my throat and into my stomach.

"You have your pack behind you, and the ancestors before you," she says. "But you must make your way up to the ring alone. We'll see you in the morning. *Agaayit ikka.*" *Gods be with you.*

I turn to leave the hall, strangely uneasy from the formality of the ceremony. I can somehow feel the *kattaka* already, coiling like a snake in my stomach, forming something in me that's not of me. As I reach the outer door to the building and step into the cold night air, I hear a sound behind me. I smell her before I feel her hand catch my wrist.

"Kier, wait."

Em's voice is quiet, just for me. I turn around and she's looking up at me, her ocean-blue eyes wide. I can smell the fear on her, wrapping around the scent of her heat and essence.

"Here. This is for you," she says, and hands me a black hair tie that she's removed from her wrist.

I take it from her, bewildered, and she wraps me in her arms and pulls herself into my chest.

"Be safe," she whispers in my ear, and I can hear the nerves in her voice. "Come home in one piece, okay? Promise me."

"I promise," I say, and pull her close. I take a deep breath, and maybe it's the *kattaka*, but for a second, the moment feels bigger than both of us. I can feel something in her, beneath the fear. Sadness, both hers and mine, but I don't know what for. And then, in a moment, she's gone, pulling away and giving me a nervous smile as she turns back to the common house.

I put the hair tie around my wrist and turn to head for the cliffs.

THE JOURNEY UP to the ring isn't steep, but it's long and winding. The *kattaka* hits you fast; I can feel the edges of my vision grow soft as I reach the first resting point. As I look up, I see the first traces of the *kiyyulit*—the Northern Lights, as mainlanders call them—beginning to appear on the horizon, dancing gently above the cliffs. They seem more vibrant than usual, as though they're pulsing with energy.

It takes an hour or so of hiking before the ring starts to come into the view. The large rocks marking the outer edge jut out against the black sky, and my breath fogs in the air like mist. It's icier up here, bone-cold and quiet. As I near the ring, the *kiyyulit* are stronger than ever, almost neon, dancing with frenetic energy. I can see them pooling in the ring like vapors, their shape obscured by the rocks marking the perimeter.

My vision is softer now and I feel a little hazy. I've talked a good game, but now that I'm actually here, I can feel the dull hum of nerves in my chest. My inner wolf is stressed, pacing back and forth, growling in agitation for whatever's in there.

Cool it, I think. The only enemy is fear. *Especially* here.

I take a swig of water from the bottle Gabe packed for me, and slip it into my rucksack. With the other hand I feel for the knife strapped to my leg.

I can do this. It's just one night. For the pack, for Em. For us, and our future.

Then I turn the corner, and head for the arch that marks the entrance to the ring.

As I walk in, the lights are so bright they're almost blinding. They start to swirl around me, encircling my limbs like smoke, like magic. My wolf panics.

It's the kattaka, I think to myself. *You're seeing things. There's nothing here.*

But then I look up and I see her. In the middle of the ring, maybe some thirty feet from me, is a woman looking out at the vast expanse of the sea below. The outer edge of the ring is empty, the cliff's edge raw and unencumbered by rocks.

The woman is made of light and mist. The *kiyyulit* wrap around her like thin layers of translucent fabric, blue and green and purple, dancing over her skin. But it's not just her clothing— her whole body is glowing, pulsing with energy.

"Móra," I whisper, walking towards her and falling to my knees. Is *this* my challenge? To wrestle the Goddess herself, like Tayyakuk?

She turns around slowly, eerie, her hair floating around her as though she's in water.

"You," she says. I look up as she steps closer, raising a finger from a lazy hand. Her face carries the shadow of something familiar. For a second, in motion, she looks like Emerson, but it's not her. The goddess is older, her bone structure stronger, her eyes dark.

"You can't save her, you know," she says. Her voice feels like it's coming from a thousand miles away and from inside me all at once.

"What?" I ask, woozy.

"Emerson. You know you can't save her," she says, stepping closer to me. "No one can. After all, look what happened to me."

And that's when I hear the growling behind me.

7

EMERSON

I can't sleep.

Each time I close my eyes, I think about Kieran in that ring. I think about Seb, the night he went to go fight. How me and the guys stayed up until two in the morning, drinking and laughing, excited to welcome him home as the first elder among us. The look on Gabe's face when we saw him stumbling down the mountain, covered in blood, a huge gash in his left leg. The frenzy around us as the healers decided this was too much for their magic, and he had to be transported back to the mainland. The sinking in my gut as I realized: he might not make it. We might lose him.

The heat that's been brimming in my body for weeks feels softer now, edged out by my anxiety like humming in the background. The only thing I feel on the surface is fear, blind and feral.

I sit up in bed and look out of the window, in the direction of the cliffs. You can't see much from my room—it's too far away, and we're facing just the wrong way—but I can see traces of the *kiyyulit* above us, dancing their way towards the highest cliff's

47

edge. There's no way I could see any of what's happening from here. But maybe if I go upstairs, to the library…

I slip out of bed and make my way to the bedroom door, then into the hall. It's dark and quiet, and in the cold of midwinter I can smell the last of the smoke coming from downstairs, embers of a fire in the hearth that we were all too anxious to enjoy. I take a deep breath, stilling my mind, sensing. The quiet is deceptive; most of the *fika* is still up. Seb is tense, I can feel it. Gabe is somewhere, numbing a sadness. And Maren?

I head up the stairs to the third floor, then down the hall to the library, where there's a turret that goes up one more floor for a view of the west side of the island. As I open the door, I see a light in the corner of the room, and slippers at the base of the stairs.

Looks like she had the same idea I did.

I close the door softly behind me and walk towards the turret to peek up the spiral steps.

"Hey," I say. "Can't sleep?"

"Nah."

I climb up the steps to find her with her knees curled up against her chest, an open book sitting beside her, ignored. She's looking out of the window, in the direction of the cliffs.

"I'm still not used to it," she says as I crawl to sit next to her.

"Used to what?"

"That you guys can just see the Northern Lights here almost every day."

"Well, until spring. Then they only start up again in October," I say, nudging her gently with my elbow. "And you're one of us now. You should probably start calling them the *kiyyulit*."

"*Kiyyulit*," she says after me. You can hear a touch of the mainland in the way her L's come out, broad and lazy. "*Lit* is light, right? What's *kiyyu*?"

"*Kiyyu* means soul. We believe the lights are the souls of the ancestors, coming to visit us."

"And fight you to the death, I guess," she says, her voice flat. "Or, at least, to lifelong pain and injury."

I swallow. "Is that why you can't sleep? You're thinking about Seb?"

She shakes her head. "I can't sleep because Seb can't sleep. He spent the whole evening pacing, as soon as he got back from the ceremony. I came up here to get some rest. So much for that plan." She smiles at me softly, and I can see she's teasing.

I scooch closer to her and lean my head on her shoulder. Her scent is warm and complex: like honey and mainland laundry detergent, even though she's been living here for months.

"I don't get it, to be real with you," she says, and rests her head against mine. "If the ancestors are on your side, why do they go so hard? Why would they almost kill you?"

"They do it to help you," I say, almost as if by rote. They teach us this in school, drilling Fakari culture and history into us so hard that the words that come out of my mouth are barely my own. "You don't *have* to do the rite. Only if you want to become an elder on pack council. And to do that, you need to overcome your biggest weakness by wrestling with your greatest fear. If you can't do that, you're not strong enough to lead the pack."

"Do you really believe that?"

I think for a moment.

"I think so," I say finally. "It makes sense that, if you're blinded by your own fears, you can't see clearly enough to vote for the good of others."

"But, like, *physically* overcoming them?" she asks. "I feel like my biggest fear is making a mistake on my taxes and going to IRS-prison. How many people have a biggest fear you can actually physically fight?"

I shrug, my shoulder bumping against hers. I've had that thought before, too. I mean, *my* greatest fear might take the shape of a person. But how many people can say the same?

"Has Seb ever told you what he fought up there?" I ask.

"No. He says you're not allowed to share it. But he told me *some* of what happened—the okay parts, I guess. It's personal, for me."

"What he fought in the ring—it's about you?" I ask, looking up. Maren moved here three years after Seb's rite.

"In a way. It's complicated," she says, and smiles softly to herself. I can see it's not a story she's going to tell me. It's probably not really hers to tell.

I look out of the window again, in the direction of the cliffs.

"I'm scared," I say quietly.

"I know," says Maren, and puts a hand on my knee. "He'll come back. He'll be okay. And even Seb is okay, after what happened to him. It's not... it's not wrong to be like Seb."

"No, no, of course not," I say, my eyes stinging. "I don't mean it like that. I just..." I swallow. "I don't know how to be without him. I need him to be okay."

She nods. "He will be," she says, and we watch the lights dance over the cliffs in silence.

At five the next morning, Kieran still isn't back.

Same for six. At half past, the sun is beginning to rise over the cliffs, and I'm getting antsy. The members of our *fika* have made our way to the common house, waiting for Kieran's return.

I look around at the others. Saga, Isolde, and my aunt Dagmar stand close together, holding empty mugs of what used to be tea close to their chests. Seb has his arms around Maren, his head resting on her shoulder. She looks as tired as I feel. And Gabe isn't waiting with us, but I can sense he's awake. He's somewhere nearby, waiting on his own. Watching for Kieran to come down for the cliffs.

I feel the tension simmering in my body. My inner wolf is jumpy and skittish, and I shove her down. I wrap my sweater tighter around myself, warding off the cold winter air.

"I'm just gonna go to the house to get some water," I tell Saga. I can see from her eyes that she doesn't believe me, but she nods, and I go before Seb or Maren can stop me.

I start walking up the hill, in the direction of our *fikarig*. But where the path splits off towards the cliffs, I follow, keeping an eye on the horizon for Kieran's figure. The grass on the hillside glimmers with frost. I keep my eyes ahead, looking for any sign of him. Finally, after about ten minutes, I turn a corner and think I see it up in the distance: his large white wolf, staggering down the hill.

"Kieran!" I call, and I start running. My hands jump to my pockets to check what I have on-hand: salve, disinfectant, bandages. I don't have water with me, but we're not far from the *fikarig*. I can run to get some if he's too weak.

I smell the blood in the air before I see it on him. It's a mix of fresh and dried, and the scent of it sends my inner wolf into a panic. I break into an all-out sprint and reach him half-way up the hill.

"Kier," I whisper, falling to my knees in front of him. His wolf form is massive, and when I'm on the ground he towers over me. He stops and opens his mouth, dropping his bag to the ground. I take in the marks where he got hurt, but it's hard to tell at first glance where the injuries are. The fur on his left side is matted down with blood, but the blood on his chest is still fresh: bright red and wet. His front two paws are painted, too. I reach out to touch him, and his body unfurls before me, shifting back into his human form. His clothes from the rite are gone, but I see the body armor peeking out from his bag. At least he had time to prepare for the shift, I register.

"Are you okay?" I ask, and I reach out to touch his face. He winces and moves his head away from me.

"Don't touch me," he snaps, his voice hoarse. "What are you doing here? You should be back at the common house with the others."

I feel like I've been slapped, and as much as I hate it, I feel my eyes start to sting. But I swallow my feelings away. He's tired.

"I came to find you. I was worried. Here, let me look at you, please." I reach out for his face again, where I can see a bruise forming around his right eye, and another at his temple. "Were you hit? Did you fall unconscious?"

As my hand touches his skin, he shakes his head to get away from me, and rises to his feet.

"Get the fuck away from me, Em," he snaps. "I'm serious. You shouldn't be here, it's not safe. Go back to the *fikarig*." He reaches down for the bag he dropped, pulling out his black wool sweater. I can smell the blood on that, too. So he was bleeding even before the shift.

"Oh, um. Okay. I brought you, um, disinfectant. For your cuts, or anything." I reach into my pocket to pull out one of the tins of salve I made. My voice is warbly, betraying my feelings.

Kieran sighs as he pulls the sweater over his head. With the movement of his arms, I see him wince. Some kind of pain in his shoulder, from whatever happened up there.

"Hey, Em, I'm sorry, I just—"

"It's fine. You're tired. We'll talk later," I say, and I drop the salve at his feet and walk back towards the house.

8

KIERAN

What the fuck?

Whatthefuckwhatthefuckwhatthefuck.

It was real, right? It had to be real.

The day passes in a blur, and this is all I can think, over and over again. People come in and out of my room at the infirmary to see me. Saga, checking my wounds, pulling me onto my side as I lose the contents of my stomach into a bucket. Gabe, feeling my forehead for fever. Seb, hanging back in the corner of the room, watching me. At some point I hear Heimig muttering something to Saga, asking some kind of question.

My mind is slow, foggy, but I can feel my wolf trying to wake me up. He's nudging me, trying to get my attention. Something about Em. And I realize: if everyone is here at the infirmary, looking after me, she must be at the *fikarig* alone.

I groan and try to sit up, and Saga comes to sit on the bed beside me.

"Em," I mumble, but my mouth feels like it's full of marbles.

"Here, *piu*, have some water," Saga says, and hands me a cup.

I gulp it down, suddenly parched. But the taste is disgusting—sweet and savory—and I gag.

"Sorry," Saga says. "For rehydration. You've lost a lot of fluid."

I look over to the side of the bed, where the bucket that was there earlier has magically disappeared. My brain slowly comes to focus. She hands me another glass, and I swallow it in one gulp.

"Good," she says, nodding approvingly. "You're very tired, but you'll be just fine. The *kattaka* is just working its way out of your system."

"You have to go to Em," I say hoarsely. "You have to protect her. She's not safe."

Heimig looks down at Saga, his brow furrowed.

"This is the lingering effects of the *kattaka, piu,*" she says gently to me. "Whatever you saw was the ancestors, challenging you."

"No, it was real," I say, my head shaking. "You have to go to her, she's not safe. He's—"

Saga lifts a hand to me. "Stop," she says, her tone gentle but firm. "Emerson is safe. What you saw in the ring was a vision. And you cannot tell me what it was, or you risk the ancestors' anger."

I fall back onto the bed, looking up at the ceiling. It had to be real. There's no way a mirage could have fought me the way he did.

My hand finds its way to my stomach, checking for the gash brought on by his claws. At the pressure, I wince, but it feels more like a bruise now than an open wound.

"We've siphoned most of the wound already," Saga says, noting the confusion on my face. "You were injured, but nothing vital was hurt. Helen did some of her best work. You should be fully healed in a few days."

My brow furrows, trying to make sense of it through the fog of dehydration and the last of the *kattaka*. There was so much blood. I couldn't possibly be better so quickly, even with the faster healing we experience as shifters. Unless they're right, and it wasn't real…

"Em," I mumble, closing my eyes. My fingers find their way to her hair tie on my wrist, and I run my thumb over it. Did I put her in danger?

"She's not here right now," Saga says. "You get some rest. I'll make sure there's someone to help you through the night, if you need anything. And congratulations, pack elder."

I hear her move away from me, and she and Heimig walk out of the door of the infirmary. I rest my thumb on Em's hair tie, thinking of her face. And for the first time in years, I fall asleep without her in my arms.

THE NEXT TIME I wake up, the light coming through the windows is gold and amber. I sit up in bed, looking around. The sun is low in the sky—either sunrise or sunset.

"About time," Seb says from a chair next to the bed. "You slept for over twenty-four hours. I was just about to start hacking at a tree with a chainsaw to get you to wake up."

"Hey." I sit up and instinctively put a hand on my stomach.

"They were able to heal all of it," Seb says, his voice flat. "You'll make a full recovery."

I swallow, thinking of the blood I lost in the ring, the blinding pain of claws tearing into my body. I can only imagine how much worse it was for him, if they could heal me this fast but couldn't save his muscle.

"I can't believe it wasn't real," I mumble.

"I told you, man. Don't let it fuck with you. Come on, I'm supposed to get you ready for the party."

"Party?"

"Yeah, it's evening already. You came back from your rite yesterday morning. That means we celebrate."

Ah, right. I'm a pack elder now—there's usually a big get-together. We didn't do one for Seb until months later, when he was fully healed and back from the mainland.

"It's soon?" I ask, still a little bleary from sleep.

"Yeah. But we can get there late, if you want. Gabe made some food, too, if you need to have that first."

I shake my head and move my feet over the side of the bed, trying to get my legs under me. Seb comes up alongside, wrapping an arm around my middle to help me as I rise onto my feet. My muscles are sore, but to my surprise, that's most of the pain. I look over at him, groggy, still waking up.

"It wasn't real?" I ask.

"It wasn't real," he says. "But it can still do some real damage."

I nod, and suddenly my mind flashes to Em and our meeting on the path up to the cliffs. I groan, closing my eyes.

"Em? Yeah, that kind of damage, too," he says.

"She told you?"

"She told Maren, and Maren told me." Seb loosens his arm, and once he sees I can stand on my own, he steps back. "But yeah. Nice going."

"*A skeia,*" I groan. *By fate.* "I'm such a dick."

"Yeah, but it happens. She'll forgive you. Maren's cheering her up right now, helping her get ready for the party."

"She'll be there?" I ask. To be honest, I assumed she'd have left by now—if not because of what I said, then because of her heat around the corner. I know she was waiting it out to do my *kattaka* ceremony, but I figured she'd leave right after.

"Yeah." He gives me a look, like he's thinking what I'm thinking. "*That*'s between you two. But you can apologize when you see her. The *kattaka* messes with your head almost as much as the rite. She'll understand."

"I hope so," I say. My stomach rumbles. "Man, I'm starving."

"I figured. I'll grab the food Gabe made, and then we can get you dressed."

9

KIERAN

We get to the *fikarig* after nightfall, and I can hear the raucous noise coming from inside as soon as we're on the property. The second I walk through the door, the hall erupts into cheers.

"Congratulations, *jenge!*" says Heimig, coming over to me to slam me into a hug. "Looking much better than yesterday morning, thankfully."

"Thanks," I wince, looking over his head through the crowd of faces. I can catch Em's scent somewhere in the air, but it's distant, and the room is so crowded that I can't find her face.

Viggo comes up to congratulate me, and I'm pulled into a conversation with him and Dagmar, then with Caspar, who I'm surprised to see Saga remembered to invite. The evening drags on and there's no sign of Em. I'm getting tired, and the beer someone pushed into my hand—who was it, Quinn?—doesn't help. But from the top of the stairs, I see Maren coming down. She's wearing some ridiculous dress, something that looks like it should be a man's button-up shirt. Mainland fashion will never stop confusing me. I walk over to her.

"*Heij*. Where's Em?"

She crosses her arms in front of her chest. "Oh, I'm pretty sure she's staying the hell away from you, like you asked *so nicely* yesterday morning."

"No offense, Mare, but this is none of your business. If I wanted your opinion, I would have asked."

She raises a defiant eyebrow. "It became my business when Emerson came to me crying yesterday."

My gut twists. "Yeah?"

"Yeah. Nice job."

"I…" I run a hand over my face. "Okay, listen, do you know where she is? I want to say sorry."

"She isn't feeling well."

My inner wolf growls in agitation, and I push past her to head for the stairs.

"Stop," she stays, holding a hand up. She gives me a look, then lowers her voice. "Don't go to her room. She's in the library."

"*Takka*." I thank her, setting my beer down, and head up the steps. My legs are tired, still achy from the hike up to the cliffs yesterday. As I near the second floor landing, then the third, the sounds of the party fade away. Down the hall, the door to the library is slightly ajar, and I can see the faint glow of lantern light spill out into the hall.

I walk towards the door and rap lightly against it with my knuckles. Nothing.

"Em?" I ask.

I hear an indignant sigh, and I know she's in there.

"Em, please." My voice is strained, over-eager after too many nights away from her. "Listen, I'm sorry. I was a dick, I know. I was just scared, and still high out of my mind—"

I push the door open and walk into the library. The scent of her is everywhere, intoxicating, overpowering. She's sitting on the windowsill, arms crossed, wearing something I've never seen her in before. It's red and silky, skimming over her body until just past her knees, with a slit that comes up high to expose the milky white skin of her thigh.

"*Agaayu.*" My voice breaks out of me, raw and husky. "*Uikbaane*, what are you wearing?"

That was the wrong question.

"What, you don't like it?" she snaps. "Oh, well, sorry. I did my best to—what was it? 'Stay the fuck away from you,' like you said. You're the one who followed me up here."

"No, Em, I'm sorry, I..." I can't help it. I feel a smile tug at the corner of my lips.

"Oh, now you're laughing at me," she says, throwing her hands in the air. "Nice. Can you please leave?"

I look behind me and shut the door, so the people downstairs don't hear us argue.

"Em."

"What?"

I sigh, raking my hand through my hair, and wince at the pain in my shoulder. I see it register in her face; a pang of worry, despite herself. I step towards her.

"I'm not laughing at you. I just... I smiled because I like this side of you."

"Oh, so you *like* making me angry." She rolls her eyes, crossing her arms again and looking away, but I can feel something in the air change just a little.

"No, I just—" I run a hand through my hair again, trying to find the words. I wish shit like this came easier for me. "I like the part of you that doesn't hold back. The part that feels safe enough to yell at me."

She looks up, her body still turned away from me. The moonlight is skimming over her skin, accentuating the rise and fall of her chest. *God give me strength.*

"So you *do* like making me angry." Her tone is challenging, but there's a playful edge now. My inner wolf registers it immediately, dipping his head low and wagging his tail, ready to play.

"I like that you feel safe being angry with me," I say, and step closer to her. "I like that you feel safe enough to show me how you really feel."

She holds my gaze, waiting. I swallow.

"Okay, look, I'm sorry for what I said on the mountain. I was a dick. You deserve to be pissed at me. If you want to yell, you can. I deserve it."

"I don't want to yell," she says, and sighs. "But I *am* hurt. I spent all night worrying about you. I spent weeks preparing for this. I just wanted to see if you were okay."

"I know." I want to pull her towards me, to hug her and make it better with my arms in a way I don't know how to with words. But I hold off. "I was scared. The thing I fought up there—I can't tell you about it, I know. But it made me scared. For you. *Because of you.*"

She looks up suddenly, her eyes wide with some kind of realization, something close to wonder. "The ancestors, the thing you fought—it was for *me?*"

"What do you know?" Has she felt it, somehow? No, she can't have. If she knows what I saw, the look in her eyes would be closer to terror.

She eyes me for a moment, something happening in her mind that I can't figure out.

"Nothing," she says finally, and looks away.

"Tell me." I come closer to her, so there's just a few inches between us.

She says nothing, thinking, then looks up.

"So you don't like the dress?" she asks finally. There's a little playfulness in her eyes—flirty, bold.

I shake my head. Maybe it's the beer, or the last of the *kattaka,* but for once, I don't stop myself.

"You look beautiful. I like it too much."

She raises her chin just slightly, and it feels like an invitation. My eyes fall over her body again, and I know she's watching me as I take her in. I admire her exposed shoulders, bare and elegant in the moonlight. The thin red straps are tied into little bows, undoubtedly some mainland fashion Maren bought for Em just to make me lose my goddamn mind. The silk in the front of the dress dips low between her breasts, skimming over them—soft, small, full—and falls around her waist and hips, accentuating the shape.

As she watches me take her in, something in the air grows thick and heady. Her breathing grows heavier, and it's unmistakable. She's getting turned on. I feel myself grow hard before I can help it.

"Em," I groan, looking away. "I'm sorry, I shouldn't have come up here. I'll give you some space."

I turn, but her hand reaches for my wrist, pulling me back.

"I don't want space."

"You're only saying that because you're going into heat soon," I manage to get out. "When I offered and your head was clearer, you didn't want this."

"I did. I do," she says, her breathing labored. "Kieran…"

She pulls me towards her until our bodies are pressed together, a thousand dreams I never let myself have. I take a deep breath. She smells divine, like sex and heat and lush, decadent wild, but also still like Em: soft and sweet, a trace of rose water and cardamom. I straighten my body and push myself away from the sill.

"I can't do this to you," I say, my voice thick and raspy with desire. "You're not yourself. You can't make this decision right now."

"Kieran, I'm still *me*. I'm not drunk, I'm not out of my mind. I'm not even in heat yet. And if I were, I'd still be able to make this decision."

I don't respond. I can't.

"You... you said you like the part of me that doesn't hold back," she says. "The part that feels safe telling you what I really feel. So... let me."

Her voice is nervous, and I can see a tremble in her hand as she takes my right hand and lifts it, placing it gently on the side of her neck and resting hers on top. Then she reaches for my left hand and rests it on her hip.

My whole body goes taught. I'm afraid to move.

"I know you don't see me this way," she says quietly. "You said it doesn't have to mean anything. So let's just have... one night. To pretend."

She looks up, her eyes hopeful and yearning, and I can't hold it anymore.

In seconds, my mouth is on her, tasting the sweetness of her mouth, feeling the fullness of her lower lip between mine. I press her into me and feel her melt, a low moan escaping from her as she kisses me back. My hands skim down to her waist, over her hips, to all the places I've never touched, never let myself imagine. It's better than anything—better than every dream, every flicker of fantasy I ever let myself have. My lips move over hers slowly, savoring.

Just one night. If this is the only time, I'm making it count.

I lean down to kiss her neck and her head dips back. She gasps as I taste her skin, delicate against the roughness of my beard.

"Sorry," I say, raspy, pulling away.

"No. More." Her hand finds the back of my head and moves me towards her again, and I groan as I find a place just at her collarbone that makes her breathing grow heavy, a few inches below where her mate bite would go.

The scent of her arousal is intoxicating, and it mixes with mine, the hardness of my cock pressing between her thighs as she gasps.

"*Iija,*" she whispers. *Yes.*

I lift her and carry her to the window, then set her down on the sill. I come down to kiss her collarbone again, then her chest, and stop at the space between her breasts.

"Yeah?" I ask.

She nods, her eyes bold, holding my gaze. Her fingers reach up to the ties at her shoulders and gently pull on the strings until they come undone. The silk in the front of her dress falls down to her waist, exposing the lace of her bra.

Damn, I was wrong. I *love* mainland clothing.

I press my face between her breasts, kissing her, nipping gently at the skin as she gasps. My hands come up to her chest, and instinctively she bucks her hips, the movement so sensual that I almost lose my self-control and want to have her right there. But I steady myself, focusing on her body, studying what makes her moan and pant. I want this to last. I want her to remember. I want it better than anything she's had before.

I cup her gently, moving over to kiss one breast over the lace of her bra. Desperately, her hands clasp behind her back, unhooking it.

"Fuck, Em." My voice is guttural as the pale skin of her breasts becomes visible, her nipples peaking under my thumbs. They're dark and beautiful, and a low groan escapes me as I take one into my mouth, sucking gently.

"*Agaayu*," she gasps, writhing under me. "Kieran, oh my God."

I keep going, and as she bucks against me, something in her changes. I feel a warmth blooming under her skin, coming to the surface, blossoming as she throws her head back. Everything intensifies: in her, in me, in the air between us. She looks down to meet my gaze, panting, primal. Her eyes are dark with desire, the pupils blown wide.

"Is this...?" I ask, looking up at her. But I know.

"Heat," she nods.

"Is this still okay?" I ask, my voice hoarse.

"Please."

Thank God.

I sink down to my knees before her, my hands moving over her supple body, taking in her waist, her hips, her thighs. I slip my hands under her dress, parting the thigh-high slit, lifting it so the fabric pools around her waist and I can see the lacy fabric of her underwear, provocatively cut to expose the roundness of her hips. A rose petal of wetness is visible in the fabric at the cleft between her lips.

"Agaayu, Em," I groan, leaning my head against her stomach. "You can't do this to me."

"For you," she says, her breathing shallow.

I look up, questioning.

"I wore them *for* you."

For *me.*

Just for tonight, my brain reminds me.

I feel my cock straining against the fabric of my pants, and I'm dying, I need her, the way a man in the desert needs water. But still, I wait. This *will* be good for her. I reach up to tug the fabric down over her ass, exposing the dark blonde curls between her legs. She spreads her thighs for me, an invitation, and I don't think twice. I lift her hips, letting her ass rest fully against the windowsill and slipping her knees over my shoulders. Delicately, reverently, I begin by kissing her inner thighs, then up to her slit. She writhes for me, moaning, impatient, and I grin against the softness of her skin.

I've held back ten years for this. She can wait.

I kiss along the outer edge of her lips until she's begging, wild.

"Kieran, please. I can't take it anymore, please. I need you."

My mouth finds its way to her clit, and I go slowly, running my tongue over it. I want to devour her, but I know too much pressure will ruin this.

"*Oh,*" she gasps, throwing her head back, her hand clamping down on the window frame.

I go gently, patiently, insistently. She groans, her hips writhing, at one point arching so hard I'm worried she'll lose her balance. I wrap one arm around her leg and bring my hand up to her waist, pressing gently on her stomach to hold her in place. Her fingers find it and lock with mine.

"More," she begs. I take my free hand up to my mouth to wet my index finger, then bring it to her entrance. Meeting her eyes, I gently press it into her, moving slowly as she takes me to the knuckle.

"Oh," she gasps, rocking against me. I slide it slowly in and out of her, bringing my mouth back to her clit. The pace is steady, building as her moans grow louder and more rhythmic.

"More," she whispers again, and I remove my hand to add a second finger.

"No," she gasps, shaking her head. "You. I want you."

My vision grows cloudy, and I stand up, looking around. We're in the fucking library. There's a sofa, but I'm not going to have her on an old couch like we're at some mainland movie frat party.

As though thinking the same, she walks to it and removes one of the pillows, dropping it onto the rug. My inner wolf pants at the sight of her, wild with the scent of sex and hunger and *me*. She looks untamed—hair mussed, the red silk of her dress hanging haphazardly off of her hips—and it's the hottest thing I've ever seen. I walk over to her, reaching for her body, but she shakes her head and pulls at my shirt.

"Off," she commands.

I do as I'm told, reaching for the bottom hem to pull it over my head. As I lift it, my shoulder hurts and I wince. She helps guide it off, exposing the bare skin of my chest and the gauze wrapped around my stomach.

"Oh," she gasps, and the air between us grows still, sweet.

Her hands are feather-light on the bandages, touching me, checking me, her brow furrowed with concern. Something in my chest hurts, seeing that look on her face.

"I'm okay," I say, my hand coming to rest on top of hers.

She looks up at me, ocean eyes wide. "Do you still want to…?"

"*God*, yes," I say, and sink to my knees on the floor.

She lifts the red dress over her head and looks down at me, her whole body exposed in the moonlight. Like this, she looks like a goddess: wild, free, too beautiful for this earth. Her skin smooth like marble; her frame perfect, the faded stretch marks on her hips and the tender shape of her stomach only making me want to devour her more.

She comes down to the ground for me, lying back so her head comes to rest on the cushion. I lean forward to lean over her, my hips between her legs, my mouth returning to kiss her neck and chest. I want to work my way back down, to make her come before I enter her. But she uses one foot to tug lazily at the waist-band of my pants.

"Off," she says again, playfully now.

I've never seen her like this: languid, sensual, confident.

"Impatient." I smile against the skin of her neck, sucking on the spot that makes her gasp. Her back arches under me, her breasts pressing against the skin of my chest.

"I've waited long enough," she says, and it's true for both of us.

I remove my pants, then my boxers, exposing myself. My cock is hard, thick with desire, glistening with precum. Her eyes go wide as she takes me in.

"Woah," she whispers.

"Thanks."

She rolls her eyes, joy tugging at her lips. "Arrogant much?"

"Just a little." I come to lean over her again. "But I can back it up, I promise."

Something changes in her face. Just before I enter her, she stops me.

"Kier?"

"Yeah?"

"Promise it'll be the same tomorrow," she says, her voice suddenly nervous. "Promise you'll still love me the same."

Something in my chest aches. The same tomorrow; right back to how it's been all these years. *Just one night,* I think to myself. But I can't help myself. I bring my face over hers and kiss her slowly.

"I promise I'll still love you the same," I say, and mean it.

She nods. "Go slow for me, okay?" she asks, and I nod.

I take myself in hand and guide my cock down her slit until I find her opening.

"*Agaayu,*" I mutter. She's so wet, so hot as I enter her. It takes all my self-restraint to do as she wants and go slow, easing in just an inch and then back out. Her head dips back with a gasp, and I press a little deeper, then pull out. Then again, until I'm almost at the hilt.

"Kieran," she gasps. "God, it's so good."

"More?" I ask, straining.

"More. All of you."

I bury myself into her and she cries out, dipping her head back.

I feel her inner walls clamp around me and go faster, finding a rhythm that matches the subtle rocking of her hips. Her moans are wild and hungry, and I make myself notice it, all of it. Every look on her face; every sound from her mouth; the way her back arches when I hit the right spot and she loses all control.

I prop myself up, and my hand reaches between us to find that delicate bundle of nerves again. As soon as my thumb reaches it, I see her body respond, aching, needy. I circle it gently, thrusting into her, and with another cry, her back arches as she finds her peak. Her hands grasp wildly around her—at the rug, her breasts, her hair—as she rides it out, her hips bucking. I'm close, so close.

"Yes," she cries out. "Kieran."

It's the sound of my name on her lips that does it. I break, leaning forward over her, losing myself in her body, her hips, her pleasure. I come hard, spilling myself into her just as she rides out the last waves of her climax. Finally, I come to rest over her, my face against her chest.

"Oh, Kieran," she says again, her hands coming up to play with my hair.

"*Kiyyuni*," I whisper, before I can stop myself. *My soul.*

10

EMERSON

When I wake up the next morning, Kieran is gone and I'm alone in the library, naked.

Oh my God.

I roll onto my back, remembering. *I asked him to have me. I basically begged him. And when he did…*

Warmth blooms in my stomach as I remember. His hands on my skin. His face between my legs, tasting me. The look on his face as he lost himself in my body.

Kiyyuni, he whispered. My soul.

I can't get it out of my head. I think about it as I clean up the library, fixing the couch cushions and opening the windows to let in the cool, fresh air. I think about it as I sneak down to the shower, washing my hair; scrubbing myself hard enough that I hope no one will be able to smell him on me.

Kiyyuni. A word no one has ever used for me before. A word you save for someone you love.

The house is oddly quiet as I walk downstairs to the kitchen. I step inside to see Maren, sitting at the table with her laptop. She's wearing the emerald sweater I knit her for Karstmis. The second I walk into the room, her nostrils flare. Her eyes snap up at me, then go wide.

"SHUT UP," she says.

Agaayu. I should have showered twice.

"Shh, shh," I say, walking to her with my hands raised. "Don't."

"You didn't!" she shrieks. "Oh my God, you two. *Thank God*, honestly. About time."

"Maren, I swear," I say, looking over my shoulder.

"Relax, we're alone," she says, laughing. "Some kind of last-minute council thing, I don't know. They all left an hour ago, and Gabe's working on Halssel today. It's just us. Okay, tell me *everything*. How did it happen? I *knew* it, when you guys didn't come down all night. I fucking *knew*."

"I…" I consider lying, but I can't stop the smile from spreading over my face. I collapse into the chair across from her and pull my knee up to rest my chin on. "Okay, it was great. It was amazing. But you can't tell anyone, promise me. It was a one-time thing."

"Oh please. I said the same thing about Seb, and look at me now." She tugs at the neckline of her shirt to show Seb's mark, nestled between her neck and collarbone. The bite cements the mate bond, when two partners claim each other for life.

"No, seriously," I say, and I feel something in my chest deflate with the truth. "We agreed, it was that time only. I don't think I would have done it if it weren't for my heat. He doesn't see me like that."

"Girl, are you stupid? The man is so in love with you it practically hurts to look at."

I chew my lip. If that were true, he wouldn't be going out with a new girl three nights a week. He would have stayed all those years ago, instead of leaving for his training on Keist. He would have come back for *me*, not Seb's rite.

But *kiyyuni*, he said.

"Wait, hang on," Maren says. "You said he doesn't see you that way. Do you see *him* that way?"

"No."

She grins. "Admit it. You're in love with him."

"I *love* him. Like a friend. Like how I love you and Seb."

"You'd *better* not love Seb the way you love Kieran, or we're gonna have some stuff to talk about." She laughs again.

"I don't have feelings for him." Somewhere deep inside me, under a hundred layers I use to keep her away, I can feel my inner wolf yip at me in irritation. *Liar*. "But he is..."

Everything to me. The person I love most. The most beautiful man I know.

"Attractive," I settle on. "I need to get out of the house. I don't think it's a good idea for me to be near him when I'm like this."

"'Cause you're gonna jump his bones the second you see him again."

I laugh. "Stop. Because I'm hormonal, and I don't want the rest of the *fika* to have to think about that. And yes, because hormones make you stupid and I don't want to make a dumb decision."

She grins. "Not gonna lie, I kinda want you to make a dumb decision. *Again*."

I get up and start making coffee for myself. Maren already has her personal vat beside her, giant French press almost completely empty. I lift the bag of coffee grounds in her direction, my eyes questioning, and she nods yes.

"Kier and I are real people, Maren," I say, starting on coffee for both of us. "Not a soap opera to keep you entertained. And if we mess this up, it's gonna ruin everything. Not just for me and him, but for the whole *fika*."

"Oh please. How?"

I sigh, filling the water kettle. "Like, if things ended badly. Imagine if he left—it would be way harder for you, me, Seb, and

Gabe to get a *fikarig* without him." I put the kettle back and turn it on. "Either you or I would need to do the rite to make up for the lost council seat, or we'd have to ask Seb's cousin Quinn or something. We can't risk what we've been working for just because I'm..." I gesture in the air.

"Horny." She grins.

"Hormonal."

"Girl, you're future-tripping. There's no way Kieran would leave us. *Especially* not you."

I swallow. Not true. She just wasn't here last time.

"Besides, we could do the rite," she says. "I believe in us."

I snort. *"You,* maybe—you box, at least. I don't think I've exercised on purpose since I was in school."

"Come on!" She claps her hands in front of her. "It would be fun. We could train together."

"Who's future-tripping now?" The water finishes boiling, and I stamp down the grounds I've scooped into the top half of the Fakari-style coffee pot. I reach for Saga's spices and add some cinnamon on top, then pour the water over the mix. "Neither of us have to do the rite because we already have two seats, and Gabe agreed to do his rite in March for the third."

I bring the pot over to the kitchen table, setting it between us.

"Anyway, the details don't matter. I just meant, the stakes are too high for me and Kieran to mess around and see what happens. Which means I need to figure out where I'm gonna hunker down for the next few days."

"So you don't jump him."

"So I don't jump him," I say, my tone resigned.

She grins, victorious. "Where are you thinking of going?"

"I don't know," I say, resting my head on my knee again. "If I'd planned ahead, I would have rented a cabin somewhere, just for me. But my heat came earlier than I expected, and honestly, I was too stressed about Kier's rite to think about it. The prices will be sky-high now. If I want to get out of here without paying a fortune, I should probably just go to our place on the north island."

Maren wiggles her eyebrows at me.

"What?"

"Nothing. I'm just saying. Shit goes down at the north island."

"*Agaayu*, don't remind me." She and Seb got together there during Fire Week last summer.

"How long do you need a place for?"

"Just a couple days, I think." I look up at her, hopeful. "Want to come with me? It could be fun. Like a girls' trip."

"Nah. Seb and I are releasing the salt scrubs this week, and I *need* them to go well. He's having a hard time living here with the elders, and now that Kier's done his rite, all that's standing between us and our own *fikarig* is Gabe's rite and the money for a new place. It's all hands on deck."

"Oh, of course." I try to mask my disappointment. A few days at our massive north island house, by myself, is going to drive me almost as crazy as being around Kieran would. "Well, I'm sure it'll be fine. I'll bring my paint supplies. Oh, shoot."

I look up, thinking.

"What?"

"I need the car to get to the north shore, for the ferry. I don't want to leave the whole *fika* without a car for a week, but I also want to get out before Kieran and the others get back. Any chance you can drop me off?"

"Yeah, sure, no worries," she says, and pours some of the fresh coffee into her mug. "Just let me know when you're ready to go."

PACKING TAKES JUST under ten minutes—I always have a duffle ready under the bed, just in case. At Maren's insistence, I also borrow her little purple suitcase and fill it with my water-color painting supplies, some paperbacks she lends me, and enough snacks to tide me over for the first day or two. I consider bringing Mom's old book of poems, but decide against it—I won't be gone that long. We load them into Saga's old Jeep and get in the front, Maren in the driver's seat.

"Thanks again," I say, looking over my shoulder at the woods in the direction of the common hall. "I think it's smart for me to get out of here before Kieran's back."

"Oh noo, I hope we don't have any engine trouble." She gives the key in the ignition a half-turn to make the car sputter.

"Don't."

She grins and turns the car on for real, then adjusts her mirrors. Our *fika* uses the car for transporting goods, mostly—because the others shift, we don't use it often for getting around. People on the mainland drive every day, and even though Maren lived in a city for the last few years she was there, she's still more comfortable behind the wheel than I am.

"Here, you put on some music," she says, and drops her phone in my lap as we pull out of the driveway. I pick up the phone—huge, practically a tablet, with a giant plastic knob on the back so she can hold it more easily—then swipe through the apps to find her music, tapping on a suggested playlist. The sound of artificial horns and a heavy beat flow from the Bluetooth speaker Maren's hung off the head of her seat.

"Oh my God, this song is so old," she says, turning onto the main road.

"New to me," I say, moving my head with the music.

"What *isn't* new to you guys? I could bring a stack of post-its back from the mainland and tell you I invented them."

"What's post-its?"

She gives me a look as we turn for the woods. "You're kidding."

I laugh. "Yeah, I am. But for real, I don't know this song. It's fun."

"If you like this, you're gonna love her newer stuff."

Maren names a few albums I should add to the queue, and then gives me a hopelessly complicated walk-through of this artist's dating history, and that of a few others I've never heard of. Every once in a while, I interrupt her to call out directions. We make our way through the trees and forest separating the *fikarig* from town, then into the town center, and eventually the plains and farms behind, heading for the north shore. The clouds ahead are growing more ominous, and I look up the weather forecast to see that it's going to snow soon.

After about an hour, I glance in the side mirror and see something in the distance far behind us. It's a large white blur, and for a second I think my eye is just imagining that it's moving towards us. But then—

"Oh my God, I think that's Kieran," I say. "Stop the car. Pull over."

Maren looks in the rearview mirror and pulls over to the side of the road. I climb out, wrapping my coat tighter around myself to brace against the winter air. It's colder now, the nip in the air from this morning more of a bite. Kieran's wolf barrels towards us, and I can tell even from here that he's running at all-out speed. I expect him to slow when he sees that we've pulled over, but he doesn't. As he nears, his body snaps forwards, unfolding into his human form. He comes to a halt in front of me so force-fully I almost think he's going to slam into my body, but throws out an arm to brace himself on the car just in time.

"Get back in the car," he growls. He's panting, his hair loose around his face and damp with sweat. I do my best not to look down at his bare chest; not to remember that same body on me last night, between my legs, inside me.

"Why? What's going on?" I ask.

Behind me, I hear Maren's door opening as she steps out onto the road.

"You can't be here. It's not safe."

"This again," I say, rolling my eyes. "I'm taking some time away. You know, for my…" I gesture awkwardly.

"I don't care. You can't do that right now. Get back in the car, go back to the *fikarig*."

"What's going on?" I ask again, my voice starting to betray my annoyance.

Maren turns the corner and immediately turns her head away.

"God, I am *never* gonna get used to you guys being naked all the time," she mutters, presumably at the sight of Kieran's bare ass. "Hang on, I think Seb left some clothes here last week." She opens the trunk of the car, and Kieran looks behind him, distracted.

"Kieran, *tell me*," I say. "What's wrong?"

"There was an attack on the south shore," he says, turning back to me, still breathless. "They think it's rebels from the southern isles. I'm not letting you go anywhere by yourself. Now get in the car."

11

KIERAN

Em brings a hand to her mouth, her eyes going wide. "What? What kind of attack?"

Maren shuts the trunk and shoves a ball of clothing into my hands. They smell like Seb and sweat and things I'm not gonna let myself think about.

"No islanders were hurt," I say, stepping into his sweatpants. They come up a few inches above my ankles. "Listen, we need to at least *talk* about this in the car. I don't feel good just standing out here."

With visible reluctance, Em opens the door on her side and folds the front seat down so I can climb in the back. Once I'm in —my knees rammed against the leather of their seats—she gets in front. I duck my head into the sweater, pulling it over my shoulders and arms, uncomfortably tight. Maren gets into the driver's seat.

"Take us back to the *fikarig*," I order her.

She gives me a look in the rearview mirror. "Excuse me?"

"Mare, I don't have time for this today."

"You're not the boss of me. I agreed to take Em to the north shore and that's what I'm doing unless she tells me otherwise." She shifts the car into drive and pulls back onto the road, driving north.

"Kieran, tell us. What happened?" Em asks, turning in her chair to face me. She puts her hand on mine, and her thumb brushes against the hair tie she leant me, still on my wrist. The feel of her skin is electric; I can feel the edge of her heat simmering under the surface, and instinctively pull my hand away to steady myself.

"They called us to an emergency council meeting," I say. "One of the farms on Saroe's south shore was razed. An entire field of sheep was slaughtered. Not for food—they were trying to send a message."

"It wasn't a wildlife attack?" she asks.

"Girl, everything on this island is a goddamn wildlife attack," Maren mutters under her breath.

"*No,*" I say, ignoring her. "They wrote something on the wall of the barn. *Hayyala,* in blood."

"Oh my God," Maren says in disgust, just as Em gasps,

"There's no way."

"It has to be," I say.

"Hang on, what are we talking about?" Maren asks.

"It's shorthand for the slogan of a militant group from the nineties," Em says, turning to face her. "The group called them-selves the True Remnant. They were against your and Seb's dads' attempts towards cultural exchange with the mainland. They attacked some of our smaller islands back then, as a warning shot. Their slogan was *Hayyala fast.*"

"What does it mean?"

"It's Fakari for *hold firm,*" I say. "As in, don't abandon the old way. Stay close to your own culture. Your own kind."

I see Maren's brow knit in confusion in the rearview mirror. "Wait, hang on. They speak Fakari on the southern isles?"

Em shakes her head. "Sort of. It's an offshoot, I think. I don't know, really—we haven't had any communication with them since the failed peace agreement in the nineties. That's where..."

Her voice trails off.

"That's where Gabe's dad died," I add, for Maren's sake. Everyone in Em's *fikarig* has been trained never to talk about Saga's late husband. Maren couldn't be blamed for not knowing Ben ever existed.

"But, Kier—" Em says. "I don't understand. Why would they be back?"

She turns to look at me, and I swallow. I can't tell her what *I* think.

"Seb thinks it might be about the asylum seekers his mom mentioned at dinner," I say finally. "But the council doesn't think that makes sense. They wouldn't want to come here *and* attack us for opening our shores."

"Could it be about Maren?" Em asks. "Or maybe something with the increased salt trade we've been doing with the mainland?"

I meet Maren's eyes in the rearview mirror.

"I don't think so," I say. "If it was about Maren or Saroan Salts, I feel like the attack wouldn't have been on a farm. This felt like it was meant to scare the whole island."

"It's horrible," Em says quietly. "Whose farm was it?"

"Anja and her husband, Tamu."

"*Ayagaayuni*," she says. *Oh my God.* "Saga was just there a few days ago."

"Exactly," I say, leaning forward. "This is why I don't want you going somewhere by yourself right now. It's not safe. The attack was too close to home. And they found the remains of two boats on the southern shore. The rebels are still *on* the island."

"But I'm going to the north island. Isn't that safer than being back at the *fikarig*, if they're still on Saroe?"

But I'm at the fikarig, I think. *I can protect you.*

"Listen, Em..." I say, running a hand through my hair, trying to figure out what I can tell her. "They found footprints and food in a cave by the south shore, near the remains of the boat. They think the rebels have been on the island for a few days. Since *before* my rite."

"Okay…" she says, looking blankly.

I look up. *Uikbaane*—wolfsbane. What am I allowed to say?

"If they knew a safe place to hide out, and they're currently hiding somewhere on the island… someone in that group must know the Fakaris well."

Recognition dawns in her eyes. "You think my dad is with them," she says flatly.

"Yes."

She shakes her head. "No, no way. For him to come back here would be a death sentence. I'm pretty sure Viggo would tear him limb from limb the second he laid eyes on him."

I set my jaw.

"And besides," Em adds. "The Remnant was anti-Fakari and anti-integration. My dad was *for* the mainland connection back then. It just doesn't make sense."

"What if he has a score to settle?" I ask, desperate. "Please, just listen to me—"

"A score with *me*? I was nine, Kier." I hear something in her voice: soft and sad. The shadow of the girl she was then.

"Or, or, I don't know. With Saga, or someone. With Viggo and Dagmar."

"You just said this can't be about Maren, because it wouldn't have been an attack on a farm. This doesn't sound like it's personal."

I stifle a growl from my inner wolf. She's right, but I *know* there's more going on.

"I just need you to trust me," I say. "Please."

"Do any of the other elders share your suspicions?"

"No," I admit.

"So what do they think?"

"Seb and Viggo aren't worried." I sigh. "They think it's a group from the southern isles who came here to cause some havoc, but got stuck after their boats broke down. Maybe teenagers or something. There's a search crew now, trying to find them before they do something else."

"So why do *you* think my dad is involved?"

Because I saw him in the ring, I think. *Because I know he's here. Because of what the ancestors told me...*

"I can't let something happen to you. I'd never forgive myself. If you come back to the *fikarig*, I can keep you safe. If you go somewhere else, fine, but I'm coming with you."

"I don't want to go back there right now," Em says, shaking her head. "I don't want to inconvenience the others with what's going on with me. And I think it's best if you and I don't..." She blushes. "Maybe you can send Gabe or something, if you're so worried. But even then, I don't really want them around me when I'm like this."

"I'm not sending Gabe," I say, annoyed. "If someone's going to protect you, they need to be the strongest person we have, and that's me."

I see the flicker of Maren's eyes rolling in the rearview mirror, but I'm right, and she knows it.

"I'm coming with you," I say. "Sorry."

"I don't..." she murmurs. "I don't know if I can trust myself around you when I'm like this."

Memories come flooding back to me from last night: Em on the windowsill, grinding her hips into my face; her, naked in the moonlight like a goddess; the look on her face as she cried out my name. I try desperately to think of something else, knowing Maren will scent something in the air as soon as it gets too charged between us.

"It's for your safety," I say, and my voice comes out hoarse.

"I think this is a great idea," Maren says brightly. "Em, you were just saying you'll be lonely at the north island all by yourself. This is perfect."

"*Mare*," she mutters in admonition. But for once, I'm grateful for her transparent attempts to get us together.

"Come on," I say to Em. "We'll have fun. I'll make sure of it."

She shoots me a look, and I know she's thinking what I'm thinking. Fun, alone together, is the thing she wants to avoid.

Just one night, I remind myself.

"If it's so dangerous, shouldn't you come with us, too, then?" Em asks Maren. "Aren't you scared?"

"I'll call Seb after we get to the north shore, but if he's not worried, I'm not worried." If Seb was anxious, she'd be able to feel it through the mate bond—even at this big of a distance.

"Besides," she continues. "It sounds like Kieran is the only one who thinks it's personal. As long as the rest of the *fika* feels safe, I'm fine."

"Em, *please*," I beg. "I won't be able to sleep if I think you're in danger."

"Fine," she says finally. "But only for a few days. And you're staying at the other end of the house."

"*Takka*," I say, and I mean it.

"Perfect. We're here," Maren says. She pulls over at the harbor on the north shore. I can see the ferry in the dock, the folding ramp down, with just one or two people standing on the deck.

She turns to Emerson. "Do you feel okay about this, for real? If not, I'll take his ass back to the *fikarig*."

I growl in protest, and Maren gives me a look.

"Seems like your knees are pretty jammed in tight back there," she says. "For once, I think I can take you."

Em glances at me, chewing her lip.

"Yeah," she says finally. "I think it'll be okay."

12

EMERSON

We get to Halluk just past five. It's already dark outside, and I'm exhausted from fighting my body on the whole ferry ride over. Kieran looks uncomfortable in Seb's clothes—the sweater clearly too tight, the pants too short—but he still looks *good*, and my body can't help but notice. The shape of his muscles, the cut of his waist.

"You look tired," he says as we step onto the dock.

"Thanks."

"No, I mean—you look good, you always look good. You just... I don't know."

I smile to myself. "It's fine. I *am* tired. It's been a long few days and I didn't—"

Get much sleep last night, is what I wanted to say, but I stop myself in time. I can tell from his face, though, that it registers.

"Um. Right. Yeah. We should... we should get you back to the house. I can shift, we'll get there faster."

"That's okay. I think it's best if you don't."

I can't handle the feeling of his beast under me right now, between my legs. He must catch on to the reason behind my answer, because I feel the tension in the air grow thicker. I laugh uncomfortably.

"Come on, Kier. We said it wouldn't be different."

"It's not different."

Everything's different. I know what he feels like now. I know what the sound he makes as he loses himself in my body. *Kiyyuni,* he said.

Agaayu. Shut up, brain.

I sling my duffle bag over my shoulder and grab the little purple suitcase, but he takes it from my hand before I can take a step. Wordlessly, we walk to the exit of the docks, turning left on the path along the shore that takes us towards the house. It's cold, and I tighten my coat around me.

"You must be freezing in those clothes. I sound like my mom, but I'm cold just looking at you."

"Nah, I run hot."

I laugh. "Gotta keep that ego in check," I joke, and as I do, I remember his words just before he entered me: *I can back it up, I promise.* Warmth pools in me at the memory, and I immediately bring myself back to the moment. *Agaayuni.* My heat is bad this year.

"No, really," he says, keeping his voice light. "No jokes this time. It's just shifter biology."

He's right—I always forget this, since it's been years since I let myself shift. Our wolf side stays warm easily, even in the snow. The more you let yourself take the shape of the wolf, the closer to the surface it is and the more of its qualities you have access to—even in your human form. Kieran shifts more than most people, and rarely needs more winter clothes than a light jacket.

"These clothes aren't really my style, though," he says as we turn right and near the base of the hill.

"Yeah, I don't think I've ever seen you wear this much black. It doesn't suit you."

It's not just that. I realize I don't like the scent of these clothes on him: the way his skin blends with Seb's and Maren's scents with them on. I don't think I realized until today that he doesn't just smell like wood and leather and amber, but also a little bit like me.

My inner animal *wants* him smelling like me, I realize, and feel myself blush.

We begin the trek up the hill, and up in the distance, the beach house starts coming into view. It's a large, shingle-style house, painted dark blue with a curved roof. The buildings on Halluk are different in style from those on our home island—this island was settled later on, and a lot of the houses on this shore were built to be vacation homes, so they're not set up for multiple families to live in together year-round. Our *fika* only bought this place a few years before I moved in, and while the house is a little smaller than our Saroan *fikarig*, it's also nicer and more modern on the inside. Bigger bathrooms, a new kitchen, and painted walls instead of the wood and exposed brick we have at home.

We walk the rest of the way in silence. After a few minutes, we near the front steps, where Kieran finds the lockbox under the porch for the key. I have a moment to take it in: the gentle roar of the ocean and the cool air on my face. I haven't been here since the summer. It's too dark to see now, but behind the house is a view of the beach. On the other side of the hill are the woods leading to the quarry and, not far from that, the house where Kieran grew up.

He gets the key out and straightens, walking past me to open the door.

"*Takka*," I say, and step inside.

The house is dark, but as soon as I'm through the door the scent of it hits me: beach days and bonfire nights, salt and smoke mixing with the soft scent of plaster. I walk to the light switch and flip them on as Kieran follows me inside.

"I should go upstairs to find some clean clothes," he says, walking past me.

"Wait," I say, and he stops at the base of the stairs. "Which room are you taking?"

"Oh. Right."

"You can have the master, I guess?" I offer. "I'll take one of the smaller rooms down the hall."

"You sure? I don't need much space."

I don't, either, but it's more about the space I can keep between us than anything else.

"Yeah, it's fine." I smile at him, conveying how extremely fine it is. How much everything is just like it was the day before yesterday.

He nods and disappears upstairs. I unbutton my coat and hang it over the railing, then kneel down to unlace my boots. Once they're off, I tie my hair out of the way and head upstairs with my bags, turning on the lights as I go.

I pick a small bedroom all the way down the hall—the blue room with a view of the sea. Setting my bags down on the bed, I unzip the duffle and take out a cozy outfit. Navy blue sweatpants Maren brought me from the mainland ("joggers," she always calls them, and I want to sound cool so I'm trying to do the same) and my loose-knit yellow sweater, once knit for me by Aunt Dagmar. There's a little sunflower pattern along the sleeves, which makes it one of my favorites. I pull out my painting supplies from the purple suitcase and head out to the hall.

As I reach the stairs, I see the door to the green room is open on a crack, and peer in to see inside. This was my room, *that* night—Fire Week the summer Kieran left for Keist, some ten years ago. I've done my best to avoid staying in it ever since, and I'm half-surprised to see that it looks exactly the same. Like a time capsule.

Shit goes down at the north island, Maren said. If only she knew.

I head downstairs to the kitchen, then into the den to turn on the lights. The room is soft and cozy—well-loved after many summer trips here. I go through the chests in the corner of the room to find what I want: blankets, pillows, candles that I set on the coffee table and light.

After about ten minutes, I hear Kieran come downstairs, then the sound of rustling and doors opening and closing in the hall. I walk over to see him putting on shoes and a jacket from the hallway closet, and lean against the door frame.

"Where are you going?"

"I want to head to the store before they close. Get us some real food, instead of whatever carby crap you have in that suitcase."

"That carby crap is called Triscuits, and I love them. Maren brought them for me."

"You know, you shouldn't trust mainland food. They add all kinds of garbage to it." He gives me a look, and I see his eyes sparkle with a touch of humor.

"Maybe, but the garbage makes the food delicious."

"I can't promise whatever I make will be good, but I can promise it'll be better than Triscuits."

I smile and watch as he zips up his jacket, checks his pockets for his wallet and keys, and leaves.

When he comes back, a little more than a half hour later, he's carrying two huge paper bags of groceries. I'm sitting in the den, wrapped in a blanket, my sketchpad leaning against my legs. I'm working on a new drawing—Gabe cooking, a dishcloth slung over one shoulder—that I'm hoping to fill in with watercolors tomorrow. When Kieran walks into the kitchen, I look up.

"Do you want me to help?" I ask.

"I think it's better if you stay over there."

"Okay. I can do that."

He prattles around in the kitchen, looking for a cutting board. After a minute I hear what sounds like success, although just a second later, he drops a sheet pan so loudly I practically jump a foot in the air. It's when he starts chopping an onion and I hear him hiss, cursing loudly, that I get up.

"Did you cut yourself?" I ask, walking over.

"No."

"Then why are you running your thumb under cold water?" I glance at the cutting board, where a large knife is lying on its side. "Give me your hand."

"Em—"

"I'm a healer, Kieran. Give me your hand." It's a command, but my voice is gentle. I never have to push with him.

He turns the water off and brings his palm to me so I can inspect the cut: about a centimeter long on the side of his thumb. I put one hand over it and close my eyes, pooling my energy. This is one of my weaker skills, and among the hardest for healers to learn. An experienced healer like Helen can not only ease pain, but stop bleeding and even heal deep wounds. I'm nowhere near that yet, but a small cut like this is easy to take the sting from, at least.

After a few moments, I can feel the darkness from the cut ease, replaced by just the little gash of the wound in my mind's eye. I haven't done much of this yet, but I'm curious, and Kieran's energy is open enough to my presence that I can afford to probe around a little. I move my hand above his just slightly, nudging the wound to close. At first I feel resistance, but slowly it gives in to me, coming together until just a small amount of the gash is left.

"Woah," I hear him whisper.

I try to push harder, closing it completely, but I can't. Finally I give up and open my eyes. Where there was a slit just a moment ago is now something more like a papercut, soft and pink, as though it happened a few days ago.

"Ooh, that's so cool!" I say. "That's the first time I've done that. I can't believe it worked."

"How did you do it?"

"I just started training for this." I beam at him. "It helps that I know you. It makes your body less resistant to me."

"That's amazing, Em," he says, and his voice is low and warm. "I'm proud of you."

I don't think about it, and for a moment I pull him towards me, resting my head against his chest in a half-hug. It's a mistake —I know it instantly in the way he stiffens, the way my whole body goes warm and loose for him.

"Sorry, sorry," I say, stepping back. *Agaayu,* this is why I wanted to come here alone. So you guys don't have to see me like this." I laugh uncomfortably.

"No worries," he says, but his voice sounds like he just swallowed gravel. "You go back to the den and I'll make dinner."

"Uh, no. Sorry Kier, but I just used most of my healing energy. I can't let you finish this meal by yourself, or you might bleed out on the floor."

He cracks a smile, and it eases the tension a little.

"Come on. Let me help you," I say, and turn to the counter. "We won't touch each other. What are we making?"

"Uh, salmon. And I got some potatoes and vegetables for in the oven. I texted Gabe for advice."

"Aw, you shouldn't have bugged him. We could have come up with something."

"No offense, Em, but it takes more than mainland crackers to keep my body like this."

He's joking, but my eyes immediately fall to his frame, more familiar to me now than it should be.

"Sorry. It was a joke," he mumbles.

"It's fine." I shake my head and try to focus on the ingredients before me. "Okay. Show me what we're supposed to do."

He pulls out his phone and shows me Gabe's texts, which are

so detailed it almost seems he thinks neither of us have ever touched a stove before. The sheet pan needs to go in first, so we get to chopping, me the vegetables and him the potatoes. I focus, making my slices perfectly even.

"Man, I suck at this," Kieran says, and laughs. "*Takkagaayu* Gabe loves to cook or we'd all be in trouble."

"I never cook either, anymore."

"Did you ever?"

I shrug. "With my mom, sometimes."

I feel his energy shift, growing careful.

"Tell me." It's a probe, not a command. I know I can say no— I usually do. But it feels okay today.

"She loved to cook," I say. "She was really good at it. She used to sing whenever she was happy, and I heard it most often when she was gardening or in the kitchen."

"What kind of stuff did she make?"

"Traditional Fakari stuff." I smile, remembering. "*Bakka* bread, *kalgaali et ekka*, broths. She used to make this amazing risotto with *perre*. What's the English word?" I gesture in the air, looking for it.

"Leek."

"Right, leek. It was so good. I haven't had it in forever."

"We should make it sometime."

"Yeah, maybe." I shrug. "It wouldn't be like how she made it."

"It could still be nice, though."

I feel some emotion deep down, and change the subject before it comes too close to the surface.

"What kind of stuff did you eat, growing up?" I ask. "Any famous Halluki recipes I should know about?"

He shakes his head, his red-brown hair brushing against his shoulders with the motion. "Nah. It was mostly my dad who made dinner, and honestly, it was usually pretty bland. But some-times my mom made *weijnotbrod*, the Fakari walnut bread. I guess you ate that too?"

"Nope," I say, shaking my head. "My dad was allergic to nuts. The first time I had *weijnotbrod* was when I moved in to our *fika*."

"Well, you missed out. My brothers and I would fight to the death for the last slice."

"You had a full house, right? Not a *fika*, but…"

"Yeah, just my family. But with three older brothers you have to fight for table scraps."

I smile. "Something tells me you did just fine."

"I had to."

I glance up at him, studying his face. It's hard to imagine Kieran—all six-foot-five, two-hundred-something pounds of him —ever feeling small. But I guess that's why he looks out for me. Because he knows what it's like to feel vulnerable.

"Do you have any nice memories with them?" I ask.

He shrugs. "Sometimes we'd go swimming in the grottos along the northern shore of the island. That was fun."

"No way," I say, smiling. "We used to do that, too. My mom would take us to the grottos on the eastern shore that only the locals know. The caves look directly out at the sea. We'd spend an afternoon there and bring picnic food and books."

He looks at me, his eyes gentle. "She sounds great."

"She was. She made every day special."

I feel the sadness welling up in me again, and Kieran must see it, too, because he changes the subject.

"I think these are done," he says, looking down at the potato massacre on his cutting board.

"That looks perfect."

He laughs. "You're such a liar. This looks like shit. Look, the pieces are totally different sizes! Half of them are gonna burn."

"I'm sure it'll be fine," I say. "Come on, next step."

We coat them and the vegetables with oil and herbs, then put the sheet in the oven. I take over seasoning the salmon the way Gabe instructed, and Kieran finds a cast iron pan. We shouldn't start cooking the fish until the vegetables are close to done, so after I have everything laid out, I head back to the den to work on my sketch while Kieran looks for drinks.

He comes back five minutes later, a beer in his hand, and hands me a rose soda.

"Oh, I'm surprised we still have these," I say, opening it.

"They didn't have anything for you in the fridge, so I went down to the cellar and we found a case."

"Thanks," I say, and take a sip.

"What are you drawing?"

I turn my sketchpad for him to see, and he turns his head. "Gabe," he says, nodding in recognition. "It's good. You can see the way he laughs. I love your paintings."

"They're hardly paintings."

"Don't sell yourself short. They're great," he says, and takes a seat on the couch. I can feel my inner wolf register the nearness of him. It seems he feels the same, so he scootches a few feet over.

"You should show me your sketches for the wedding arch you're making," I say.

"I don't have anything with me." He takes a swig of his beer. "I wasn't planning on coming here. I'm lucky there's still some clothes that fit upstairs."

"You didn't have to come."

"I didn't want to leave you alone," he says.

"I would have been fine."

"Maybe. But if you weren't, I wouldn't be able to live with myself."

I look down at his open hand, lying in the space between us, my black hair tie still on his wrist. I still don't really understand why I gave it to him, but it does something to me to see him wearing it, and I don't want to ask for it back.

Carefully, I lift his hand in mine to see where his cut was. I run a finger over the little pink line, admiring my work.

"Em..." he says softly. "I don't know if this is a good idea."

"No, probably not," I say, and I look up to meet his eyes. "But I want you to know that I don't regret it. What happened last night."

I wait. I want him to tell me, *me, neither*. I want him to tell me he wants me again like that, today and tomorrow and the tomorrow after that. I want him to call me *kiyyuni*.

But he says nothing, and I find myself blushing, dropping his hand back into his lap.

"Em—"

"No, you're right. It's not a good idea. I'll go finish the salmon," I say, and stand to go to the kitchen.

13

EMERSON

I'm six years old, sitting in the hallway closet with my knees curled up to my chest.

"Emerson, go," she said. But I can hear them in the living room: him shouting, her crying. The scent of fear and fury in the air.

I rock back and forth. Stay here, she told me. But at the sound of something breaking, my panic rises higher, and I reach for the handle and crawl out into the hallway.

Don't do it, my inner voice says. *This is a dream. Wake up.* But I don't.

I walk into the hallway and see them: my dad in his wolf form, feral with rage; my mom lying on the ground, crying. Scratch marks in the wall, in the carpet.

"Stop it," I say, trying to make my voice big, and their heads both snap to look at me. He snarls, all cruel eyes and sharp teeth.

"Emerson, baby, go upstairs," she says.

"But Mama—"

My dad barks at me, a warning, and at the harshness of the sound, a wave of fear cracks through my body. I panic, and can't help it—I snap forward, folding into my wolf form, small and soft. Still a pup, even smaller than my child self.

He turns his attention back to my mom, bearing his claws, towering over her.

"Janus, please, not in front of Emerson," she begs, but he just snarls, bearing his claws, and slashes at her. His claws hit her arm and I see red: on the floor, on her dress. She screams, and he turns his back to her and thrashes against the wall again.

I yip, trying to get their attention, trying to make it stop, but they don't hear me. I try to shift back, but I'm too young to control it, and whenever my feelings get the best of me it's my wolf in control. I hear my mom's crying, my own whimpering, the snarls of my dad's rage. I'm afraid, trapped in my body, unable to help. Unable to make it stop.

I SIT UP IN BED, breathing heavy, panting from the nightmare. I look around. I'm in the blue room on the north island. *He's not here. I'm an adult, I'm safe,* I try to remind myself, but my voice breaks out of me, small and sad, and I can feel the grief and adrenaline rolling through my body. My wolf is closer to the surface than usual, scared and wanting comfort. I shove her away.

Behind me, I hear the door to my room open. I look over: Kieran in black sweatpants, no shirt, his face groggy from sleep. Within a second he's on the bed behind me, wrapping an arm around my waist and the other over my shoulders, pulling me towards his chest.

"Hey, it's okay, I'm here," he says, his voice low. "I'm here, okay? You're safe."

I should tell him to leave, but I don't want to. I wrap my arms around his neck and pull myself close.

"You're okay," he murmurs, the warmth of his breath in my hair, on my skin. "Come, you can sleep."

He pulls me down to the bed, and I feel my breathing slow, returning to normal. My face is wet with tears, and he kisses my cheeks and my forehead. Something in me warms, soft and hopeful. We lie there for a few minutes, quiet, breathing in the scent of each other.

"Do you want me to shift?" he asks.

I shake my head. "No. I want you the way you are."

The space between us grows tender. He pulls me towards him, my face in his neck, his hand on my lower back, our legs tangled together. It's different since last night, even if we said it wouldn't be. His body is just a little more familiar now; parts that used to be off-limits just a little more safe.

"Do you know I love you?" I whisper, before I can stop myself. I almost don't know what I mean by it—which kind of love. I feel his body grow still, like he isn't sure either. But he nods.

"I love you more than anyone else," I say, and I mean it.

Something in the air grows sad, and I don't know why. It's his sadness and mine, mixing together; wistful, melancholy. I want to figure it out, want to say whatever I need to make it better. But I'm tired, and some things are better left until morning. Instead I close my eyes and draw myself as close to him as I can, letting myself fall back asleep with his arms to keep me safe.

WHEN I WAKE up in the morning, he's gone, and I smell breakfast. I go downstairs in my pajamas and hear him in the kitchen, talking on the phone.

"It doesn't look like when you do it."

I smile, hiding behind the arch of the doorway. Someone on the other end of the line—Gabe, it must be—says something.

"I don't know. Like, browner. Or like, more... dry, or something? I'll send a photo."

I exhale sharply, trying to suppress a laugh. I hear him grow still.

"You can come out, you know," he says. "I can smell you anyway."

"Rude." I blush and walk into the kitchen.

"It's a nice smell," he says, and I hear sounds of protest from over the phone.

"A room? We have a whole house to ourselves," Kieran says. "But okay, I'm gonna go. Thanks for the help."

He hangs up and gestures proudly to the stove to show me what he's made. Scrambled eggs and something that looks like it used to be bacon, twenty minutes ago.

"I can't believe you made me breakfast," I say, lifting myself up to sit on the kitchen island.

"Gabe couldn't, either. He told you to come home if you can't choke this down."

"I'm sure I'll manage."

He makes me a plate and I eat it happily, even if it's easily less good than anything Gabe's ever made. Breakfast. *For me.*

"So what are you doing today?" Kieran asks, leaning against the sink.

"I wanna finish the thing I'm painting for Gabe. And Maren gave me some of her books to borrow, so I want to tell her what I think of the first one so far. I was gonna take a walk in the woods and send her some voice messages."

"Cool. I'll lace up my shoes after you finish eating."

I swallow my bite of eggs. "Oh, I was planning on going alone."

"Em," he says, crossing his arms. "You can't go by yourself."

"I didn't realize I needed to ask."

"You said you'd let me look out for you while we're here."

I put my plate down beside me. "I agreed to let you come with me to the house. I didn't agree to you coming with me for everything I do."

He lifts an eyebrow. "You want to take a walk in the woods, alone, when some True Remnant nutjobs are slaughtering a field of sheep and writing things on the wall in blood?"

"You're being dramatic. *If* it's even the real Remnant, they're on Saroe, not here. I don't need your permission to take a walk."

"Em, if anything ever happened to you—"

I jump down from the counter. "You wouldn't forgive yourself, I know. You know, this whole overprotective thing isn't as hot as you think it is."

I see a flash of anger in his face and instantly feel guilty. But before I can apologize, he says,

"I don't do this to be hot for you, Emerson. I'm just trying to keep you safe. The world is a dangerous place. Not everyone has good intentions."

The indignation hits me like a bucket of cold water to the face.

"You think I don't know the world is dangerous? I'm not naïve, Kier. There isn't a thing out there you can protect me from that isn't already worse than what happened in my own house."

I see some emotion flash across his face, but I don't have the time to figure it out.

"I didn't say you're naïve," he says. "I just want to make sure you're okay."

"I'm fine. You're letting your fear get the better of you."

"You don't know what I know."

"So tell me, then."

"I can't."

I sigh. "Nice. So not only do you have to protect me from what's out there, but you *also* have to protect me from *knowing* what's out there."

"It's not like that—"

"I'm not a child, Kieran. I don't need you to protect me from myself."

"I protect you because I *love* you."

My brain sputters to a stop. *We're best friends*, I remind myself. *That's what he means.* I take a deep breath.

"But I need you to know that you protect me because I *let* you," I say finally. "Not because I can't protect myself."

His brow furrows. "Okay, but you *do* let me. If I don't make you feel safe, why do you let me sleep in your bed every night? Why do you want me there whenever things get hard?"

Because I'm in love with you, you idiot.

I shake my head, caught off-guard by my own emotion. I don't know what I'm upset about anymore, which part of it. What we're even arguing about.

"Hey. I just want to keep you safe," he says, reaching out to hold me.

I shrug his hands off, and the words come out of my mouth before I have the time to think about them.

"So then what happens when you're not here? What happens when you leave again?"

"Em." I see surprise in his face. "I had to go."

"Not true, and you know it." I feel the tears come to my eyes, and I bring my hands up, using my ring fingers to wipe them away before they hit my cheeks. "*Agaayu*, this is so embarrassing. I'm sorry. It's not about that. It's just because I'm hormonal and we're here again that I'm thinking about it."

"Hey." He reaches out to me again. "Hey, it's okay. You don't have to cry." He pulls me to his chest, and for a second I feel better, but then I shake my head and push him away.

"No, you know what? It *is* about that. It's *also* about that." I swallow, crossing my arms in front of me. "Listen. You live in a world where I need you to keep me safe. And you *do* make me feel safe, Kier, you do. But the hardest stuff I've ever had to do, I did without you. The worst parts of my life, I survived before I met you. And do you know when, in my adult life, I felt the most vulnerable?"

He shakes his head. I swallow, looking up at him, meeting his eyes. Hazel, gold.

"It was when I stood upstairs in *this* house and I asked you to stay, and you *left* me. For *two years*, Kieran, you left. You didn't say a word until Seb's rite brought you back. I got through *that* on my own. So no, I don't need you to follow me into the woods. I know how to take care of myself."

And with that, I grab my coat and shoes, and storm out of the house.

14

KIERAN

She winds through the paths in the woods, trying to lose me. I hang back, maybe some forty or fifty paces—far enough to give her some space, but close enough that she knows I'm still there.

I can feel her anger ease as she walks farther. After about forty-five minutes, the thick clouds ahead finally give way to snow, and she leads me where I knew she would—the quarry.

She takes a seat on the rocks and looks out at the water. I hang back in the trees, giving her her space. After a few minutes, she looks over her shoulder and meets my eye. She nudges her head towards the water, and I follow, coming to sit next to her.

In my wolf form, she seems so small and delicate next to me. When I sit on my haunches, her head only comes up to my mid-chest. But today she doesn't lean against me. There's anger in the air as she looks out at the water.

"Do you remember when we met?" she asks.

Ah. So I'll have to earn it.

My body rolls forward, shifting into my human form, and I

can see her resolutely look away from me. She reaches into her bag and pulls out a blanket and a black sweater.

"Of course I remember." I pull the sweater on and wrap the blanket over my lower half.

"Tell me then."

"Well, I was—what was it, you were nine? So I would have been eleven. I was playing by myself in the woods, because my asshole brothers had just locked me out of the house. And then I heard a scream from the quarry."

"It was *not* a scream."

"Right, my mistake. I heard a *voice* coming from the quarry."

"Better."

I smile. "So I ran over to see what it was. And I saw this little girl with long blonde hair and two kids from her *fika*, standing at the edge of that rock."

I point up to the rock a few meters above the water, which we use to cannonball from in the summer. I can see it now: her in her yellow bathing suit, the one her mom made that she wore for three summers, even after it didn't really fit. Holding her arms around herself, stepping backwards towards the edge as Seb and Gabe goaded her.

"And what were they like?" she asks. "The other kids."

"*Incredibly* stupid. You could just smell it off them. Even now—"

She laughs softly, and I can feel something in the air warm.

"Okay, okay," she says. "So then what?"

"I saw Seb holding a frog, trying to scare you with it. Gabe was kind of half-stopping him, but laughing along. And you were scared."

"So what did you do?"

"Well, I did what I had to. I punched Seb in the face."

She cracks up for real now, folding over with a hand on her stomach, the laughter echoing off rocks around us. "*Agaayu*, I still can't believe you did that. And he's never forgiven you for it."

"Yeah, but he's also never tried to scare you with a frog again, has he?"

"I guess not." She looks up at me, and I see the warmth in her eyes.

"That was the first summer I was happy," I say, before I can think about it.

"What?"

"Nothing."

"No," she says softly. "Tell me."

I swallow. "I… I don't know. I didn't have a great home life. Nothing like you, of course. I know what you had to go through is—" I stop. "Anyway. I was just lonely, I guess. The summer I met you was the first summer I didn't feel alone."

She smiles. "It was the summer we became a family. Me and the guys, I mean. And you, I guess. It all changed when we met you."

She looks back out at the water and tentatively leans her head against my shoulder. I feel a small part of my world fall back into place.

"Yeah?" I ask.

For a minute or two, she says nothing—so long that I almost wonder if she didn't hear me. But finally, she speaks.

"I moved into the *fikarig* the night after Mom died." Her voice is quiet, and I can hear the emotion in it. The wolf inside her that she's pushing away. "They didn't like me. Seb and Gabe had their own thing—the only kids in the *fika*, and all that. And when I came, I was an imposition. They teased me a lot."

I feel a growl escape from my inner wolf, and clear my throat to cover it.

"It wasn't like *I* wanted to be there," she says, bringing her knees up to her chest. She's still in her pajamas under the coat, and I watch as a few snowflakes land on the red flannel. "I would have done anything to be with her, instead. But, I don't know. We were kids. And I guess because I wasn't happy, when they teased me I'd cry, and that made it worse. So I stuck to myself. Or I'd hang out with Saga and make myself helpful around the house."

I think about little Em, hanging out with the grown-ups. Helping Saga with her then-new business. Trying to make herself indispensable. Trying to earn her place in the *fika*.

"That summer... I don't know," she says. "I didn't know how to stand up to Seb, and when you did for me, I felt safe. Instantly. It was like you stood up to him and I just..."

She brings her hands together, like magnets.

"And then the real Em came out. So once you were there, the guys got to know me. That summer we got close for the first time ever. It was the first time I had a family after my mom died."

I wrap my arm around her, pulling her closer to me.

"I feel that. You guys became my family, too. Especially once my parents split and my mom moved us to Saroe."

The air grows quiet, and I know what she's thinking.

"So then why did you leave?" she asks finally.

I swallow. "My training—"

"There are carpenters on Saroe, Kier. Why did you have to go all the way to Keist?"

I think back to that summer. The night I left—from *here*, their vacation house on the shore in Halluk. Em had just turned eighteen, and I was a hair over of twenty. It was the summer I realized I loved her.

"You were dating Oskar," I say weakly.

She rolls her eyes. "You were dating Astrid. And then Charlotte, and then Ester, if I remember correctly. *Next*."

I look up at the sky, running a hand over my shoulder, massaging the muscle, trying to think. The snow is falling harder now, but I'm still not cold.

"Do you remember that night?" I ask.

"Yeah."

"What do you remember?"

She turns her body towards me, her knees resting on my leg.

"We were here," she says. "The guys had a fight. I don't remember about what, but it was a shouting match, and I panicked. It was the first time you saw me shift."

"The only time," I say quietly.

She swallows. "You and I were alone in the room upstairs. And I was so scared, I couldn't control myself. I shifted, and I couldn't go back. And you... you held me, for the first time. Until I felt safe enough to control it. Until I could get back into my skin again. And then, when I did..."

I set my jaw, feeling the shame wash over me. When she shifted into her wolf form, she'd torn through her clothes. I was holding her when she shifted back, so she ended up naked on my lap.

It had been a few months since I'd known I was in love with her. She had a boyfriend. I had Astrid, or Charlotte, then—I don't remember which, but it should have mattered, and it didn't. I couldn't stop myself, and I kissed her. It could have been five minutes, it could have been an hour. It's a miracle we didn't go any farther, with how badly I wanted her even then.

"I knew you were deciding on your traineeship," she says quietly. "And I asked you to stay. So me, you, and Seb and Gabe could make our own *fika*."

"I wanted that," I say. I still want it, now—more than I know how to say.

"So then why?"

"I didn't want—" I groan, trying to find the words. "God, Em, I'm not good at this stuff. Do we have to talk about this?"

"You know, for years I thought I was a terrible kisser."

I bark out a laugh. "*What?*"

"Yeah. It took until I was dating Arjen for me to learn that my mouth wasn't, you know. Cursed."

"I— Em." I can't help but laugh, and she gives me a look.

"*That's* what happens when we don't talk."

I swallow, pulling away from her. "Okay. I don't know. But I remember I kissed you and something in me… took over, I don't know." I shake my head, unable to meet her eyes. "When I went out with the guys to get firewood, we came back and saw you and Oskar."

"*He* was kissing *me*. I was confused."

"You kissed him back. And I didn't want to make you choose."

"Kieran," she says softly. "It would have been such an easy decision."

"I couldn't—" I shake my head. "You were younger than me. I saw how you looked at him. I saw how *he* looked at *you*. I hated how he looked at you."

"I know," she says, laughing softly. "I remember that part."

"I didn't want to make you choose. Not to spare you the decision, although I guess that would have been bigger of me. But because—and this sucks, but it's true—if I asked you to choose and it hadn't been me…"

She puts a hand on my arm. "It would have been you."

The air between us grows heavy. It's snowing harder now, the snowflakes pooling in her hair, on her clothes, in her eyelashes.

"You must be cold," she says.

"I'm not."

She looks out at the water again. "I'm sorry about what I said. I know you always protect me. But I want you to know that it's because I let you. I'm not weak."

"I know," I say, and I mean it. "Your strength just looks different than mine."

She rolls her eyes. "Maren would call that a cop-out."

"Maren's wrong. You *are* strong. But my strength is… I don't know. I get mad, I break stuff. I punch Seb when he's holding a frog. It's good, but it's not like you."

"So what kind of strong am I, then?" She raises an eyebrow.

I feel a sharp pain in my gut, remembering my rite.

"You've been through more shit than anyone I know," I say. "And you're still Em. You're still… I don't know. Soft. You know how to love people. I don't think I could go through what you've been through and not let it break me."

She tucks her chin. "I wish I could be strong your way, sometimes. I wish I didn't jump when someone drops a sheet pan." She gives me a look, humor tugging at her lips.

"But you're strong like I'm not. And you don't need my kind of strength, because when I'm here, I'll always stand up for you. We can fill in the gaps for each other."

"Maybe," she says, and brings her head back down to my shoulder. "You *do* know how to love people, you know."

"Not like you. You remember birthdays and stuff."

She snorts. "That's easy. I just write them down."

"No, really," I say. "You make people's favorite cakes. You pick up on something someone said a year ago and then surprise them with it for Karstmis. I don't know how to love people like that."

"You know how to love me."

I don't know how not to love you. But I can't find words for it, so I wait.

"You know how to make me feel safe." She looks up at me and I see a hint of nervousness in her face.

I swallow. The air is changing. She's trying something for me, something I don't know how to do. Closing the distance between us.

"You called me *kiyyuni*," she says, her voice quiet, hopeful. "Did you mean it?"

"*Iija.*" *Yes.*

I move my mouth towards hers, slow and hesitant. She brings

her face to mine, and our lips brush gently against each other. I kiss her again, more firmly now, but she pulls away.

"What does it mean? If it happens again?" she whispers.

"I don't know. It depends on what you want it to mean."

She turns to look at the water, and I can scent the disappointment in the air.

"Em." I put a hand to her face and draw it up to look at me. "We said just one time. But I..." I swallow, pushing away my nerves and self-doubt. "It doesn't have to be just once. I want... I don't know. I want this. I want... I want you. If you—"

What happens next is so fast that it takes my brain a second to process. In a second she's on me, crawling onto my body, straddling my lap, kissing my face. She takes me in her hands and kisses me hard, her teeth on my lower lip, her tongue brushing against it. I bring my arms around her and pull her against me, but she pushes me down onto my back, into the snow.

I feel myself grow hard, and I notice the second it registers in her body. The way her hips press against me just a little bit harder; the scent of her heat and arousal in the air. She grinds gently against me and I can't suppress a groan.

"Kieran," she says, pulling away, and I can see the bloom of hope and love and heat in her eyes.

"Yeah?"

"Take me home."

EMERSON

He shifts for me and I climb on his back, feeling the warmth of his beast between my legs. The animal of his body is powerful, strong as anything. He moves his head down for me, an instruction: *get low.*

I wrap my arms around his neck and lie my body close to his, drawing myself as near to him as possible. And then he runs, barreling forward through the woods, ducking through paths that he must have learned from a hundred childhood days out here, wandering through the woods before I knew him.

We near the edge of the forest and I can see the house up ahead on the top of the hill. As we get inside the front door and he shifts again, back into his human form. I hand him the blanket and he wraps it around his lower body, looking down at me, his eyes hungry.

"You're all dirty," I say, running my hand over his shoulders, his arms. There's some mud on him from the path through the woods.

"It's not so bad."

I shake my head, looking up at him. I feel my heat pulsing through me, making me bold. "No. We should shower."

"Together?"

I nod.

I take off my coat and shoes and take his hand, leading him up the stairs to the master bedroom. Attached to that room is the biggest bathroom in the house, with a tub and large shower. I pull him inside and reach into the shower stall to turn the water on, then turn to face him.

He reaches for me, but I take a step back and bring my hands to the bottom hem of my pajama top, pulling the soft red knit over my head, exposing my bare breasts and stomach.

"Em," he groans, looking at my body, then up at my eyes. I keep eye contact and slip off my pants, pulling them down over my hips and my ass, my underwear with them. I hear his breathing grow heavy, admiring me as I step out of them. Completely naked, I step towards him.

"Now you," I whisper, running my fingers under the hem of his sweater.

He pulls it over his head, dropping the blanket I'd brought to the woods for him. In a second he's naked, our bodies pressing together. I can feel his hardness against my stomach, making my knees weak. I pull his face down towards me, kissing his lips, his beard, his neck. He groans against me, pressing his hips into me, and I feel my body respond, warmth and wetness pooling between my legs.

The heat of the shower is starting to steam up the room, and I grab his hand and lead him into the water with me. He towers over me, and I watch as the water slides over his head, soaking into his red-brown hair, beads running over his body.

"Em," he murmurs, pulling me close. "God. You feel so good. *Ijekayyatik.*" *I love you.*

"I love you," I whisper back, bringing his face towards me again, kissing him. I run my hands up his body, up to his neck, his shoulders, down his back. I take in everything, savoring every curve and line of his body, every muscle.

"You're so beautiful," he says, and in his eyes, I feel it. I've always felt like there's not enough of me. Too short, too thin, too quiet; the shape of my breasts too small, the curve of my waist and hips too minor to be interesting. But in Kieran's eyes I feel like I'm everything. The warmth of the sun, the glow of the stars. The peace of the lakes and the power of the ocean. I feel confident, bold. Sensual in a way I don't know how to be even with myself.

"I love you," I say again, reaching up to kiss his collarbone, the muscular curve of his chest, his shoulder. "I love you." I run my hands over his stomach, feeling his muscles, taking in the cuts and bruises where the rite hurt him.

I want him—under me, around me, inside of me—but this is more than that. It's reverent. Devoted. He runs his hands over my body, taking me in, memorizing me. We take our time, accounting for every detail, every freckle and scar.

He brings his mouth down to mine, tasting me.

"You know how many showers I've stood under, trying not to think of you?" he murmurs, making his way to my throat.

"Tell me."

"Hundreds. Thousands." I feel him smile against my skin. "You won't believe my water bill."

I laugh, but then he nips gently at my neck and I feel my heat flood through me, hungry and primal. My wolf is in there somewhere, wanting him, too—wanting him to mark me, take me as his mate.

"Again," I whisper, and he kisses me harder, scraping his teeth across my skin and biting gently.

"Oh, God. Kieran." I bring my hand down to his erection, and the energy between us changes. His head rolls back, and he groans as I run my fingers up and down the length of it. After a minute he tries to brush my hand away.

"I want to take care of *you*," he says, reaching for my hips.

I shake my head. "I want *this*."

I reach for him again, stroking him, watching what it does to him when I go faster or slower, when I make my grip tighter, when I run my hand over the head and then come back down. I make the space between our bodies smaller, bringing myself so close that the back of my hand brushes against his abs and my fingers brush against my own stomach as I stroke him.

"Fuck. Em," he groans, panting, the water spilling over us. He grabs onto my hips to hold himself steady, and I go a little faster, the pace becoming needy, insistent. My own breath quickens in pace with his. I like seeing him like this: guard down, lost in pleasure for *me*, at my hands.

"Too good," he groans, and pushes my hand away. He reaches down for my hips and lifts me up, pressing me against the wall of the shower. I wrap my legs around him and gasp as I feel his hardness brush against the sensitive place between my legs. I think he's going to take me, but instead he holds me in place against the wall, kissing me, working his mouth down to the places in my neck that make me gasp and go wild with desire.

He's studied me, I realize. He's learned what I like.

He brings his mouth lower, sucking and biting along the spot between my neck and my shoulder. I notice his body grow taut as he takes his time, nuzzling into me, nipping lightly at the skin of my neck. It's the place where his mark would go, I realize. And as I see what he's doing—lingering, savoring, *imagining* how it would be to claim me—I feel my whole body flood with need.

"Kier," I breathe.

He sucks on the skin, and I feel his teeth run lightly over it. Instinctively, my hips grind towards him.

"*Iija*," I groan.

"Em." He pulls away, his eyes dark with desire. "I want you."

"You have me."

"No. I *want* you. Where?"

I point through the glass of the shower to the bedroom. He lifts me higher onto him and I wrap my legs tightly around his waist. He reaches to turn off the shower handle and carries me out of the bathroom, laying me down on the bed, climbing over me, our bodies still wet.

"Fuck, Em," he says, kissing his way down my body. I gasp at the familiar warmth of his tongue on my clit, the feeling of one finger dipping gently in and out of me.

"You're so wet," he murmurs. "God. I've been dreaming of this."

His finger curls up, brushing against some spot inside me that makes me buck instinctively. I moan, my hands grasping for him, fingers tangling in his wet hair. He dips his finger in and out, his tongue moving faster, and I feel my vision start to grow hazy. He works me until I'm close, and it takes all my self-control to drag his face up to mine.

"I need you," I gasp.

"Okay," he says, but then he hesitates. "But... Your heat. What about—"

"Oh," I say, realizing. Birth control. "I take something. I have for years, just in case."

He nods. "I didn't think that night. I only realized the next day, and I wanted to ask."

"No, we're fine. We're good," I say, pulling him towards me, but he keeps himself in place.

"It would have been okay," he says softly, looking into my eyes.

His words catch me off-guard. I swallow back whatever complicated emotion I'm feeling and pull his face in to kiss him hard. Not because he said this. Not because I believe him. But because I realize this is a man who loves me; a man who has thought about all our forevers.

He positions himself between my legs, sliding his cock between my lips, then pressing gently at my entrance. We both gasp as he enters me. I'm more ready for him now, more prepared for the length and girth of him than last time, and as he thrusts himself into me, my head falls back.

"God, Kieran," I gasp.

He pulls back and then thrusts into me again. I moan and he picks up the pace. I can feel the pressure building faintly somewhere in me, bringing me higher.

"I want to try something," he says, reaching for a pillow from the head of the bed. "I want to put this under your hips, okay?"

I nod and he pulls out of me, and I find myself groaning in protest.

"Impatient," he jokes, just like that night. His amber eyes are dark and sparkling, and God, I need him.

"Stop joking and fuck me, please," I say, and he laughs.

He folds the pillow in half and slides it under me as I lift my hips, then comes to lean over me.

"If you don't like it, tell me," he murmurs into my ear, and then he enters me again.

Agaayu, it's so good. The angle is different, and I feel him in me, filling me, reaching that place his fingers found earlier. The sound that comes out of me is primal, and the feeling building in me gets stronger as he thrusts into me again.

"Good?" he asks.

"So good," I gasp.

"Touch yourself for me," he says, his voice low. "I want to see the look on your face when you touch yourself."

He lifts his upper body higher, and my hand reaches between us to find my clit. As my middle finger starts to circle it, I hear the sounds I'm making change, my tone getting higher. The pleasure rocks through me, and his pace changes in response.

"Kieran," I gasp. "Oh my God."

"Fuck. Em," he groans. "You look so pretty like that. You look so pretty touching yourself for me."

He brings his mouth to my neck again, kissing and biting

gently at the skin as he thrusts into me, and I feel a flood of desire rush through my whole body, making me weak. I *want* him to mark me—to claim me as his, so I always belong to him. At the thought of it, I feel my inner walls clench tighter around him, and he gasps.

"You feel so good," he groans, his hips moving faster.

I'm bucking for him, gasping, when I hear a buzzing from the other side of the room.

"What's that?" I ask, looking up, breathless.

"Who cares?" he asks, burying his face into my neck, kissing me.

"No, really."

He lifts his head reluctantly, following my gaze. "Oh, my phone. Whatever."

"What if it's important?"

He pulls away, looking at me with humor in his eyes. "Em. There is literally not a single person in the world I would rather talk to than be doing *this*."

He thrusts into me again, rounding his hips, and my mind goes soft. As his pace grows faster, more insistent, the rest of the world falls away. He's groaning, panting, losing himself in me. I feel my eyes grow glassy as I near my climax.

"What do you want?" he murmurs into my ear. "How do you want to come?"

"I wanna be on top."

He nods, pulling my body towards him, then rolls onto his back. I gasp as the angle of him changes inside me. Straddling his hips now, I reposition myself, pushing the pillow out of the way, feeling him deeper than before.

"Kier," I moan, putting my hands on his body to steady myself. I begin to rock my hips back and forth, finding a rhythm that feels good, riding him.

"Oh, God," he says, his voice labored. "I don't know how long I can have you do that."

"Good," I purr, going faster. His hand finds my clit and I gasp. My hips buck—wild, needy, chasing my pleasure and his.

This time, it hits him first. He groans, grabbing onto my hips with his free hand, pressing up into me, and I can feel him spill himself inside of me. The thought of it overwhelms me, and seconds later I'm coming, my climax shaking through me. I'm gasping, wild, saying his name.

"Kieran. Oh my God, Kieran."

"Em," he whispers.

As I come down, I look at him under me, his gaze all warmth and devotion. I lean myself down onto his chest, slipping him out of me, looking into his eyes.

"I can't believe this is real," he murmurs, wrapping his arms around me, kissing the top of my head.

"Promise me you'll never leave," I whisper.

"I promise."

16

KIERAN

When Em comes back from washing up, she picks up my phone from the table.

"Someone's calling again." She tosses it gently towards me, and it lands on the bed. As she comes to lie next to me, curling up in the crook of my arm, I lift it to see the screen.

"It's Seb," I say, and pick up the call. "Hey, what's up?"

"Dude, where the fuck have you been?" His voice is tense. I can hear people talking in the background.

"What? I was busy. What's going on?"

"There was another attack. They came for the harbor, in broad daylight."

"What the fuck?" I sit up in bed. Em looks up at me.

"What is it?" she whispers. I bring the phone down to put it on speakerphone.

"They attacked the harbor? On Saroe?" I ask.

"They destroyed it. Someone tore through the sails of all the fishing boats. They flipped Heimig's car and lit two of the shops on fire."

"*Uikbaane*," I curse. "Is Heimig okay? Is anyone hurt?"

"No one's hurt. He was there, but he wasn't in the car."

"How many of them were there?"

"Ten? Twelve? I don't know, dude. We're having a council meeting in twenty minutes."

"I can't get there in time," I say. Not that it would do much good, anyway.

"No, don't bother. It's better that you guys are safe."

"Are you thinking of coming here, too?" Em asks.

"Oh, hey Em," Seb says over the phone. "I don't know. Saga says that if we leave now, we're giving them what they want. And I'd rather have me and Gabe here at the *fikarig* to protect the place if they get too close. But Maren is scared, so we're talking about it."

"It would only take you a few hours to get here, right?" Em asks. "So if you're not sure, but something changes…"

"Yeah, Gabe said the same thing."

"I'm sorry, man," I say, running a hand through my hair. "I should have been there."

"Nah, what are you talking about? What could we have done? There were ten of them, at least."

"Yeah," I say, but it doesn't feel right. "If you need me, you'll tell me. Okay?"

"That's not gonna happen. But yeah, okay."

"Call us if anything changes," Em says. "And if you need to come here, don't hesitate."

"Will do," Seb says, and we say goodbye and hang up.

"*Agaayu*," Em says, curling her knees up to her chest and looking up at me. "It's so horrible. Why would they do this?"

I set my jaw, thinking.

"You're worried it's my dad," she says.

I nod.

"Kier, you said this morning…" She brings a hand up, twisting a lock of wet hair, trying to find the words. "You said I don't know what you know. Do you have a real reason to think he's here?"

"Yeah," I say. "I think so."

"Something from the rite?"

"Yeah. But I don't… I don't know, with the *kattaka* and every-thing. I'm not sure how much of it was the ancestors and how much was my own mind."

"Saga says you can always trust the spirits," she says quietly. "You know, Seb told Maren something about his rite. Part of it was about her, somehow. She doesn't know everything, but she knows some."

I swallow. Seb can make his own choices, I guess, but the edicts in the ancient books are clear. You can't tell another soul what you see in the ring. No matter how much I want to.

"I'm not supposed to tell you," I say. "It fucks me up that I can't. It doesn't feel right. But I just need you to trust me."

"I do," she says, and takes my hand in hers. She brings it up to her face, eyeing the mark where the cut was last night, and kisses it, running her finger over the hair tie she gave me. "It's not that. It's just that I knew that Seb's rite involved Maren. And when you told me in the library that some part of your rite was about me… it made me hope." A small smile tugs at her lips.

"Hope what?"

"Hope that maybe I am for you what Maren is for Seb."

"My mate?" I ask, and pull her close. I want it to be her. I lost myself in the shower, my wolf taking over, imagining how it would be to see her wear my claim on her neck.

"Maybe. Is that crazy?"

"I don't think so."

I pull her towards my chest and think about the things I can't tell her. The words that have kept me up at night, after she falls asleep. The things I wish I didn't know.

"You can't save her, you know," she says. Her voice feels like it's coming from a thousand miles away and from inside me all at once.

"What?" I ask, woozy.

"Emerson. You know you can't save her," she says, stepping closer to me. "No one can. After all, look what happened to me."

And that's when I hear the growling behind me.

I turn and stumble backwards as I catch sight of him. The wolf behind me is massive: fur dark gray and matted, his body full of hunger and raw power. His teeth are bared, his head low to the ground as he walks towards me, stalking his prey.

Seb's advice comes to me fast. Don't shift too soon, or you'll break out of your body armor. I stagger back, feeling for the knife strapped to my leg. As soon as I reach it, the wolf lunges, all teeth and claws, and I run out of the way just in time. But he doesn't reach me. Instead, as I run to the side, he reaches the goddess, tackling her to the floor.

She cries out as he pins her down, his claws bared, his paws pressing down on her forearms. She thrashes against him, crying. And then I hear it.

"Stop it."

The voice is small, and I turn behind me to see a little girl. Em.

I know her immediately, even though she's so much smaller than even when we met. She must be five or six at the oldest. She's wearing blue pajamas with a yellow sun on the front.

"No," I say, reaching out to her. I want to keep her out of this. But the wolf hears her voice, and he and the goddesses both turn to look at her.

"Emerson, baby, go upstairs," the goddess says. But it's not Móra, I realize, and the realization hits me like a gut punch.

It's Em's mother. Lena.

I'm in a memory. Em's memory.

"But Mama—"

The wolf barks at her, the sound so harsh and loud that it startles even me, and I fall to my knees. I see a wave of fear hit Em, her eyes going wide. Her breathing gets erratic, tearing through her, and I know what's next. I've seen this before, in kids—the way the wolf overtakes them, before they learn to control the shift. She gasps and falls forward, tumbling into her wolf form before me, her fur tan and white.

"Em. Em, it's okay," I say to her. "You're safe, okay?" But she's whimpering, scared, and I realize she doesn't hear me. It's like I'm not here.

"Janus, please, not in front of Emerson," I hear behind me, and then I hear a scream and smell the scent of blood.

Agaayit, I think, looking at the pup before me. She's so small. Smaller than she should be for her age. Too small to see this. She's yipping, panicking, and I can feel her fear in the air.

"Make it stop," I say, my voice weak. Not for me—for her.

"Are you ready for more?" asks Lena, and now she's like the goddess again: floating over me, the slate wiped clean. The smell of blood disappears from the air, Emerson's wolf form vanishing into mist. I turn around to see the gray wolf stalking me, prowling around the edge of the ring.

"No," I say, but it's too late. The scene snaps to something different: their family at dinner, Janus shouting at Lena in the kitchen, holding a knife while Emerson sobs under the dining room table, rocking back and forth, hands to her ears. The wolf is still stalking the ring, watching me as I take it in.

"Again," the goddess says, and now Lena is crying on the couch, Janus looming over her in his wolf form. Emerson stands between them, facing her mother. She's almost the girl she was when I met her: she must be eight, maybe nine. She's holding a stuffed rabbit under one arm, stroking her mother's hand.

"It's okay, Mama," she says, as her mother cries. "I can help you. You're gonna be okay."

Janus lifts his paw, claws bared, and I lunge.

"No!" I shout, trying to tackle him to the ground before he hurts them. But as I reach them, the scene vanishes into mist, and what comes through the vapor is the wolf that's been prowling around the ring, watching me.

Now that I've seen the memories, I know it for sure. Janus, her father. He's a little older, but it's recognizably him, his body massive, just a little harsher and more angular than it was then. I move quickly, unstrapping my knife from my leg, and take a fighting stance.

I've always hated him. I hated him from the first goddamn moment I saw how Em reacts when someone raises a voice, or the way she jumps at a loud noise. But now, seeing what he did to Lena, seeing how young Em was for myself, I feel the anger coursing through me, pushing me, controlling me.

I want him dead.

He lunges first, fangs and teeth bared, and this time I don't run out of the way. He's so large and strong that he barrels into my body and slams me into the ground. I gasp, the breath crushed from my lungs, but I only have a second to act. He lifts a paw and slashes at my left arm, just as I manage to get the right one free and sink the knife into his side. As the blade meets his flesh, he yelps and stumbles back from me, retreating to the edge of the ring.

The air fills with the scent of blood, his and mine. It's warm on my hands, and I feel it starting to soak through the fabric of my sweater. It hits me with confusion that this is so much more real than the memories I saw a moment ago. I bring a hand to my arm, then back up to my face.

The blood is real. This is all real.

"Is he really here?" I ask Lena, the goddess, whoever she is. Maybe both at once.

"He's here."

Janus prowls the edge of the ring again, growling, watching me. Agaayu, how will I protect Em from this? I need to kill him before he can find her. I think, drawing on my memories from my training. I need to shift. It'll be easier to overtake him in my wolf form.

"You can't save her, Kieran," Lena says again, interrupting my thought. "What's done is done."

"It's not over. I'll kill him." I start to walk around the ring now, too, watching him, unwilling to turn my back. I need to get my body armor off. I reach to take off my sweater without looking away from him.

"He can smell her on you," Lena says.

My breath clouds before me as I reach for my protective vest and undo the straps. As my hands fumble together, I feel the hair tie Em gave me.

Wait—is that how he found me? Could he smell her on me somehow, when I came up to the ring? No, that doesn't make sense—

"No," Lena says. "Not from your clothing. Because you're her mate."

Her words catch me off-guard, and I fumble as I finally get the vest off. Which parts of this are real? Which parts am I supposed to believe?

"You know that, don't you?" she asks. "Deep down."

"I don't— I don't know," I stammer. Don't I?

"I know you love her," she says, and her voice is sad. "But you can't protect her from what's going to happen. You can't take her destiny from her."

"What do you mean?"

The lights grow brighter, more vibrant. Suddenly she swirls through the air, flowing around me and then appearing behind my body. Her voice is rushed and serious in my ear.

"He's here, Kieran," she says. "And he will find her."

And then he lunges for me again.

17

EMERSON

We spend the rest of the day in bed. Kieran makes me come four, five times, until my knees are weak and my legs are shaky. He tells me he loves me, again and again: in my hair, against my neck, kissing his way down my stomach. In the evening he insists on making me dinner, and this time I let him. I sit on the kitchen counter across from the island, sketching him as he works his way through a recipe Gabe sent over. That night, we go to sleep in his bed, and when I wake up in the morning he's still there, his arms wrapped around me.

Mine. And I'm his.

I turn to face him, admiring his nose, the freckles over his face, the cut of his jaw. Kieran's fully Fakari, but like me, he's fairer in coloring than Seb or Gabe. The thing that gives it away are his broad, blunt cheekbones and the golden ring in his eyes, a sign of the wolf buried within.

I climb out of bed, not wanting to wake him, and slip into the bathroom to wash my face. Standing in front of the mirror, I take in my own eyes, dark gray-blue. They have an amber ring, too, but it's thin and faded, barely perceptible anymore after all these years of keeping my wolf hidden away.

As I wash my face, I think of Maren, who spent years unknowingly suppressing her wolf with creams, pills, and tonics before she came to the Fakaris. When I met her, her eyes were a rich, warm brown, but nothing indicated she might be a shifter. Once her wolf finally came to the surface—and especially after she spent months learning to work with her inner wolf with Seb —it was like her whole face changed. She glows now. As though the gold that brought its way to her eyes also wove its way into her skin, her posture, her bearing.

I straighten from over the sink and pick up a towel to dry my face. As I do, I look in the mirror, wondering. What would I look like, if I let my wolf in? Would I glow, too?

But then, in an instant, I remember how it felt to be trapped in my own skin: even smaller than I am now, but not able to speak or defend myself. How it felt to slip into a version of myself without wanting to, whenever a strong enough emotion overtook me. Thrashing against my own body, trying to take control of a part of me that felt uncontrollable.

No. It's better this way.

I slip out of the bathroom and walk down the hall to the blue room, where my bags are. I change out of my pajamas, into dark jeans and a blue-and-white striped shirt. It's cold outside, so I add my warm yellow knit sweater on top, a Karstmis gift from Saga a few years ago.

I look out of the window at the sea below. The sun is just beginning to rise, painting the sky pink and amber. Kieran probably won't be up for another hour, and I'm dying to tell Maren what happened yesterday. I rummage through my duffle bag and find my phone, putting it into my back pocket. I'll take a short walk and be back before he wakes up.

Once downstairs, I lace up my boots and grab my coat to head out of the door. There's a thick blanket of snow on the ground—

the snowfall yesterday didn't stop until the evening, and now the earth is coated in it, muting everything. I'll walk along the beach, I decide. Kieran won't be happy that I'm out by myself, but it's not his decision. And at least this way I'll be in an area I know.

I make my way down the hill and towards the shore, where a strip of sand is visible between the blanket of snow and the icy blue sea. I pull my phone from my back pocket and open the app Maren and I use for audio messages.

"Heij," I say after hitting record, and my voice is still groggy from sleep. "I hope your product launch is going well, and that you're not too freaked out after what happened yesterday. I have so much to tell you. You won't believe what happened with Kieran. Or, well, maybe you will, but I still don't…"

I tell her about the argument we had in the morning and our conversation in the woods later that day. That he took me home and we spent all day in bed together.

"I can't believe it," I say, looking up at the sky. I'm nearing the edge of the beach now, where the sand of the shore starts to turn into forest. "I think this is *real*. Like maybe this is really it, you know? We finally found our way—"

I stop, seeing something between the trees. It can't be.

"Hang on," I say, walking closer. But I see the shape again.

"Uh, Maren, I have to go. I'll tell you the rest later." And I tap to end the recording.

Through the trees, I can swear I see her. Blue floral dress, golden hair.

I freeze. It's been years since this has happened. Kieran would want me to stay here. He would tell me not to go chasing visions through the woods. But Kieran still has both his parents. He doesn't know what it's like.

My feet make the decision for me. I start walking towards the trees.

"Mom?" I say quietly, almost under my breath. If it's real—if this is her spirit—she'll be able to hear me regardless.

She slips away again, but I know she'll be back. I reach the edge of the woods, stopping just before the tree line. Still in view of the beach house.

"Mama," I say, and my voice breaks. "Mom, I'm here. Come out. Let me see you."

She appears again in my line of vision. She's beautiful. Beautiful in the way your mom is when you're a kid. Beautiful in the way someone you love is after they're gone.

"Emerson," she says, and she smiles softly. "Who let you get so big?"

My throat feels thick with the tears.

"It's okay, baby," she says, and she steps forward. She's still ten, maybe twenty feet from me.

My breathing tears through me, and I feel tears spilling over my cheeks, hot against the cold winter air.

"Mama," I say, and I feel like a little kid again. "I think about you every day."

"Do you?" she asks, turning her head to the side. Like she knows.

"I— I don't know." I swallow, bringing my hands up to my face, using my sleeves to wipe away my tears. "I think if I let myself, it might kill me. But I *feel* you every day. When I sing in the shower. When I use your brushes to paint. When I put cinnamon in my coffee, like you used to."

"Oh, *piu*," she murmurs. "You don't have to be sad."

"But I am," I say. I feel my wolf in me, closer to the surface than ever. "I always wondered if I'd ever see you again. It's been so long since the last time."

"You'll see me very soon," she says, and I feel my brow furrow.

"What?"

"Follow me." She lifts a hand to me. An invitation.

I hesitate. I can almost hear my own voice in my mind; the part of me that always calls out to myself in a dream, telling me *don't go, come back.* I can hear Kieran telling me he wants to protect me, that *I just need you to trust me.*

"You can trust yourself," she says.

Can I?

I hear something from the top of the hill, and instinctively I glance over my shoulder, looking towards the noise. It's a fox, exploring the deck of the house. I turn back to my mom and suddenly she's just a few feet from me, her eyes serious.

"Emerson, listen," she says, her tone earnest, words coming fast, like she doesn't have enough time. "You will have a choice to make. When the moment comes, remember. You have everything you need to do this."

"What moment? To do what?" I ask.

"You'll know. Be strong. Who you are is enough."

"What?"

And then she disappears.

"Mama, no. Wait," I cry.

I have so much to tell you, I want to say.

I'm grown now. I'm becoming a healer, like Saga.

I have a man who loves me, and I love him more than anything.

You'd be so proud of me, Mom.

"Come back." My voice is quiet now, broken. "Please, come back."

But she's gone and I'm alone, standing at the edge of the forest. Wondering what would have happened if I'd been brave enough to follow when she asked.

18

KIERAN

When I wake up, it's close to ten. I stretch and roll over to find the space next to me in bed is empty.

"Em?" I call out. Nothing.

The adrenaline jolts through me immediately.

"Em, where are you?"

There's no reply, and I jump out of bed and rush out into the hall.

"Emerson," I call out. She's not in the blue room, so I go down the stairs. I'm relieved when the scent of her hits me as I enter the kitchen. She's in the house, at least. Finally, I find her, sitting on a chair at the dining table, knees up to her chest.

"Hey, what's wrong?" I ask, coming towards her. She looks up at me. Her eyes are rimmed with pink, and I can see she's been crying.

"Are you…" I don't know how to ask. "Did something happen? Did you… did you change your mind?"

I see a flicker of confusion in her eyes. "About us? Oh, no."

I let out a sigh of relief, embarrassed the thought crossed my mind. I pull out a chair and sit down across from her, leaning forward.

"What's wrong? Are you scared? Is this about the attack on the harbor?"

She shakes her head. "I... Kier, I saw my mom."

I can practically feel my heart stop. "What? Where?"

"At the edge of the forest, outside."

"You went *outside*?" I ask, and instantly feel bad. *Come on, man. Get yourself in check.*

"I don't want to do this right now," she says, shaking her head.

"You're right, you're right. Okay. What happened?"

"She told me something."

Agaayu. My mind flashes through the things her mother said to me in the ring. Words I can't get out of my head. The things I'm afraid they mean.

You can't save her, you know.

You can't take her destiny from her.

He's here, Kieran. And he will *find her.*

"What was it?" I ask, but she shakes her head.

"I don't want to talk about it yet. I need to think about it first."

"Em, please." I reach for her hand, taking it in mine. "You don't have to tell me. But was it—was it about your dad?"

She shakes her head, then hesitates. "Maybe. I don't know."

For days I've been poring over the memory, trying to separate the *kiyyulit* from the *kattaka*, figuring out what's true and what's just my biggest fear: that she'll get hurt and I can't stop it. That he'll find her, and she'll die before I can save her.

"Em, this is serious. I know I can't tell you what I saw up there, but I... I heard something in the ring." My gut twists as I try to figure out what I'm allowed to tell her without invoking the ancestors' wrath. Without making this worse—dooming her or myself to whatever our lives would be without their protection.

"What is it?"

"I've been trying to figure out if it's true. If your mom told you the same thing, we'll know. We can figure out what to do."

He's here, I want to say. *He's looking for you.*

"I'm sorry, Kier. I can't think about this right now. I need some time to process."

Her phone buzzes on the table next to her, and we both jump. She grabs it, picking up immediately and bringing it to her face.

"Hello?"

I know in my body before I even see her eyes go wide, before her hand comes to her mouth.

"*Ayagaayuni,*" she says. *Oh my God.* "What happened?"

She stands, and instinctively I follow, watching her face for any sign of what's going on.

She gasps. "*Nekka.*" No.

"Em. What's happening?" I ask, putting a hand on her shoulder.

"They attacked the common house," she says, pulling the phone down from her mouth. "Gabe's hurt."

19

EMERSON

They arrive at the house just after nightfall: Seb and Maren, Seb's cousin Quinn, and Gabe, his leg set in a full splint going up to his hip, using crutches to walk. Kieran and I spent the evening doing the only thing we could: preparing the house. I made dinner for more people than we needed; he shoveled the walkway to make it easier to bring Gabe inside. As they walk into the house, I rush past Seb and Maren, immediately to Gabe.

"Are you okay?" I ask, checking his bandages. I can feel the shape of the wrappings under his sweater, and I put a hand on his chest, closing my eyes to see what's happened. I see it in my mind's eye: deep gashes in his chest. Claw marks, now mostly healed by Saga's skill. A cloud of bruising at his ribs, but those are healing as they should be. And—I wince—the broken femur in his leg. Snapped completely through.

I grit my teeth. Our healer's power works for flesh wounds, but bones are much harder to heal, and take a kind of skill that no living healer on the Fakaris has. I open my eyes, looking down at the splint. Saga and Helen have set it the mainland way, wrap-

133

ping it in a plaster cast. It'll be months before it's healed. There's no way he can do his rite this winter.

"Gabe. I'm so sorry," I say, and I pull him into a hug.

"*Heij*. It's okay. I'm good," he says. "It could have been worse."

"I should have been there," I hear Kieran say behind us. "I could have fought them off."

"We tried, man," Seb says. "There were just too many of them."

"They went for Gabe specifically," Maren says quietly.

"What?" My head snaps towards her. "You didn't tell me that."

"I wasn't there when it happened," Maren says. "Quinn told me."

I look at Quinn. She's lean and lightly muscular, almost as tall as Seb and with the same tawny skin and dark hair, though the bottom half of her short bob is bleached. Usually sporting a *don't fuck with me* attitude, today even she looks shaken, her face gray.

"What happened?" I ask.

"I was there when they came in," she says. "They were looking for Gabe for sure. One of the older ones saw him across the room and sicced the others on him. The one who got there first was large. Female. She pounced on him and just tore into his chest."

"*Uikbaane*," Kieran says.

"Come on," I say, making my voice sound stronger than I feel. "We should get you guys settled in. I made dinner, if anyone's hungry. Did you guys bring bags?"

Maren nods.

Seb and Kieran go down the hill to get them, and I bring Gabe, Maren, and Quinn into the den. We prop Gabe's leg up, and I make them all a plate of food and then watch as they pick at it wordlessly, no one having the energy or desire to eat. Once

Seb and Kieran are back, they come into the den, too. The mood is like a funeral service.

"Why does the council think they went after you?" Kieran asks.

"I don't know. Maybe because of my mom," Gabe says. His expression is grave, and his voice, usually light and jovial, sounds tired.

"They think it might be a warning shot to the rest of the island," Seb says. "Since Saga's the *reijna*, and such a big figure in the community. That they're trying to cause unrest."

"I'm so sorry, Gabe," I say, putting my hand on his arm. "I can't believe this."

"Did they say anything? Anything to indicate why they'd do this?" Kier asks.

Seb nods. "They came in wolf form, but one of them flipped back to shout something as they left."

"What did he say?"

"*Hayyala fast.*"

I shake my head. "It doesn't make sense. We haven't heard *anything* about the Remnant since the nineties. How old were these people? Your parents' age?"

"No, younger," Quinn says. "The one who attacked Gabe was young, our age. There were maybe one or two elders."

"Not—" says Kieran.

Seb shakes his head. "No one we'd know."

"So what now?" I ask. "What are they gonna do?"

"There's a search party trying to find the rebels, since they need a boat to leave the island," Seb says. "Saga, Isolde, and your aunt and uncle are staying on Saroe. They've left the *fikarig*, just in case, and they're staying with another *fika* where they'll be protected now that we're gone."

"Why stay?" Kieran asks. "Why not just come here?"

"Because now that it seems targeted, if my mom leaves the

island, people will panic," Gabe says. "And that's what they want."

"It's the wrong call," Seb says. "We should all have left."

"They had a huge fight," Maren mutters as an aside to me. "Not just about that, but the whole thing with the asylum seekers."

"What? Why?" Kier asks. "Who cares about that right now?"

"*We* do," Seb says, gesturing to Gabe and himself.

"This is even more proof we need to let them in," Gabe says.

"You can't be serious," Kieran says. "They slaughtered Anja's farm. They destroyed the harbor. They brutalized you, *on purpose.*"

"But the people doing this aren't the same ones asking for asylum," Gabe says. "And if this is the kind of violence they're facing in the southern isles..."

"You're right," I say, and I hear Kieran bristle.

"It sucks, though," Gabe says with some effort, repositioning himself on the couch. "It's gonna be another year until we can get our own *fikarig* now. I won't be healed in time to do the rite this winter."

"Don't worry about that right now," I say. "You just focus on getting better."

"I mean, yeah, but it does suck," Seb says. "We were looking forward to getting our own place soon. Mare and I have been saving, and I know Kier had some money he set aside."

I glance up at Kieran. He's been working hard this fall and winter, between training for the rite and taking on extra orders to save for a place. The reminder that he's doing all this for *us*—for me—fills me with a kind of warmth.

"I still don't get why we need three council seats to buy a house," Maren says.

"You don't," Quinn says. "Anyone can buy a normal home. But if you want a *fikarig* big enough for multiple families, you need at least three elders to make a bid."

"Why, though?"

"So that we preserve pack life," Gabe says. "So that the *fikarigs* don't just go to the people who have the most money."

Seb sighs, and as I see the frustration in his face, I feel for him. His arguments with his mom and Saga have been getting worse lately, and with him and Maren getting together, I know he, especially, really wanted our own place soon.

"Really, we shouldn't be thinking about this right now," I say, putting a hand on Gabe's good knee. "We just need to focus on getting Gabe back to normal and getting through the next few days here while they find the rebels."

"But it doesn't have to be Gabe, right?" Maren asks. "Anyone could do the rite?"

Seb waves his hand. "We decided a few years ago that Kier, Gabe, and I would do it."

"But now it can't be Gabe, at least not for a while. So why not someone else?"

I look up at her, feeling a shiver go over my skin.

"We don't need our own place that badly," Kieran says. "It's not a big deal to wait another year."

"No, she's right," I say, sitting up straighter. "Why not someone else? We're getting older. We're partnering up. It'd be nice to get our own place soon. And just because we agreed Gabe would do it a few years ago, doesn't mean that still makes sense now."

"Em," Kieran says, a warning. I can hear in his voice that he knows what I'm thinking.

I can't do this, right? I haven't even shifted in years. But I've never really felt like I belonged here, in this *fika*. I was always the add-on, the extra limb. The little sister they finally made room for once Kieran joined.

I meet Kieran's eyes, remembering the chant the council sang over and over as he made his way to me for the *kattaka*.

It's time for you to prove your worth. It's time to earn your place.

"She's right," Quinn says. "One of us could do it."

"Who?" Kieran says dismissively. "You? Maren?"

I barely hear them over the sound of the blood in my ears. I think of my mom's spirit at the edge of the woods.

You can trust yourself.

When the moment comes, remember: you have everything you need to do this.

Maybe I can finally learn to be strong for them, in the way they always have been for me.

I look up. "It should be me. I'll do the rite."

20

KIERAN

"Absolutely fucking not."

"Why?" she asks. "Women have done the rite before. Saga did it. My aunt Dagmar, too."

"It's not about being a woman," I say. "It's about the fact that there's a gang of bloodthirsty zealots running around the island, and I'm not gonna let you climb up a mountain high on drugs while they're still around."

"First of all, you don't get to '*let her*' do anything," Maren says.

"No offense, Mare, but you can't girlboss your way out of this one," I snap. "The rite requires serious training."

"I need at least a month, right?" Em says, glancing at Seb for confirmation. "I could take Gabe's slot in March. That gives me six weeks. There's no way they won't have caught the rebels by then."

"This is insane," I say, bringing a hand to my head. "You can't be serious. Guys, back me up."

"I mean, yeah, it's rushed. But it's an idea," Seb says. "Why not try, at least?"

"Because Em doesn't train!" I snap. "I'd been training every day for *years* before I did the rite."

"Okay, but the amount of time you spend working out is *not* normal," Gabe says. "Seb trained for, what? A month?"

"Yeah, and look what happened to him," I snap. "And he was in better shape than Em is now. He's got, what? Six inches and forty pounds of muscle on her? She can't do this!"

"Please don't tell me what I can't do," Em says quietly.

I look down at her, sitting on the couch between Maren and Gabe. Even between the two of them, she looks small, ethereal, delicate. Like a fairy, not a warrior.

"Em, listen to me," I say. "My rite was brutal. The amount of blood I lost was unreal. We fought until daybreak."

"Okay, but every person's rite is different," she says. "The ancestors change the challenge for the person. We won't fight the same thing."

"*We* will," I say weakly. "Tell me you don't know what you'll see up there."

She looks at me, silent.

"Well, *I* think it's cool as fuck," Quinn says.

"Yeah, same," says Maren.

"So one of you do it, then," I say, throwing my hands in the air.

"I would," Maren says. "I'd try the training, at least. But if Em wants to do it, I'm not going to take that from her."

"This is insanity. How can you guys not see how insane this is? People have *died* doing the rite."

"That hasn't happened in decades," Gabe says. "Not even since our parents' time. Worst case, she taps out, and then we're back where we started."

"Is *that* the worst that happens?" I ask. "Some people leave their rite in pain for the rest of their lives. Some people *in this room*, in fact."

The words come out of my mouth before I can stop them, and

instantly, I feel awful. It's not Seb's fault, what happened to him. But it's true—his leg has been fucked since the night of his rite, and even the years of physical therapy haven't been able to take the pain away. I'd do anything to go back in time and do it differently. To be in his training pack. To stop him from fighting too early.

"She can learn from my mistakes," Seb says. "I'm not saying it's a good idea. But if she wants to do it, we can try. I can try to train her."

"Dude." I look at him. "Would you let *your* girl go up there and risk her life for this? For a *house?*"

"I trust Maren to handle herself," he says. "She doesn't need my permission to do what she wants. If Em wants to try, we should let her try."

"Wait, since when is Em *your* girl?" asks Quinn.

"We don't have time to unpack that right now," Maren mutters.

I cross my arms in front of my chest. "I'm not doing this. I won't let this happen, I'm sorry."

"I don't need you to let it happen," says Em from the couch. Her voice is quiet but firm. "If I want to do this, all I need is four people in my training pack. It doesn't have to include you."

I feel a cold wave of anger flush through me.

"*If* you did this—you, who's never trained for anything like this before, who hasn't even taken her wolf form in a *decade*—you would need the best fucking training pack there is, and if that doesn't include me then it's a goddamn death sentence."

The look on her face is like I've punched her in the gut. I can see her breathing grow faster, anger and indignation pulsing through her. She stands up and walks out of the room, and I follow her. Behind us, I hear Seb let out a low whistle.

"Em. Em, please," I say, following her through the kitchen and into the foyer. "Please, just listen to me."

She turns around. "I don't need to listen to you, since you've made your disdain for me perfectly clear. I know you're worried about me. I know you want to protect me. But being the person I trust with myself and my safety is a *privilege*, not a *right*."

"Just—*agaayu, vaare*, listen to me. People train for years for the rite. Seb did it in a month, and he'll be in pain for the rest of his life. Gabe started his training months ago. You can't just do this without preparing properly."

"I'm not stupid, Kier," she says. "I can train for it, and if it turns out that I'm not ready in time, then I can always drop out and Gabe can do it next year. If that happens, we lose nothing."

"But why would you put yourself through this?" I ask, grabbing her arm. "Why take the risk? Do we really need a house that badly? Is what we have now really so terrible?"

She crosses her arms in front of her, thinking. When she finally speaks, her voice is quiet.

"If I can do this, it's my way of earning my place in the *fika*. Giving back for what they've given me."

"*Piu*," I say, putting my other hand on her shoulder. "You know you don't need to earn anything, right? You *belong* in this family."

"Don't patronize me," she says, looking away.

"Is that what this is about?" I ask. "You *are* a part of this family. No one is going to kick you out overnight."

"Why would you say that?"

"You think I don't know that you always have a packed bag under your bed, just in case?" I ask. "You think I haven't noticed that your bedroom furniture is the exact same as the day you moved in? Come on, Em. You never let yourself believe you belong here. But getting yourself killed in the ring is *not* the answer."

She steps back from me, shrugging my arms off her. Something in the air is different between us. I've broken something.

"You don't know me," she says.

"I know you better than anyone."

"You don't know me better than I know myself." She swallows. "Is that really what you think of me? That I'm so weak? That I'm completely incapable? That I'm so stupid that I'll just walk up there to my death?"

I shake my head.

"Em, I— it's not about strength. You're, what, five-five? I could lift you over my shoulder with next to no effort. It's not about what you can or can't do, it's just the facts. It's just the way it is."

I see her swallow, and her face grows bitter. "Maybe you're right, Kier. Maybe I'm insane to want to do this. But if you loved me, you wouldn't shut me down. You would help me train, so I have the best possible chance."

"Em, this is a death sentence."

"*Not* if you help me."

I shake my head. "I can't do that, I'm sorry. I can't let you risk your life for this."

"Then leave," she says, and turns back for the den.

21

EMERSON

My aunt and uncle take Kieran's side.

"*Piu*, is this wise?" Aunt Dagmar asks over a video call. She, Viggo, and Saga are crowded on the other side of the screen, sitting at the *fikarig* of some family friend.

"I'm not saying I'll absolutely do it," I say. I'm in the den with Seb and Gabe on either side of me. Kieran is standing in the doorway, arms crossed with his back to us, pretending not to listen. "I'm just saying that I want to try. If we near the date of the rite and we don't think I'm ready, I can always drop out."

"I would never want Em to get hurt," Seb cuts in. "If I have any concerns, I'll say so."

Saga nods, thinking. "With Gabriel stopping his training, we don't have anyone else slated to complete the rite in March. There's not an *official* reason not to have you sign up, at least."

"But in the midst of all this?" Dagmar asks. "They're not on Saroe. They don't have access to the training gym."

Seb shakes his head. "There's a gym here we use to train in the summer. That won't be an issue."

"What about her mentor?" Viggo asks. "If they stay on Halluk until the rite, she won't be able to meet with someone."

"I don't think we'll be here until March," I say. "You'll catch the rebels before then. And besides, Seb can be my mentor."

Dagmar shakes her head. "*Nekka*, can he?"

"The only requirement is that the person have been on council for three years, which Seb has," Saga says. "Typically we'd want to set a trainee up with someone they don't know so well, but under the circumstances…"

"Seb helped Maren learn to shift," I say. "I think he could help me, too."

The three of them look up, as though the thought of me needing to learn to shift for this hadn't even occurred to them.

"I think it should be alright," Saga says finally. "If Seb and Gabriel are with you, and they help you prepare. And if you boys promise to be honest about what she's capable of, and to tell us if you don't think she's ready—"

"We will," Gabe says next to me. "We'd never let anything happen to her."

From the corner of my eye, I see Kieran bristle again.

"Good thing you prepared the training salts for Kieran, Emerson," Saga says. "Now you can make your own, as well. I'll ask one of the Halluki leaders to bring you the ancient salt in the proper ratios. I imagine you can get the rest from Seb?"

Seb nods next to me.

"So who will be in your training pack?" Uncle Viggo asks. "Seb, Gabe, Maren, Kieran?"

"Not Kieran," I say. "Quinn. She's a gym junkie, and she said she'd be happy to help."

"Why isn't Kieran helping you?" Dagmar asks. "He's just done the rite."

The three of us say nothing.

"Did something happen?"

"We don't... really see eye to eye on this," I say, glancing his way.

"I see," Saga says. "Is he still with you, at the house?"

"*Iija*," I say. *Yes.* For now.

"You know we love having you all at home, *piu*," Dagmar says. "You don't need to do the rite this winter. We'd be happy to have you all here for another year."

"I know," I say. "But still. I want to try. I just... I need to do this."

"Alright," Saga says. "I'll let the council know about the change in plans. And you'll keep an eye on Gabriel's healing? I know you haven't had too much luck with siphoning wounds yet, but—"

"Actually, I tried it the other day on something small, and it worked. So if you want me to try with Gabe in the coming days, I can see what I can do."

"Okay," she says, and gives a small smile. "Be careful. Don't push too hard. And *tekanni*," she says, turning to Gabe. *My son.* "You should be very careful with the leg. Don't do too much. It won't heal as fast as your other wounds, and you can't put weight on it for the next few weeks."

"Yes, *Ama*," Gabe says. "You told me."

"You kids be good," Dagmar says. "They'll catch the rebels in a few days, and then you can all come home."

"Okay," I say. "I'll see you guys soon." And we hang up.

"Well," Seb says, leaning back onto the couch as I turn the phone screen off. "I'll go to the gym in the morning and set it up for your first day. You all can meet me there around nine. Em, make sure you eat at least an hour before so you don't get sick."

"Okay," I say, and I glance at Kieran in the doorway, still not looking at us.

"It's late. We should get to bed," Gabe says. "Which rooms are you guys in?"

"Kier's in the master. I'm in the blue room," I say.

"You guys aren't…" Seb asks. *Sharing a room*, I assume he wants to ask.

"No," I say firmly. I hope it hurts Kieran to hear it.

"Okay. Then I guess Maren and I can take the room next to you, and Quinn can have the green room. We should set up a bed downstairs for Gabe, so he doesn't need to use the stairs."

I nod. "You figure out the pull-out couch, and I'll go find some clean sheets."

I stand and brush past Kieran without another word.

THAT NIGHT, when I fall asleep, I slip into memory.

It's a carousel of greatest hits. My dad shouting at my mom while I cry under the dining room table. Him slamming her into the wall while I watch. Us at my school, when my mom says something to the teacher I see instantly he doesn't like. The cold realization that he'll make her pay for it when we get home.

"You can't be mine," he says to me through the closet door as I hide on the ground, behind my own clothes, hoping he won't find me. "Any child of mine wouldn't be so *weak*."

The sound of him shaking the closet door. The smell of my own fear as I try as hard as I can to make myself invisible. And just as he manages to open it—

I sit up in bed with a gasp. I can feel the anxiety in my chest, the rattling in my bones.

I'd always wondered if it was true, what he said. I wondered if maybe I didn't belong in our family: if maybe there was a mistake at the hospital, and I should be with different parents, with a dad who loved me. Who didn't see my mom as yet another porcelain thing in our house he could break.

But if I wasn't his, I wouldn't be hers either. And, half asleep, too tired to stop it, I think about my mom. Her painting watercolors at the dining room table in the early hours of the morning. The hydrangeas and rhodoras she kept in the front yard; the book of poems by her bed, by the poet she named me for. The old Fakari song she sang to me every time it rained. Whenever it rains, I still think of her.

I wrap my arms around myself, and it's at that moment that Kieran comes through the bedroom door, groggy and still half-asleep.

"Hey, you're okay," he says, approaching me and climbing onto the bed. He wraps an arm around me, but I push him away.

"I'm good," I say. "I don't need you. Go back to bed."

"Em—"

"No. Go," I say.

The air between us grows soft and sad, and I can scent his hurt in the air. But he's hurt me too, and I don't have the energy to protect him from the consequences of his own actions. Without another word, I wrap the blanket around myself, and I listen as he walks out of the room, closing the door behind him.

22

EMERSON

When I wake up the following morning, it's practically still dark outside, the first traces of sunrise just starting to paint the horizon. I get out of bed and head downstairs, where I find Kieran in the kitchen, making scrambled eggs with vegetables.

"You're still here," I say, walking into the kitchen and leaning against the island. "I'm surprised."

"You shouldn't be." He keeps his eyes on the stove as he talks to me. "I made you a promise."

"That was before. Things are different now."

"Not for me."

Oh. I feel something in my chest soften.

"Did you talk to the elders?" I ask, my voice gentler now. "Have they found anyone? Any sign of the Remnant?"

"Saga called this morning," he says, stirring the pan. "Nothing. There's a party searching the island, but there's just too much ground to cover. They're focusing on the southwest part of the island first, since that's where the attacks were. And they asked around—a few people said they saw what Quinn saw, that it was definitely targeted against Gabe. So it's good we're laying low here."

"Okay," I say, stepping closer to him. "You're up earlier than I'm used to."

"Yeah, well. You need a good breakfast, if you're gonna get your ass handed to you today."

I cross my arms. Kieran turns off the stove and grabs a plate, which he piles with eggs, vegetables, and sliced avocado, and hands to me.

"Eat."

"You changed your mind?" I ask. "You're helping me train?"

"No. I think you're insane to do this, and I'm not gonna help you get yourself killed. But I'm not leaving, either."

I purse my lips. I'll give him that, at least.

AN HOUR LATER, Quinn, Maren, and I walk down to the gym together to meet Seb.

Quinn is wearing traditional Fakari clothes. They're a little more masculine than what I usually see women wear, even to train: a loose black shirt and flowy pants, with clasps to accommodate her shift and a leather jacket that I assume she won't take into training. Maren, for her part, came dressed like she's in a Viking-themed B-movie. A black mainland sports bra with more straps than can possibly be necessary, under a semi-sheer long-sleeve shirt, with high-waisted black leggings that hug her wide hips and end in yet another strappy configuration at the ankle. She's braided her thick, curly hair into two chunky braids going down her head, adding little gold ring clasps here and there for decoration.

"I'm so excited for you!" she says, clapping. "She's in her villain era now, ladies."

"Who?" I ask.

"*You*, dummy. The big buff dude thought you couldn't do it

and now you're gonna prove him wrong. This is the beginning of your hot-girl-kicks-ass montage. I can practically hear 'Eye of the Tiger.'"

I say nothing. That's not how it feels for me.

We make our way towards the cobblestone streets of the town center. It's a cool winter morning, and Halluk's streets are quiet. The north island is typically pretty empty outside of the summer, and as we pass a handful of closed shops, I think about Kieran and his childhood here. We walk by a school, where I can see kids in little Fakari-style school uniforms lining up to go inside. Would he have gone to school here? Or somewhere closer to his house, on the other side of the forest?

"So how much training have you done before this?" Quinn asks, pulling me from my thoughts.

"Oh, nothing. I don't think I've run on purpose since we did the yearly 3k in high school."

Quinn looks me up and down. "Brave girl."

"How about you, Quinn?" Maren asks. "What kind of training do you do? I feel like I never see you at Seb's gym."

"I have another gym I go to, closer to my apartment. I do a mix, mostly lifting and FMA."

"What's FMA?" Maren asks.

"Fakari Martial Arts," I say. "Seb never taught you?"

"No. I have my own training routine, so we never really did that stuff together."

"What kind of training do you do?" Quinn asks.

"I run, and I did spinning and kickboxing a few times a week when I was on the mainland," Maren says. "On Saroe, mostly just boxing."

"Cool," I say as we near the gym. "So I'm by far the least-prepared of the three of us to do this."

"That's why we're in your training pack," Quinn says, and she leads us inside.

The gym is separate from the rest of the buildings on the

street, and from the outside it's pretty nondescript: white facade with a Dutch gable, like most of the buildings on Halluk. It has a black door and traditional thatched roof, but the inside is dark and modern. It's smaller but nicer than the gym Seb and Kier go to on Saroe, attached to our common house. There's a large boxing ring in the center, and next to that, an area with mats on the floor. Around that runs what looks like a small indoor track, separating the inner area from the machinery and equipment that runs along the walls. Along one side are rows of complex-looking black-and-silver machines, and at another, a large weight rack and a few benches, where I see two older men working out.

Seb looks up from the mats, where he was bent over his gym bag.

"Hey, *morlaa'*. Right on time," he says.

"Good morning," Maren says sweetly, walking over to give him a kiss on the cheek.

"Did you bring everything I asked?" he asks. "Water, towel, clothing that can shift?"

I nod nervously. I don't even own any shift-appropriate clothing, so I had to borrow a top from Maren and some pants from Quinn. I'm practically swimming in Maren's sweater, but luckily Quinn's pants are a close enough fit, even if they pool at the ankles.

"Alright, great. I'm gonna have you start up with a few laps around the gym to warm up your muscles, then we'll stretch and get started. Put your bags down and go."

I drop my duffle onto the mats and take off my winter coat. Quinn and Maren put their stuff down, too, and I see Maren do some quick stretches: standing on one leg and stretching the other thigh muscle, then switch, followed by some lunges. I try to copy her, but she moves quickly, intuitively, and by the time I get into my first lunge, she's already done.

"Ready? Go," Seb says, and Quinn and Maren start a light jog around the gym's track.

I follow. It's a pretty slow pace, and for the first twenty seconds I'm already mentally congratulating myself on how well this is going. *See? You're in pretty decent shape. You can do this.* But then Seb tells us to go faster, and Quinn and Maren speed up with ease, while I feel an uncomfortable stretch in the backs of my legs.

"Switch. Run in the other direction," Seb commands, and we turn on our heels and go counterclockwise around the ring.

"Good. Faster," he says. Quinn and Maren pick up the pace and I try to keep up, but after a minute or two I can feel my breath get raspy, scraping through my throat. My face is hot, and I feel sweat starting to build on my forehead.

Seb calls out more orders, making us switch directions in less and less time. After about five minutes he tells us to stop, and I'm panting, my face red. Maren is just slightly out of breath, and Quinn looks totally fine.

"That was the warm-up?" I ask breathlessly.

"Yep. Now come to the mats and we'll stretch."

Quinn leads us through a stretching routine as my heartrate slowly returns to normal. We do something with our arms that feel mostly performative—I can barely feel anything—and then she has us stretch our hamstrings and quads. Those are awful; I can barely get my knees down to the ground when I'm sitting with my back straight, and when she tries to get me to do a stretch on my back, with one leg up in the air using a band, I can't get it nearly as far as Maren.

"We're gonna have to work on that," Quinn says, sitting up with her hands on her knees. "I'll have you do some foam rolling tonight."

"Okay," I say. *What on earth is foam rolling?*

"It's good enough for now," Seb says, grabbing a clipboard and a pen from his bag. "I want to do a test of your current level and then we'll have your first lesson."

He takes me on a tour around the gym. Quinn demonstrates

how to do a pull-up and chin-up. She lifts herself smoothly into the air, showing me the motion, then has me try. I put my hands on the metal bar above me.

"Good, okay. Now lift yourself from the ground."

I pull on the bar, but I barely get an inch off the floor.

"Sorry, okay. Let me try again." This time I try harder, gritting my jaw. I lift myself a little into the air, but I can feel the texture of the bar grating at my palms.

"Is that as high as you can go?" Seb asks. "That's fine."

It's not fine.

"Let me try one more time," I say, bringing my hands down and wringing them together.

"No, it's okay, save your strength," he says, and writes what looks like a zero on his clipboard.

Next we go to the weight rack. How much weight can I handle if I'm on my back, pushing up? We try one set of dumbbells, but my hands shake as I bring them back down towards me, and Maren steps in instinctively and takes them from me, swapping them out for a lighter set. Next they have me leaning forwards over the bench, pulling the dumbbell up towards my chest. Quinn has to correct my form twice, and I glance with embarrassment over at one of the older men, taking a water break on his bench.

"No one's looking at you," Maren says gently. "Everyone's just here to work on themselves."

"*You're* all looking at me," I say, wiping the sweat from my face.

"Okay, fair. But we're here to help."

I nod, but I feel the sting of humiliation behind my eyes.

Seb brings me through the rest of the gym, testing how much weight I can handle on the different machines. Finally, he takes me back to the mat and tests my push-ups (four), and sit-ups (six). He releases the pressure from my feet and I fall back, catching my breath.

"Very good. Drink some water and then we'll get started."

"*Get started,*" I grumble. This fitness test was more of a workout than anything I've done in years.

"I didn't say it would be easy, Em," he says to me, standing. "You don't *have* to do this."

Yes, I do, I think, and get up to grab my water bottle.

THE LESSON DOESN'T GO WELL. Seb teaches me some boxing basics: the fighting stance, how to hold your hands to your face for sparring, how to land a punch without hurting yourself.

"We're not doing FMA today?" I ask. I've watched kids take lessons outside the common house after school, and I've always been curious.

Seb shakes his head. "Real FMA training takes months before you start combat, and we don't have that kind of time. We'll introduce some FMA concepts later, but for now you need to get used to the rhythm of combat and learn how to take a punch. For that, boxing is less complicated."

We practice a few punches in slow motion, then he has me strap into some absolutely foul-smelling boxing gloves to spar with Quinn. Maren goes across the street to do some work for the salt scrub launch, and Quinn and I climb up into the boxing ring to practice.

"Fighting stance," Seb calls out. "Good. Em, don't lock your knees, light on your feet. Yes, better. Tuck your tailbone under, strong core. Nope, too much. Yes, better. Keep your elbows in. Good."

It's a barrage of information, but I try to keep up, mirroring Quinn's body language.

"Okay, let's just throw some practice punches. Same combination I just taught you. Em, you first."

I move my hand slowly towards her like he taught me, and Quinn blocks.

"Okay, good," Seb calls out. "Em, undercut."

I do as told and she blocks again.

"Okay, great job. Quinn, now you."

Quinn throws a mock punch, and I deflect with my left arm. Then, without Seb's command, she undercuts, too, but my arm comes down too late. Her glove lands against my stomach. I let out an *oomph* as it hits.

"Sorry," she says. "I thought—"

"No, it's okay. It's what he taught us." It doesn't hit too hard, but the second her fist lands on my body, I feel a shot of adrenaline surge through me. Instantly I'm a little edgier, a little more reactive.

This is just practice, I think to myself. *You're fine. Calm down.*

"Okay, very good," Seb calls out. "Keep going, just go at your own pace. Em, you keep dropping your hands after you land a punch. Keep them up, protecting your face. And don't forget to tuck your elbows in, you're too wide."

I nod and bring my hands inwards, but I feel tense, frustrated at the amount of things I'm supposed to remember. Quinn guides me through a few of the combinations Seb taught, and when I'm landing punches on her, everything is going well. But the second it's my turn to block, I feel the panic rising in me again. She keeps having to remind me to fix my footwork, to keep my hands close to my face. Each time I do, it's too much information, and the waterfall of course-corrections and punches I don't quite block is getting me worked up. Finally, she accidentally lands a blow on my shoulder, and part of her glove hits my jaw. I stagger back, gasping, and the adrenaline in me is running so high that I feel tears starting to sting my eyes.

"Shit. I'm sorry, Em," Quinn says, stripping off her gloves. "Hey. We can take a break."

"No—I'm, fine," I say, but I'm not fine, and she can see it.

This is so stupid, I tell myself. *You're in a gym. You signed up to do this. You're safe.* But no matter what I tell myself, the shock of the hit and the resulting adrenaline only seems to surge higher, and I can't push them away. Tears spill out over my cheeks, and I turn from her.

"*Agaayu,* I'm sorry, this is so embarrassing," I mutter, using my teeth to tear one of the gloves off and bringing my hand to my face to wipe the tears.

Seb is climbing into the ring.

"Em," he says. "Hey, it's okay. You don't need to do this."

"Don't tell me what I can't do!" I snap.

I hear him pause, deliberate. For a second I think he's going to get mad, but his voice is practiced and calm.

"I didn't say you *can't* do this. Just that you don't *need* to."

"Yes, I do," I snap, and I put the glove on again.

"We should take a break."

"I don't *want* a break." I square my shoulders. I will not let them be right about me. "Come on, Quinn. Hands up. Let's go."

WE SPEND three hours at the gym today, and I'm completely exhausted. When we get back to the house, Seb is supposed to help me with some of the mental coaching, but I need a break, so I go upstairs to take a shower and let myself cry. The warm water flows over me—over my sore muscles, over the spot on my arm where I can already feel a welt forming from a blow I couldn't block. Mare promised it would take about 24 hours for the soreness to set in, but I feel it already. Everything burns.

I think back on the morning. Every move I couldn't do, every time Maren had to swap my weights, every time Quinn's glove hit and the tears sprung to my eyes when I knew she could see. Seb had me wear clothes for shifting today, and we didn't even touch on that. There must be more we didn't get to.

After about twenty minutes, I get out and dry myself off, then pull on some comfortable clothing. I know Gabe and Kieran were planning on making lunch, so I go downstairs. I can see Seb walking into the kitchen, fresh from his own shower, and after a second I hear voices. I stop outside, listening.

"How'd she do?" Kieran asks.

"It wasn't great."

I feel the sting of Seb's words like a slap, even if I know he's right.

"I told you, man. She's too new at this," Kieran says. I hear the clamor of something—plates, I think. "Six weeks was never gonna be enough time."

"Yeah," comes Seb's voice with a sigh. "I've never trained someone completely from scratch before. Even Maren had never shifted, but she's—"

"Maren," Kieran says, as though that's enough of an explanation. As though it's obvious a girl like Maren could do things I never could. His words burn.

"Em has grit, I'll give her that," Seb says. "I gave her a few chances to stop or take a break, but she didn't budge. She just kept going."

"Do you think it'll be enough?"

"I don't know," I hear Seb say. "I'll give it three weeks. If she's not improving, we'll have to have a hard conversation."

Three weeks, I think, sucking my teeth. Not three weeks to get good at it. Just three weeks to get good *enough*. To show them I can do it.

I can do three weeks.

23

KIERAN

E m comes into the den at five p.m., reeking of sweat and exhaustion and failure. It's her sixth day of training, and I know from Seb they were going to start shifting practice today. From the scent of her shame and the expression on her face, it didn't go well.

She looks like shit as she collapses next to me. Her ponytail is loose and lopsided, her long blonde hair tangled as it falls down to her waist. There's huge bags under her eyes, and with a growl of anger, my inner wolf takes note of the bruises forming on her skin: one on her right arm, and another on her left thigh, peeking out from under her gym shorts.

I stand up and walk to the kitchen to fill a bottle of water, then grab a bowl and fill it with some almonds from the pantry. I walk back into the den and set them on the coffee table before her.

"I'm not thirsty," she mutters.

"The hell you're not."

She holds out for a few seconds, but by the time I'm back on the couch, she reaches for the bottle and starts gulping down the

159

water. She finishes most of the bottle in one go, then sets it back down.

"*Takka.*"

"You're welcome. Now eat. You need protein after a workout."

"I shouldn't, I'm going on a run before dinner."

I bristle. "*Agaayu*, I can't watch you do this."

"Then close your eyes," she says spitefully.

"No, Em—treating yourself like this. You're up every morning before the sun to run. You're training all day with Seb, then coming home and doing God knows what kind of exercises with Quinn in your room. And I saw you with Gabe last night, trying to build your healing power. You need to *rest*."

"I need to *train*."

I feel frustration roil in my gut. I'm angry—angry at her, I realize, for doing this to herself and putting herself in harm's way.

"Recovery is half of training," I say. "If you keep going like this, you're going to die from exhaustion before you make your way up to the ring."

She pulls her knees up and I see her wince. My mind registers immediately: sore hamstrings, maybe glutes. And I can see from the way she's holding her neck that she has some tension in her shoulders.

"Is Seb having you do ice baths?" I ask.

She furrows her brow and shakes her head.

"Is someone massaging the sore muscles at the end of the day?"

She shakes her head again.

"How much are you sleeping?"

"I don't know. Six hours? Sometimes I'm too tired to fall asleep."

I curse. "*Uikbaane*, what are these *nagaayit* doing to you out there?"

She ticks off her fingers. "Stretches, foam rolling, running, a little bit of boxing, basic FMA combinations, and I just started shifting practice today. Oh, and Seb wants to start me on mental coaching later this week."

"That's insane. That's way too much."

"Well, as you pointed out to me, I guess I'm in terrible shape," she says bitterly.

"Em, baby." I put my hand on her arm. "You need to slow down."

"Don't *baby* me." She pulls her shoulder back, and I see her wince with the movement.

"Come here," I say, rolling my eyes. "Let me rub your back."

"*No*. We're not like that. Not anymore."

"Not for sex," I say, irritated. God, I'm so bad at this. "For your recovery. I can see from the way you're holding your neck that your lats are sore, and if you keep overcompensating in your posture, you're gonna run yourself into an injury."

She sets her jaw. God, she's so stubborn. The wolf in me respects it—likes the challenge—and I tell him to mind his own goddamn business.

"Come on, you're a healer," I say, trying to make my voice softer. "You know the whole body's a system. If you overcompensate for muscle soreness in one area, you'll fuck up another."

She sighs. "The salts and salves haven't been working."

"You don't need healing magic for muscle soreness," I say, and I can't help but smile. "This stuff is a little more manual. Here. Turn around for me."

Reluctantly, she turns her back to me, changing her legs to sit pretzel-style on the couch.

"There," I say, resting my hands low on her shoulders and digging my thumbs into the muscles just under her shoulder blades. I hear a low breath escape her mouth as I ease the muscle, and I can feel her relax a little.

"Good?" I ask quietly.

"Yeah."

"How's this?" I move my hands up, rubbing the tendons connecting her shoulders to her neck. She rolls her head forward, responding to my touch. I feel the energy in the room shift, and I force myself to focus. She really *does* need to get some recovery before she hurts herself. I'm not gonna let my dick get in the way of her best interest.

I move my hands down to her mid back, massaging the muscle. A few minutes later, I can feel her body starting to give way, her posture becoming soft and pliable.

"Your legs are sore," I say finally. "Let me help you."

I can sense momentary resistance, but her body needs this, and that wins out.

"What do I need to do?" she asks.

"I want you on your stomach."

I climb off the couch and she lies down flat, her arms coming up so she can rest her face sideways on her hands. I take a look at her legs, long and lean. There's a large bruise forming on the side of one of her thighs, and now that she's spread out for me like this, I see the hint of another on her right calf.

"One sec," I say, standing up and walking towards the pantry.

"What are you getting?"

"Grapeseed oil."

I come back a minute later with a blend that Saga made for me last year, which I'd brought to the north island during Fire Week but forgot to bring back. I come to kneel next to the couch and use the dropper to put some into my hands, then bring them up to her legs.

She groans in discomfort as I put my hands on her left leg and guide them gently down, digging my thumbs into the sore muscle. I ease up on the pressure a little and move my hands out to the sides, and her breath hitches. I breathe out, loudly enough for her to hear; a nudge. She exhales too, and slowly her breathing syncs with mine. *In, out.*

I massage up and down the back of her thigh until I feel the muscle loosen in my hands, becoming less hard and resistant, more open to me. I bring my hands down to her calf and she hisses in discomfort. I breathe in and out for her again, an instruction, and she syncs her breathing to mine as I gently force the muscle to relax and release.

After a few minutes, her whole body eases. As I make my way to the other leg, the sounds she's making grow less tense, less frustrated. Slowly I feel her body relax for me, *from* me. Under my hands.

I want it to mean more than it does. I want to bring my hands back up, to her thighs, to her ass, which I know is sore too. I want to give her more relief. The wolf in me wants to reward her, to make her feel good, to show her how proud I am of her for pushing through and not giving up.

But I hold off. She doesn't want me like that right now, and if I look at it from her side, I can't blame her. Even if I also think she's being an idiot for putting herself in this position.

I won't help her kill herself, but maybe this is a way to take care of her, still. To help her, even. Even if she doesn't want me.

I take my hands from her body and rub the extra oil into the backs of my hands.

"No running tonight," I say. "You should be running three days a week right now, max. And the salts for this stage of training are more effective if you combine them with food. Bring the samphire salt down from your room and I'll make sure it's in your breakfast tomorrow."

"Okay," she says, sitting up and pulling her knees towards her. With satisfaction, my inner wolf recognizes that there's no wince this time. *I did that.*

"Thanks," she says quietly.

"Yeah. No problem," I say, and I get up and leave to take my first cold shower in days.

24

EMERSON

Three weeks.

It's what I think to myself every morning as I stretch, prepare my training salts, have breakfast.

Three weeks, as I do my warm-up, as I learn whatever new thing Seb has for me, as I practice with Maren or Quinn and feel my inner wolf panic the second a punch lands.

On the bad days, where I can practically *feel* my body tearing in half: *It's only three weeks.*

And on the days where I have enough energy to push myself harder: *I only have three weeks.*

We fall into a sort of routine. Gabe calls his mom in the morning, asking for news about the search party. Still nothing, but they've cleared the caves on the southern shore and are now starting on the forest around Moon Lake. Kier and Gabe make breakfast, with Gabe calling out instructions and Kieran doing the work. The whole gang eats together, and afterwards, Seb and Maren do some work—the salt scrubs *were* a huge success, and now they're coordinating a restock—and I study up on my healer's training. And then, once the food has settled, we train.

Every day of training is different. Boxing is getting a little easier, so Seb's introduced some self-defense: how to get out from under someone, how to get someone off of your back once they've grabbed you. For that, I can only practice with Quinn, who's the closest in the group to my build even if she is a head taller than me.

I'm starting to like Quinn, I realize. She intimidated me when we were growing up, so I used to avoid her. But ever since our first day of training, she doesn't treat me like I'm fragile. When I don't block a punch, or she pins me down and I panic, she's the only one in the group who doesn't react to the tears in my eyes. And the first time I get out from under her and slam her body into the mat, her whole face lights up.

"Good," she says, catching her breath. "Really good, Em. Again."

Slowly, *so* slowly, I'm getting better. I can do one and a half pull-ups now, and I'm lifting almost twice the weight I was before—though starting at eight pounds, that's not much. But still, the training is brutal. FMA is the hardest; if Seb isn't constantly yelling out corrections, it's Quinn, *showing* me how I need to correct by taking advantage of my weaknesses. We train for hours, until everyone's exhausted and I'm the only one trying to hide it. When we get back—usually around one or two in the afternoon—I have an hour to rest before shift practice with Seb. And that's where it all goes wrong.

Today we're outside, on the shore. I couldn't get myself to shift in the gym, and Seb thought bringing me somewhere where there's no one to see would help. But that's not the issue. *I'm* the issue.

"Pool your energy," he says, putting a hand on his stomach. "Close your eyes."

I try, following his lead.

"Now bring your attention to your gut. Try to connect with that part of your body. Breathe towards it."

"Okay," I say, and I do so, although I don't really know where the breath should be going. The soft roar of the ocean, and the bite of the wind, distracts me. I can barely feel anything in my body.

"Do you feel your inner wolf?"

I shake my head. "I don't feel anything."

I hear a hitch in his breathing, which I take to be frustration. "Okay. We're trying to find the part of you that reacts first to tension. Maren doesn't feel her wolf in her stomach but in her pelvic floor. Does that work?"

I open my eyes and bring my hands up to my face. "Seb, no offense, but I don't really wanna talk to you about my pelvic floor."

"Your rite is in *five weeks* and as far as I know, you haven't shifted in a decade. I'm trying to help you. If you don't let me, I'm going to tell the council I don't think you can do this."

I grit my teeth and try again, closing my eyes and putting a hand on my stomach. After a minute, I look up again.

"I really don't feel anything."

"Do you ever feel your wolf in you?"

"Yeah, sometimes."

"When?"

"When I get scared. When I think about my dad."

He nods. "I think that's part of the problem."

"Hm?" I cross my arms, bracing myself against the cold sea air.

"For you, shifting is about being scared. A lot of kids have that, because they can't control their shift yet, so it just happens whenever they have a strong feeling. But if you haven't let yourself shift since you were a kid, and if your childhood was mostly..." His voice trails off.

"My childhood was mostly feeling scared, yeah," I say flatly.

"Okay." His voice is gentle—less judgmental than I expect. "Do you ever feel your wolf other times?"

"Um. Yeah, I guess."

"When?"

"This is gonna sound weird."

He shakes his head. "It won't."

"With Kier, sometimes."

He nods. "Okay. So what moments with Kieran?"

I feel myself blush. "Seb, I don't really know how to—"

"We have *five weeks*, Em. I know you guys are sleeping together. Or were, at least. You can spare me the details, but I can handle hearing that you're an adult."

"Maren *told you*?"

"No, dumbass." He rolls his eyes. "We could all smell it on the two of you as soon as we walked into the house. And honestly, it's been like ten fucking years, so it wasn't a huge surprise. Now tell me. When do you feel your wolf?"

I swallow. "Okay. I feel it when I'm happy with him. Or when I'm... caught up in the moment." I wave my hand to indicate what kind of moment I mean.

"Your wolf is not an *it*, she's a *her*. If you make her into a state of being instead of a part of you, she'll be harder to access. Try again."

I sigh. "*Agaayu*, so many rules. Okay, *her*. I feel *her* when I'm happy, or swept up in a feeling."

"Any other times? Ever when you're by yourself?"

I think. "Lately, sometimes I feel her when I run."

He nods, his eyes lighting up. "That's good."

"Yeah?"

"Yeah. You want her near the surface. And the more your brain can associate her with moments where you're in flow, and not just the times that you're scared, the easier it'll be to let yourself shift."

I nod. "Okay. So how do I do it?"

"You can't just like... give in to her, in those moments?" he asks. "When you feel her in you, you can't let her take over?"

"I don't know. I never tried. How?"

He shakes his head, thinking. "Fuck if I know. This is the first time I'm teaching someone *how* to shift. With Maren we had to focus on reining her wolf *in*, and that's what I had to learn to do, too. With you, it's the opposite. I don't know how to describe it, and what we've tried so far hasn't worked."

"What if we go on a run?" I ask. "And when I start to feel her, I'll tell you, and we can just try to figure out what's next?"

He nods. "Worth a shot."

WE START ALONG THE SHORE, picking up pace as we get to the trail at the edge of the woods. At Seb's suggestion, he runs behind me so I can focus on myself. It helps in part because, in his human form, running is also harder for Seb since his rite. I know if I see him limping, even if he says he's fine, I'll fixate on his discomfort instead of myself.

For the first few minutes, I focus on the rise and fall of my breath, and the rhythm of my feet hitting the ground. But after a while, the outside world starts to fall away, and I find myself getting wrapped up in flow. My mind starts to wander. I think about the rite, about Kieran, about the outfit Maren wore to breakfast this morning. I start to think about what I'll do tonight: practicing my healing skills with Gabe, then painting. And as the thought hits, I feel my wolf somewhere, deep under the surface.

I keep running, not wanting to say she's here too early and ruin it. So I focus my thoughts. Painting. I'm going to paint purple rhodoras today. I want to paint the way the light falls on my favorite coffee cup.

My wolf is there, under the surface. She's happy.

I try to send my breath towards her, like Seb said.

Hey, I think. *I'm glad you're here. You're allowed to be here.*

But just as I think that, I feel a glimmer of tension run

through my gut. Is it true? Do I want her here? And the second I think it, she disappears.

No, I want you here, I think. *You belong here. In me.*

Nothing.

I grit my teeth, the feeling of the run becoming more visceral again: the rasp of the cold air in my throat, the rhythm of my feet on the dirt path. Okay. Painting. I'm going to paint rhodoras. I'm going to paint my mug.

Nothing.

Frustration starts to roin in my gut. I don't want to disappoint Seb; I want this training to work. So I try something different.

My dad, holding a knife to my mom in the kitchen. Pinning her down on the floor of the living room. Red; the scent of blood. Him standing outside of my closet door.

You can't be mine, he said. *Any child of mine wouldn't be so weak.*

I feel my wolf now, rising panicked in my chest. She's scared.

Okay, I think, and I focus harder. His wolf, snarling, angry, barking at me to stay in my place.

I feel my own wolf just under the surface and I let myself give in to her. I don't really know what's happening; I just let my conscious brain fall away, and I let the feelings rolling through my body take over. I can feel her, so close to my skin that she's almost me, that I'm almost her, and then suddenly I'm crashing forward, my body folding, everything cracking. It hurts and it feels good and then I'm close to the ground, the fabric of my clothes flying off of me.

"Good! Good, Em," I hear Seb say, but I can't stop running. She's in control and the panic is all around me now. Her fear is mine, and it's everywhere, and I feel like I'm sinking, drowning, dying, like I'll never be safe again. I go faster and faster, and I can hear Seb's uneven footsteps get farther away. I sense it in the air the moment he shifts, taking his wolf form so he can match my pace, but I don't slow down. I run and run and run, until I find myself on the other side of the trees and I'm looking out at the rocks of the shore.

I stop, breathless. I'm drowning, I'm dying. He's here, I can feel it. I can't escape.

Seb's wolf form comes up behind me, and he drops a bundle of clothing—his and mine, snapped off when we shifted—from his mouth onto the ground. He makes a gentle sound from the back of his throat, and his eyes are kind, but I don't know what he wants from me. I'm so much smaller than him when I'm like this; smaller than any other wolf I know. How could I ever be safe if I let this part of myself take the lead? How could she ever protect me?

Seb must realize that I'm not going to be able to get myself out of this, so he shifts back into his human form and pulls his clothes from the bundle with mine on the sand, snapping the magnetic clasps until he's covered up.

"Look at me, Em," he says, his voice calm but firm. "You're okay. He's not here. You're safe. You can take control of this."

But I can't. I yip and scratch, and as he reaches out to calm me, my claws catch on the back of his hand. He hisses in pain, and immediately I feel terrible.

"Em," Seb says, grabbing his cut hand with the other. "Look at me. *You can do this.* Slow your breathing. Find the edge of your consciousness."

I try, and somewhere in *her*, I find *me*. The conscious part of myself.

"Yes, good," he says, picking up on some imperceptible change in my body language. "Give over to yourself. Take control."

Control. Somewhere in the wolf, I clasp on to the edge of myself and I pull, letting my conscious brain rise. And suddenly my body is folding again, unfurling, and I'm me—the human me —sitting naked on the bank of sand.

"*Ayagaayuni*, Seb, I'm so sorry," I say, scrambling in the sand for my clothes. I snap them onto me until I'm covered, and then I take his hand and look at the marks of my claws.

"It's fine," he says, but his voice is brusque.

I put my hand over his and close my eyes. In my mind's eye I see the streaks of my claw marks, three dark gashes, and I find the energy in Seb. It's frustrated, angry—angry at *me*, I realize—but it's open enough to my presence that I can coax it, goading it around his wound, nudging it to bring the sides of the small gashes together.

After a minute, the gashes are gone from my mind, and I'm able to siphon out the sting of the wound. I open my eyes and see Seb is staring at me in some kind of mix of wonder and confusion.

"Does it still hurt?" I ask, looking down. His hand is back to normal. You can't even tell what happened.

"When did you learn to do that?" he asks. "The last time you tried this on me back at the *fikarig* a few months ago, you couldn't do anything."

"I've been practicing with Gabe," I say. "And I feel like the training is helping, actually. I'm getting stronger. It's easier to do." It's true, but I'm exhausted now—my body feels hollow with the energy it took to do this.

"That's crazy, Em," he says.

"Thanks."

"But—" He sighs. "I'm sorry. I don't think this is working. It's not that you could *never* do it, it's just that you can't do it *now*. We don't have enough time. And we spent so much time trying to get you to shift for the first time that we haven't even started the real mental work of preparing for the rite."

I shake my head. "No. You said three weeks."

"What?"

"I heard you, in the kitchen with Kieran. You said you'd give me three weeks. I still have six days left."

"Em." He shakes his head, his eyes firm. "Six days is nothing.

If it's not getting better, why would you torture yourself? Look at how good you're getting as a healer. Why not focus on that? You'll overtake Saga soon enough."

I shake my head. I can't explain why, but that's not enough for me.

"Six days," I say.

He sighs, looking down at his healed hand.

"Fine," he says finally. "Six days."

25

KIERAN

When Seb and Em come home that night, I can tell something's happened. Seb and Maren eat in their room, and Em immediately disappears to go shower upstairs, even though she already showered after their morning training session. When she comes down again, she goes directly to the formal living room, where we set up the bed for Gabe.

I walk in to find them sitting on the couch together. His shirt is off and her hand is over his chest, a few inches between them. I can see her head bowed, pooling her concentration. I watch as the scarring on his chest seems to move under her hand. It's not healing, exactly, but it's… *reacting*, somehow.

She lowers her hand and lets out a sharp exhale, as though she'd been holding her breath.

"Sorry. I used most of my healing energy on Seb today."

"What? What happened?" I ask, and she looks over her shoulder to look at me.

"Oh. I shifted," she says, and I feel surprise and—I can't help it—pride overtake me.

"Hey, that's awesome!" Gabe says.

"Yeah. But I couldn't shift back, and I panicked. I scratched his hand by accident."

I can scent the disappointment and frustration coming off her, and I walk into the room and sit on the couch across from them.

"Still, that's amazing, Em," I say. "You haven't done that in years."

"I guess." She turns to Gabe. "I'm sorry I can't help, though. I was hoping we'd get rid of some of this today."

"Nah, it's fine," Gabe says, sitting up straighter on the couch and grabbing his shirt. "I didn't expect this to respond to any more healing magic, after what Mom and Helen already tried. The fact that you've healed so much of it is amazing. And it'll help you in the ring."

"Huh? How?" I ask.

He looks at me like I'm stupid. "When a healer goes into the ring, she can heal herself if she gets hurt. That's what my mom did, way back. So if you bring enough energy, you can buy your-self more time. And it might make up for what you lack in other areas."

"Like strength," Em says quietly.

I look at her. It's only been two weeks, but she's already changing, her body more susceptible to muscle as a shifter. I can see the slight cuts in her arms, showing the first hints of triceps emerging. When I massaged her back yesterday, I could feel some of the new muscle definition coming in. It's slight, but it's there. My wolf respects it, mostly because it speaks to her inner strength—her commitment, her unwillingness to take no for an answer. I wonder if she gives herself that credit.

"We should eat," I say, standing. "You need to get some of your energy back."

"Where are the others?"

"Seb and Maren are upstairs," Gabe says. "And Quinn's at the gym, teaching an FMA class."

"Wait, really?" Em's eyes go wide.

"Yeah. The owner offered her a teaching trial, since he saw you guys together," Gabe says. "She was telling me earlier. She's psyched."

"That's so cool!" Em says. "I wish she'd told me. I would have gone."

I laugh. "Five hours a day of training isn't enough?"

Em smiles and leans down to help Gabe up. "No, it's not that. I'd just love to support her."

Gabe gets to his feet slowly, the full leg cast coming off of the couch with some difficulty. I watch the way Em helps him up, knowing intuitively where to put her hands. I'm surprised she can handle the weight of his body. She really is changing.

I swallow and walk to the kitchen without them.

AFTER DINNER, Em cleans up the kitchen while I help Gabe back to the couch.

"Things are going well between you two, huh?" he asks.

"Shut up."

"Come on, dude. Just apologize."

"I can't," I say, setting him down on the couch. "I can't apologize if I don't think I'm wrong. And I'm *not* wrong. She may be doing better in training, but she's just not ready and she's going to hurt herself."

Gabe gives me a long look.

"What?"

"Nothing, man. You're not ready to hear it."

"Fine. If you can spare me touchy-feely shit today, I'll take it. I'm gonna go help her with recovery."

"You do that," he says, and I ignore the goading edge in his voice. But as I walk for the door, he stops me.

"Hey. How much longer do you think we'll be here?"

I turn and lean against the door frame. "Until they catch the rebels. It can't be long now, they started on the woods this week. Why?"

"I don't know, man. I'm going stir-crazy. At least you guys have things to do. I'm just house bound. I'd love to go back to Saroe, where I have my own stuff."

"You're part of her training pack. None of you guys can leave without each other."

"Yeah, but how about you? I heard you on the phone with Caspar this morning. You could bring some stuff back for me."

I sigh. I wasn't planning on being out on Halluk at all, and definitely not for longer than a few days. Our orders are piling up, and I need to finish the wedding arch in the next two weeks. That's work Caspar can't take over for me.

"I'm probably gonna head back for a week or so, then come back up here," I say.

"I'll make a list of some things you could bring. And as soon as something changes. If they find them—"

"Your mom would tell you," I say. "But if I found out first, you'd be the first to know."

"Alright. *Takka.*"

"Yeah, no worries," I say, and walk to the den.

I find Em in a state of half-undress, her shorts hiked up to expose more of the leg muscle, wearing just a blue sports bra. Maren's oversized shifting top lies in a pile on the floor.

Agaayit. It's been two weeks since we've slept together—in either sense of the word—and my wolf craves her. These nightly massages are the only nearness I get, and while I love it, it also hurts. It's not just my inner animal that needs her. *I* miss her. I miss when the rhythm of our days was wound up in each other; the soft sound of her laugh. The feeling of her body near mine, even when we're just sitting on the couch.

"*Heij,*" she says softly as I walk into the den.

"*Heij.*" I grab the oil from the side table and put some in my hands. "On your stomach."

She does as told, and I feel my wolf respond with approval. Even more so as I lay my hands on her back and she sighs happily.

"Thanks for this," she says, after a minute. "It's really been helping. I feel like my time in the gym is getting easier."

"That's not just the recovery," I say, gliding my hands down to her lower back, pressing so firmly she lets out a soft little moan. *Fuck. God help me.* "You're also getting stronger."

"Yeah? You can tell?" she asks.

"Yeah, of course."

"Tell me."

I swallow, not wanting to admit the ways I notice her. But I can feel the hope and vulnerability in the question, and I don't know how to say no.

"I can see it here," I say, sliding my hands up to the backs of her arms. "In the way your muscles are coming in. Here, this one." I move my thumbs along her triceps, and she lets out a little sigh of relief as I ease the tension.

"I see it here," I say, bringing my hands to her shoulders and her upper back. "Not in the muscle, but in the way you carry yourself. How you helped Gabe up earlier, and it was so easy for you."

"I thought you might be jealous," she says softly. "I see you watching us when we're together."

"I'm not watching the two of you together," I say, pressing gently into her back so that she lets out a sigh. "I'm watching *you*. And if I'm jealous, it's because you let him be close to you in a way I can't be right now."

"Says the man reaching his hands under the back of my bra."

"What, you don't like it?" I say softly, teasingly, and I press into her muscles in a way that makes her moan just a little.

"I like it fine," she says, and I can hear the smile in her voice.

It's quiet as I move my hands down her lower back, then skip over her ass to get to her legs. The bruises are healing, large yellow-green splotches that I hate to see. Still, they don't take away from her beauty. I like the new muscle coming in on her, I realize. Not because it's hot on its own, but because it's Em —*Em*'s legs that are growing stronger, *Em*'s arms that can do more now than they could two weeks ago. I think I'd like her any way she was. Any way her body changed.

"I see it here," I say, sliding my hands gently up the back of one of her thighs.

"Yeah? How?"

I clear my throat. *Things are different now*, she'd said a few days ago. They're not for me, but she's the one who started sleeping in a room down the hall, who kicked me out of her bed a few nights ago when she had a nightmare. I can't just comment on her body anymore.

"I can just tell. You're doing squats. I can see that."

"I'm not *just* doing squats," she says. "I'm doing good mornings and kickbacks, and I'm using the Smith machine."

"Let me guess. Maren is running this part of your training."

"How did you know?"

I laugh, the sound a low rumble. "Because Maren got you that red dress, and I think she likes making me a little crazy for you."

"Is that so hard to do?"

"The easiest thing in the world."

It grows quiet for a minute, and I can feel her thinking.

"Show me where you see it," she says finally, softly. An invitation. My wolf lowers his head, ready to play.

Man. Am I really doing this?

I bring my hands up slowly to her ass, gently squeezing the outer curve on each side.

"I see it here," I say, my voice low.

"Mm," she says, and I can hear her breath hitch.

"Are you sore?" I ask, bringing my mouth close to her ear. "Do you need some relief?"

"Maybe. Just a little."

"It would be easier to massage you if I could be on top," I say.

She presses herself up to look at me, and I can see her eyes are dark with desire. The hormones of her heat are already fading away, but I can still sense the edge of it on her. Without a word she climbs off of the couch and onto the rug, lying on her stomach, putting her head on the backs of her hands.

"Like this?" she asks innocently.

I straddle her, sitting lightly over the backs of her thighs, and I slide my hands gently under the hem of her shorts. She lets out a sigh and I feel my body respond, growing hard at the way her breath catches, the way she reacts to my touch.

"These are in the way," I say as I reach for the waistband of her shorts.

"I can—"

Before she finishes her sentence I pull them higher, so the front seam of the shorts pulls in against her slit. I hear her gasp, her back arching from the sensation.

"That's better," I murmur.

"Kier," she breathes.

Agaayit. I shouldn't be doing this. But my wolf is hungry for her, and he's in control now.

"Where else do you want me to touch you?" I ask. "Where else do you have some tension you need to release?"

I bring my hands low on her ass to dip my thumbs between her thighs. I run them over the seam of her shorts, where I can feel the shape of her lips under the fabric. She moans at my touch.

"Does that feel good?" I murmur.

"Yes," she breathes, and I slip one of my thumbs under the fabric, running it over the seam of her.

"How about this?"

She gasps in reply, her back arching for me, breath growing heavy. I dip my thumb between her lips, and my whole body responds as I register the wetness pooling there for me. I slide down to her clit, and I can see the second I reach it, her whole body tensing.

"I— Em," I manage to get out. I swallow. *Agaayu.* I can't believe I'm doing this. "You said things were different for you. Do you... do you *want* to be doing this right now?"

God. Please say yes.

She hesitates, and I sense the moment her desire takes a back seat and her higher consciousness kicks in.

"I— I don't know," she says finally.

I climb off of her, giving her some space so I can sit next to her on the floor. She sits up, one leg curled to her chest, and I can smell her arousal in the air, see it in her eyes.

"I want you," she says. "Trust me, I do..."

"Em," I say softly, resting a hand against her face. "So then what are we doing?"

"I don't know."

"Are we together? What's going on?" My voice is desperate. I sound like a lovesick schoolkid, and I hate it.

"We're not *not* together."

"Then why aren't you sleeping in my bed? Why are we keeping our distance all day?"

"Because you hurt me, Kier," she says, and she swallows. "And I thought it was just about the rite, but it's not. It's not *just* that I don't want you to think I'm weak. I also don't know if I can be with someone who doesn't... who doesn't..."

I fill in the gaps. "But Em, I *do* love you. I love you so much."

"Do you love *all* of me, though?" she asks. "Do you know how to love me in a way that doesn't just look like protection?"

The words hit me like a blow to the chest, and I stare at her, unsure. Isn't that how I'm supposed to love her? Isn't that the thing she's always wanted to feel? Safe?

"I thought it was new, this overprotective thing," she says, looking down. "And it is, in a way, because you've never been like *this*—not wanting me to leave the house alone, stuff like that. I know that's left over from the rite. But…" She swallows. "I don't know. Is the other stuff new? Have you always thought I couldn't take care of myself?"

"Em." I lean forward, putting a hand on her knee. "I *know* you can take care of yourself. You've had to take care of yourself since you were a little kid. But I *like* taking care of you. And if I do, you don't have to worry about it, and you can focus on the things that make you happy."

"I think that maybe, right now, fighting for myself *is* the thing that makes me happy."

"Okay," I say weakly. *But don't risk your life. Don't kill yourself in the ring. Please.*

We look at each other for a long time, like we're both waiting for something to change. Finally, she speaks, and it's not what I expect.

"Can I ask you something about your rite?" she asks.

"You can ask. I don't know if I can answer."

"I'm not going to ask what you fought, although I think I can guess." She comes closer to me now, putting a hand on mine. Her thumb runs back and forth against the elastic she gave me. "I know the ancient book says *nekkatik veijtanna kiyyu unbeijnkit—* you can't tell another soul what you saw. But I also know we face our biggest fear in the ring. And I know that ever since that night, you're scared that my dad is here on the Fakaris. So for weeks, I've been trying to piece together why your biggest fear would be my dad."

I think back to that night. My certainty that the wolf I fought was real, and that it was just Lena and the memories that came from the *kattaka*. If that was true, then my biggest fear isn't her father, but what Lena said to me. What it might mean.

"Maybe my biggest fear is losing you," I say, and my voice comes out husky.

"Kier…"

"But I don't know," I say, looking away. My voice comes out

angrier than I mean it to, and I see it register in her posture. "Because I didn't defeat *that* that night, did I? I brought it home with me. And now we're both paying for it."

"What do you mean?"

"It's costing me *you*. Us. This. What we could be."

"Kieran." She takes my face in her hands and pulls it towards her, stopping a few inches before her face. "It doesn't have to be this way. Tell me you think I can do this. Tell me you believe in me."

"I..." I swallow. "I believe you're strong. I believe you're going to fight like hell. I believe you won't quit."

She drops her hands, and her voice grows bitter. "But you don't think I can do it."

"I don't know, Em." I sigh, exasperated. "Can you trust me when I say that I *hate* this? I don't want to feel this way. I don't like to see how it hurts you. Do I think you're going to give it your all? Yes. Do I think you're kicking ass in training? Yes. Am I proud of you? Yes—so, so proud. But do I think you can train for the islands' biggest challenge in *six weeks,* with no preparation? No, I don't. And that's not personal. I don't think *anyone* can do that."

She nods.

"We almost lost Seb," I say, my voice hollow. "He only trained for a few weeks, too, and he almost *died.* Wouldn't you give anything to go back and change it?"

She sighs, and I can't read the look on her face as she gets up and starts walking for the door.

"Hey, Em. Wait."

She turns around. "What?"

"I—" God. I sigh. The timing of this is terrible. "I have to go back to Saroe for a little bit, to finish some work orders. But I want to be clear, this is not me leaving. I'm coming back, okay? It's not about this."

"Sure. Whatever," she says, and turns around.

"No, wait," I say, and get up. I walk to her and put my hands on her shoulders, turning her to face me again. "Listen. I want to be really clear, because I need you to know I'm telling the truth. I'm not leaving. Not today, not ever."

She looks at me, her mouth tight, her eyes a deep, rich blue—and for the first time, a little gold. I can see the amber ring around her irises coming in a little stronger, and it catches me off-guard. I swallow and focus.

"I know we're figuring some shit out right now," I say. "But I made you a promise, and I meant it. So you can be fucking pissed at me, and maybe I deserve it. But I'm still gonna be here, okay?"

"I don't know, Kier," she says. "I don't know if I want you here, if you don't know how to support me."

"I'm trying," I say.

"I'll see you when you get back, okay?" she asks, and she turns to walk to the stairs.

26

KIERAN

The morning I leave for Saroe, I take the first ferry of the day.

I feel like shit. Em's been ignoring me since our last conversation, and even though I was training on Halluk, I moved my schedule to work out in the afternoons so she could have the gym to herself in the mornings. My body misses the routine almost as much as it misses her.

Caspar picks me up at the north shore and takes me straight to the woodworking workshop. On the drive over, he fills me in on the orders he's fulfilled, and which new ones have come in. I'm half-listening, but I'm also watching the people on the streets as we head into town. Things feel different—a little quieter and more edgy than when I left. I notice that most of the kids that play out in the streets now have a parent watching from the doorway.

"How have things been since the attacks?" I ask.

"Tense," he says, taking a left. "You know Ingela Tayyuni? Her car backfired near the harbor yesterday, and people scrambled like it was a gunshot."

"Man," I say. "That's crazy. Even in the nineties, I don't think it was like this."

"Yeah. At least then, they left after each attack," Caspar says. "It's been different since they stormed the common house. There's a curfew now, and the marshals asking people to volunteer for the search crew."

"Who's involved?" I ask.

"Right now it's just the two marshals and the volunteer fire squad looking full-time. I helped them out on Tuesday, but this week has been too busy at the shop. I think Viggo's involved, if you want to talk to him about volunteering."

"Yeah, thanks. I'll think about it."

Caspar pulls into the street with our workshop and drops me off outside, then heads back to his place to park the car. I pull my keys from my front pocket to unlock the front door. Once I'm in, I switch on the lights, taking in the scent of sawdust and lacquer.

It's good to be back, I realize. I missed a bit of my sense of purpose on Halluk, with mostly Em to care for and the Remnant to worry about from afar. It'll be good to lose myself in my work again, if just for a little bit.

I head up the steps for the loft, where Caspar's and my desks are located. First I make some coffee—just instant stuff, not nice the way Em makes it—then refamiliarize myself with my latest projects. The most important is the wedding arch, and I take a look at the design I was working on when I was last here.

I spread out the papers on my desk. Four pillars curving into arches at the top, forming something like a trellis. I'd imagined carvings in the arches: grapes and pomegranates, doves and sparrows. But looking at it now, it feels wrong. The beams look thick and clunky, and the symbols don't ring true.

I set the papers aside and take out some clean sheets to take another stab at the design. I try for something a little more abstract: tree branches overlapping to create separate arches, crossing each other in something like a stained glass window.

But it looks like an elf door from one of those fantasy movies Maren made us watch, and I start over. At some point, I hear Caspar get to work downstairs, starting on a dresser I designed a few months ago. By the time I think to take a quick lunch break, I'm four redesigns deep, and I hate each one as much as the last.

It's just past three when we hear a commotion from outside. First a woman's scream, and the sound of metal clanging from down the hill. I stand, looking through the front windows, and see Caspar turn to look behind him.

"Do you think it's..." he asks. But before he can finish his sentence, I'm running down the stairs and towards the door.

I throw it open just in time to see a group of wolves tear past me, making their way to the heart of town. I look to the left, where they came from, and see Heimig's book stall turned over in the street, a bushel of apples spilling onto the ground from the market. Behind them, a woman is gathering her children inside, all three of them crying.

"Caspar, the rebels. Come," I yell, and I shift and follow the group.

They tear through the cobblestone streets, and as soon as they realize that Caspar and I are behind—both in our wolf forms now—I see one of them give a signal, and they split. I can sense more of our own kind running up behind us: Heimig and two other elders, whose scent I can't quite catch in the air. A few of the rebel wolves break off down a side street, and Caspar and Heimig turn to follow them. I follow the main group—there must be five or six—as they head for the heart of town.

I get close, trying to bite at the tail of one of the smaller wolves running in the back. She's a female, with a small frame and gray fur. I think of what Quinn said. The wolf who attacked Gabe was female. Could this be the one who cost Gabe his rite? Who started all this?

But just as I lunge forward, trying to catch her, I feel a body barrel into my side. Another female wolf, this one silver-gray and absolutely massive. She tries to slam me out of the way, getting me off of the smaller one. I look up to see where she came from, and realize she's run in from one of the side streets, from the group Caspar and Heimig chased away, now trying to rejoin her pack. I pick up speed, but she runs faster, trying to worm herself between me and the smaller one.

No—*this* must be the one who attacked Gabe. The smaller wolf wouldn't have enough weight to break his leg by jumping on him. This one, though, is a beast.

Caspar and the other wolves he broke off to chase don't return to the pack, and I hope he's subdued them somehow. Looking up ahead, I can see that the sound of the chase has alerted others to what's happening. Viggo and Saga's wolves are coming up ahead with a pack of other elders. I'm chasing the group in the direction of the central plaza, and I know there aren't enough exits for them to escape if the elders come in from the other side.

I take my chances. I pounce on the large silver-gray wolf, aiming my bite for the back of her neck. As the weight of my body hits her, she turns onto her back and falls under me, the rest of the group running on without us.

The silver wolf wrestles under me, snapping and baring her teeth, but she puts up a less fight than I expect for an animal of her size. As I crush her front paws under mine, pinning her down, she rolls her neck to see what's going on ahead of us. I look up, too. The elders have met the rebel pack, and what's unfolding now is an all-out brawl, with the rebels clearly outnumbered. I see Viggo fighting with one of the males, while another Saroan elder, Iena, has managed to pin down the smaller female I was chasing earlier.

I snarl at the silver she-wolf, baring my teeth. But where I expect her to fight back, she mostly writhes under me, giving the appearance of fighting without any power behind it. And then— I'm surprised—she shifts. Within seconds, in the place of the massive, muscular gray wolf from before is a young woman, tall but lean, her hair a wild mess of curls and waves, her facial features sharp and refined.

I shift, too, to get a better grip on her. In a second I'm towering over her, pinning her forearms down with my human hands, pressing one knee over her leg to keep her down. She wriggles as though she's fighting me, but she's barely pushing back.

What the fuck is she doing?

"Please listen to me." Her words come out fast, with the cadence of something practiced. "My name is Thalia Nayakka and I'm here with my sister, Nomi. When they take us, separate me from the others. I'm willing to talk. I have information that will help you. I'll make you a deal."

"Like you're in any place to negotiate with us," I say, and I feel my hands clamp harder down on her wrists.

The sounds up ahead are changing, and I glance up to see that the whole pack of rebels has been subdued. A marshal is running up to Saga, and I see the volunteer fire crew coming in too, bearing clubs and rope.

"Please," says the woman from under me. "Listen. You may not trust me, but you need to give me a chance. My sister and I applied for asylum but were denied multiple times. We had no way to get to the islands except to go with this group. We need your protection."

"I need to protect these islands from *you*."

"If you don't do it for me, then do it for my sister. Please."

I swallow, registering the fear in her eyes. There's a marshal walking towards us with rope.

"Promise me that you'll at least tell the others," she whispers.

"Okay," I say finally. "I promise."

27

EMERSON

Just after Kieran leaves for the ferry to Saroe, I show up at Seb's and my usual spot on the shore. My physical training is going well—my shifter nature lets me pick up skill and strength faster than I knew was possible—but the wolf training isn't getting any better. Seb has tried a few more times to get me to shift on command, but on the rare occasion I can do it, I can't change back. I can tell he's getting frustrated, counting down the days till our deal is over and we call it quits. The pressure only makes it worse.

I stand on the shore, waiting for him. The minutes tick by, and I start to get nervous. Is he backing out? But finally, fifteen minutes after we agreed to meet, Quinn and Maren make their way down from the house.

"Hey. What's going on?" I ask.

"I thought we might have more luck than Seb," says Quinn.

"He's giving up?"

"No. We just want to try something different."

Maren smiles. "And besides. Sometimes women just get it."

I nod my head, and I wonder if either of them could possibly understand. Maren with her effervescent energy, her full self-confidence that anything she tries will always work out. Quinn, strong and self-assured, kicking my ass every day in the gym and never seeming rattled by anything. I doubt either of them could understand this.

"So. What's the plan?" I ask.

"I wanna try something from FMA," Quinn says. "Seb thought we didn't have time for theory, but I wonder if maybe that's what you need. Come on. Let's take a walk."

"Okay…" I glance at Maren, wondering what we're about to do. She shrugs, and we follow Quinn towards the woods.

TWENTY MINUTES LATER, she brings us to a clearing in the trees, loosely marked by boulders in a circle.

"What's this?" I ask.

"Probably just a place teenagers come to smoke at night," Quinn says, a wry smile pulling at her lips. "But for us, it's perfect. We just need some clear space and privacy. Okay. Fighting stance."

I move my feet the way Seb taught me: a little wider than shoulder-width apart, knees slightly bent, core strong, my hands up and open. Maren does the same.

"Good," Quinn says, and her voice takes on a new quality, still firm, but soft and smooth. Her teaching voice, I realize. "Now close your eyes. Connect to your life force. Your inner strength."

Strength. Okay. I close my eyes and think of my time in the gym. The way it felt when I did my first pull-up. Landing a punch for the first time. The sense of victory when I first got out from under Quinn's weight.

Fighting. Proving myself.

"Em, I see your shoulders tensing," Quinn says. "This doesn't have to be strength the way you typically think about it. Think about *your* strength, the way the *agaayit* made you."

I take a breath, wanting to take her correction the way I do with boxing, and suddenly Kieran's words that day in the woods come to me. *You know how to love people.* Memories flood to the surface: Maren lighting up on her birthday when I gave her that emerald sweater, the first I'd ever made. Seb's wound coming together under my hand. Gabe's chest healing for me.

"Alright, good," Quinn says, as though she can see something in me change. "Okay. Now imagine that strength pooling in you, like energy. You can picture golden light, or something that feels more like you. Imagine it flowing down from your center, into the earth, taking root underground. Connecting you to the dust you came from."

I imagine the energy in me pooling, swirling through my body. It's not gold, but green and blue and purple like the *kiyyulit*. I picture it going down to the earth, hooking into something far below me: the heart of islands, the center of the earth.

"Alright. And now for that same energy, I want you to bring it upwards and connect to something above you," Quinn says. "Imagine it flowing up through the crown of your head, up to the ancestors' space. Have it hook in somewhere. You can imagine it looping around a star, if it helps. Traditionally, we imagine the moon."

I try to imagine the *kiyyulit* doing that, but it feels dopey and comical. I hesitate, trying to figure out something that feels right.

The ancestors' space. I think of my mom, wherever she might be: somewhere beyond me, in a place I can't know. And without my conscious mind being aware of it, I feel the energy do something different than what Quinn said, but it feels right. It doesn't hook or take root, but it blends with the *kiyyulit* in the ancestors' space. I don't know where it is, but I picture it somewhere beyond me, tying me to her. To all the ancestors; the people who came before not just me, but her, too. All of us.

"Ground yourself in the moment," Quinn says softly. "Take note of where you are. Now open your eyes."

We do as told, and Quinn is standing firm, looking directly at me.

"Your life force comes from the soil below you, and the ancestors above. It was forged for you by the *agaayit*. It's not too big or too small for you, but just right. It's safe for you to trust."

I doubt how much of this message is traditional FMA, and how much Seb or Gabe has told her about my issues. Still, it reaches something in me. My eyes sting, and as I take a deep breath, I feel something in my stomach ease. Somewhere in there is my wolf, small but present.

Not scared. Just *there*.

"We're gonna run now," Quinn says gently. "The three of us together. Em, you lead. If you feel you can shift, let it happen, and we'll shift with you. And once you're there, find this feeling again. If you get scared, find *this* feeling, and let it bring you back to yourself. Okay?"

"Okay," I say. I don't know if I want this. But I only have two days left before Seb makes his call. And I can trust myself, right?

That's what Mom said. *You can trust yourself.*

We do some quick stretches, and I wait for Quinn to take us out of the clearing. But she looks at me expectantly, and I remember. Right. I'm in charge now. I glance at Maren, who gives me an encouraging smile.

These people support me. They want what's best for me. So, ignoring the nerves in my gut, I gather my courage and I start to run.

I lead them through the trees, towards the quarry and then up and around it. After a minute my nerves and the rhythm of my feet fall away. First, I find myself slipping into muscle memory. I think of my dad; I think of Seb making his decision soon, and the way Kieran looked when he told me he wanted to believe in me but just couldn't. I feel my wolf grow tense, but then I catch myself.

No. We're doing something different today.

I tap into that connectedness again; the *kiyyulit*-like energy flowing through me. I let myself think about my mom, watching me from wherever the ancestors are. I think about her painting at the dining room table in the house we got, once it was just the two of us. I feel that stinging in my eyes again, but it feels good this time. My wolf comes closer to the surface, but I don't push her down or to the forefront. She's just there.

I think of my own painting, and the moments I feel the most in flow. The way I feel when I'm swimming in the summer, when the water's all around me and I feel like a part of something bigger than myself. I think of the garden behind the *fikarig*, the glow of the purple rhodoras; the way I feel when Kier and I are out there, laughing and letting the sun soak into our skin. And then I think of Mom again: the way she used to sing when she felt free. The way I felt when I was with her. Like I mattered. Like no matter what happened, we would be okay. We would find a way through.

I swallow, and I realize I'm starting to cry, but today I don't stop it. Quinn and Maren are on either side of me, making room for me, for my strength and my weakness, and for once I'm not ashamed.

You can trust yourself, Mom said in the woods. I feel my wolf at the edge of my skin and let my other mind fall away until she's in charge. My body folds forward, shifting, bending, unfurling. And then I'm her, in her skin, just as we reach the edge of the woods and I see the sand and rocks of the shore before us.

Maren and Quinn shift beside me, Maren's form strong and black, Quinn lean and gray. I don't worry about the clothes we're leaving behind, and I run and I run and I run. For the first time, I feel the joy in this body: the strength and delight, the playful edge of it. The part of me that feels free.

We run along the shore, Quinn dipping back and Maren beside me, and I feel myself wanting to laugh. A yip breaks out of my chest, and I run towards the edge of the water, dipping my paws in. It's cold, but in my wolf form it just feels cool, calming.

Quinn comes up to us, carrying the fabric of our clothes in her mouth, and drops them on the sand of the shore. She gives me a nod.

Your lead.

I feel for the other side of me—the edge of my conscious mind, somewhere inside myself—and lean into it. And suddenly I'm unfolding, unfurling, back in my skin, buck naked and laughing at the edge of the sea.

Maren shifts beside me, then Quinn.

"Oh my *God*, girl. That was so freaking cool," Maren says. "How do you feel?"

I grin as Quinn tosses my shirt to me. The water splashes at my feet, but it's not too cold. The warmth inside me takes up my whole body. I throw my head back, and a laugh—joyful, victorious, free—breaks out of me.

"Honestly?" I ask, looking over at her. "I feel incredible."

28

KIERAN

The marshals, Sigur and Ivo, take all ten of the rebels into custody. We don't have a jail cell, so after some quick improvisation, they and the volunteers take them down to the basement of the common house. Viggo and I help with transport, and Saga follows behind. I've got the wolf girl, Thalia, by the arm, and some of the elder women have found blankets for the rebels to cover their bodies.

We lead them down into the basement, where Ivo has us tie them to metal chairs that we bind to each other, back to back. Saga goes to the apothecary to get salves with *trotsayyit* and *uikbaane*—witch hazel and wolfsbane—that she can use to prevent them from shifting, and I head outside to call Gabe.

"Hey, man. We caught the rebels."

"Woah, that's great," he says. "Where did you find them?"

"We didn't," I say. "They ran into town to commit another attack. It looks like they were heading for the school, but we cornered them in the plaza."

"That's awesome. So we can head back?"

I sigh. "I don't know. I don't think this is all of them. None of the people we caught are formerly Fakari. And I think, if they were able to hide out so long and knew how to identify you, there's got to be someone who knows our islands well enough to direct them."

"So you want us to say here," he says, his voice flat.

"I think that's smart."

Gabe sighs. "What does my mom think?"

"I haven't talked to her yet, but I'll let you know. But, hey, there's something else."

"What?"

I look out at the woods before us, and the path up to Moon Lake. The sun is starting to set, painting the sky like cotton candy. I'm nervous, I realize, and I don't know why.

"Can you describe the wolf who broke your leg in the common house?"

"Uh, yeah. She was gray. Massive. Bigger than any female wolf I've seen before."

"Okay." I swallow. "I talked to her—I was the one who caught her, when we stopped the attack. She says she's an asylum seeker."

"*What?*"

"Yeah, I don't know. Maybe it's a bit, you know—buying more time and sympathy or something. I'm gonna have to check with Saga to see if the names line up. But she says she and her sister came here seeking asylum, and this was the only way to get to the islands after we denied their requests."

"Huh. Okay. So what now?"

"I don't know, dude. She asked me if we can separate her from the others. She's willing to talk if we can make her a deal. I told her I'd bring it to the council, at least."

"*Agaayu,*" he mutters.

"I know."

"You have to do it," he says. "If she has more information—"

"I don't know, man. She could be talking out of her ass."

"Yeah. Maybe. But if she's not…"

"I'll let you know after I talk to your mom," I say. "How are things over there?"

"Good. Em shifted to her wolf form and back today, on purpose. The girls are celebrating."

I feel a grin spread over my face. "That's amazing. Can I talk to her?"

"Uh, let me ask."

I hear a rustling at the other end of the line, and some mumbling.

"Sorry, not right now," Gabe says when he comes back. "She and Maren just put on these disgusting green face masks and they look like hags, so they can't talk. Hey!—" I hear a soft thud as something seems to hit him, presumably a couch pillow. The sound of laughter comes through the line, and I can make out Em's giggle, soft and flowing like a brook. My inner wolf responds eagerly to the sound, wanting to play.

Not now, dumbass.

"Yeah, now's not a good time," Gabe says. "But I'll tell them about this. She'll probably call you later to hear more for herself."

"Okay. Thanks." I swallow. "Talk later, then?"

"Yeah, talk later. Bye."

We hang up, and I see Saga walking to the common house with a bag of salves. Even from here, I can smell the *uikbaane* and wrinkle my nose. I walk up to her as she nears the door.

"*Heij*, Saga."

"Oh, Kieran. I didn't have the chance to welcome you back to the island yet. It's good to have you home, *tekanni*." *My son.* I'm not her kid, of course, and I'm not even formally a member of her *fika*. But the term feels like it acknowledges my role in their pack in a way I really need right now—especially with Em putting so much distance between us. I swallow the feeling in my throat.

"Thanks, Saga," I say. "You, too. Hang on, I need to talk to you." I reach out a hand to stop her before she heads for the door to the common house.

"What is it?"

"Is the name Thalia Nayakka familiar to you? Or Nomi?"

She furrows her brow. "Vaguely… Why? What's going on?"

I swallow. "The wolf I caught—I'm pretty sure she's the one who hurt Gabe. She says she and her sister originally tried to come here as asylum seekers. She's willing to talk to us in exchange for—I don't even know what. Protection or a place on the islands, or something."

I see it in her face the moment I mention Gabe's injury. Her mouth tightens, and she shakes her head as she answers me.

"We can't negotiate with these people. If she attacked Gabriel, she's not someone we can let onto our shores, asylum petition or not."

"She said she had no other way to get here."

"She should have waited for us to approve her request."

"But—" I run a hand through my hair, remembering the argument we had over dinner a few weeks back. "We weren't going to approve it, were we? We denied her twice. The second time you didn't even bring it for a vote."

She shakes her head. "I'm sorry, *piu*, I can't have this conversation right now. I need to go see that we stop them from shifting. But we can discuss it later. Are you coming to the *fikarig* for dinner? Now that they're caught, I think we can return home."

"Is that safe? This can't be all of them. They knew the island too well to all be southerners. But if we talk to the girl, maybe she can tell us—"

"Later, Kieran. We'll discuss this later. If you want to join us at the *fikarig* for dinner, you're welcome to."

I DO EAT at Em's *fikarig* that evening, in spite of my wariness about who else may still be lurking on the island. It's just me and the elders tonight—Viggo, Dagmar, Saga, and Seb's mom Isolde. Since Gabe isn't home to cook, I bring takeout from Hilde's, the seafood restaurant on Saroe's south shore.

"Heij, jenge," Viggo says as I walk through the front door. The house feels strange without Em and the others—the scent is different, and I can tell from a faint mustiness that no one's been here for the last few weeks.

"Hey, Viggo. Good to see you."

He pulls me into him, clapping me on the back.

"Well done at the plaza this morning," he says. "It's good to have you back to defend the islands."

"Yeah. Thanks."

"Oh, is that Kieran?" asks Dagmar, walking into the hall, holding silverware. "Good. We've already set the table. Come in."

I follow her into the dining room and set the bags with our dinner down. Isolde comes in and begins unpacking, and Saga takes a seat. We divide up the dishes, and once everyone's plate is full, Viggo lifts a glass.

"Kututkuk. To the restoration of peace, and our children coming home soon."

"Kututkuk," we say in unison, and the others begin to eat.

"Viggo," I say, putting my glass down. "I wanted to talk about that. I don't feel right about Em and the others coming back until we're sure we have the whole group detained. Caspar told me you're involved with the search crew. Did you learn anything about where they were hiding?"

"No, nothing," he says. "And the ones we've caught have given nothing up. But we should be able to get it out of them soon enough." He raises his eyebrows and gives a jovial look to Isolde, who sits still, stoic as ever.

"Did Saga tell you what I told her, about the black she-wolf?" I ask.

"Ah, yes, she said. She wants to make us a deal."

"It might be worth it to get what information she has, if it means finding the rest of their group."

"But what will she ask of us?" Dagmar says, wiping her mouth with her napkin. "Surely we can't give her a place on the islands if she came here as a terrorist."

"Besides, who knows whether her information is even valuable?" says Isolde. "She may send us on a wild goose chase just to secure herself a place on the islands."

"We should find out, at least," I say.

"We would need a council vote on any negotiation," Saga says, shaking her head. "We can't decide to negotiate without raising it to a vote."

"Can I at least get permission to talk to her? See what she wants, before we bring it to the council?"

"*Iija, 'ts kut,*" Saga says, waving a hand. *Yes, that's fine.* "Now, please, let's enjoy dinner."

AFTER THE MEAL, I climb the stairs to Em's room. As soon as I open the door, the scent of her hits my nostrils, and my wolf registers it happily. I take in the familiar sights: her bed, fitted with white cotton sheets. The healer's training book sitting on her bedside table. The watercolors she's pinned up on the walls.

I walk around the room, looking at them. She swaps them out every few weeks with new one's she's made, the older ones returning to a pile on her desk. When we used to sleep here together, I'd notice them change from time to time but didn't think much of it. Now that we're barely talking, I feel the need to really take them in—to hang on to any piece of her.

I look at the ones above her desk: hydrangeas in a glass vase by the window. Saga's blue-and-white Fakari coffee pot.

Dagmar's hands stirring honey into her tea. On the wall over her bed are the ones of us: Seb and Gabe in the lake. The five of us running through the woods—Seb, Gabe, Maren, and me in our wolf forms, with Em riding on my back. Her and me in the garden, lying on our backs next to the bushes of deep purple flowers. She has one in her hair, and the sight feels vaguely familiar.

I walk to her desk to look at the painting I framed for her, still lying face up in its wooden frame. As I pick it up, I see a stack of older paintings underneath, bound together with red string. I've never seen these before, but in the top one I see my own face, partially obscured by the knot. I pick up the stack, trying to suppress the feeling that I'm invading on something private.

Sitting on her bed, I carefully untie the string.

The first painting is me, asleep. My face is partially obscured by my hand, curled up near my head, and I can see her knee and long blonde hair in the bottom corner of the illustration. I pick it up and put it at the back of the stack. The next is us in the lake, her facing me with her arms around my neck. But the one after that surprises me. For a second, I think it's Em, bent over in the garden, planting the purple flowers we have behind the *fikarig*. But the clothes don't feel like her, and the hair is a touch too dark. I look down in the bottom corner to see, in Em's slanted, loopy handwriting: "Mom in the garden." And suddenly, I remember that it was Em who insisted we plant these same purple flowers behind this house.

I feel my phone vibrating in my pocket and slip it out. My inner wolf yips happily to see it's her calling.

"*Heij*," I say as I pick up, trying to hide the desperation in my voice. "How are you?"

"*Heij* Kier." Her voice feels firmer than I want it to be. "You asked Gabe to talk?"

"Oh, yeah. I wanted to congratulate you. I heard you shifted today."

"Yeah, I did."

"That's awesome. How's it feel?"

A sigh. Something easing, just a little.

"Okay, I guess. I'm gonna keep practicing. Actually, you know what? It feels really good. I'm proud of myself. I feel like I'm finally doing it. What no one thought I could do."

Something in my chest hurts. "Listen, Em—"

"I don't want to hear it right now. I'm celebrating today, okay? I don't need to deal with our stuff."

I swallow. "Okay."

She asks me about the rebels we caught, her voice betraying surprise when I tell her about Thalia trying to strike a deal for her and her sister.

"Is the council going to do it?"

"I don't know. Your *fika* elders are against, but I think it's smart to at least hear what she wants. I'm gonna try to talk to her tomorrow."

"Okay. Be careful, please."

"Why?"

"Just that you have a thing about protecting the underdog. Don't let her manipulate you."

I bring a hand to the back of my neck, thinking. Is that what's happening here?

"Hey, I have to go," Em says, interrupting my thoughts. "Quinn and Maren and I are going out for dinner to celebrate. I'll talk to you soon, okay?"

"Okay. But wait, before you go. I have a question."

"Hm?"

I look at the painting in my hands. "What's the name of the purple flowers you planted in the garden out back?"

"Rhodoras. Why?"

"Nothing, just—I remember how much you like sitting out there in the summer. You were the one who planted them, right?"

"Yeah."

"Why those? Are they special for you?"

She lets out a breath. After a second she says, "They were my mom's favorite. She got them from the Ralph Waldo Emerson poem, 'The Rhodora.' That's who she named me for. The poet."

"I didn't know that."

"Yeah. She used to keep a book of his poems by the bed. But I have to go now, okay? I'll call you later."

"I'm gonna call you tomorrow, okay?"

"I might be too busy tomorrow," she says. "We're gonna do some new mental training for the first time."

"Doesn't matter. You don't have to pick up. But I'm gonna call."

"Okay," she says finally. "We'll see."

29

EMERSON

"It's been three weeks," I say, walking into the gym. I asked Maren and Quinn to hang back today, so I could see Seb alone. I glance around the gym to see that there's no one else here. *Good.*

"*Morlaa'kut* to you, too," he says, looking up from his seat on the mat.

"You said I would have three weeks to prove myself. I can do four pull-ups, I've more than doubled the weight I can lift, and Quinn says I'm getting a lot better at boxing and self-defense. Let me keep training."

"Em—"

"Seb, I have everything in me that I need to do this. I can run three miles and shift on command. *And* my healing is stronger, which Gabe thinks I can use to buy myself more time in the ring."

Seb sets his jaw, eyeing me. "You shifted on command *once*, on a run in the woods. Do you think you can do it again, now?"

"Yes."

"Show me."

I take a deep breath and put my feet into fighting stance. I remember Quinn's words in my head. *Pool your energy. Root below into the earth. Send it up into the ancestors' space.*

I exhale and try to connect to my inner wolf. The second I feel her, I bow my conscious mind over to her, and suddenly I'm tumbling, rolling in on myself, and folding into my wolf form.

I look up at Seb, victorious.

"Good," he says nodding. "Now back."

My wolf wants to run and play, but I do my best to find my conscious mind and let her take control. A few seconds later, I'm unfurling, my arms and legs unfolding, and I scramble to my feet.

Seb looks at the ground to give me some privacy. I pick up Maren's shifting shirt and the pants I borrowed from Quinn and snap them into me.

"So?" I ask.

"Well, it takes too long and you look like shit doing it. And we need to train you to shift back onto your feet, not your ass. But okay."

"Yes?!" I say, jumping up and down. "You're saying you'll keep training me?"

"Yeah. But it's gonna get harder from here, not easier."

"Okay," I say, nodding. "I can do harder."

"Not physically. We need to start the mental training."

"Okay. I can do that."

He nods. "We'll start that this afternoon. For now, let's get a workout in. Run for five minutes around the track."

I start walking towards it.

"No. In your wolf form. Go."

WE GET HOME in the afternoon and find Quinn and Gabe in the kitchen. Gabe still can't put weight on his foot, but he's leaning on his crutches while Quinn follows his orders on how to make lunch.

"Hey guys," I say, walking in. "Guess who's allowed to keep training?"

I put my hands up and do a little twirl for them.

Quinn grins at me. "That's awesome, dude. You deserve it."

"I start mental prep with Seb today," I say, leaning against the counter. "What are you guys making?"

"Frittata. It should be done soon," Gabe says.

I look down at my watch. "I have some time to practice my healer skills before lunch, if you want, Gabe."

"You're not too tired?"

"No. Actually, I feel like I have more energy from this morning. Come on, we can go to the living room so we don't disturb Quinn."

He nods and I follow him to the living room on his crutches. Once there, he positions himself over the couch and gently lowers himself down, and I take the crutches from him.

"Alright, let's take a look at this," I say, unfastening the clasps of his shirt to expose the scarring on his chest. "Oh, this is looking way better. It may not even scar at all."

"That's all you," he says, leaning back a little as I put my hands over the scars. "I can't believe you did this much for it in three weeks."

"Well. It helps having someone to practice with every day."

"Do you think your training is helping?"

I look up. "What do you mean?"

"I don't know. I don't think it's normal for someone to be growing their skills so fast. Could your shifter training be helping, somehow?"

I shrug. "Maybe. I considered that for the physical training, but for shifting I didn't really think about it."

"Makes sense, right? You're building your power in other ways, so…"

"Could be," I say, nodding. "But okay. Give me a minute to focus."

I close my eyes and pool my concentration, feeling in my mind's eye for the wound. Most of the internal wound has healed, so I pull back a layer to look at the thick scar tissue that's formed on his chest.

I've never trained to work on scarring, so I'm not quite sure what I'm doing. But I focus on the thick lines, which, in my mind's eye, look puffy and have the color of a shadow—less dark than the deep gashes from before. Saga's and Helen's healing magic has been almost completely pushed out now, and I can only feel my own, swirling around his chest, around the bruising in his side. It makes his energy more open to me, now that mine is familiar to the wounds and muscle.

I spread out my fingers, trying to coax the scarring to ease, but that does nothing. I move my hand a little, as though smoothing the dark clouds of his scars, but they don't respond to that, either. Hm.

"It's weird not having Kieran here," Gabe says.

I open my eyes. "Is it?"

"You don't miss him?"

I suck my teeth, annoyed. "I don't know. Shouldn't I be working on your scars right now? Why are we talking about this?"

"Can I be real with you?" he asks.

I feel my inner wolf snap in defiance, but my mouth says, "Yeah, of course."

Stupid people-pleasing brain.

"Stop wasting time."

I give him a look.

"I'm serious," Gabe continues. "Not everyone gets a chance to love someone like that. *You* do. Stop throwing away time you could be happy together."

I swallow. "I don't know, Gabe. It's complicated."

"I've seen the way you look at each other. How complicated can it be?"

"I don't want to talk about this," I say, shaking my head. "You and Quinn seem to be getting along really well, though."

He laughs. "You know Quinn's gay, right?"

"*What?*"

"Yeah. Man, you're obtuse."

I think back for a moment to a conversation I overheard between her and Maren the other day, where they were joking about short nails. Maren's bi, but I chalked the conversation up to yet another one of her pop culture references I didn't get. But suddenly, I wonder…

"Anyway," Gabe says. "Even if she wasn't, I couldn't see her like that. We practically grew up together."

"So did me and Kier," I say.

"That's different. You guys are mates."

I meet his eyes. "You can't know that for sure."

"No, but *you* can. And you do, don't you?"

I swallow. "I guess. Maybe."

"Come on. Was there ever anyone else?"

I shake my head. "No. Not really."

"So stop messing around. I'd kill to have what you guys have."

"Oh, come on. You'll find your person soon enough."

"I don't think so."

I blink in surprise. "What do you mean?"

"I don't think there's someone out there for me. Or, well. I don't know." He looks at me sheepishly. "Maybe there is. But I don't think I'll find her again."

"Again?"

"It's a long story," he says. "I'll tell you some other time, when we're back home, and I can walk, and you and Kieran have finally gotten your shit together. Deal?"

"Yeah, okay," I say, even as I want to probe and ask. I've never seen Gabe hanging around someone before. Who is he talking about? But he looks down at his chest, and I take the nudge.

I put my hand to his body, closing my eyes and probing his energy again. I try the same tricks as earlier: moving my hand around, spreading out the fingers. Again, they don't work. Finally, I decide try something new. I bring Quinn's words to mind and sink my energy into the earth and sky. And then I bring my hand close to his skin and let out a long, slow breath. I send my energy into the wound, and as it goes, I whisper to it.

"*Takka aka leif deij Gabe da tik heim tso nateyyaka,*" I say. *Thank you to Gabe's body that you've protected him so well.* "*Takka feij al ta kantaaye mekot. Eije ek nakiyya veilije.*"

Thank you for all your hard work. He's safe now.

"Woah—" I hear Gabe say, but I can feel something happening in the wound, so I tune him out, focusing on the scars in my mind. I send more of my energy in, blue and purple and green, swirling like the *kiyyulit* in my mind. I feel Gabe's body warm under my hand, opening to it. The clouding of his scars feels softer now. Pliable, like clay.

"*Teij makka de nakiyya leijkayyu.*" *You can let go now.*

"Em, what's happening?" Gabe asks, and at the panicked edge in his voice, I open my eyes. In the inches between my hand in his chest *is* the *kiyyulit*—or at least, what looks like it. The energy is dancing between us, green and purple and blue. Instinctively, I snap my hand away.

"What the hell is that?!" I ask.

"I—Em. The scarring is gone."

I look at his chest, and he's right. In the place where three pink, puffy lines were a moment ago is just... his chest. There's a faint red mark where my energy was, as though the skin was just touched by something hot.

"How did you do that?" Gabe asks, looking at me. "I've never seen that before."

"I don't know," I mumble. "I just... made it up."

He looks at me, his brow furrowed. "You should call my mom."

"No. I don't know. It's nothing."

He grabs my hand, his eyes serious. "This is *not* nothing. My mom has been a healer since before I was born, and I've never seen her do something like this. Hell, I've never even seen *Helen* do something like this."

I blink. I don't want to call Saga. I want to call Kieran.

But suddenly the exhaustion hits me like a wave, and the thought of talking to anyone feels like too much. I lean back against the couch.

"Hey. You good?" Gabe asks, dropping my hand.

"Yeah, I'm just tired." I bring a hand to my head. The world feels fuzzy. At that moment, Seb walks into the room.

"Hey, guys. Woah, Gabe—what happened to your chest?"

"Em happened."

I look up at Seb, who's staring in bewilderment at me.

"*Uikbaane.*"

"I need a little time to rest before we do the mental training," I say.

"Yeah, that's fine. I wasn't going to get us started until two, anyway."

I nod. "I might take a nap."

"Okay. Do you want me to wake you up at, like, one thirty?"

"I don't know. I may just rest here," I say, and I walk over to the couch opposite Gabe's and lie down. My exhaustion feels like a blanket, falling over me, weighing me down. Within a minute, Seb and Gabe's voices fall away. In two, I'm fast asleep.

30

EMERSON

Seb wakes me two hours later, and by two o'clock, I've had some coffee and my energy is mostly back to what it was. I'm still poring over what happened in my mind and what it may mean. Seb wants to have this session outside, in the forest, and I can feel my body protesting as we walk through the woods. I'm tired. I need recovery.

I need Kieran.

He leads me to the clearing Quinn took me to yesterday, and we sit on two of the boulders, facing each other.

"So. Tell me what you know about what we face in the ring," he says.

I force my mind to focus, in spite of my exhaustion. "Your biggest fear," I say, as if by rote.

Seb shakes his head. "No, you face your biggest *weakness*."

"Right. In the form of your biggest fear."

He moves his head from side to side, like *yeah, sort of*. "It's more complicated than that. The ancestors come to teach you a lesson. Maybe they bring you a message, or they show you something you need to learn."

I remember what Kieran told me about his rite. *I heard something in the ring.*

"What kind of lesson?" I ask.

"Something to help you grow, and continue to overcome the weakness after you leave."

"Okaaaay," I say, thinking. "So it's not about your biggest fear, but your biggest weakness. But you do fight…"

"Right," Seb says, nodding. "The *kiyyulit* take the form of an adversary, to help you uncover the weakness within you. And that may *look* like your greatest fear, but the point is not the fear, but the weakness in you. The fear is a path to uncovering your weaknesses."

"Sorry, I'm too tired to follow this," I say, shaking my head.

"Okay. Let's try it in practice. Some people already have a feeling for what they're going to face in the ring. Do you?"

I nod. "Yeah. My dad."

"Okay. So tell me about your dad."

I sigh. I knew this was coming.

"He was a fisherman," I say. "We lived near the west shore of the island. Just him, my mom, and me."

"Was?" he asks.

I give him a look. I know he knows this stuff already. But the point, I guess, is for me to share it, not him to hear.

"Was. I don't know what he does now. He was banished to the southern islands when my mom died."

"How did she die?"

"They say it was his fault," I say, looking down at my hands, lying limply in my lap.

"Was it?"

I swallow. "I guess. *I* think so, but it wasn't so obvious. He didn't, like, lash out and kill her one day. He killed her slowly, over years. Eventually it got too bad, and Viggo and Dagmar helped us move out. But then she got sick, and they think he caused it. Like the stuff she suffered had already broken her before we left."

Seb nods, watching me, saying nothing. I know he wants me to tell him more. I know he thinks it's best for me if I share details; if I cut myself open for him and let out all the dark and horrible things that wake me up at night, like every therapist Aunt Dagmar made me see as a kid. It doesn't help—it didn't then. And if he wants me to talk about it, he'll have to ask.

I wait, but he doesn't. We sit there in silence, for five minutes, ten. The quiet begins to prickle at me, unpleasant and uncomfortable.

"Can I ask you something?" I say finally, looking up.

"Sure."

"What's *your* biggest weakness?"

He lets out a chuckle, and it catches me off-guard.

"You know I can't tell you what I fought, right?" he asks.

"You told Maren."

"I told Maren *some*. And besides, she's my mate."

"Fine. But that wasn't my question. I asked, what's your biggest *weakness*?"

"My anger."

I nod. He's not wrong, but I wonder how you can fight your own anger in the ring. How it could take so much from you, like Seb's rite did from him.

"So what was your lesson, then?"

He doesn't hesitate. "That I can have what other people have, if I let myself accept it."

My brow furrows. "What?"

"Yeah, I didn't get it then, either. The ancestors gave me a message, but it didn't make sense until a few years later."

"When you met Maren."

"When I met Maren."

I bring a knee up to my body on the rock. "So what's Kieran's biggest weakness?"

He shakes his head, waving a hand. "That's between him and the ancestors."

"No, it's not," I say, and I find that my words surprise me. "We all live together. We all see each other, every day. If you don't see the people you love, it's because you're not paying attention. What do you see?"

He cocks his head, thinking. Finally he says, "I think he spends a lot of time protecting people he sees as vulnerable, so he doesn't have to feel vulnerable himself."

"Huh." I look down at my feet. I don't know what I would have said. And I wonder for a moment if *I've* been seeing Kieran this whole time. I've been so angry that he's not seeing me. But have I really been paying attention?

I look up at the trees around us, and I think about Kieran as a kid, wandering these woods by himself after being kicked out by his brothers. I think about what he said about making himself big, before he even met me. *I had to.* And then, like a sucker punch to the stomach, I remember what he said about the night before he left for Keist.

I didn't want to make you choose. Not because I wanted to spare you the decision... But because if I asked you to choose and it hadn't been me...

I look up at Seb. "You're smarter than I give you credit for."

He laughs. "I do okay. I think we all forget, sometimes."

"That you're so smart?" I roll my eyes.

He laughs. "No, dumbass. That the rest of the *fika* is growing up around us, just like we are."

I nod, eyeing him. Trying to see him through new eyes: not as the angry little kid I grew up with, but as the man he is now. Maren's mate. A leader in our *fika*-to-be. And he is, in a way. But he's also just Seb.

"So what about me?" I ask finally. "What's my greatest weakness?"

He shakes his head. "That's for you to figure out, in these woods in the coming weeks. Knowing the *kiyyulit* will take the form of your dad in the ring is easy. Understanding *why* is the key to overcoming him when the time comes."

I nod. "You know, this first session is nothing like what I thought it would be."

He shrugs and stands up. "I'm going to walk back to the house. Sit here for a while and think. See what comes to you. I have some prompts for you in the coming days, but for today, I just want you to reflect on what you think you'll see in the ring, and why."

I nod and he starts the walk towards the house. As he leaves, I take a look at his footprints in the snow, unevenly spaced after what the rite took from him.

I know I should think about my dad, and why he scares me, or what I'm most afraid of. But instead, I find myself thinking about Kieran. And specifically, why Kieran's biggest demons would be mine, and what that says about both of us.

31

KIERAN

It takes another four days before the rest of the pack council agrees to let me speak to Thalia Nayakka. When they bring her in, I'm already sitting at Sigur's desk at the marshal's office. She looks like shit, and she reeks of the *trotsayyit* and *uikbaane* they're using to control her shift. Her eyes are rimmed with dark circles.

Sigur leads her in and sets her down in the chair across from me, then gives me a nod. He leaves the room, leaving the door open just a crack.

"Well. You look like hell," I say.

"Yeah," she says, her voice slightly hoarse. "Doesn't do the soul much good to sit locked up in a basement for four days with limited food and water."

I grimace. We shouldn't be treating them this way, regardless of what they've done.

"You want some water?" I ask, reaching for the bottle I had sitting on the desk.

She shakes her head, lifting a hand to say 'no.' The other

hand, tied together at the wrist with rope, comes with it. I see that the skin under the rope is red and chafed.

"Okay," I say, setting the bottle down. "So. You wanted to talk."

She nods, looking up at me. "If you can guarantee safety for me and my sister on the islands. Then yes."

"I can't decide that on my own. That's a council decision."

Her posture stiffens. "So then why are you wasting my time?"

"I got permission to ask you what you want from us, in exchange for information."

She gives me a look, like I'm unbearably stupid. *"A-sy-lum,"* she says slowly. "Like we asked for in the last two petitions, and like I told you when you slammed my body down in the street. You have a thick skull behind all that hair, don't you?"

Her accent is faint, but it's there: a slight, lilting hint of French influence, from the way the southern islands were first colonized, the way ours were by the Danish and Dutch.

"Okay, but what does that mean?" I ask. "You want, what. A house? A place to stay, for you and your sister? For how long?"

"I want it agreed that we can live here safely," she says. "I don't need a house or a hand-out. We can work and save money to earn our own keep and buy a place. I hear there's a lot of empty houses on the islands."

That's true. The Fakari population has been slowly shrinking for years. One of the other ongoing issues we have to discuss in council meetings—what to do if our way of life is no longer sustainable.

"You know it won't be that easy, right?" I say, sitting back. "No one's going to want to hire someone who set the dock on fire and tore into the *reijna*'s son at the common house."

"I'll make it work," she says icily, staring down at her feet.

"For what? To live between people who resent you? Who you had to bribe for a home?"

"I know it will be hard," she says, looking up at me with ice in her eyes. "Imagine the hell we are trying to escape in the south, if I'd rather be hated among strangers here. But sometimes you have to do tough shit to protect the people you love."

I watch her face, studying her. Somewhere in the back of my mind, it registers: a protector, like me.

"Tell me about your sister," I say.

"Why?"

I let out a sigh. "Because I'm trying to get to know you, *nagaaya*."

"Her name is Noémie," she says finally. "We call her Nomi. She's younger by four years, and she's an adult now, but she became my ward when we were still teenagers. You have someone you would do anything for?"

"Yes."

"Then you know how it is," she says with a nod. "I got us to these islands. I will get us a place here. For her."

"Why do you want to leave so badly?" I ask.

Her eyebrows raise in surprise. "Ah. So the man they send to interrogate me hasn't even read my petition."

"I wasn't on the council yet when you sent it," I say, but I feel my own irritation as I say it. She's right. I could never bother with this stuff, but I should have made the effort. "Why did you want to meet with *me*, anyway?"

She sighs, and I can scent the anger coming off of her. "Because you made me a promise, and I could see in your eyes that you meant it. I trust you more than the elders who withhold food and water from us in a musty basement."

"Okay," I say finally. I have no idea what to do with this. I have no idea what I *can* do with this. "Listen, I want to help, if I can. But how do we know that the information you have is worth trading?"

"It is."

"But how do we know? How can we make sure we don't

make a deal and you end up giving us information that's worthless, and then we let two terrorists onto the Fakaris?"

"I'm not a *terrorist*," she snaps.

"You tore into my friend's chest in the common house."

"I was careful to stick to the places I knew would be easiest to heal. I didn't go too deep."

"You snapped his leg clean in half."

She looks up, shock registering in her face. "What?"

"Yeah. You broke his leg, and we don't have healing magic for that anymore. He'll need months to recover, and it cost him the chance to do his elder rite this year. So, nice work."

She's visibly stunned, her large gray eyes momentarily filling with worry. The scent in the air changes, and I can sense her honest regret. For the second time this week, I find myself surprised by her.

"That was an accident," she says finally. "I didn't mean to break any bones. I was careful. The Remnant leaders had their suspicions—"

"Hang on, which ones are the leaders?" I ask, looking at the page Sigur gave me earlier, with a list of the names of those we detained. This is the first piece of information she's let up.

Thalia gives me a long look, as though deciding something. "Matis. And Blaise," she says finally.

"They suspected you of…?"

She waves a hand dismissively, the other coming with it, tied at the wrist. "That I wasn't in it for the cause. I needed to prove myself, so they had me do their dirty work." She chews the inside of her cheek, and her big eyes stare up at me. They have the shifter ring, too, but hers is cooler and more silver toned than I'm used to, and I find myself unnerved by her gaze.

"I tried to steer clear of any lasting damage," she says finally. "My mother was a healer. I knew which wounds heal fastest. I didn't mean to break bone."

"Why go after Gabe?" I ask. "Is it because his mother is high-up in the council?"

"Give me asylum and I'll talk."

I sigh. "Thalia, I believe that you know something. I want to make a trade with you, I do. But I need *something* to prove to the council that you're not just talking out of your ass."

"So you won't trust that I have information to share, and I won't trust that you will offer me a place in exchange for it. It seems we're at an impasse."

I set my jaw. If the information she's hiding is just stuff about why they came here, or what's happening on the southern isles, I don't give a shit. There's only one thing I want to know, and I decide to come out with it.

"Are there more of you on the islands? People we didn't catch?"

"Slow learner, aren't we? I told you, I won't talk without an agreement. If not for me, then at least for Nomi."

I throw my hands up. "I *want* to help you—"

She scoffs. "No, you don't. You want to help yourself, and you will reluctantly consider helping me to do it. Very noble."

I breathe out sharply through my nose. She might be funny, if she weren't so awful.

"Okay, well, I tried," I say, standing up. "You said you wanted to talk to me, but it seems like you don't have anything to say. I'll have Sigur take you back to the common house."

"Oh, that's the grand plan, hm? And then what? Keep us there forever? Send us back to the southern isles, like you do with all the other prisoners you're too good to keep here?"

I blink. "People who break pack code don't belong on our islands, Thalia."

"So you just dump them on our shores?"

I cross my arms. "How often does that happen? Once a decade or more?" Em's father was one of the last cases, and that was almost twenty years ago.

"It happens enough." She's angry now, and her words come faster. "Oh, you have it *so good* here on the Fakaris, with your pack houses and your money and your mainland trade. And what, you think you earned this? What gives you the right to dump your cast-offs onto us, and then deny good people's requests when they need safety?"

"I, uh—" I sputter, trying to collect myself. I never paid much attention in school when they taught us about this, and I wasn't ready for a debate today. "The southern isles are unincorporated. People don't need an agreement to come there."

"Un*incorporated*, yes, but not un*inhabited*. What do you think it does to a people, to a culture, when we get the violent hand-me-downs from the wealthier islands?"

"I..." I swallow and run a hand over my hair. I wasn't prepared for this. "I'll tell the council you want a guarantee of asylum in order to talk. And I'll tell them you're not willing to say anything to verify that you have valuable information. Sigur will take you back. I'll come talk to you if I hear anything."

As I walk for the door, her voice comes from behind me, lilting and mock innocent.

"I hope Emerson's okay."

I turn around in an instant.

"*What?*"

"Emerson. Janus Stenberg's girl." She looks at me with doe eyes, but there's a hard edge behind them, the outer ring almost looking silver. "I hope she's well."

"What do you know?"

"I. Want. Asylum."

My breathing comes faster, and I feel the rage and adrenaline coursing through my body. I don't bother to stop it.

"Listen to me," I say, grabbing hold of her chair and bringing my face close to hers. "If anything happens to her—if she gets so much as a goddamn *papercut* and I find out that you had the knowledge to stop it—you'll finally get your wish to stay here, because I will tear you limb from limb until there isn't enough left of you to pick off the fucking floor and mail back to the southern isles in a box. *Do you understand?"*

I expect her to wither, but instead, a slow smile creeps across her face.

"I'm not afraid of you," she says coolly. "Do you know why?"

"Why?" I snap, seething.

"Because I know that I have what you want," she says. "I know you will not let harm come to me so long as you think my knowledge will serve you. And because—" and now she makes her voice a whisper "—I know how it is to make yourself big. So what I see behind that tough exterior is a scared little boy who has *somebody* on this island he will do anything for. And I think I just learned who."

She leans away from me again, sitting up straight in her chair. "Go ahead and send me back to the basement. You'll be back to talk to me, even if your council can't agree."

She's right. Anger and venom coursing through me, I slam her chair back against the desk, so she has to brace her bound hands not to fall. Without another word, I storm out of the office.

32

KIERAN

"She won't talk unless we give her asylum."

We're in the common house, each of the pack council elders seated on the ground in a large circle, with community members who want to listen in sitting behind them. I've sat in on votes here many times, basically since Seb became a pack elder. It feels wrong that the first council meeting where I can vote is without him here.

"That's the end of it, then," says Saga, sitting across from me. The spot behind her, where Gabe usually sits to listen to the council discussion, is empty. "If she were able to give us information that shows that she's really on our side, we would reconsider the plea. But it's clear she's only interested in helping us to save herself."

"And her sister," I add.

Saga gives me a look. "Don't make the mistake of empathizing with her, *tekanni*. If anything, she's committed more violence than the others. *They*'ve destroyed property. *She* hurt my son."

"I'm not empathizing," I say. "But she may know something

that can help us."

"Whatever information she has, the others in her group will, too," says Viggo, sitting next to Dagmar on the other side of the room. "If we can't get her to talk willingly, I'm sure there are other ways to get it out of them." He gives a sly smile.

Ingela, another pack elder, on my right, looks up. "Surely you're not alluding to torture."

"No, no, of course not. But we can see to it that they're not comfortable. We've been keeping them hungry and tired. If we can trade information for extra food, water…"

I set my jaw, remembering how Thalia looked when I saw her in Sigur's office.

"How likely is that to work?" asks Heimig. "I was there when we brought them in. They've all been completely silent, except the sisters."

Sigur nods. "Ivo and I have separated each of them and tried to talk to each. None of them say anything but *Hayyala fast*, except the two women. The younger one has only asked to see her sister. And Thalia, the older, has asked to speak to Kieran."

"Still?" I ask, looking up. Our conversation was three days ago now, and I haven't been able to get it out of my head. Every day that I'm working on that arch at the workshop, every time I'm in the gym, I'm thinking about what she said. *I hope Emerson's okay*, in that mocking, goading voice.

"Still," Sigur nods.

"I should talk to her again." Instinctively I look to Saga, as if for permission. "If she wants to talk, maybe she would share more information without an agreement."

"If we'd do that, we need a plan," she says, shaking her head. "And we shouldn't leave it to our most junior pack elder. Perhaps Sigur or Ivo, the professionals. Or myself or Viggo."

Sigur shakes his head. "I tried. She refuses to talk to us. Only Kieran."

"But why?" asks Viggo.

Because you guys are trying to starve them out, and at least I kept my promise, I think.

"Let me talk to her again," I repeat. "I can use Viggo's idea. Food, water, something small to trade. It could be important."

Isolde, usually quiet in pack council meetings, shakes her head. "To learn why they came here?"

"I mean, yeah, but more importantly, to learn if there are more of them hiding out," I say. "We can't have caught them all. Someone in their group must know the Fakaris well, for them to have stayed hidden so long. If there are more of them hiding, what Thalia shares with us could save lives."

Heimig shakes his head. "There are former Fakari people on the south islands who could have prepared them without coming along for the trip. Even a map could account for them hiding. I see no reason to believe there's more of them. It's been almost a week since the last attack."

"And how long was it between that one and the one before?" I ask. "Let me talk to her. If any harm comes to another pack member and we could have stopped it, I'll never forgive myself."

Saga shakes her head slightly, the move barely perceptible, and I find myself growing agitated.

"I told you she knew Emerson's name," I add, this time speaking directly to her. "I need to make sure she's not in harm's way. Why can't we just *try*?"

Saga meets my gaze.

"Every time we speak with them without a plan of what we're willing to trade, we put ourselves in a position to be manipulated. And any step we make towards allyship with this woman is a step closer to offering her a place on the islands. We cannot do that without thinking through the consequences."

"You're overthinking this," I say.

"No, I'm thinking *through* this." Her voice is corrective, like a schoolteacher, and I feel my wolf grow defensive. "And that is the job of the council. If the elder Nayakka truly had good intentions, she would tell us what she knew as an act of goodwill and hope for our mercy. The fact that she won't, and that she's the only one of the group to have harmed a pack member, tells me she's not trustworthy. For all you know, she'll tell you false information just to make things worse."

I grit my teeth. "Why can't we fucking try?" I snap. "What's the harm in asking? Do you really want another pack member to get hurt? Are you willing to sacrifice Emerson's safety so you can stew in indecision? Think about the people you *love*, Saga."

"Don't you dare speak to me that way, *tekanni*," she spits, her eyes glinting gold. I can see her wolf in there, prowling under the surface, and my own wolf sits up. "You're worried about harm coming to Emerson, I know. But *all I do* is sit here and think about the people I love. I have lost a brother and a husband, each of whom sat on this council with me before you were even *born*. And right now, my only son is on another island to stay away from the prisoner you are so eager to trade with, *igaa*."

Pup. I swallow, her words hitting me like a slap.

"So yes," she continues. "I think about *each* loved one I've lost, and am at risk of losing, as we make a decision. And I think about the many people on these islands whose fates are in our hands, who we are supposed to protect with our choices. I cannot make this decision for your sake, or Emerson's. My role as an elder is to think about *all of us*. As is yours."

Frustration rolls through me. I can't help but feel like we're sitting here, wasting time that we could be spending solving an actual problem.

"We're nearing the end of the meeting time," says Wim, our council secretary, from the corner of the room. "Should we bring it to a vote?"

I nod wordlessly and Heimig leads the call. 29 in favor of me talking to Thalia again, in the hopes of a negotiation; 31 against.

I glance at the empty place where Seb would be sitting, a few seats over from Saga. His vote wouldn't have made the difference, but he's a better speaker than I am. I can't help but wonder how it would have gone if he were here.

Heimig brings an end to the meeting, and I get up with everyone else. I see Saga heading towards me, probably to make it right and invite me to dinner, but I don't want to talk. Instead, I head for Wim.

"*Aftnu'kut*," he says, looking up from his laptop. "How did you feel about your first council meeting?"

"Yeah, fine," I say, nodding. "Council records are available to any pack council member, right?"

His brow furrows. "Sure. What do you need?"

"I'd just like to read up on some past stuff."

"Past… stuff?"

"Yeah. To be better prepared for future decisions."

"We keep everything upstairs. I can get you anything you need."

"No worries. I can look myself."

He nods slowly, eyeing me. "Okay. Well. If you need help finding a particular topic, you know where to find me."

I swallow, lowering my voice, though I don't really know why. "The asylum petition for the Nayakka sisters?"

"We organize by year," he says, nodding. "I think they've applied the last three or four years in a row, if you look through the filing cabinets."

I can feel my head jerk in surprise. "Four years? I thought this was just the second time."

He shakes his head. "They're not the first asylum petition we've had, either. Start there and come back if you need something else."

I nod. "Thanks."

"Yeah, any time."

I glance over my shoulder to see Saga waiting to talk to me, but I'm not in the mood. Before she can approach, I turn for the stairs to find the archives.

33

EMERSON

It's been days since I healed Gabe's chest, since the moment I saw the *kiyyulit* coming from my hand, and I haven't been able to let it go. The house is tense, the air heavy with the weight of something he and I are both unwilling to hope for out loud. I haven't wanted to try healing again; with all of us in such close quarters, I don't want Seb catching wind of what we think may be true. Because if my suspicions are right—if whatever happened that day *is* some lost healing art—then the implications are way, way bigger than Gabe's broken femur.

From my place on the mat at the gym, I glance to my left to see Seb, walking with his uneven gait towards the weight rack. His pain comes from something far deeper than a bone break. Although he and I have never talked about it, I know from Saga that most of the trouble now comes from the mainland doctors' removal of part of his leg muscle to preserve the rest of the leg.

Even if someone could heal bone, they couldn't bring back flesh, right? You can't make something out of nothing, and reviving dead tissue seems closer to necromancy than bone healing.

But this didn't feel like *just* bone healing.

As I weigh the thought, Quinn's upper body slams into mine, pinning me onto my back. I feel my shoulder blades press against the ground, and she comes to rest her forearm against my neck, showing me she could cut off my windpipe if she wanted.

I drag my eyes up to her.

"You good?" she asks, panting. Her short half-bleached hair waves in front of her face, damp with sweat.

"Yeah, sorry. I'm… I'm somewhere else."

"I can tell." She releases the pressure from my body and sits up, catching her breath on the mat. "No offense, but I've been handing your ass to you all morning, and I *know* you know at least some of these combinations. Where's your head? Is it Kieran?"

I shake my head. "No. It's me."

"Ah. So Seb's mental training is doing its job, then." She gives me a wry grin, and for a second, I can see the hint of her cousin's likeness in her face, coming forward and then disappearing like a stone sinking into water.

I shake my head again. "Not that, either."

"Are you okay? What's up?"

I swallow, and for a second, I consider telling her. But Seb's voice from across the room interrupts us.

"What's going on?" he asks, walking towards the mats. "We've got just a week or so before your rite. Why are we resting?"

"I, uh… I'm not feeling well," I say, looking up to meet his eyes.

"You won't be feeling well in the ring if you don't train today."

"Let her have a break, man," Quinn says beside me. "She's been killing it lately."

"She has a break. Every day, *after* we leave the gym." He crosses his arms in front of him and gives me a look. "When you're in here, I need you training. Anything less is gonna get you killed. And you don't have the excuse of being tired from healing anymore, either. You finished with Gabe's chest days ago."

I look at him for a long moment, then glance over at Quinn and back. I'm not going to be able to train properly until I work this out.

"I'm on my period." The lie comes out quickly, and I see from the slight twitch in his face that it has the desired effect. "I'm really sorry. I think I need some painkillers and a new pad to get my head back in the game. I can't focus when I'm worried about... leaking."

"I... uh. Okay," he says, his posture stiffening.

"I have something in my bag," Quinn offers.

"No, it's okay." I climb to my feet, thinking quickly. "I have something specific I need to get at the house for this. But it's... complicated." I look at Seb, trying desperately to think of anything period-related that would take at least an hour. Nothing.

"It... takes a while," I say, gesturing vaguely. "The... insertion... Blood..."

Seb raises his hands, making a face. "I'm good without details. Yeah, whatever. We can just end early today and head back to the house together."

"No," I say, and glance at Quinn, who's looking at me incredulously from the mat.

Insertion?, she mouths, and I give her a look.

"You wanted to stay here and talk to Seb for a bit, right?" I ask her. "About the... FMA combinations. My next step in training."

I stare at her, pleading with her to help me, and I see the moment it registers on her face that I'm trying to be alone at the house. Or, specifically, alone with Gabe.

"Right," she says, nodding slowly. "Yes. Yeah, I do. And I

think it'll take at least… an hour?"

"If not two," I say, nodding.

"Right. Two. Two hours."

"What? What FMA combinations?" Seb looks between the two of us.

"Quinn will explain," I say, rushing for the door, where my gym bag is resting underneath the hook for my coat. "I have to go, I'm practically about to bleed through my pants. I'll see you later, at the house."

Thank you, I mouth to Quinn, and she shrugs, bewildered. Then I grab my coat and bag, and start for the shore.

I run down the cobblestone streets of Halluk's town center, still wet with the melt of last week's snow. The sun is out this morning, and the stones below my feet gleam in the light.

An hour, maybe two. That's enough time to try, at least.

WHEN I GET to the house, Gabe is in the kitchen, stirring something at the stove while leaning on one crutch. I take a breath, and my wolf registers the scent: apple, cinnamon, cardamom, and ginger.

"Hey," I say, dropping my gym bag before the kitchen island. "It's just us here, right?"

He looks up from the stove. His dark brown hair, thick and loosely curly, is damp with the steam of whatever he's making. Apple sauce, I think.

"Yeah. I think Maren is working in a cafe somewhere, and the others were with you at the gym. Why?"

"I know this is crazy, but I can't stop thinking about what happened the other day. I don't think I'm gonna be able to let it go unless we just try."

He turns back to look at the pot. "I don't know what you're talking about."

"Yes, you do. Of all of us in the *fika, you* do." I walk towards him, unbuttoning my coat. "I know Saga taught you more Fakari history than the rest of us got as kids. I *know* you had the same thought as I did after what happened. We're thinking the same thing."

I swallow, willing him to look at me.

"What if this is some kind of healing power we've lost?" I ask. "What if it could help Seb?"

He clears his throat. "I don't want to get his hopes up."

"So we don't get his hopes up," I say, shaking my head. "We'll just try, the two of us, until we're sure. And if I can't get it to work on you, he never has to know what we thought."

Gabe turns off the stove and faces me. I take in his expression, his thick brown brows knit, dark eyes clouded.

"I was thinking about it," he says finally. "Our healers lost the art of bone healing, but it wasn't that long ago that we could still do that here. We have records—we know what it looked like. But it wasn't like what you did. I don't *know* what you did."

"Me either," I say. "But it felt real. I think it's… I don't know. Something lost, something ancient. It came from the ancestors. And they wouldn't give it to us if they didn't want us to use it, right?"

"Shouldn't we talk to my mom, or Helen?" he asks. "You just started healing this year. You won't know how to wield it yet."

"They won't, either," I say, shaking my head. "Nothing in my healer training told me about this. And I don't want to make them think it's something if I can't do it again. I just want to try, for Seb. Will you let me?"

He hesitates, then lets out a low laugh. "We haven't had bone healing in generations. And you want to use it as a warm-up."

I nod. "Yeah. I do."

"Alright," he says finally, nodding. "I guess it's not the craziest idea you've had recently. Let's give it a shot."

He leads me to the living room, and I help him down into the couch. I come to my knees on the ground before him, looking at his leg cast.

"I'm just gonna try for a bit, okay?" I say. "I need to close my eyes for this. If something changes, or if something hurts, you tell me and I'll stop."

"Okay." He nods.

I swallow and bring my hands over the leg, closing my eyes. I've never even probed a body for bone breaks before; we know that art is lost to time, so trying to feel for one as a trainee feels more like ego than anything else. But I bring my focus towards his leg, feeling for the energy of his muscle, then going deeper.

I can see the bone in my mind's eye: two blurry gray shadows separated by a jagged break. The sight of it makes me sick. It's a bad break, and seeing that this is what Gabe's been dealing with makes me hurt for him. I try not to show the reaction in my face.

I take a deep breath and move my hands the way I do for flesh wounds. I know it won't work, but I can sense my own nervousness in the air, and I need to ease myself into this. I can feel the muscle around the bone respond, but the break stays immobile. Gabe lets out a low breath.

"Bad?" I ask, eyes still closed.

"Yeah. Don't do that."

I nod and take a deep breath. "Okay. Sorry, I just wanted to try. Give me a second."

I ground myself in my body, breathing out slowly, then send something from my core down to the earth. Next, I tuck in my chin, letting the crown of my head rise up, lifting my energy.

"What are you doing?" he asks quietly.

"Grounding myself and connecting to the ancestors," I say. "I learned it from Quinn, sort of, but I do something a little different than she taught me. I don't know how to describe it."

I let out a low breath, feeling for something. Each time I've done this before, I've vaulted some part of my energy up to the ancestors' space, not quite knowing where it goes. I still can't see where I send it, but this time, I feel a soft buzz of warmth at the back of my mind, and then my shoulders and back. It's dancing, playful, brushing around my body like heatless flames. I'm not just sending my own energy up; the *kiyyulit* are here with me.

I feel a shiver go over my spine. It's going to work, I know it. They wouldn't come down if they didn't want to help.

Something forms in my gut, strong and certain.

"Okay, Gabe, are you ready?" I ask, and I hear my voice waver. Eyes still closed, I reach my right hand out for his without quite knowing why.

"Yeah. Okay," he says. He's nervous, too.

"I think it might hurt." I swallow. "I think it may have to hurt, to heal. If it's too much, you tell me."

"Okay."

I move my free hand over the leg again, feeling for the bone beneath. I can see it clearer now, the shape sharper around the edges. They're letting me see it. And I *feel* something. It's not mine, but it's *in* me somewhere. His pain.

"Do you trust me?" I whisper, unsure if I even trust myself.

"Yes."

I nod.

"Aka leif deij Gabriel geij ikka takkani, feiyya nateyyakata fast." The words come out quickly, breathlessly, from a place somewhere deep in my mind that I can't reach: *To Gabriel's body I give my thanks, for your steadfast protection.*

"Takkata feiyya vuuromgeija dat kiyyuime, eijtna geijaim kasayya deija verut bavakka."

Thank you for giving shape to his soul, and for giving him a means of moving through the world.

"It's happening," I hear Gabe say from somewhere far away. I can sense the nervousness in his voice, and I feel his anxiety somewhere in *my* body. In my mind's eye, through a cloud of mist, I see myself, kneeling before him. The *kiyyulit* between my hand and his leg is a faint flicker, but it's there.

I'm seeing through his eyes, I realize.

"Ije seijatta vayyatik," I whisper to his body. *I see your pain.* And suddenly, a cloud of darkness overtakes me.

I'm not Em anymore. I'm Gabe, somewhere. Gabe in his own mind, in his self-perception. I'm seeing the ceiling of the common house through his eyes, the big silver wolf on top of him. I feel his fear.

In real-time, somewhere far away in the living room where my physical body is, I hear Gabe cry out, the grip of his hand clenching tight around mine.

"I need you to trust me," I hear my own voice say. But it doesn't feel like me. My body feels paper-thin; not a person, not a shell, just a wisp of something between Gabe and the ancestors. The *kiyyulit* are everywhere. I can feel their energy around me, through me, but I can't see them.

I see the black wolf. I feel the weight of her as she lands on his leg; the blinding snap the moment the bone broke.

His first thought as he feels it break: *I won't be able to do the rite.* His body washes with relief, and then he's crushed by shame. He sees Seb and Kieran in his mind's eye; he fears their disappointment.

The wolf tears into his chest and he sees his own blood. A blinding crack of fear; something slicing. There's so much blood. He thinks he may die here.

Is this where it finally happens? he thinks. *Is this where I die for them?*

"What?" I hear come from my own mouth, somewhere far away.

The wave of feeling and memory is overwhelming, and the part of me that's Em feels like it's slipping away. I'm letting it overtake me; I'm becoming the veil, some thin barrier between life and death, and if I can't find the edge of myself in here, it's going to eat me alive. Somehow, I know that I need to take back control of my body. If I want to use the *kiyyulit* to heal him, I need to be strong enough to nudge them without losing myself.

I'm exhausted but I try, searching for myself in the mist of light and fog and Gabe's memory. Somewhere in there, I find my conscious mind. Just like when I'm shifting, I give her the reins, and my sense of gravity shifts, like I'm falling back into my skin. I realize now that I'm saying something, muttering, the pace of the Fakari words coming so close together that it sounds like rain on a tin roof. I can barely make it out.

My hand is moving. His bone is shifting for me, yielding. I can feel Gabe's pain, so bright it's blinding. He's groaning.

"We're almost there," I hear myself say to him. "I need you to trust me."

But then there's something else. There's more pain, something deeper, and then the memories are coming closer together, flashing. The moment he knew Seb loved Maren, when he saw them walking on the shore together. I see myself and Kieran through his eyes, happy in the back garden when we thought we were alone. I feel Gabe's sadness, his loneliness.

It's not meant for him, he thinks. He will give himself up for us.

What?

Now, in his memory, I see a little girl with big green eyes. They're climbing a tree together. She tells him she's scared to go back. He takes her hand. He says something I can't hear.

I hear Gabe cry out beside me, and the light I'd felt building in his body grows brighter, blocking out my vision. It hurts so much. I feel his pain in my body, but I know we're close to the other side. The white light glows brighter, brighter, and I feel his bone click into place. I see the kiyyulit swirling around it, turning golden, binding it together.

"I think we're there," I say, my voice hollow with exhaustion.

Then I hear a *boom* and then the world goes quiet. So quiet, I almost think I'm dead.

I open my eyes, afraid to see what I've done. But we're just in the living room. Gabe is on the couch, breathing rapidly, eyes wide. But he's okay. And the rest of the world is unchanged.

"What the fuck happened?" he rasps.

"I think I healed the bone," I say, as much to myself as to him. But I don't think. I know.

"You saw my memories."

"I saw your memories," I repeat numbly.

He looks up at me, his eyes wide with confusion and fear. "What the fuck, Em?"

"Gabe," I say quietly. "Who is she?"

34

KIERAN

"*Heij, jenge!*"

"Hey, Heimig," I say, walking into the bookshop.

"Not often I see you in here without Emerson," he says. "Are you here to pick up something for her?"

I shake my head, then pause. "Well. Maybe, sort of. I don't know."

"What do you need?"

I look down at the table to my left, covered with a large display of new hardcovers.

"You probably don't sell poetry, right?" I ask.

"Sure I do. What are you looking for? Some Neruda, perhaps?" He gives me a knowing smile, but I don't get the joke and shake my head.

"Um. Ralph Waldo Emerson?"

His eyebrows raise appreciatively. "We do have some. Any particular collection?"

I nod. "Something with 'The Rhodora,' if you have it."

"I'm sure we can find that," he says with a wink. "Follow me."

He leads me through the narrow aisles of the front of the store, towards the stairs that take him to the lower level where the second-hand books are kept. I've been in here a few times with Em, when she was looking for a particular book on Fakari history or healing. But Heimig leads me to the left, where a small shelf at half-height is marked with a sign reading 'Poetry.'

"Here," he says, reaching for a thin blue book with faded letters on the spine. He flips through it. "Yes, see? 'The Rhodora.'" He clears his throat dramatically. "'In May, when sea-winds pierced our solitudes...'"

"Right, yeah, that's perfect," I say quickly, looking around in case anyone can hear us.

Heimig closes the book and gives me a smile. "Do you want me to ring this up for you? Or are you looking for something else?"

I hesitate. I'd only come for this today—Em's been finding every possible reason not to talk to me in the evenings, and for the lack of her closeness and scent, I find myself scrambling for any trace of her. But now that I'm here...

"Can you take that up to the counter? I'll be there in a few minutes. I'm just going to look around."

He nods, his eyebrows raised. "Sure, *jenge*. I'll have this behind the register for you when you're ready."

I nod, and he leaves for the stairs while I turn to the used books Fakari history section, where Em usually goes whenever she used to take me here. I take a few minutes to see if there's anything of interest. I see some translations of the *Fakari Eijna*, the ancient text which contains both our moral edicts and folklore. There's a handful of old books, pages yellowed and spines peeling, about Fakari religion and language. My eyes practically glaze over as I skim just the titles. And then I see one book that may help me.

It's large and fairly thin, just about a hundred pages or so, and the style of the spine makes me think it's probably a hundred years old. The letters on the back read *Atgabrayyit Gast-naejet dat Fakarieilat*. A Comprehensive History of the Fakari Islands.

I pull out the book, and my inner wolf recoils at the scent of mildew and old paper. But as I open it and flip through the first few pages, I see it's what I want. Maps, island history. There's stuff about the southern isles in here, too.

Perfect.

I bring it with me up to Heimig's counter.

"This too, thanks."

He nods, scanning the book and the collection of poems. "Didn't take you for much of a reader."

I shake my head. "I'm not, really. Just… trying to learn."

"I heard from Wim you're also looking into council records?" he says, packing the books into a paper bag.

"Yeah. Doing my best to live up to my new role, I guess. Especially while Seb's gone. Someone's gotta hold down the fort."

"Good for you, *jenge*. That'll be ₭101.49 *króna*."

"A *hundred?*"

"It's an old book," he says, shrugging apologetically. I sigh and get out my bank card, tapping it against his machine. Serves me right for trying to read.

THE NEXT WEEK moves slow as tree sap. I spend my mornings at the gym and my afternoons at the workshop, working on the wedding arch. In the evenings, I try to reach Em. I call every night, but she always seems to have a reason not to talk to me, or to get off the phone as soon as possible.

I miss her. My stupid wolf doesn't understand why we're not talking, and he hounds me every night, wanting to get nearer to her. For the lack of her presence, I spend my evenings reading the poems—a small window to her world, or her mother's, at least. I want to start with 'The Rhodora,' but I wait, working my way through the book from front to back, even if I'm not sure that's how you're supposed to read a poetry collection. Hopefully, by the time I finally get to her mom's favorite, I'll have enough of an understanding of the language to appreciate it.

If the poetry is tough to adjust to, the council records and history book are way harder. This stuff is so much more complicated than I'd realized. The details in the asylum petitions are brutal; it's worse than I ever thought on the southern isles, and sometimes I find myself sympathizing with Thalia—or, at least, the person she might have been if the violence there hadn't made her what she is. But even though it feels important, trying to read the meeting minutes and the old history book—in *Fakari* no less—is practically beyond me. This is stuff for Seb, or Gabe: people who have always been interested in pack code and island politics. Still, they're not here, and I am, so I push through. When it gets to be too much, I go to the gym or the workshop to turn my brain off.

We're getting close to the deadline to ship the arch out, but none of my redesigns are doing the thing I want, so I start building the one from my first design as a back-up. As I work on it, shaving away wood to form the doves, the grapes, the pomegranates, I imagine the couple who will get married under this arch. I mutter a prayer to the *agaayit* for them: for a happy marriage and a lifelong union. And almost always, as I do, I think of Em.

Em who still won't pick up the phone. Em who still won't talk to me.

My prayers for the couple slowly become prayers for her. For her courage and her forgiveness. For me, maybe. To be able to love her the way she wants.

The days get lonelier. I'm sleeping mostly at my own apartment now, instead of the *fikarig*. Not because she's gone, although it does feel less like home without her. But because whenever I'm there, I end up arguing with the *fika* elders about Thalia and the Remnant. If we have to argue, I'd rather save it for the council meetings, which are about nothing else lately. Even so, despite all our bickering—and Sigur and Ivo's continued pressure on the rebels to share more information—we learn and decide nothing. Every council meeting defers a decision to the next, leaving me more and more frustrated.

As the days pass by, I start to wonder if maybe the others are right. Slowly, the anxiety of the attacks is lowering, and after another week passes without incident, I begin to wonder if maybe I was wrong, and somehow we *did* catch the whole pack when they tore through town. Which is why it's such a shock, one Wednesday morning, to hear commotion outside and smell smoke.

I pull on my shirt and sweats and run outside, trying to see what's going on. In the distance, I can see thick plumes of black smoke rise into the sky from somewhere along our eastern shore.

I weave through the gathering crowd towards the marshal's office. There's an air of nervousness on the street; I can hear the chatter of neighbors trying to figure out what's safe. I see Saga gesturing towards the crowds to go inside and shut their windows.

Once I get to the marshal's office, I see Sigur and Ivo standing outside, and hear the sound of sirens growing nasal, changing pitch as they drive into the distance. Our volunteer fire squad must have just left.

"Hey, Ivo," I say, approaching him. "What's going on?"

"Two houses caught fire this morning, near the west harbor."

"Do you think it's—"

"I haven't gone myself yet, but the owner says it smells like petroleum. We think it's intentional."

I feel my inner wolf sit up, all attention. I fucking knew it. He *is* here.

"You're going to investigate?"

He nods. "We're leaving in just a few minutes."

"Take me with you. I know this is crazy, but I have a feeling."

Ivo eyes me, uncertain. We're not close, but I know him through the gym and his role in my training pack. I lean in, hoping he'll see reason.

"Please. You have to. You know I spoke to Thalia."

He eyes me for another second, then finally nods, gesturing for me to follow him to the van. I hear Sigur taking a second car behind us. As we drive towards the eastern harbor, I watch as the thick clouds of smoke get bigger and take up more of the sky. I'm racking my brain, thinking about what Em told me about the place she grew up. The places she and her family used to go for trips, along the eastern shore.

As we near the beach, I see the rocks along the sea, and it finally hits me.

"Do you know the grottos?" I ask.

Ivo looks at me quizzically.

"Here, here, take a right," I order, and at my direction, he turns off of the main road onto a small side path leading towards the rocks of the shore.

"What do you know?" he asks.

It's all clicking into place now. How could I have been so stupid?

"Em grew up near here," I say. "She and her parents used to come to these grottos for day trips. She said it's completely isolated, and if you're on the beach you can't even see inside. It would be the perfect hiding place."

Ivo pulls into the parking lot and I run out of the car, up towards the rocks. With the adrenaline coursing through me, I scramble up them in seconds. The scent hits me as soon as I'm in: sweat and unwashed clothes, urine, the last remnants of food. I look around and see empty cans and the food wrappers of preservatives, along with the peels of a few oranges and a soggy carton of cigarettes. But no people.

I hear Ivo climbing up the rocks behind me and turn to see his face as he enters the grotto.

"*Uikbaane,*" he mutters as the scent hits him.

"They were staying here."

"The scent is fresh," he says, wrinkling his nose. "It would have been as recent as this morning."

"How many people do you think were here?"

He sniffs again, and I can see the gold ring in his eyes flash. "I can't tell from the scent—the ocean has taken too much of the smell. But this can't be enough food for more than one person, *maybe* two, for the week or more they would have had to hide."

"Where would they have gone?" I ask.

Suddenly the walkie-talkie at his hip goes off, the rattle of static noise echoing through the cave. Sigur's voice comes through, nasal and flattened by the device.

"Reports of a boat stolen from the west harbor. Looks like the suspect is taking the straight between Saroe and Keist, heading south."

I look out towards the sea, where I can make out the very farthest parts of Keist's shore in the distance. The stolen boat should be visible soon, if it's heading that way.

"How many are in the boat?" Ivo asks into the walkie-talkie.

"Just one. I'm radioing the volunteer squad on Keist to take boats from the cape and block him before he gets farther."

"I'll do the same for the south shore," Ivo says.

I half-listen as he makes a call to the volunteer security at the southern harbor, which we set up after the first attack. As he talks, I look down at the remnants that the person staying here left behind. The cigarettes are completely waterlogged; they must have come with the group on the first boats, and gotten wet when the boat crashed on the rocks. I kick over one of the food rappers. Walnuts.

Wait. Walnuts?

I try to think back to that day with Em at the Halluk house, before the others arrived. She'd never had *weijnotbrod* until she moved into the *fikarig*. Her dad was allergic, she'd said.

Ivo's voice gets louder, his words coming faster now as he describes something in the distance. I turn to follow his gaze and look out again at the ocean. There it is, a white speedboat tearing through the water, heading south. And, clear as day: just one person in front. He's too far for us to see his face, but I make out tawny skin and a full head of dark hair. Far younger than Em's dad would be by now.

I feel something cold roil in my gut as it hits me. Have I really been so stupid? Letting myself get hypnotized by the *kattaka* to believe in ghosts, when the truth was in front of my face the whole time? Em's dad can't have been here. Maybe he knew this group before they left, and gave them instructions on how to navigate Saroe. Hell, if the group had access to a phone, they could have even called back to him for advice after their boat crashed.

I think of Thalia's words—*I hope Emerson's okay*. Was it a threat, or a lucky guess because she'd met Janus and just hoped the name would land?

I pore over it in my mind, trying to see it from every angle. As Ivo takes us to the west harbor to see where the boat was stolen, I think. As Sigur takes a witness testimony about the man who started the fire—dark hair, no older than 25—I think. And as we head back to the southern shore, and Ivo gets a call telling him that the Keist volunteers were able to apprehend the man in the boat—a 23 year old man named Laurent—I think.

We get back to the southern shore and I walk back up to my apartment, feeling numb. The sun is setting now, and it's freezing cold outside, the clouds up ahead knitting together, promising fresh snow.

For weeks, ever since my rite, I've been letting my fear drive me. Pushing all my actions and decisions, keeping me from Em and the kind of love I want for us. Would I have believed in her if I didn't think her dad was here somewhere, waiting to hurt her?

Maybe not, if I'm honest. The answer floods me with shame.

I unlock the door to my building and walk up the stairs to my apartment. Once inside, I walk over to the bed and lie down, for once completely exhausted by the emotional, not physical, weight of the day.

I think over the last few weeks, retracing my steps. I've been making this about Em's dad, and the fear of him hurting her was absolutely at the front of my mind. But that wasn't the thing that hurt her. It was that I couldn't bring myself to support her. And that has *nothing* to do with Janus, I realize, and everything to do with me.

I sit up in bed and grab the phone, calling Gabe. He picks up on the third ring.

"*Heij*," he says. "I just talked to my mom. They caught the last Remnant member?"

"Oh, you heard. Listen, can I talk to Em?"

"Uh, I think she's—"

"I know she's not busy, man. Let me talk to her."

I hear him sigh and the rustling of something on the other end of the line. A minute later, he's back.

"Sorry, I don't think now is a good time."

"Again? What the hell is going on over there? Is she okay?"

"She's... going through some stuff. She's really tired, and she's figuring some things out."

I feel a cold snake of fear uncoil itself in my gut.

"Figuring stuff out about me?"

"No. Bigger than that."

"Okay," I say finally. "I... Okay. Listen. You don't have to tell her this, but. I don't know, dude. I think I might have been wrong."

"No shit."

My inner wolf snarls immediately, ready to fight. "*A skeia.* Remind me not to talk to you about important stuff again."

"Okay, sorry. Tell me, what's up?"

I sigh, but the truth is, I don't fully know yet.

"Do you remember the morning Seb came down the mountain?" I ask.

"Yeah, of course."

"What did you think when you first saw him?"

"I… I don't know, man," he says, and I can hear him lower his voice, like he doesn't want to be overheard. "Why?"

"It matters. Just tell me."

He sighs. "I remember looking at his leg and thinking there was no way to come back from that. I thought we were gonna lose him. And that maybe…"

He can't finish the sentence, and I think back to that day. Me, Gabe, and Em standing with the others outside the common house, waiting for Seb to come back victorious, the first elder in our group. I could still feel the alcohol flowing through my body from the night before, when we celebrated after he left for the cliffs. We were so fucking young—so stupid. As we stood there, I wasn't even thinking about Seb, but about Em and how beautiful she looked. How much I'd missed her in those two years on Keist. How I'd hoped the time apart would have gotten me over her, and all it had done was make me love her more.

When Seb finally came into view, covered in blood, dragging his leg behind him—muscle hanging off like tattered fabric, bone almost completely exposed—it felt like my whole world flipped upside down. Everything I'd believed about us: that we were young and invincible; everything I'd believed about myself as a good and loyal friend, a protector—it all broke in that moment. Why had we been so fucking *stupid*? Why hadn't I come back to help him train? Why did I let my own issues with Em get in the way of me being there to support him, keeping our *fika* safe?

"You know what I thought?" I ask. "My first thought was: *this is my fault.*"

"It wasn't," Gabe says. "You know that, right?"

"Does it matter, if I've spent the last three years living like it's true?"

I hear him sigh. "So this stuff with Em. It's about Seb, in the end? His rite?"

I shake my head. "Yeah. And no. It's about me. I don't think I got that until today."

A silence falls between us as I think it over.

"So now that they caught the last guy, do you think we can come back?" he finally asks.

"I think so. You tell me when, and I'll come and pick you up at the harbor."

We talk logistics, and after we hang up, I lie back onto the bed. It's not fixed yet, but I'm going to fix it. I'm going to make it up to her.

I reach for the book of poems by the bed and flip to the page for today's reading, and as I read the poem through, it feels like a sign. I read it again, and again, thinking of Em. And finally, I realize what's been missing from the arch.

35

KIERAN

Three days later, I take one of the vans for Saroan Salts and drive to the north shore to pick everyone up. Saga's Jeep wasn't big enough for a group this size, but I hate driving the van. To be honest, I barely passed my license exam, and we drive so rarely on the islands that I'm still not used to it.

I get to the north shore a half hour early and wait. After a few minutes, I can start to see the ferry roll in, and my inner wolf perks up in anticipation, dying to see her. When the boat docks, only a few people step out, and as soon as the gang is visible, my eyes go straight to Em.

Agaayu, she looks incredible. She's five and a half weeks into her training, and with her shifter nature, her body has picked up muscle faster than I knew was possible. She's still truly, undeniably Em—small and slender, with her same delicate facial features—but I can see the new strength on her. She's wearing jeans today, and I notice that she's filling them out differently, the new muscle accentuating the slight curves she had before. Most noticeably, though, she carries herself differently. Her chin is a little higher, her shoulders back. I can see the confidence in her posture.

I walk towards them as they step onto the dock. Gabe says something to greet me, but I barely hear him. I come to stand before her.

"*Heij*," I say.

"*Heij*." Her face is beautiful, glowing, and I note with surprise that the rings of her irises are different now. The thin gold line was always there, but now it glows, radiant. And I realize that's what's changed the most. She glows, as though not just the ring around her eyes but the whole of her is gold.

"You look… Yeah, I don't know," I say. "You look great."

"Thanks." She smiles, but I can see some kind of sadness in her eyes.

"We should get to the car," Maren says. "Come on guys, let's give them a minute."

The rest of the group walks to the van, and Em and I stay standing there, staring silently at each other.

"Listen, Kier—" she says.

"I'm sorry." My voice comes out broken, husky. Not for the first time, I hate how weak I sound when I'm around her.

She shakes her head, looking down at the ground. "I don't know. I get it, I guess. Seb told me the rite really messes with your head. I know you thought—"

"Don't let me off easy," I say, stopping her. "It's not just about that. Yeah, the rite messed with my head. But if it hadn't happened, I still don't know if I would have supported you how you wanted. And for that, I'm *so* sorry. That was because of me and my shit—*not* because of you."

I step closer to her, feeling my pulse in my throat.

"I have some stuff I need to work out," I say. "But I need you to know that me not supporting you was *never* because of something wrong with you. It was because of something wrong with me."

"Yeah?" She looks up at me, a smile tugging at one side of her mouth. "I'm kicking ass, you know."

"I know," I say, nodding. "I believe it."

"To be honest, I don't think I believed in myself for a long time, either," she says quietly. "I think that's why it hurt so much when you didn't."

From behind us, I hear one of the van doors slam closed, and I look over my shoulder. The gang's crowded into the back of the van, leaving the front two seats for us.

"We should head back to the *fikarig*," I say. "But I want to make this up to you, and I have some stuff I need to tell you later. Not as an excuse. Just so you… understand."

She bites her lip and nods, and the blue and gold of her eyes feels like it softens for me.

"I have stuff to tell you, too," she says. "Big stuff. Crazy stuff."

"Okay," I say, and we start to walk towards the van. As we do, she surprises me by grabbing my hand. And I feel a tiny part of my world slip back into place.

WE DROP Quinn off at her apartment first, then head back to the pack house. Saga and Dagmar have prepared a big welcome-home dinner for everyone, and the house erupts into noise the second we walk through the door. For once, the dinner conversation is jovial—everyone has questions about Em's training and rite, about Maren's latest product launch, and about how Gabe's healing is going. He's still in his full-leg cast, but he looks a lot better, and I notice Em look around nervously when Saga asks about it. For all the happy conversation, I know that talk about Thalia and the rebels will erupt into disagreement, so I change the subject every time we get too close to the topic.

After dinner, as Isolde and Viggo clean up the table, Em takes my hand.

"Let's go upstairs," she says. "Maybe to the library?"

I swallow at the look in her eyes. "I'd love to. And later tonight, yeah. But first I need to talk to Seb, okay?"

She furrows her brow. "What about?"

"I'll tell you after."

"Okay," she says, and turns for the stairs.

I walk outside and find Seb and Maren sitting on a bench on the back porch.

"Good to be home?" I ask.

"Weird, mostly," Seb says.

"I actually didn't mind it, with the six of us on the north island," says Maren. "It's a preview, I guess. For how it'll be once we get our own place."

Seb nods. "Actually, speaking of. With Em doing her rite in the next week or so, I think we can afford to start looking at places soon."

"Yeah?" I ask.

He nods. "I've heard there's a few places on the other side of Moon Lake that are for sale."

"Those places are pretty pricey, right?" I think of the massive houses I've seen at the far edge of the lake, close to the woods. They're beautiful, and I never imagined I'd be able to live in a place like that. Although I guess with Seb's salt business and how much money I've saved in the last few years, it might actually be feasible.

"We can look, at least," Maren says. "We were thinking of doing some tours later this week."

I nod. "That sounds good. Hey, Mare, you mind if I talk to Seb alone for a few minutes?"

"Be my guest," she says, standing up. She leans over to give him a kiss on the cheek, then walks into the house.

I take a seat on the bench beside him.

"What's up?" he asks.

"I, uh. I need to talk to you. About the rite."

"Yeah? What's going on?"

I swallow. "You told me before I went up there that I shouldn't let whatever I saw get in my head. I don't think I listened."

He rolls his eyes. "Big surprise."

"Yeah, yeah, I know. But really. I saw some shit up there—or, specifically, I *heard* something that really got me. And it's been haunting me. Not just in the ring, but in the weeks after."

"Is this behind the stuff with Em? The fight?" he asks.

I nod. "Part of it. And… Em heard from Maren that you told her some stuff, I guess, about your rite. I don't know how much, and neither does Em. But I guess your rite involved Mare, somehow?"

He nods wordlessly.

"Right. So, mine was about Em. And the stuff I saw, and learned up there—I don't know, dude, it's killing me. I want to be able to tell her, to explain why I've been acting like this. But we can't share what we see up there."

He nods again.

"So, I…" I sigh, trying to find the words.

"You want to figure out how much you can tell her."

"Yeah. What did you tell Maren?"

He leans forward, resting his forearms on his knees, mirroring my body language.

"Do you think Em's your mate?" he asks.

"What does that have to do with anything?"

"It has to do with this."

I shake my head. "I don't know."

"Yeah, you do. Come on, tell me."

I sigh. "I think so, yeah. I hope so."

"Do you *know* so?"

I think about it for a long moment. The way I feel when I'm with her; the way she gives every day meaning. The way, when we're together, I somehow feel more myself than when I'm alone.

"Yeah. I do."

He smiles. "Congrats, man."

I find myself smiling, too, and try to suppress it. "Thanks. Now we'll just see if she'll have me."

"Please. I'm not worried about that *at all*. But okay. Do you remember what the ancestors said about how mate pairs are made?"

"Yeah, what is it, again?" I say, waving my hands. "It's like, the lights, and the ancestors or something…"

He laughs. "Man, you really didn't pay any attention in school, did you?"

"I did fine," I say, defensive.

He shakes his head, still laughing. "The ancestors believed that, in the place before this, the two souls in a mate pair have already found each other. They're woven together. And when the souls are separated to be born on the islands, they're too closely woven for a neat split. Each soul comes here with a small piece of the other, and you spend your life—or, if you're lucky, just your early years—looking for the person who already has a part of you, and whose soul is already in your chest."

"I… okay," I say. "This stuff is a bit too mystical for me, man."

"Alright, but bear with me. What do you know about the rules for what we can tell others about what we see in the rite?"

"'*Nekkatik veijtanna kiyyu unbeijnkit,*'" I say, repeating the words from the *Fakari Eijna*, the ancient book. They drill some of the edicts into us as kids, and this is one of them. It practically falls out of my mouth before I can think about it.

"Okay, so you did pay *some* attention in school. Translate."

I think. "'You cannot tell another soul.'"

"Almost," he says. "Try *unbeijnkit* again."

I think. "Different. Separate, unknown."

"Right," he says. "Not, 'you cannot tell *another* soul.' You cannot tell a *separate* soul. So what does that mean if Em's soul is a part of you, and if yours is a part of her? If your souls are knit together?"

I think about that night in the library, and the words that slipped out of my mouth. *Kiyyuni*, from a place in me I couldn't even consciously reach. It just came out of me, as though some primal place *knew*.

"Are you telling me that we're allowed to tell our mates what we see up there?"

He shrugs. "I'm telling you it's complicated. It's all a little mystical, and the earliest records we have of the *Eijna* are more than a thousand years old. You either believe it or you don't. But if you *do* believe it, then don't rule out the full scope of the story. The ancestors believed that you couldn't tell another soul about the rite, yes. But they *also* believed that our souls are tied together. If you tell Em something in good faith, because she needs to hear it to understand you, I don't think they'll punish you for that."

I nod, thinking.

"And if you think about it," he continues, "if your souls are tied together, a part of her was with you that night, already."

I look down at my hands, where Em's black hair tie is still wrapped around my wrist.

"How much did you tell Mare?" I ask finally.

"Not everything. But enough for her to understand." He swallows. "My rite was *about*, and *for*, me. But she made an appearance, in a way, and that shaped the way I acted when we were getting to know each other. When I figured out she was my mate, I owed it to her to explain."

I bring my head down, resting it in my hands. "I just wanna say I'm sorry, man."

"To Em?"

"No. To you."

"What? What for?"

I swallow and look over at him. "For abandoning you before your rite. I left because of shit with Em, but I should have come back to help train you. And I can't help feeling like, if I'd gotten over myself and come back to help, if I'd been there—"

"Come on, dude. When are you gonna let that shit go?"

His words catch me off-guard. "What?"

"That whole Atlas, carrying-the-weight-of-the-world, thing." He shakes his head. "It wasn't your job to save me from my own decisions. My rite was supposed to go the way it went. I *had* to learn those lessons."

"But if you'd been better prepared, you wouldn't have ended up like—"

He puts a hand on my back.

"I don't regret it," he says firmly. "No, I don't like living in pain. Yes, I spent years wondering what would have happened if I'd prepared better, or if I hadn't let them transport me to the mainland for medical care. But I can't live in regret. I need to see what I have now, and build *forward*, instead of staying stuck in the past. Maren taught me that."

I look up at him, and I feel a knot in my throat.

"You know, I spent years hating myself for what I let happen to you," I say finally.

"I know," he says, nodding. "But, no offense dude, my rite wasn't about you. You're not *that* important."

"Whatever," I say, letting out a low laugh. He laughs too, and then the air grows still.

"Seriously," he says, after a minute. "My rite was designed for me to learn a lesson I had to learn. Yeah, I could have prepared better, but that's not on you. And maybe letting go of all that over-responsibility is part of *your* lesson."

I give him a look. "So you're telling me you spied on me in the ring."

"I'm telling you I know you better than you think. Now, come on. Go upstairs and tell that girl she's your mate, because the rest of us have been waiting for years for you two to figure it out."

I smile and get to my feet.

"*Takka*," I say, nodding at him.

"Any time."

36

EMERSON

Kieran finds me upstairs, sitting in the library. I'm on the couch by the window, scanning through a book.

"Hey," he says, walking in.

"Hey." I look up as he shuts the door behind him.

"What are you reading?"

"An old healer's book I found. I think this one belonged to Saga's mentor, or hers before that. It was published in the forties, so the information is a little different than in mine."

"Yeah? Anything interesting?" He walks towards the window, taking a seat on the couch next to me.

"Not yet. I'm trying to figure something out, but I haven't found what I'm looking for."

He nods. "Gabe's looking great. I can't believe his chest scarring is totally gone."

"You don't know the half of it," I say quietly. Gabe and I haven't told anyone about what happened yet, and we decided to keep his cast on until I can figure out what on earth I did to heal his leg. It took me days to recover from how much energy it cost, but I've gone back to check, and the break is healed. I'm dying to tell Kieran, but before I can muster the nerve, he puts a gentle hand on my knee.

"Can we talk?" he asks. "I want to finish what we started earlier."

"Yeah, of course." I close the book and put it aside.

"I have some stuff I want to say. I need you to know why I've been like this."

"Okay," I say, scooching nearer.

"It's two things, I think," he says, and I can see the nervousness in his face. "First—and this is part of what I needed to talk to Seb about... His rite really impacted me. Seeing what happened to him changed me, and ever since the way he came back, I've been blaming myself for not helping him. For not *saving* him and stopping it. And I think the truth is, if something happened to you..."

"You'd never forgive yourself," I say. "I know."

"No, it's not that." He shakes his head. "I say that, and it's true. But honestly, I don't think I could survive it. You're everything to me, Em. You mean more than anything and anyone else. So for years, I've been keeping you safe because, I think... I need to know you're safe, so *I* can feel safe."

"Oh." The word comes out like a whisper.

He looks down at his hand on my knee. "It wasn't fair. I should have supported you doing this. If I wanted to make sure I didn't have the same regrets as with Seb, I should have helped you do better, not try to hold you back."

I put my hand on his, running my thumb over the back of his hand.

"The truth is," he says, looking up. "I don't know if anyone could do this rite in six weeks. But you're the strongest and the most amazing person I know. You never stop surprising me. If *anyone* can do this, I know it's you."

I swallow, feeling a stinging in my eyes.

"Kier," I say, and my fingers interlace with his. "Can I ask you something?"

"Of course."

"I heard you with Seb in the kitchen, after my first day of training. He said he'd never trained someone from scratch, and that even Maren had never shifted on purpose before. And you said, but she's Maren. And I just..." I feel my voice warble, and I swallow. "I don't know. I just wanted to say that that really hurt to hear. That you think someone like Maren is so different from someone like me."

"Em," he says, his eyes widening. "*Agaayu,* I'm sorry. I didn't mean it like that. I just meant that Maren had been shifting by accident before she started training. Her wolf was close to the surface, and you had to learn how to bring yours back. I never meant you couldn't do it. Just that you it was a different situation."

I nod. "It still hurt."

He nods, his thumb running over my knuckles. "Hey. Maren's great. And I know Seb thinks she's amazing. But she's *nothing* compared to you."

I smile a little, despite myself. "To you, maybe."

"To me, definitely. I know I was wrong for underestimating you. And I want to tell you the second thing. It's about my rite— about what I saw and heard, so that the last little bit makes sense."

I feel my eyes go a little wider, and something in my chest softens.

"Like Seb told Maren?"

"Like Seb told Maren."

"But... Kier," I say. "You know the edict. You can't tell another soul."

"What if you're not another soul?"

He gives me a look, and suddenly I realize what's happening. He must see it in my eyes, because a small smile tugs at his lips.

"I guess you paid more attention in school than I did," he says.

"*Ayagaayuni*, don't ruin this with your dumb jokes," I say, laughing, feeling my eyes sting. "Wait, hold on. What are you saying?"

"Em." He grabs my other hand and looks at me gently. "I love you. I've loved you since—*agaayu*, I don't know. I think I loved you since that day I first saw you, in your yellow bathing suit at the quarry. I loved you the night we first kissed on Halluk, and I loved you on those *agaayit*-forsaken years on Keist. All I can do is love you. I don't think I know how to do anything else."

I can feel the tears welling up in my eyes.

"I'm not gonna ask you anything now. Not because I don't want to, and not because I don't think you're my mate, because I *know* you are. But 'cause you deserve something more special than me asking to claim you in the library."

I let out a soft laugh. "I don't know. Some special things have happened in this library."

He nods, grinning. "Yeah. But you deserve more than that, for something like this."

I scooch closer to him, putting his face in my hands, looking up at his eyes.

"You're it for me, Em," he says quietly. "There was never anyone else. There never will be. You are the other part of my soul."

He swallows, and I can hear his voice waver.

"Will you love me?" he asks. "Will you let me love you?"

"*Iija*," I whisper, kissing his cheeks. "Yes, yes. *Kiyyuni*."

He kisses my mouth, and the feeling is soft and gentle. I take in the scent and taste of him; wood and amber, a little salt from the sea air this morning. After a minute, he pulls away.

"Hey," he says, leaning his forehead against mine. "I wanted to tell you this now, instead of at, like, some fancy dinner with candles or something, because I need to tell you about my rite before you go up to the ring."

"Okay," I say, pulling back. "What do you want to tell me?"

He swallows. "That night in the ring, I saw your father."

"Yeah, I know," I say, nodding. "I figured that much out already."

"No, but I really, really *believed* I saw your father. And your mom was there."

I feel something in my chest twist. "My mom's spirit came to you?"

He nods. "When I walked into the ring, it was me, your mother and a large gray wolf. At first, I thought she was Móra, and he was just some animal. But then he attacked her, and I think... I think she showed me your memories."

I blink, feeling a patter of anxiety in my chest. He nods, putting a hand on my leg.

"We don't have to talk about it. But it felt wrong for you not to know what I'd seen. And as the ancestors were showing me your memories, the wolf was still there, prowling the outside of the ring."

I nod, thinking. "But it was still the *kiyyulit?*"

"It didn't feel like the *kiyyulit*. It felt like a real beast. After the last memory, he attacked me, and we each drew blood. The wolf I saw in your memories was like a mist when I tried to touch him. This one felt real."

I shake my head. "But the *kiyyulit* do take a physical form for you to fight. If that wasn't the case and it was always a mirage, nobody would leave the ring with injuries."

"I guess," he says, shaking his head. "But I asked your mom if he was really here, and she said yes."

"Here like, in the ring with you? Or here as in, on the island?"

"I don't know. I guess I just said 'here.' And she said..." he swallows, like he's still not sure how much he can say. "She said

I can't save you. That I can't prevent you from your destiny, and that he'll find you."

I nod, thinking.

"Can you describe the wolf to me?"

"He was big and gray, maybe as big as my wolf. His fur was matted. He looked hungry, but strong. Angry."

I nod. "And his face?" I ask.

Kieran shrugs. "Just… I don't know. A wolf. Why?"

"No scarring?" I ask, and he shakes his head.

"That's my dad from my memories," I say resolutely. "Not the real him."

"What? How do you know?"

I clear my throat. Even with the training I've been doing with Seb, I find this stuff hard to talk about. But I do my best.

"The night my mom and I moved out, a few months before she died, they had a really bad fight," I say. "I mean, they were always bad, but it seemed like they were getting worse over time. We lived in a pretty remote place, and we didn't have a lot of nearby neighbors. But that night, a trader came home late from the harbor, and he heard. He called the marshals."

I see him nod, watching me.

"They came and had to separate them. It was horrible. There was so much blood. My mom was sick already, from the illness that eventually got her. But after the marshals came, Viggo and Dagmar came to pick us up so we could stay with them for a while until my mom found a new place. And when Viggo saw what my dad had done, he just lost it."

"What happened?"

"He attacked my dad. Dagmar had taken me and Mom away already, but Viggo stayed, and apparently they had a massive fight. Viggo tore into him so badly that had all this new scarring, also on his face. And apparently—I didn't know this, at the time —but because Saga and my mom were friends, she couldn't bring herself to heal him. Helen, the other healer, was still living on one of the other islands. And Saga was so angry at my dad that she couldn't get her healing magic to work. So he scarred over."

"Em," Kier says softly, stroking my hand.

"Anyway. I never knew that. I used to see my dad around the islands, sometimes. Like a ghost, but I always worried he was real. Finally, around the time you left for Keist, I told Aunt Dagmar. She told me the story, and after that, it helped separate the wolf in my mind from the real thing. Whenever I thought I saw him, I would tell myself that it couldn't be real, because my real father had scarring that the wolf in my memories didn't. So," I say, smiling softly at him. "You didn't fight my father. You fought the father from my memories."

He nods slowly. "But then what about what your mom said?"

"He *was* really there, wasn't he?" I ask. "*To you*, he was there in the ring. And she was right that he would find me. Because next week, I'll be climbing up to the ring to fight him, too."

I see him swallow, thinking.

"This has to be it, Kier," I say, coming close again. "She said you couldn't save me from my destiny, and she was right. You wanted to protect me from going into the ring, but what *I* had to do for myself was finally face my fears and fight for myself."

He nods, finally, looking up at me.

"If your dad really *was* there, in the ring…"

"He couldn't survive for more than a week," I say, shaking my head. "I had to do a plant unit for my healer training. The cliffs are too high up for larger plants to grow. All he'd be able to eat would be weeds and the unprocessed *kattaka* plant. If he really *was* there during your rite, he would have died within a week if he didn't come down."

Kieran shakes his head, thinking.

"I'm sorry I didn't believe in you," he says finally.

"I'm sorry I got so angry," I say, climbing onto his lap, taking his face in my hands. "I know you were just trying to keep me safe."

He nods, kissing me, pulling me close. I feel his mouth on mine, the scratch of his beard against my skin; his hands slipping up the back of my sweater. I grind my hips lightly against him, feeling his body respond with desire.

"Mm. Em," he groans. "God. It's been too long."

"We have the rest of our lives," I whisper, kissing my way down the column of his neck, to his throat.

"I want you," he groans.

I smile, kissing the side of his neck, running my teeth lightly against the place where my mark would go.

"*Agaayu*," he says. "I want to mark you. I want you to claim me."

"What happened to all those promises of a candlelit dinner?" I say sweetly.

"I'll do that too," he breathes, pressing his erection up against me in a way that makes me moan. "But we've wasted so many goddamn years. I don't want to waste another second."

I pull his face close to mine.

"They weren't wasted to me," I whisper, kissing him. "I'm not in any rush. We have time, *kiyyuni*. I promise."

And with that, he throws me down onto the couch, and we desecrate the library for a second time this year.

37

KIERAN

We spend the next few days in something that feels like heaven. Every night I get to sleep next to her, and every morning I wake up with her in my arms, the soft scent of cardamom and rose water reminding me that I'm home. Saga expects Em's rite to be in just a few days, but a cold snap freezes over Moon Lake, and the elders determine that the path up to the cliffs will be too icy to be safe for another week.

I don't mind. More time means more days for her to prepare. In the mornings, she goes to the gym or to be coached by Seb, and I head to the woodshop. She doesn't have to work in the afternoons—those training for the rite who aren't self-employed have a reduced workload during the preparation—so a few days after the group comes back to Saroe, she starts joining Seb and Maren in touring new *fikarigs* for us.

I'm grateful for it. I didn't feel any pressure to get our own place soon, but ever since we caught the Remnant members, tensions at the *fikarig* have been high. If it's not me arguing with Saga and Viggo, it's Seb or Gabe. It's gotten so bad that, five days after the group returns from Halluk, Gabe asks if he can spend the afternoon at my place instead of being stuck at home with them.

"Make yourself comfortable," I say, letting him through the front door of the apartment.

"Thanks." He limps through the front door, his leg still immobilized by the full-length cast.

"When do you get that thing taken off?"

"Officially, full recovery is at least twelve weeks, even for shifters. And sometimes as long as a year."

"Damn," I say, shutting the door behind him as he walks to my small dining table. "And unofficially?"

"Unofficially… Em's been trying some stuff."

I glance over at him. "It's a bone break, right? What can she do?"

"You should talk to her about that," he says, lowering himself into a chair. "I know she wants to tell you, but she needed to figure some stuff out first."

"Okay…" I say. I want to ask, but I see Gabe lean over the table, looking at the scattered books and papers.

"What are you, writing a book report?" he asks.

"I've just been doing some reading after our last council meeting. Hang on, I'll clear the table."

"No, wait." He puts out his hand, stopping me. "Can I look?"

"Sure. Honestly, I've had a hard time getting through it. This stuff was always more your and Seb's deal."

He tilts his head as he opens a folder and looks at the scans inside. "The Nayakka petitions?"

"Yeah. There's four of them, going back six years."

He nods slowly, reading over a random page. "Man. This stuff is rough. I never felt right about what we do with their islands."

"I never thought about it," I say, sitting down. "But yeah. Meeting someone from there, it feels different. I picked up some books on old Fakari history. Did you know in the old days, all the islands were considered *pakka*? Even the south."

He nods again. "Yeah, I did."

"That girl, Thalia," I say, "the one who broke your leg. She's been asking to meet with me almost every day."

"And? Have you seen her?"

"Not since the first time. The council's against it. They don't want me talking to her unless we can come to an agreement about what kind of deal we'd make. And now that it seems we've caught everyone…"

He shakes his head dismissively. "They would never have made a decision, anyway. I know sitting in on council meetings is newer for you, but honestly, they can never get a majority on anything. It's good you're able to vote now. We need more young people on council who are willing to actually *do* something."

"I feel you," I say, thinking back on the last few meetings we've had. "It's already driving me crazy. We can't decide anything, and everything undecided is following us home. I haven't had an evening not talking *about* the Remnant in weeks. And at the same time, we aren't doing shit."

"So we should do something," he says, looking up.

"Like what?"

"Talk to the Nayakka girl. She's asking for you."

I shake my head. "The council decided against. I can't go directly against a decision, they could take my council seat."

A smile spreads across his face. "They didn't forbid *me*, though, right? And she broke *my* leg. Maybe I just want to get an apology. And you're there for moral support."

I raise my eyebrows. "That doesn't sound like you."

He sets his jaw, looking down at the papers again. "I've been sitting on my ass all winter. I'm sick of the bickering, and I don't like my mom using what happened to me as a reason to vote for something I'm against. Maybe it's time for something to change."

GABE CALLS Ivo just after lunch, and we make our way down to the marshal's office about an hour later. Thalia's already there, sitting in the same wooden chair across from Sigur's desk. I'm expecting a sardonic *"About time"*, but when we come in, she's quiet, her head bowed over.

"Heij," I say, walking in.

She looks up, and I can see she has a black eye. The silver-gray of her irises seems even brighter in contrast.

"Agaayit. Did one of us do this?" I think immediately of Viggo, who said they'd find a way to get the information from the people we've caught.

She shakes her head. "They let us see the sun yesterday, and Blaise attacked me. They barely trusted me and Nomi to start with, but I guess they heard I've been asking to speak to you."

"Fuck. I'm sorry," I say, shaking my head.

She shrugs noncommittally. "It's life. Most people cannot keep their violent instincts contained."

I swallow and head for Sigur's chair to sit, but realize Gabe is still on his feet, and gesture for him to take it. He limps over and lowers himself into the chair.

"This is Gabe," I say.

"Ah, the man I maimed." There's a sarcastic edge in her voice. "They've brought you here to fill me with regret, have they?"

"No. I came because there wasn't an easy way for Kieran to see you otherwise."

"Ah. Well." She shakes her head. "I *am* sorry, for what it's worth. I hear I cost you the chance to do your elder rite. And I imagine you're in quite some pain."

Gabe nods wordlessly, then looks up at me. Right.

"You've been asking to talk to me again?" I ask.

She nods. "Please tell me you came to a decision."

"I'm sorry. Still nothing."

She mutters some curse I don't know, shaking her head.

"How hard can it be? Haven't you read the petitions? Haven't you seen what we're trying to escape?"

"I have. But the council—"

"Ah. Well at this rate, I imagine I'll spend seven years in this basement if we leave it to your council."

"You can't blame them," I say, crossing my arms. "You put yourself in a bad position, Thalia. You're the only one of the group who's hurt an islander. You didn't want to share information, which made them question your motives. And honestly, I don't know that whatever information you have is going to sway the council. Now that we've caught the last of you—"

"What?" she asks, wrinkling her forehead.

"The last one of your group, Laurent, lit a fire on the west shore last week and fled. Fishermen from Keist were able to catch him before he left."

She hesitates, eyeing me.

"He's being held on Keist, now, away from the rest of you."

"You still want to talk to me," she says.

"Yeah, so you say, but you haven't managed to convince anyone," I say. "I don't think this is working the way you want it to. The council doesn't trust you. Some people want to hear you out, but you lording this information over us isn't going to bring you closer to what you want. Maybe if you *tell* us what you know first, it'll be easier for the council to agree to a deal—"

"Oh, so you cannot trust me, but you expect me to trust you?" she snaps. "The people who keep me chained in a basement? How do I know I won't tell you and you'll *still* betray me, hm? And then I've sold out my fellow citizens and you send me back to our shores together, where they can rip me into shreds?"

"I—" I shake my head. When she puts it that way... "I can't do this by myself, Thalia. I can't make a deal for you. You have to play ball."

"I'm trying, aren't I?" she spits. "I'm here in this god-forsaken office, trying to plead for my life and my sister's freedom with a man who doesn't spare me a second thought. Why even come here, if you're just going to toy with me? Please." Her voice gets low, her eyes pained. "It's so brutal there. Please push the council to come to a decision. And if you decide not to let us here, then at least put us on the ferry to the mainland. Don't send us back to the southern isles."

Gabe's brow furrows. "You'd rather be undocumented on the mainland than sent back to your home?"

"It's not my home," she says bitterly. "Not anymore."

He nods, looking at her. Something's happening behind his eyes, but I don't know what.

"Can I ask you something?" he asks.

Thalia purses her lips, leaning back in her chair.

"Do you know an Ilse? She's from the southern isles, too."

I expect her to shut him down, but she waves her hand dismissively. "The islands are big. There's many people I do and don't know. A name is nothing."

"I don't know her last name." He swallows, nervous. What is he talking about? I've never heard of this.

"Her dad was a delegate," he continues. "She came here with him for the peace treaty that broke down, after the last attacks."

Thalia looks up, her brows knit. "Ilse Tanayyu?"

He shakes his head. "I don't know. She'd be 28 or 29 now, I guess? Green eyes, curly hair."

Thalia nods. "I knew her. She's dead."

I see the reaction in Gabe's body, his shoulders tensing as he sits up.

"*What?* What happened?"

"She died ten, eleven years ago," she says with a wave of her hand. "She fell into the ravine at the heart of our largest island. They found her days later. You knew her, then?" she asks, noting his reaction.

"Sort of." His voice is hollow. I've never seen him like this, and I find myself feeling like I'm watching a movie I'm completely outside of. I don't even know who he's talking about.

"Well. I'm sorry for your loss." She doesn't sound sorry; her posture is tight, her tone almost derisive. I give Gabe a minute to respond, but his hand is on his mouth and he seems lost somewhere inside his mind.

"So *this* you can share," I say, "but something that'll keep our islands safe, you'll only save for a deal?"

"It's different. He knew the girl." I expect her to raise her chin defiantly, but she looks tired, worn-down, and her voice is softer now. "But if it makes a difference to your council, yes. Tell them I helped. Tell them whatever they need to hear. Just get us out of there, please."

"I'll bring it up, but I can't guarantee anything. I'll see if we can get a decision to you in the next few days."

"Please," she says quietly. "Please do."

38

EMERSON

A week after we return to Saroe, I wake up with that heavy knowing in my bones. I bring a hand to my stomach, feeling a patter of anxiety begin to flutter in my chest. Today is my rite.

I turn in bed to look at Kieran, fast asleep next to me. His red-brown hair is half over his face, swaying slightly with each exhale. I bring my fingers up to brush it out of the way, behind his ear.

"*Kiyyuni,*" I whisper, and kiss his cheek. He turns but doesn't wake up. Swallowing my nerves, I slip out of bed, changing my clothes and heading downstairs.

When I get to the kitchen, I see Gabe's already made breakfast. The stove is piled high with eggs and sausage, and there's a pitcher of protein-heavy Fakari yogurt on the counter. Saga's sitting by herself at the kitchen table.

"*Heij*, morning," I say, coming in. "I guess you told Gabe?"

"Yes, and he was nice enough to make all this for us."

I nod, looking at the display. I haven't seen much of Gabe the last few days—he keeps going off to spend time alone. Something's up, clearly, but here he still is, taking care of us. I start preparing a plate as Saga gets my rite salt mix ready.

"And how are you feeling, Emerson? Nervous?"

"Honestly, yeah," I say, glancing over my shoulder at her. "I don't know. It's really happening. I don't think I really thought I'd get here, somehow. Did you feel that way?"

She thinks for a moment, then shakes her head. "*Nekka*. I was laser-focused back then. I felt I had something to prove."

I nod. "Yeah. I want to prove myself. But still, all of this... it's a big change for me from where I was a few months ago."

"Well, the boys tell me you've come a long way in six and a half weeks," she says as I walk to the table with my plate. "Both in training *and* healing. But from one healer to another, be thoughtful with your healing in the ring today."

"Yeah?" I ask, sitting down.

She nods. "You can use it to your advantage, but healing work is exhausting, too. The more of your healing energy you expend, the less you'll have left to fight. So be wise with how much you use. Don't use it unless you really have to."

"Okay. *Takka*. I'll be careful."

She smiles at me and reaches out to put her hand on mine. "You're the first healer to go into the ring since my rite, thirty years ago. I'm so proud of you."

I swallow, thinking of my mom. I wonder if she'd be proud. I hope to find out tonight.

Just then, Maren walks into the kitchen through the arch behind Saga. She eyes the massive pile of scrambled eggs on the stove and then looks at me, a huge smile brightening up her face.

"Is today the day?"

I nod, and she squeals and jumps up and down, clapping her hands together.

"Oh my God, this is so exciting. When do we start preparing

for the ceremony? Seb and I were gonna go look at some *fikarigs* near the north shore today, but we can totally cancel."

"Oh, no, don't bother. I need someone to help me with stretching in the afternoon, but we won't start the preparations until seven or eight."

"Okay, good, because I'm low-key excited to see the houses." She walks to the stove to start piling her plate with food.

"Send me photos," I say. "We're looking at a place for four families, right?" Seb and Maren, Gabe and his future partner, Kier and me, and, tentatively, Quinn if she wants to join.

Maren nods happily. "I'm so psyched. With the salt scrubs doing so well and the houses we have available here, we have way more than enough money for something great. And we can renovate it to make it perfect."

"And if you *can't* make it perfect, you girls can always stay with us a little longer," Saga says gently.

"We're not in any rush, *Aja*," I say—though that feels less true now than it did a few months ago, with how much the guys have been bickering with our *fika* elders. "But it's exciting to take the next step in all our lives together. Especially now that two of us have found our mates."

Maren grins at me as she sits down at the table. "I fucking told you. At *this very table*, might I add, when you came down after you and Kier—"

"*Heij, heij*, none of that," I say, laughing nervously and looking between her and Saga. None of the adults need to know what happened in the library. Twice now.

Saga smiles. "It seems like you two would benefit from some girl time. I'm going to speak to Helen about the *kattaka* ceremony. Emerson, if I don't see you before tonight—good luck."

"Thanks, Saga," I say, and take a bite of my eggs.

THE DAY PASSES QUICKLY. I take my rite salts in the morning, and Kier and I go on a walk to help steady my nerves. He leaves just after, since he has to stop by Halssel to send a few orders to the mainland this morning.

I get back to the common house in the early afternoon. Quinn helps me with stretching my hamstrings and quads, which are always tight, and then I go into my day-of ritual: scrub, sauna, cold plunge. Around seven, Seb, Maren, and Gabe make their way to the common house and help me get on my fighting gear.

I strap my clothes on. A base layer with magnetic snaps for shifting; body armor; a loose sweater overtop. The pants can accommodate shifting, too, and we attach a knife to each leg so I have options. Maren braids my hair into a tight crown around my head, since a ponytail or loose braid can be used against me in the ring. Once she's done, Seb takes a few minutes to go over strategy with me.

"Don't shift too early, before you can think about it critically," he says. "Though I don't think that'll be an issue with you. And you can use your healing power to help yourself, but I'd wait until you get near the end and feel like you're losing."

"Got it," I say.

"And remember: the ancestors are trying to uncover your greatest weakness. Whatever you see is going to mess with you. You may think you know what to expect, but they could always surprise you. Don't let your default behavior take over. Take the time to think. Be smart."

"Okay," I say, trying to take it in.

Quinn and I go over some last-minute self-defense combinations, though I think it's mostly to take the edge off my nerves and not because I need the practice—I won't be able to remember anything new I learn today, anyway. Finally, just after nine, it's time.

Quinn and Maren each hug me goodbye.

"Good luck, girl," Maren says, pulling me close. "You're not gonna need it."

"Thanks," I say, and squeeze her tight. "And thanks for always being in my corner."

They leave the locker room, and then it's just me and Seb.

"Nervous?" he asks.

I take a breath, checking my gut.

"Yeah," I say honestly. "I guess. But I'm also… I don't know. I'm kind of excited, as weird as that sounds."

His brow furrows. "Yeah?"

I swallow as the realization hits me. "Because I hope I see my mom again."

He smiles. "I hope so, for you. And Em—"

"Yeah?"

He gives me a hug and squeezes me tight. I let go after a second, but he hangs on.

"What are you doing?" I ask. I hear him swallow, and I realize he's getting choked up. For a moment, I worry he's taking stock, in case this is goodbye. But he pulls back.

"I'm proud of you," he says, taking me by surprise. "You were always the smallest of the us, but you were never the weakest."

I smile. "Thanks, Seb."

"You ready?"

"Yeah."

He leads me out of the dressing room, and we head for the ceremonial hall.

It's dark, the room lit only by candlelight, and I can feel a chill of goosebumps go over my skin as I hear people shuffling, making way for me. The first thing I see is Saga and Helen, standing in the middle of the room in our healers' gowns. Seb leaves my side, and he, Gabe, Maren, and Quinn line up on either side of the doorway. The women from the elder council fill in the rest of the way to the healers. I find myself looking instinctively for Kieran around the perimeter of the room, but I don't see him, and I feel a flush of nerves. As everyone gets into place, I take a deep breath.

They begin beating their chests and thighs, singing. The song as sung by women is higher-pitched than it was for Kieran's rite, but it still feels like an ancient rhythm: unusual to my modern ears, beautiful in its brutality. I realize for a moment that this is the song my grandparents would have heard when they did their rite, and their great-grandparents before them.

Daughter of Tayyakuk, valiant warrior, the voices chant.

I begin walking towards the healers, feeling the drum of nerves in my gut. My wolf paces nervously, and I let her get close to the surface.

It is time for you to prove your worth, the elders sing. *It is time to earn your place on the islands.*

I come to stand before the healers, and Saga steps forward.

"Emerson Stenberg, daughter of Tayyakuk," she says, raising the bowl of *kattaka* between us. I can smell the mixture, the scent musty and herbal, as she lifts it to my lips.

"May the ancestors guide you and uncover your weakness. May you rise to the fight. May you wrestle into submission the weakness within you and return to us."

She tilts the bowl and I part my lips so that the *kattaka* slips into my mouth. The mixture is thick and cool, the texture earthy. I choke as the last bit reaches my throat, and swallow, feeling it slither down to my stomach.

"You have your pack behind you, and the ancestors before you," Saga says. "Now you must make your way up to the ring alone. We'll see you in the morning. *Agaayit ikka.*"

I nod and turn for the doors, every moment feeling slightly unnatural. Is this the *kattaka* already, or does it just feel weird that it's actually happening?

As I pass the elders, then the people from my training pack, I get encouraging nods and smiles. And as I walk out of the door into the night, I see Kieran.

Warmth floods my body, and I hear the heavy door to the common house close behind me. I walk up to him.

"We aren't supposed to see each other once the ceremony is over," I whisper.

"That didn't stop you."

I smile, feeling the patter of my nerves in my chest. He grabs my hand.

"I didn't get why you gave me the hair tie," he says. "But I liked having a piece of you with me when I was up there. I brought you something."

He pulls a hand out from behind his back and opens it. In his palm is a purple blossom. A rhodora.

I gasp in surprise. Already, the *kattaka* seems to be having an impact on me, and my voice feels almost exaggerated to my own ears as I ask, "Where did you get this? They're not in season."

"It's not real," he says. "There's a woman on Halssel who makes flowers out of crepe paper. I paid her to make it, and picked it up this morning when I shipped the arch. I know it's stupid—"

"It's not stupid," I say, picking it up and twirling the wire stem between my fingers. "I love it. Thank you."

"It's like you," he says. "I read about rhodoras. The flowers are beautiful, but the plant grows in the hardest environments. Its beauty doesn't take away from its strength."

I slip the flower behind my ear like my mom used to, feeding the wire into part of my braid to keep it in place. I swallow and pull him close.

"Thank you," I say. "Not just for the flower. For believing in me."

He kisses the top of my head. "Always. Now go kick some ass."

"I will," I say, and I pull away and head for the cliffs.

I CAN FEEL the *kattaka* hitting me after just a few minutes. The path up the first hill is winding, and at first I feel it in the softness at the edge of my vision, and a weird swirling in my gut. I see the first hints of the *kiyyulit* as I near the top of the first hill, and they're more vibrant than I've ever seen them, dancing like wisps of neon light.

I'm coming, Mom, I think, and walk on.

By the time I near the third turn of the path, I'm starting to feel the *kattaka* in my whole body. My knees feel loose, my body liquid, every movement strangely exaggerated. The *kiyyulit* are stronger now, and I can see them pooling at the top of the cliff, their shape obscured by the black rocks jutting out against the night sky.

After about an hour, I reach the top of the cliff, the ring now fully visible. It's quiet up here—quiet as death, quiet as bone, with barely a breeze to distract me. I look down at my feet, where I can see the frost on the grass and weeds. The ice from last week has thawed, but it's still slippery getting up to the cliff.

I look up ahead to see the arch, marking the entrance to the ring. I can see whatever's in there, behind there, moving. Waiting for me.

A shiver runs over me as it sets in that this is really happening. I feel a flicker of doubt. I've come a long way, but I'm still weaker than Seb and even Quinn by a lot. Am I really strong enough to do this? Do I really have what it takes to survive this, let alone win?

Instinctively, I bring a hand to my gut. I run through my mind every piece of advice I've been given for this, the words pouring over me like a waterfall in the same way Seb's corrections did that first day in the boxing ring.

Don't shift too fast.

Wait to use your healing power until the end. Any energy you use for healing, you can't use to fight.

Don't let your default behavior take over.

"I can do this. I can do this," I whisper. And then I pool my energy into my gut, sending it down into the earth and up into the heavens. Even with my eyes closed, my own energy feels vibrant and sharper, my perception of it impacted by the *kattaka* just like the actual *kiyyulit*. I see my energy swirling up into me, this time hooking into the Northern Lights, centering me *here*, in this moment, at the edge of the cliffs.

I swallow and open my eyes, and step towards the ring.

As I near the entrance, I see the lights everywhere, so bright they're almost blinding. I brace myself. My father could be anywhere, but I find myself instinctively looking for my mom, hoping to catch a glimpse of her, hear some words of wisdom. Feel her close to me again.

And then I see her, standing at the edge of the ring, near the raw edge of the cliff with her back to me. But she's not here, really. She's at the kitchen sink, somehow, and I realize it's a memory. I know which one instantly.

She's singing the rain song for me, and although I can't see myself in the memory, I'm watching her from where I was—my seat at the kitchen table. He comes in from the rain, and immediately the energy in the room shifts. He's shouting, angry about something that isn't her fault. She tries to stand up to him, and in minutes it all coalesces in horror. Screaming, crying, violence.

I force myself to breathe deeply. *Stay grounded. He's not here yet.*

A new memory forms before me. We're at the beach on the west shore. My aunt and uncle were visiting that day, and Mom and I are at the edge of the rocks with Dagmar, looking out at the sea. She lifts a leg up to herself to rest her chin on, and I notice the bruising on her. Dagmar asks,

"Lena. Is everything okay?"

"Oh, I'm fine," Mom says, and makes up some excuse. But I can feel the change in the air. Dagmar doesn't believe her, and somewhere behind us my dad has heard our conversation, and I can scent his anger. I know what's to come.

As I watch this scene, I see something moving at the edge of the ring, and a bolt of adrenaline hits me.

It's my dad, big and strong.

It's my dad from my memory, I tell myself. I note his face, free of scarring, and the size of his body. It's not even my dad as he truly was then. The *kiyyulit* have made him to scale from my memories, so he towers over me the way he did when I was a kid.

I know it can't really be him, but the animal of my body reacts like he's here. The anxiety courses through me, making me panic, and I force myself to breathe.

Don't shift. Don't shift, I remind myself. Stay calm. Be rational. It's not him. But the *kattaka* is blurring the edges of my mind, and somehow, I feel I can't be sure. Could his scars have healed by now? Is there any way...?

The lights in the center of the ring shift again, and now it's the night mom and I were taken away. There's so much sound, so much fear in the air. Blood, screaming. I hear sirens. It's all so much.

I feel my anxiety rocking through me, harder now, but I force myself to breathe. Connect to the ground. Connect to the *kiyyulit*.

I'm here. I'm an adult. I'm safe.

My father's wolf prowls into the center of the ring, towards the memory. He walks through the mist of the scene, coming directly at me. Instinctively, my hand goes to my thigh, to find the knife strapped there between the clasps of my pants. I grab it and take the fighting stance.

My mom is still in the mist of the memory, wailing on the floor. The sound feels like it's all around me, in me, my mother's grief and fear punctuating every moment of this, wrapping itself around every sinew of my body. And my dad's wolf is so big, at least two heads taller than me.

I'm tempted to run. I'm tempted to remember Kieran's words, weeks ago now—that this isn't worth dying for. But I've been running from these memories and the shadow of my father since the moment I first saw him hurt her. And as I look into his eyes, I tell myself I don't need to be afraid anymore.

This is the *kiyyulit*. It's only as real as my mind lets it me.

"Hey, dad," I say weakly, and he lowers his head, ready to pounce.

39

KIERAN

"Kieran," Ivo says as I walk back into the ceremonial hall. "Thalia wants to speak with you."

"Not now, man," I say, shaking my head. "It's a big night. I just want to be with family until Em gets back."

"I know, I told her. I said we had a rite tonight, but she got even more upset."

I shake my head. "We haven't come to a decision. You can tell her I'll talk to the council tomorrow or Thursday and get back to her."

"Kieran," Ivo says, grabbing my arm. "When I told her about the rite, she freaked out. I tried to get her to talk to me, but she won't. She'll *only* talk to you. Please. I think it's important."

"Fine," I say reluctantly, and I follow him to the marshal's office.

When we get there, Thalia is tied to her chair again, looking around wildly for me.

"Kieran," she says as soon as I walk through the door. "Kieran, please, I need to talk to you."

"I'm here. What's wrong?"

"Shut the door behind you," she says. I don't want to, but the look on her face is grave, and reluctantly I do so. I come to sit before her in the office chair at Ivo's desk.

"What's going on?" I ask.

"He said there's a rite tonight. Is this the rite where you go to the cliffs?"

"Yeah. Why?" At the fear in her voice, I feel a shiver run through me. "What were you guys planning?"

She shakes her head, then looks away. She's exhausted, I can see it; her posture looks almost brittle. She's wrestling with herself, somewhere in her mind.

"Please, Kieran. Tell me you spoke with the council for me. Tell me you have an agreement."

"Nothing yet. And honestly, Thalia, I'm exhausted. If you don't have something urgent, I'll come back tomorr—"

"Has the person already left?" she asks, interrupting me. "The one doing the rite?"

"Yeah, why?" I ask. "Thalia. What's going on?"

She lets out a shaky breath. "Okay. Okay. You told me yesterday that it would be wiser to tell you what I know and hope for the council's mercy. But I can't live with myself if something happens and I don't prevent it. I'll tell you."

I feel another shiver run over my skin and set into my bones. *"Tell me what?*

"You didn't catch all of us."

"I know. We caught Laurent the other day, when he passed Keist."

"No." She shakes her head. "There were two others. Laurent, and Janus."

My blood runs cold and I stand up. "Janus Stenberg?"

She nods and reaches out a hand to me, trying to keep me in place.

"Please, listen to me," she says, her eyes wide. "He was the one who brought us here. The others, the young men, they had their own agenda. For Janus, it was personal. He was the one who ordered we go after Gabe, the son of the woman he says betrayed him. He was the one who forced me to attack."

I shake my head. "So he's somewhere on the island."

"Kieran, he's *at the cliffs.* He hung back from each attack because he didn't want his scent in the air, and this time Laurent stayed with him because he was injured at the common house. He told us several times that the eastern shore caves were the most remote place on the island, except the cliffs. That the cliffs were only ever used for the rite, a few times per year in the winter. If you found the caves, there's only one other place he'd go to hide."

I shake my head.

"But you've been in custody for weeks," I say. "There's not enough food up there for him to survive."

"We had brought food reserves. Not enough for this whole time, probably, but I wouldn't put it past him to find a way. If no boats have been stolen, if no one's left the island in the night, he's still here."

"*Ayagaayuni,*" I say. "Em. She's going up there."

"Emerson? His daughter?" she asks.

"Yes his fucking daughter," I snap. "But you knew that, didn't you? Wasn't that always part of the plan? Isn't that what you taunted me with, when I was first here? That you hope she's alright?"

She shakes her head again, her eyes wide. "He had no plans to see her. I only knew her name because he spoke of her once. I said it so you thought I knew something, in case it would spur you to speak with the council. The fact that you knew her was a lucky guess."

I'm barely listening, my mind doing the math. How long ago did Em leave? Could she have reached the ring already? Is there any way to stop her before she gets there?

"I'm sorry," she says, her voice panicked. "I would have told you before, if I'd known. I only heard from Ivo today that someone was doing the rite. Last I'd heard anything about it, you had said that Gabe couldn't do it anymore. I thought it was safe."

"*Takka*," I say, walking for the door.

"Kieran," she calls, as I reach the front door of the marshal's office.

I turn and give her a quick glance.

"Please. I told you this for my conscience, not for a deal. But please, don't forget about Nomi and me. Now that I've betrayed the others, if you don't let us stay—"

I shake my head and run out of the door.

40

EMERSON

I ground myself in my fighting stance, and the memory behind my father fades away, replaced just with the vibrancy of the *kiyyulit* surrounding me and my father.

Not my real father, I tell myself, studying his face. Just the image of him. It's not real. It's not real. It can't be real.

I let out a long, slow breath, and then he pounces.

His body hits me in seconds, slamming me into the ground, and in a jolt of adrenaline, my muscle memory takes over. There's no time to think, and the combinations I learned from Quinn just come out of me. I slam one foot into his left hip at the same time I crash my forearm into his throat. I see my arm crush the wind out of him, and as his hips turns inward on the side I hit, I use my arm on his throat and the power from my legs to get him off of me, pushing him onto his back into the ground on my left.

His legs are powerful enough to get me off of him, so I avoid them like Quinn taught and go straight for his exposed stomach. In one clean slice, I cut through his torso from chest to stomach, and then scramble back ten, twenty feet, waiting, regrouping. There's blood in the snow, on my hands, in the air. I wipe my hands on my pants, waiting, but he doesn't move.

This was too easy, I think. *It's not over. This isn't the real test.*

His body stays limp, motionless, and now the *kiyyulit* are dancing harder, faster, frenetic around me. They're enveloping me, swirling around my arms, over my hair like a breeze. I put out my blood-soaked hands in front of me, and I see the lights swirling around my wrists, through my fingers, dancing around the knife, and on my empty palm like heatless fire.

It really does feel like a breeze now, and I feel a brush behind my ear as Kieran's paper flower slips out, guided seemingly by the lights into my blood-stained palm.

"What's happening?" I whisper. I'm scared now, and instinctively I want my mom here, her wisdom with me.

And then I hear her voice.

"Emerson."

I look around, frantic. The lights are swirling around me faster and faster.

"Mom? Where are you?"

"When the moment comes, remember."

"Remember what?" I ask.

The lights are choking me, blinding me, coming so close that I can't see the ring anymore. Everything is light: green and blue and purple, brighter and brighter until they're white and I can't see anything.

"You have everything you need to do this. Be strong. Who you are is enough."

And then, in a snap, they're gone.

"Mom?" I ask, looking around. But the *kiyyulit* have disappeared, and now I'm standing in total darkness.

I can't see anything. It's so dark here that for a moment, I wonder if maybe I'm dead, and the beast of my father killed me in the ring. But I still hear the soft roar of the ocean far below the cliffs, and something else, too. A whine.

It takes a moment for my eyes to adjust, and it's so quiet up here, so dark. Finally, the edges of the rocks of the ring come into view. I look to the entrance of the ring and see that the massive body of my father's wolf, the memory of him, has faded.

I'm alone.

Or—am I?

I hear something. A rattling, a whisper. It's coming from the center of the ring.

I walk closer, the shape of something—a body, or some kind of wounded animal—coming into view. Its frame is large, but it's clearly sick, its breathing tearing through it too fast.

"What...?" I mutter, trying to get close enough to see without making myself vulnerable. At the sound of my voice, it snaps at me, furious, wicked. I can smell the *kattaka*, somehow, from somewhere far away.

I grip tighter onto my knife, taking the fighting stance, and realize as I hear the rustling of paper that the little flower is still resting in my other hand. I'm scared, and it's a different fear than when I saw the mirage of my father. That fear was frantic, rattling through me, close to the surface. This one is deep, primal, as though somehow my body knows something my mind does not. Stripped of the lights and any semblance of what's happening, I feel my own mortality closer than ever.

And then, as the beast turns its large yellow eyes to me and I see the scarring warping its face, a horrible realization slithers over my body, sinking into my skin, wrapping itself around my bones.

It's my father.

Not my father from memory. Not my father but from the *kiyyulit*. My actual father.

"What?" I gasp, my mind doing the math. Kieran's rite was

almost two months ago. There's no way he fought my father and that he's been up here this whole time, waiting. The cliffs are too remote, and there's not enough food up here to survive more than a few days.

At the sound of my voice, he barks at me, snapping. But his body is weak, and he can't seem to get up. I look closer. There's something wrong with his back; it's twisted. He seems sick, and I can see his ribs sticking out of his side, some kind of open wound. He looks close to death.

My mind races through possibilities. Is this a mirage, too? The trickery of the *kiyyulit*? But it can't be—the dark skies feel like a message, a confirmation from the ancestors that what's in front of me is real. But if that's the case, how did he get here?

He must have come to Saroe with the rest of the Remnant group. Maybe he came to the ring after the first few attacks. I try to piece it together. He would have been in the caves with the other man, Laurent, on the day of the fire. Laurent left, and for whatever reason, my dad was left behind with the marshals close by.

Where on Saroe would you go, if you had to hide? Where is the most remote place, where no one ever goes, except for this rite a few times a year?

My breathing is coming quick now as it all falls into place. He came here to hide. The same frost that delayed my rite by a week must have kept him from going down when he wanted to, to steal another boat or hurt more people. He's been trapped up here for—what is it now? A week? Maybe more? With nothing to eat but weeds and grass.

The smell of the *kattaka* in the air. It's him, I realize. He's been eating whatever he can find. The raw *kattaka* plant.

He's panting, panicked, and I step closer—close enough for him to see me now. I watch as something registers in his eyes as he looks at the knife and the blood on my hands, and then up at my face. He barks again, but it's not at me—it's like a cry of surprise, or fear.

"*Heij*. It's me," I say, without thinking.

He snaps again. He must be hallucinating from the *kattaka*. Maybe he saw the same thing I saw in those memories. But as I see the wild fear and confusion in his eyes, I realize who he thinks is in front of him.

"Not Lena," I whisper. "It's me, Dad. Emerson."

He pants, fearful. I swallow. I can see that he's sick. I think his spine may be broken, and there seems to be some wound in his side that looks infected, even from here. But he's still bigger than I am. If I get too close and he attacks—

You will have a choice to make, my mom had said.

He's an enemy to these islands. He came here to hurt our people.

He was an enemy to my mom, for all the love their marriage was supposedly once based on.

He's an enemy to me, isn't he?

You can't be mine, he'd whispered to me, his voice furious, wicked. *No daughter of mine would ever be so weak.*

But he's sick, and from the looks of the infection and the rapid rise and fall of his chest, I know he's close to death. It must have been days since he's had real food or water.

You will have a choice to make, Mom said.

My mind is racing. I may have enough energy to heal him. But if I do and he overtakes me, I won't have enough to fight back, and there's no one here with me to protect me now. It's just me and him in the ring. Even the ancestors have left me.

I look down at my blood-soaked hands: the knife in one, the paper flower in the other. You become an elder by defeating the adversary the ancestors bring you. If I save him, will my rite even count?

You will have a choice to make.

I swallow my fear, and I drop the knife in the snow, falling onto my knees beside him, pulling my bag to my side.

"I'm going to help you," I say. "I have food and clean water, and healing salve. I need you to lie still, okay? I need you to stay calm. I'm going to help."

41

KIERAN

I race to the cliffs in my wolf form, passing the common house. Saga, standing outside with Seb, seems to catch the scent of me in the wind and looks up. I force myself to shift back.

"Saga," I gasp. "Thalia told me Janus is here, on the island. He's hiding out in the cliffs."

"What?"

"We have to save her," I say, moving forward, about to shift back.

"Kieran, wait—" calls Saga.

"There's no time."

"You can't interrupt her rite," Saga says. "We've never—we've never had this before. If you help her, I don't know if we can consider it—"

"I don't give a fuck about the council seat right now, Saga. She's up there with her worst nightmare. We have to help her. If you're not coming with me, I'm going alone."

She glances at Seb, but before they can agree, I shift into my wolf and start sprinting for the cliffs. It takes an hour on foot, but if I'm in my wolf form, I can make it in maybe twenty minutes.

It's not enough time, I realize. She left almost two hours ago. It'll be too late.

He will find her, Lena's spirit said. *You can't save her*. And *agaayu*, I know with everything in me that she was right. I can feel it in the ether, somehow—that this was how the ancestors wanted it. That whatever grand and horrible thing is unfolding for her in that ring is the way it was supposed to be. Without me there to defend her.

No. I sprint faster, harder, trying to outrun time. Somewhere in the back of my mind I register Seb and Saga shift far behind me, both running towards the cliffs, too. There may be more behind them, but they're too far for me to register, and I *will not* stop. I can't. I know I can't save her, but I have to try.

As I run, faster and harder than I ever have, for lack of anything else I can do, I pray. I pray to the *agaayit*, the gods to who made her, who knew her before her soul had a body, who watched every day of her life and every moment that led her here. I ask them for time. Not just for me, to get to her before she's hurt. But for more time with her.

I reach the first, then the second bend in the path to the cliffs, and it's only then that I realize the sky is dark. The *kiyyulit* were out earlier, weren't they? They had to be, for her rite. The realization of their absence sinks into my bones like a bad omen.

You can't save her, Lena said. *You can't save her. You can't save her.*

For every time I hear those words, I make myself remember what Emerson whispered to me: *We have time. We have time. We have time.*

I want it, need it to be true. I need more days with her; more mornings waking up together, pulling her close to me in the early hours, when the sky is still pink and there's a mist over the hills. More winter evenings sitting next to her by the fire. More summers under the sun in the back garden, hearing her laugh.

More and more and more, a thousand moments. A thousand arguments, even. All the time she believed we could count on.

We have the rest of our lives, she'd said. And I beg the *agaayit* not to cut hers short.

The exhaustion is starting to set into my body, but I make myself keep going, and that's when I see it. Somewhere far ahead, coming down from the ring, is a shadow. It walks deliberately, but I see a weight in the gait that doesn't match the way Emerson walks.

Agaayu, agaayu, *it's too late. I couldn't get there in time.*

As I get nearer, the shape of the shadow becomes more clear. And then I realize: it's someone holding a body. As I get close, the smell of blood hits my nostrils, then the scent of something else. Sickness, sweat.

I snarl, barking. *Get your goddamn hands off her body*, I want to shout. I want to kill him. I want to tear him limb from limb. I want to make good on the promise I made Thalia weeks ago, before all this: that there won't be enough of him back to send to the southern isles in a box.

But as I get closer, it registers somewhere in my wolf's mind before it hits mine: it's not Emerson's blood I smell in the air. And as I get close enough to make it out, I realize.

It's Em walking down the hill. And the body she's carrying is her father.

Her hands are bloody, and I can see the sweat and determination on her face. The adrenaline in me is too high to give form to happiness or relief. As I reach her, I shift back into my human form, panting.

"Em. Oh my God, Em. You're okay. What—oh my God."

I look down. The wolf in her arms is massive but skeletal. I realize he's still breathing.

"He's sick," she says, her voice betraying the strain in her voice. "But he's gonna be okay."

"Em—I—what the fuck?" I ask. I'm still gasping, trying to

catch my breath, and my brain can't quite catch up. She's walking forward, careful with every step. "I... what? Did you fight him?"

"I fought a version of him," she says. "But then the lights—I don't know. They were all around me, and I heard my mom's voice. And then they disappeared and he was there in the ring. The real him."

I put an arm out to stop her, but she shakes her head and keeps walking. The wolf in her arms groans, and I find myself filled by a wave of loathing.

"He's not in his right mind," she says, noting me looking at him. "There's not enough plants to eat up there, to survive, and he's eaten a lot of unprocessed *kattaka*. I gave him water, and it must have activated some of it. He probably can't even hear us right now."

"Is he dying?" I ask. He reeks of infection.

"Not anymore. When I got there, yes. He has a bad back injury and an infected wound, and he's starving and dehydrated on top of that. He wouldn't have made it another day. I healed him enough to carry him back to the infirmary, but I needed to save enough of my own energy to bring him back down."

"I... but Em. Stop. Why would you save him?" I ask. "This is the man who killed your mother. Who hurt *you*."

"Because he needed help," she says, her voice labored. "I don't care what he did. It could have been anyone. I wasn't going to let him die up there."

She shifts his weight in her arms, and I see the strain in her face.

"I... Here, let me help you," I say, reaching for him.

"*No*," she snaps. "No. I need to do this. I have to do this myself."

I'm surprised at the tone of her voice, but I see it in her face. She has to do this.

"Do you want me to shift? You can ride on my back. We'll get to the infirmary faster."

She shakes her head. "No. I have to do this myself. I need to carry him down the mountain."

"Okay," I say weakly.

I shift beside her, falling back a few paces to walk behind. This is her rite, and it's her choice. So she takes the moment for herself, and I watch as she carries her father's broken body down to safety.

I don't understand it, and it's not the choice I would have made. But it's Em, through and through. Knowing how to love people better than any of us.

Proving to me again that she's stronger than I am.

42

KIERAN

We encounter Seb and Saga on the way down, but they see me walking behind Em and follow suit. As we near the infirmary, we all shift and follow Em inside, Seb pulling some clothes from the box at the entrance for us to put on.

When we enter the infirmary room, it's like a wind storm. The room's edges are full of frantic energy: Helen and a few healers in training rushing around, getting items Em is asking for: gauze, salve, disinfectant. And at the eye of the storm, completely still, is Em. She's standing in front of the bed where her father's wolf lies. As we walk in, Saga immediately joins the busy fray, and I stand back, watching.

Em stands tall, her head held high, the braid around her head looser now but still intact. There are wisps of loose hair around her face and neck, some sticking to her face with sweat, others curling away. Her clothes and hands are stained with blood, and she's giving orders to everyone else in the room.

I've never seen her like this. She's leading without asking, without apology. Helen comes forward holding gauze and tries to push Em out of the way, but Em stops her.

"No. I'm doing this."

She raises her hand above her father's wound and closes her eyes. I see something in her posture change just slightly. Her core seems to tuck in and I see her lower her chin, like the back of her head is being pulled up by an invisible string. Then she begins to whisper.

I'm too far away to hear what it is, but I can tell from here that it's Fakari. And as she begins muttering, the whole room goes still.

Between her hand and her father's stomach, a little wisp of energy begins to form. At first it looks like a small blue flame, dancing between her skin and his. But it grows thicker, and then it's green and purple and blue, dancing. It looks like the *kiyyulit*.

I hear a whisper ripple through the room. We all watch in confusion and bewilderment as the wound under Em's hand slowly begins to disappear. The lights grow stronger, brighter, dancing more fervently. Within a minute, the wound is gone.

"How are you doing that?" Helen asks, but Em ignores her, still whispering. Her words come faster together, and her hand moves from the gash in his side to the mangled twisting of his spine.

I feel a wave of shock wash over me as I realize what she's trying to do. Bone healing is a long-lost art. She can't be...

The lights between her hand and his body grow brighter, so bright they hurt my eyes. Her father whines on the table, and I can see that whatever's happening is growing in intensity, nearing some kind of end. Em's voice grows louder, more rhythmic, and her eyes flicker open, the gaze in them hollow. Her father barks out in pain and Em twists her eyes shut tight, as though she's pooling all her concentration and effort. Then, suddenly, the light under her hand flashes outwards as a soft *boom* echoes through the room.

The infirmary is completely silent, everyone staring wordlessly at Emerson. She looks up, her gaze empty. Exhausted.

"I gave him some water, but he's still probably dehydrated," she says, her voice weak. "And he'll be out of his mind for at least the next day from the unprocessed *kattaka*. You should have someone here, and tie him to the bed, for when he comes to."

"Emerson—" Helen says.

"I don't want to see him. But if he asks who saved him, I want him to know it was me."

"Okay," Saga gently.

"I'm going to go home and sleep," Em says, and I can hear the exhaustion in her voice. "We can talk about what it means for my rite in the morning."

She starts walking towards me, her feet shuffling. Behind her, I can see her father panting, his eyes looking around frantically. His back no longer looks twisted, and though he's still thin and matted, the wound being gone makes him look almost like a different animal entirely.

How the hell did she do that?

"Emerson, no—you should rest here, in the infirmary," says Saga.

But Em shakes her head, walking past her.

"No. I want him far away from me," she whispers as she walks to me. I take her hand and lead her to the front door, waving Saga away as she tries to approach. As soon as Em and I get out of the door to the infirmary, her knees buckle, and I catch her upper body as she falls forward.

"Take me home?" she whispers.

"Yeah," I murmur into her hair. "You want me to shift?"

She shakes her head, but she's clearly exhausted, so I gently reach down to scoop her up, carrying her against my chest.

It's a ten minute walk to the *fikarig*, and she rests her head against me as I start on the path towards the house. It's unnaturally dark outside without the light of stars or the *kiyyulit*, and after a minute, I think she's fallen asleep. But then she reaches into her pocket and pulls out the little paper flower. I see the petals are stained with blood.

"Thank you," she says.

"I'll get you a new one. It was probably stupid to give you this just before hand-to-hand combat."

"No. I loved it." She rests her head against my chest again. "I did it, Kier. I beat him. But I did it my own way."

"Yeah, you did." I say, drawing her close to my chest. Within minutes, she's asleep.

43

KIERAN

When I wake up, Em is still sleeping.

I look over at her, resting beside me in bed. Her face is wan and tired; I can see the circles under her eyes, even now, a full day later. The tone of her skin has turned gray and pallid, and the fever from the *kattaka* working its way out of her system has stained her hair dark with sweat. She hardly looks herself, and I can feel the wolf inside my chest pacing at the sight of it.

I roll onto my side, pulling myself closer to her. It's the second morning since the night of her rite. I hate that she's still so out of it, but Saga has been reminding me it's normal—that this happened to me, too, and I was just too sick to be aware of it. The *fikarig* has been overactive with people coming to tend to her: Saga swapping out the bucket beside the bed for when she gets sick; Maren bringing a cool cloth to her head every few hours; Helen checking her body for wounds to heal. They all share their love and concern for her, but as soon as they leave the room, I hear the murmurs from the hallway.

What does this mean for her rite? Does it still count?

How did she learn to heal bone?

I know Gabe, at least, has answers to the second question, but I haven't mentioned it to the others. If Em wanted to wait to share this, then I'll leave it up to her.

I rest my head on my arm, eyeing her profile. She shifts just slightly, and I can tell she's starting to wake up.

"*Heij,*" I whisper.

She groans, bringing a hand to her head.

"*Mmh,*" she grumbles.

"Your head hurts?"

Em opens one bleary eye and turns her head to look at me.

"Kier?" she mumbles, her voice hoarse.

"Yeah. I'm here. You're okay."

"I'm home?" she asks.

"Yeah. You didn't want to stay in the infirmary, so they let you recover here. Does your head hurt? I can get you something."

She hesitates, as through processing the information.

"Did I do it?" she asks.

"Yeah, *piu,*" I say, bringing a hand to her face. "You did it."

"Even though…"

Her voice trails off, and I feel a sinking in my gut.

"You did your rite," I say. "They're still figuring out what it means for the council seat, and they didn't want to decide before talking to you. But you did it, *piu.* And you deserve to be an elder."

She nods again, closing her eyes and leaning her face into the palm of my hand. I can tell my words don't quite reach her.

"What do you need?" I whisper. "Food? Water? More rest?"

She shakes her head softly, and I see her breath grow heavier again.

"Okay. I think water would be good, so I'm gonna go get some for when you're up more. You stay here and rest. I'll be back in a bit."

She nods wordlessly, and I climb out of bed and make my way to the stairs, leaving the door open a bit to let some of the stale air out. As I shuffle down, I can hear voices from the kitchen.

"*Heij*," I say, walking in to see who's seated around the table. Seb, Saga, Gabe. "Em's up."

"Yeah? How's she feeling?" asks Gabe. His face is gray, too, though not from Em's rite or the aftermath. He hasn't been the same since we spoke to Thalia a few days ago, and I've been too in my own world to ask about it.

"To soon to say," I say. "She just woke up, and I think she's going back to sleep. But I thought I'd get her water for when she's awake again."

"Ah, good," says Saga, standing. "She needs to rehydrate after the *kattaka*, and she couldn't keep anything down last night. Let me make some with salt and sugar, to help."

I nod and she walks to the fridge, getting out a jug of filtered water and setting it on the counter. As she reaches for the salts above the stove, I take a seat at the table beside Seb.

"What were you guys talking about?"

He shakes his head barely perceptibly, and Gabe looks at me.

"Janus is starting to come to this morning," he says. "The council needs to decide what to do with him and the others. Mom's called a vote tomorrow night about sending them back. *All* of them."

I glance over my shoulder at Saga, standing at the counter.

"Thalia was the one who told me he was on the cliffs," I say. "She did that for Em's safety, not for her own self-interest. That changes things."

"Does it?" Saga asks, turning around. "Because last I checked, she still attacked our shores and hurt my son. And Emerson didn't need you to intervene—she survived on her own."

I feel myself bristle, and I can see Gabe's posture tighten.

"But Thalia had no way of knowing that, and neither did we," I say. "She alerted us to a threat."

"And if we send her and her sister back with them now, they'll be torn apart," says Gabe. "The others already know she met with Kieran. It's a death sentence."

"She should have thought of that before she hurt you," Saga says.

"*Ama*," he says, his voice low. "You can't mean that. You can't possibly think she deserves to die for what happened to me."

Saga looks up at him, and I watch something in her face change.

"It's not like you, *Aja*," I say. *Aunt.* "Didn't you say we need to think about the good of the islands? We have to look beyond our own *fika*."

"And besides," says Seb. "You fought so hard for Maren to come here. And look how much good she's brought all of us."

"That was different," Saga snaps. "She's family."

An awkward silence falls at the table, and I glance over at Seb. I can see Gabe from the corner of my eye, seething, and I know this conversation is only going to get worse, so I change the subject.

"You went looking at new *fikarigs* the other day, right?" I ask. "How'd it go?"

Seb shrugs. "Fine. We saw one we kind of liked, but it wasn't exactly what we're looking for. But there's another we're going to tomorrow that looks promising. It's close to the salt plant, and there's a shed in the back you could use for woodworking, and a garden for Em. It's out of our original budget, but with how well things are going…"

I nod, glancing over at Gabe again. He's glowering at his mother, and the energy in the kitchen is palpably tense. If both our businesses are thriving, at least it means we can get out of here soon.

"Sounds good. Let me know how it is," I say.

"You guys'll be back in time for the vote though, right?" Gabe asks tersely.

Seb nods, and behind me, Saga comes over and sets the pitcher on the table.

"For Emerson," she says, her voice tight.

I nod and get up. *Takkagaayu*—anything to get out of here.

I grab the pitcher and an empty glass from one of the cabinets, then head back up stairs. When I near the top, I can see Em in bed, half sitting up against a nest of pillows.

"*Heij*," I say, walking in. "You're up. That's great."

"I feel awful," she says, her voice still hoarse.

"You've been through a lot."

She nods, and I set the pitcher and glass down on the bedside table next to her, on top of her healer's textbook. I pour her a glass, and she picks it up, gagging after she takes a sip.

"Yeah, sorry, I should have mentioned. Saga added salt and sugar for rehydration."

I take a seat on the bed beside her, and Em forces the rest of the glass down, then looks up at me.

"Is my dad…?" she asks.

"He's waking up, I heard. I don't know how lucid he is. But he made it. I saw how sick he was when you brought him down. I don't think he'd still be alive if it weren't for you."

She nods, eyeing the glass in her hands.

"How did he make it?" I ask. "After we saw the caves, I was convinced it couldn't have been him."

"I saw some of his memories when I healed him," she says. "They barely had enough food to make it. The other man, the younger one, stole a bag of nuts towards the end, and my dad had to leave. The fire was his last act, before he made it to the cliffs."

"You saw all that?" I ask, and she nods.

"When I heal a bone break, I can see how it happened. I saw him slip on ice when he tried to leave the ring, during the week of the frost. That's how he hurt his back, and why he had to stay up there. I saw other stuff, too. Deeper wounds…"

I nod, waiting, but she doesn't elaborate, and I don't ask.

"I'm sorry I didn't tell you about the bone healing," she says finally. "I was still trying to figure it out. Still am."

"No," I say, shaking my head. "I get it. I mean, yeah… it's huge. How did you figure it out?"

She tells me about her weeks without me on Halluk, and the way she built up her healing skill with Gabe.

"I think it all kind of flowed into each other," she says. "FMA training with Quinn, my shifter practice with Seb, healing with Gabe. It's like it all kind of came together and helped me navigate this when the ancestors made it possible."

"So it's not you doing it?" I ask. "You think it's the ancestors?"

She hesitates. "I don't know. I don't think I'm the first healer in generations to do this because I figured out mindfulness, if that's what you're asking." She cracks a weak smile. "It's something I'm doing, but I'm only doing it because they let me."

"Maybe it's both," I say. "Maybe they're making it possible, but it also *had* to be you."

"Why me, though? What did I do?"

I swallow, thinking. "I don't know. I was thinking about what you told me in the library, about how Saga couldn't heal your dad's face after what he did to your mom. But *you* were able to heal him—not just to save him from scarring, but save his life—when he hurt you so much worse. Maybe you're the person the ancestors trusted to bring this back, because they thought you'd use it the right way."

I see her chew the inside of her cheek, thinking. After a minute, her brow furrows, and I reach for the glass from her hands and pour her more water. She takes it from me and takes another few sips, wincing at the taste.

"We shouldn't be talking about this now," I say. "You need to rest. Do you think you could eat anything? I can get you some crackers from downstairs. Or those awful Triscuits Maren got you. She left another box here somewhere."

Em shakes her head, closing her eyes and leaning back against the pillows. "I just want to lie down for a while."

"Okay. I'll let you rest. Oh, and hey, one more thing."

"Yeah?" She looks up.

"There's a council meeting tomorrow about what to do with the rebels, including your dad. I figure you don't want to be there, but I just wanted to let you know, in case there's anything you want me to say—"

"I want to be there," she says, setting her glass down and turning to her side.

"Yeah? We can see how you feel first."

"I want to be there."

"Okay," I say, standing up and brushing her hair back from her face as she closes her eyes. "Sounds good."

44

EMERSON

I feel better the following day. Not *all* the way better—but, as I remind Kieran, I'm already one day farther into my recovery than he was that night in the library. He helps me get dressed that evening for the council meeting, and he, Gabe, and I walk slowly to the common house.

"How did Saga react when you told her about your leg?" I ask, gesturing to it. They removed the cast without me yesterday morning.

"No big reaction," Gabe says, his steps still a little unsteady. The bone has healed, but the muscle is still weak after six weeks of rest. "I think you kind of gave away the big reveal with your display in the infirmary."

I smile. "Not really the plan. Sorry."

"Don't say sorry to me," he says. "I'm not the one with hundreds of years of island tradition crashing down on her shoulders. If anything, I'm sorry for *you*."

"Did you talk with Seb about it?" I ask, and Gabe shakes his head.

"No. Not yet."

I nod and look up ahead, where the common house is coming more clearly into view. There's a small crowd milling in, and I see Saga's Jeep parked in front, with Maren climbing out of the front seat. Beside me, Kieran lifts an arm to wave at them. Maren looks up and waves back excitedly, then gives a big thumbs-up.

Oh, right—they were visiting a new *fikarig* today. I guess from her signal that this one looked good, but with the weight of tonight's vote, I won't be able to ask for details until later. I smile at her, and she and Seb duck into the common house.

We walk up the steps behind them and enter. It's later than we planned to get here—my energy is still low, and between Gabe's leg and me, it took longer to walk here than we thought. The majority of the elders are already seated in their spots around the ring, and the hall is fuller than usual. As we enter, I hear a hush fall over the room.

I look around, trying to see what it is. But most of them are staring at *me*.

"Told you," Gabe says under his breath. I smile nervously and reach for Kieran's hand as we make our way to our seats.

Kier leads me to a spot near the head of the council, next to where Seb usually sits. Seb is already seated, with Maren behind to listen. Instinctively I want to sit next to her, behind Kier. But it takes me a second to remember that I'm an elder now—or, at least, I think so. Kieran grabs a cushion and seats it next to himself, beckoning for me to sit. Hesitantly, I do, and Gabe moves across the room to his seat behind Saga's usual spot. Saga herself is sitting at the head of the council today, calling the meeting to order.

"Good evening," she says, looking around the room. "We have two big topics on the table tonight, so I don't want to waste any time. Wim, the council secretary, is taking the minutes, and I see we have more than enough elders for a quorum. With that said, I'd like to turn our attention to the first issue on the table: that of our newest potential elder, Emerson."

I blink, glancing around. I hadn't prepared for any talk about my rite this evening, and I'm surprised to hear her mention it.

"Emerson's rite was unusual—both in that she returned with a person she rescued, and in that there was an effort to help her during her rite. We don't have a precedent for how to deal with this, but I don't think we need to turn it into a big discussion. After rereading the *Eijna*, the case seems pretty clear to me. Emerson." She turns to me, her eyes warm.

"Did the ancestors bring you an adversary in the ring?"

"Yes," I say, thinking of the version of my dad I fought first.

"And, without telling us what it was—did you overcome that adversary?"

I nod.

"Say it out loud, *piu*," she says softly. "For the secretary."

"Oh. Yes," I say again. "I did."

"And had you made your way out of the ring before anyone came to help you?"

"Yes."

"Then this fulfills the expectations set forth in the *Eijna*. The council affirms the validity of your rite. Congratulations, elder."

I feel a flush of warmth in my cheeks as the sound of gentle applause fills the room. Saga smiles, and I feel my inner wolf sit up happily. I don't know what I was nervous about—of course she'd see to it that my rite would count. It's Saga.

"I'm afraid that leads us to our next topic, which I suspect will be more contentious," she says, looking around the room. "We called this special meeting to order because we need to decide what to do with the rebels who made their way to our shores six weeks ago. Since we caught the first of them, we've kept them in the basement downstairs, waiting for a decision. We now know we have them all—including Janus Stenberg, a former Fakari pack member."

I glance over at Kieran, beside me.

"I think it's time to make a decision," Saga says. "The longer we keep them here, the longer they benefit from our hospitality. I move to send them back to the southern islands."

"Wait a moment," says Ingela, an elder across the circle from us. "Is that wise? They're radicals. If we let them return to their home islands, they'll just have the chance to regroup and come back stronger."

"Then we strengthen our own defenses," Saga says. "We cannot afford to keep them here. We don't have the infrastructure for prisoners. Nor am I interested in housing and feeding them with our resources."

"We're hardly feeding them," Kieran grumbles beside me.

Saga looks at him admonishingly. The warmth in her eyes when she spoke about my rite is gone, and I find myself unnerved by it.

"Isn't it—" I say, but my voice comes out weaker than I want it to. I clear my throat. "Is there another way to send them away without sending them home?"

My uncle Viggo, sitting beside Saga at the head of the council, shakes his head. "Not short of death."

"Or sending them to the mainland undocumented," adds Dagmar. "Which is almost worse."

I swallow, thinking. "And what about the Nayakka sisters?"

Saga shakes her head. "I see no reason they should be any different."

"No, hang on," says Kieran, next to me. "She traded her security for Em's safety. She told us Janus was here, knowing it could cost her her life once the other prisoners learned."

"At the last possible second, after it could make any difference," Saga says, shaking her head. "Anyone who came here as a terrorist should be sent back."

"*Ama*, this is insane," Gabe says from across the room. "You're not thinking clearly. I've read their petitions—this is clearly a different situation for her and her sister than the others."

I see Dagmar and Viggo glance at each other, and something registers in my mind. While Viggo looks stern, Dagmar's face is sympathetic, uncertain. A part of her agrees with Gabe.

"*You* are not thinking clearly," Saga says. "Your heart is too big. You're letting your compassion blind you to what's best for the islands."

"And you're letting what happened with Dad cloud your vision."

A ripple of surprise goes through the crowd, and the room goes silent. *No one* talks about Ben Taguit—not even Saga, his widow.

Saga sets her jaw, staring at her son. I can feel the anger in the air.

"These people need our protection, *Ama*," Gabe says, his voice gentler now.

"*We* need to be protected from *them*. I'm raising it to a vote. We'll decide for each group. First, the others. We cannot afford to sustain the prisoners on our islands indefinitely, and we don't have a proper place to keep them. I propose we send all those *but* the Nayakka sisters back to the southern isles, and I'll bring a proposal for heightened defenses next week. All those in favor, raise your hands."

I glance around the room. Slowly I see hands begin to raise, including those of Seb and Kieran. I raise my own hand, still half-uncertain. But we can't keep them here, right?

Saga counts, and I see Wim checking the count behind her. Once she's done, she nods.

"And against?"

A trickle of hands comes up, but clearly fewer than before. Saga and Wim conduct the count, and she clears her throat.

"68 to 18. It's decided—we send the rebels back to the south. I'll inform the marshals and we'll see that it happens this week."

"And the Nayakka sisters?" Gabe asks, his voice growing louder. "We can't treat them the same. They asked for our asylum again and again, and were denied. They came here with the rebels as a last resort, and Thalia traded her security for Em's life without even knowing her. We have to treat it differently."

Saga bristles, about to speak.

"*Ama,*" Gabe snaps.

I look over, surprised. I never see him angry—Gabe and Seb have an argument every few years, and honestly, it's always Seb at fault. But this is personal for him, clearly, and I think maybe I know what's pushing him.

I swallow, thinking about the little girl with the big dark eyes from his memory. If Gabe is right and this is about Ben for Saga, then maybe for him, it's about Ilse, the girl I saw in his memories.

"What's the alternative, then?" Saga asks. "We let them *live* here, among us?"

"Yes. We give them shelter, which they asked for in the first place."

"Or just freedom," Kier says beside me. "We don't need to house and feed them. Thalia says she wants to work for herself. We can just allow them to live here."

"I raise it to a vote," Saga says, her voice cold. "All those in favor of letting these two women—who razed a field of sheep, attacked the harbor, and hurt an innocent man in this very room —live among us in peace?"

"*Ama,*" Gabe says, his voice withering, and I find myself growing similarly frustrated. Isn't the idea behind the rite that it helps you see past your own interests? It feels like Saga can't treat this like a normal vote.

Beside me, Kieran and Seb raise their hands, and I do, too. I haven't met Thalia, but after what Kieran has told me, I know enough. I watch as a ring of hands goes up—fewer than for the first vote, clearly, but still a significant part of the room. I feel a patter of anxiety begin in my chest as Saga and Wim do the count.

"42. All those in favor of sending them back home with the other terrorists?"

"—knowing that they may be *killed* for the information they gave us to help Emerson," Gabe interjects.

A ring of hands slowly goes up, Saga and Viggo among them. I look at Aunt Dagmar, silently willing her to keep her hand lowered and abstain. But she glances at Viggo and then slowly raises her hand, too.

Saga counts, then looks at Wim to confirm. After a moment, she turns back to the group.

"42 to 42—an even split. If we cannot decide in favor of keeping them here, precedent says we send them away."

"No, stop," says Gabe. "What about the family exception?"

"What?"

"The family exception." He rises to his feet, struggling slightly to get up on his weaker leg. "When Maren wanted to come here, the decision to let her onto the islands was a tie. The tie-breaker was that you, as her family, agreed to take her in as your ward. We make exceptions for family."

"That's irrelevant," Saga says, waving a hand. "The Nayakkas have no family on the Fakaris."

"But they could," he says.

I feel a shiver go through me as I realize what he's implying.

"*Tekanni*," Saga says, her brow furrowing. *My son.* "What are you saying?"

"If she were to find a mate on the islands—someone to marry her—both she and her sister would become family, and they would be able to stay."

"But she hasn't," she says, and I can hear the edge of fear in her voice.

"But she could," Gabe says. "If I marry her. If I make her my mate."

The whole room goes quiet, and I feel a ripple of shock rush over me.

"Gabe," I whisper, and he looks over at me. I shake my head —*Don't do this*. A mate bond is forever. To tie yourself to someone you don't even love means sacrificing your one chance at happiness with the person who's meant for you.

But Gabe turns away and looks back at his mom.

"*Tekanni*, don't be foolish," Saga says, her eyes serious. "This is the woman who hurt you. How could you possibly have fallen in love with her?"

"I haven't, but that doesn't matter. Giving her and her sister shelter on these islands is the right thing to do. I've read her asylum pleas—*all* of them. I've heard her speak to Kieran. I know she told him what he needed to keep Emerson safe, even though it gained her nothing."

"Emerson would have been safe regardless."

"But she might *not* have been. And in a moment of hesitation, this woman's humanity won out. Can't ours?"

Saga shakes her head. "I cannot let you do this."

"I don't need your permission."

She blinks, and I can scent her rage in the air.

"No son of mine will bring a terrorist under my roof, no matter *how* noble his reasons."

"Then we'll live somewhere else. We have three elder seats now. We've been looking at *fikarigs*."

The room falls to silence as we all stare at the two of them, seeing whose will wins out. I look at Saga—my mentor, one of the people in the world I consider family.

She won't make him do this, right? She won't let him throw away his chance at a true mate just to bring this woman and her sister to the islands.

I glance around the room, silently begging even a single person to change their vote in favor of the Nayakkas staying. If we can get a majority, the sisters can stay here without Gabe throwing his one shot at love away.

But Saga shakes her head.

"We send the rebels out this week. If you haven't marked her as your mate by then, she and her sister will be on that boat. And if you have…"

She swallows. "Don't come home, *tekanni*."

And with that, she ends the council meeting.

45

EMERSON

Three weeks later

"*Heij.* I want to show you something."

Kieran looks up at me from the heavy wooden dresser he's moving. His red-brown hair, pulled back in a little knot, is damp with sweat, and I can see he's slightly out of breath with the effort of moving the furniture.

Our new *fikarig* is still half-empty, but with the influx of Kieran's pieces and the items Maren has been ordering, it's starting to feel like home. Tonight's the first night we'll all be staying here together.

Well, most of us. The aftermath of Gabe's decision has caused some awkward shuffling of sleeping arrangements, since he wasn't welcome at the old *fikarig* after the council meeting where he announced he'd claim Thalia as his mate. Pretty soon the rest of us didn't feel welcome, either. Gabe's spent the last few weeks crashing at Kieran's studio, and the Nayakka sisters have been staying at Quinn's apartment while she stayed with a friend. I've

319

met Nomi twice now, but Thalia still refuses to meet with any of us. I highly doubt either of them will be moving in tonight, even though technically they'll live here.

"What is it?" Kieran asks, wiping the sweat from his brow.

I hold out a hand playfully, eyeing him. "Come. I'll show you."

He grins, looking me up and down, knowing something's up. He walks forward and takes my hand, and I lead him up the stairs, to the second floor landing and towards the part of the new *fikarig* that's meant for us.

It's a gorgeous house—all hardwood floors and tall, arched windows to let in the light. I never imagined I'd live in a place like this after growing up in the little fisherman's hut my parents shared near the eastern shore. But with how well Saroan Salts has been doing, and the success of Kieran's work these last few years, our budget was way higher than we first thought. Sometimes as Maren and I laugh in the sun room downstairs, or take a walk in the garden together, I have to remind myself that this is real.

Our part of the house is a three-bedroom section on the far end of the second floor. I pull Kieran behind me, intertwining my fingers with his as I lead him to the door of our new bedroom.

"Okay. Close your eyes," I say, turning around to look at him.

He does as told, a small smile tugging at the edge of his lips. He looks so beautiful, standing there like that, and for a second I take in the curves and angles of his face; the soft edges of his beard and the freckles sprayed over his cheeks and forehead, darkening now that we're heading into spring. I want to remember all of it—commit this moment to memory. And though I'd planned to show him the room right away, I can't help myself. I bring my arms up around his neck and lean him down to kiss me.

He wraps his strong arms around me, pulling me into him.

"Is this the surprise?" he murmurs against my mouth.

I shake my head and reach for the door handle behind me, pressing down and pushing the door open.

"No. Look."

Kier looks up at the room behind me, and I watch his face as his eyes widen. He and Seb moved the bed and mattress in last night, but Maren and I spent the whole morning decorating with things we've been finding for the last few weeks. I don't have to look behind me to know what he's seeing. Soft linen sheets on the bed in different shades of ocean blue and deep teal. A little dark wood bench at the foot of the bed, with some yellow pillows and a blanket artfully placed on top (styled by Maren, of course, who wouldn't even let me sit on the bench until after Kieran had seen everything). Above the bed we've hung a large painting of the ocean, and across the room, I set up a full-length mirror next to a leafy green tree and a gorgeous wooden dresser Caspar made.

"Em. It's beautiful," he says, walking in past me.

"No white sheets," I say proudly. "And no duffle bag under the bed, you can check. I'm here for real. Together with you."

He turns around to face me, and I see his eyes go to something above my head.

"Oh, and look," I continue, gesturing to the wooden dresser. "Quite an upgrade from the chair where you had to keep your clothes, huh?"

But Kieran doesn't react, and instead he walks towards me, eyeing the wall next to the door frame. I turn around, following his gaze. Hanging there is the painting I made of us at the quarry years ago, mounted in the wooden frame he gave me for my last birthday.

"You hung it up," he says, eyeing the painting. "I thought you didn't like it."

"What, the frame?" I take his hand as he eyes it. "No, I loved it. It was so thoughtful. I just—I don't know. The drawing made me sad. It was us on the night you left."

"It was us on the night I first kissed you," he says, looking down at me.

I nod. "Yeah, I guess. But I didn't like looking at it for a long time. It made me sad to remember."

"Not anymore?"

I shake my head. "Not anymore. Those years aren't wasted to me, remember? They brought us here. To this house. To our future."

I take his hands in mine, rubbing my thumbs over the backs of his palms. He's still wearing my black hair tie around his wrist, though it's starting to come loose at the place where the two ends of the elastic come together. We're going to have to get him a new one, one of these days. Or maybe something a little more permanent.

"I have something for you, too," he says. "I was gonna save it for later, but maybe now's the right time."

"Yeah?" I ask, looking up.

He nods and leads me downstairs, then out the garden door across the wide expanse of green, and to the little wooden shed Seb suggested he can use for woodworking. Kieran's still keeping the workshop he has in town, but since we're living on the other side of Moon Lake now, we thought it might be nice to have another place for him to work.

He puts his back against the doors of the shed, grabbing the handles of the doors behind him. I can see his Adam's apple bob in his throat.

"What's going on?" I ask. "What is this?"

"I made you something," he says. "I started working on it when I came back to Saroe, when you and the others were still on Halluk. But I think, in a way... I think I've been working on it a lot longer than that."

"Okay," I say quietly.

"I... Wait, I don't know. Maybe I should do this another time," he says.

"No, no," I say, stepping forward. "Let me see."

He nods hesitantly, then turns to the doors, pulling them apart.

I feel the air escape my lungs. There, in the middle of the woodworking shed, is an arch. It's beautiful: four pillars reaching up to a canopy above, the wood carved to look like twisting vines. It's painted gold, and I can see that he's carved different designs into the pillars. Wrapped around the canopy on top and coming down over the corners of the beams are hundreds of paper flowers in different shades of vibrant purple and violet.

Rhodoras.

"Kieran," I breathe, stepping forward and reaching out a hand to one of the beams. "It's gorgeous."

"It's us," he says quietly, as my hand reaches for one of the carvings. "It's our different moments. Look, here. The quarry."

I eye the delicate shapes he's etched into the beam. He's right: there we are, our profiles in view as we look out at the rocks over the water.

"And here, at Moon Lake," he says, pointing to a different beam. I see us in the water, my arms wrapped around his neck as we're facing each other. He's carved ripples in the water around us, and I can see the shore and the setting sun etched to look like they're in the distance.

I look over the different beams, my eyes stinging. There's dozens of scenes carved into the wood. It's us. It's our story.

"And look. Sunflowers," he says, pointing to the top of the arches where they blend to meet the canopy above. He's carved golden flowers, thick and strong, into the place where the wood meets. "Because of the pattern on that sweater you wear."

"Cinnamon?" I ask, noticing little bundles of cinnamon sticks he's carved along the base of the arches.

"For how you make coffee." His voice wavers with nerves, and I look up at him.

"It's how my mom made it. And the paper rhodoras, for what you gave me for my rite," I whisper.

"No. Well, yeah, also. But also because, when you were still on Halluk…" He swallows and runs a hand over his hair. "I don't know. I missed you, and I wanted some part of you close to me. You told me about your mom's favorite poem, so I bought a poetry collection at Heimig's bookshop. And when I started reading them and I finally got to that one, I realized… it's about you, to me."

"Tell me," I say softly, stepping closer. He's still visibly nervous, and I find myself smiling as he reaches for his back pocket, looking for something.

"I—Sorry, I was gonna prepare better for this. I wasn't planning on doing this today, but I just… Hang on, let me find it."

He turns around, looking at the tables behind him, where his tools are laid out neatly, not yet used in this space. Finally, he seems to spot it—a small blue clothbound book sitting on the far end of the table. He grabs it, then walks back to me, opening to the right page.

"The poet finds a rhodora plant in the woods," he says. "He's amazed by its beauty—even the petals falling from it make the dark water on the ground beautiful. And he realizes from seeing it that its beauty isn't wasted. Here," he reads aloud. "*'Beauty is its own excuse for being.'*"

Kieran looks up at me, his eyes tinged with pink.

"I don't know," he says nervously. "Sorry. I was gonna do a whole speech, but I—"

"Stop it," I say softly, stepping closer. "I love it. Just tell me."

"You make my life better, Em," he says. "I cursed the years we spent apart, but you were right. They weren't wasted. Love is never wasted. It justifies itself—it's its own reason for being. And loving, and being loved by you, is the best thing about my life. Has been for years, even before we finally got together. And I hope you know now that you never need to earn it. Not from me."

I swallow, and he wraps his arms around me, the book pressing gently against my back.

"I spent months wrestling with this stupid arch for a client," he murmurs into my hair, "and I couldn't get it right. I realized it's because I didn't know how to make it feel true. Because I don't know how to talk about love if it's not about you."

"Kier," I say, looking up at him, the tears spilling over my cheeks. "*Ijekayyatik.*" *I love you.*

"I love you, too," he says back, kissing me. "I was going to take you out for dinner—"

"Can you stop taunting me with dinner and just *ask* me already?" I say, laughing, our faces pressed together. "I don't need dinner. I want this. I want you."

"Em." He swallows, pressing his forehead against mine. "I love you. I've always loved you. I want to spend the rest of my life loving you. Our souls belong together; I've known that for years before I could admit it to myself. Maybe since the first time I saw you. Will you—will you marry me? Will you be my mate?"

"Yes, yes," I say, kissing his face, the broad, blunt cheekbones, the bridge of his nose. I feel the tears spilling over my cheeks, taste the salt as they come between our faces, as he claims my mouth.

"Yes, I will," I whisper, pulling away. "*Kiyyuni.*"

"*Kiyyuni.*"

WANT A SPICY BONUS SCENE?

See Kieran and Emerson cement their mate bond in the scene just after this epilogue ends. To receive the spicy bonus scene, sign up at **rowan.lol/ihor-bonus** or scan the QR code below.

I send one email a month with writing and publication updates. You can unsubscribe at any time.

I love going through the reader's guide questions at the end of my favorite books. I'm under no impression that this book will be read in a book club (though if it is, <u>please</u> invite me—that sounds hilarious), but I wanted to draft some questions for the main way romance books are shared, at least in my life: through recommendations from friends. Here's some questions to talk and laugh over with the romance readers in your life.

1. If ancestral magic could help you regain any lost skill or art, what would you choose?

2. Many people on the Fakaris have their own trades: Seb has his salt business, Kieran is a carpenter, and Saga sells bath and body products alongside her work as a healer. Which of your skill(s) would you turn into a trade if you lived on the Fakaris? We are seeking a shepherd and someone to lead the community choir.

3. Why do you think Emerson is able to heal bone while healers of prior generations, like Helen and Saga, cannot? What do you think this says about the ancestors and their wishes for the islands?

4. Fakari isolationism has led to some interesting pop culture blank spots in their society. What do you think the general reaction of the islanders will be when Maren introduces them to the concept of furries? Bronies?

5. One of the central tensions in this book is the difference in how the older and younger generations look at tradition. What

does honoring the past look like for Saga, Viggo, and the elders? How about for Emerson, Gabe, and Seb?

6. Bed, wed, or make 'em dead: Gabe, Kieran, Heimig the bookshop owner.

7. Are you a Maren, an Emerson, a Thalia, or a Quinn? Which of these heroines would you choose to rob a bank with? To bury a body? Start a business? Who gets the aux on a road trip?

8. Kieran and Emerson have a major argument and spend some time apart before they can finally be in a relationship. Do you think they could have had a healthy relationship without that time apart? If not, why did they need that time, and what did it teach them?

9. Emerson's heat all but disappears about halfway through the book. Is this because in the Salt Islands universe, werewolf heat is similar to human ovulation? Or is it the result of the author's lazy writing?

10. And finally, a suggestion from my husband: "What was the most sluttiest part of this book?"

Fakiri Dictionary

Fakari and English are the two official languages of the islands, and many characters use them interchangeably. I've tried to make most Fakari in the book easy to understand through translation or context cues, but for those who want a reference, here are a few common Fakari words used throughout this book.

Aftnu'kut: good evening
Agaayu (f. *agaaya*, pl. *agaayit*): god
Ayagaayuni: oh my God
Aja: aunt
Ama: mom
Apa: dad
Et: and
Fika: a group of four or five families living together as a pack
Fikarig: a communal home for the families making up a *fika*
Heij: hey
Iija: yes
Dennani: my daughter
Jenge: boy
Kattaka: a hallucinogenic plant, consumed as an herbal drink as part of the rite
Kiyyu: soul or spirit
Kiyyulit: the Northern Lights (literally spirit light)
Kiyyuni: my soul
Kutetkuk: equivalent to 'bon appetit'
Morlaa'kut: good morning
Nagaayu (f. *nagaaya*, pl. *nagaayit*): idiot
Nekka: no

Pakka: pack. Used as an adjective to refer to people belonging to the Fakari people (as in, "she's *pakka*").
Reijna: wise woman; typically a healer, the highest-ranking woman on pack council
Takka: thanks
Takkagaayu: thank God
Tekanni: my son
Trotsayyit: witch hazel
Uikbaane: wolf's bane; used as a curse word in Fakari
Vaare: woman
Welkommit: welcome

A NOTE FROM ROWAN

Thank you so much for reading Kieran and Emerson's story. I wrote this book in the middle of the hardest year of my life, and during those difficult months, the Fakaris were a special place I could retreat to. Although Em and Kier's struggles and experiences are different from my own, they became safe and happy avenues for me to create beauty and work through my experiences. I've been so touched by the early responses to this book, and grateful that this book has meant something to others already.

If you enjoyed *In Her Own Rite*, please consider leaving a review online, or recommending it on social media or to a friend. Word of mouth makes a huge difference for authors and can help other readers find books they love. Great places to leave a review are GoodReads, Amazon, or the retailer where you got this book. But even a carefully placed Post It or creatively decorated cake can do wonders.

Either way, thank you for letting these characters into your life for even just a few hours, and for supporting independent authors.

PRE-ORDER THE NEXT BOOK IN
THE SERIES

Pre-order the next release in this story, *Worth His Salt*, featuring Seb and Maren's love story. You can scan the QR code below to pre-order, and read the first chapter starting on the next page.

WORTH HIS SALT CHAPTER 1
MAREN

The last time I was on a boat, I threw up no less than 13 times.

It was during my college orientation, when I made the mistake of choosing whale watching instead of the food tour for my day trip. My roommate insisted—and at the time, I wasn't in the habit of saying no to people who insisted on things.

In the immortal words of Julie Roberts: *big* mistake. *Huge*. The wind was rough and the waves were choppy, and not only did my tour group not see a single whale, but we all ended up hurling repeatedly over the side of the boat. It was probably Boston Harbor's most colorful day since 1773.

I learned two valuable lessons that day. First: *always* choose the food tour, and second: never let someone pressure you onto a boat. Those lessons have served me well in the eight years since, and I can't help but wonder now—as the ferry rocks back and forth so strongly I worry about a repeat incident—whether I could have arranged for an island-hopper instead.

The answer is no, of course. The Fakari Islands are hard enough to get to as-is.

First I had to book a last-minute flight from New York to

Halifax, then take a six hour bus to the northern tip of Nova Scotia. The bus ran so late that I nearly missed the ferry, and since it only runs three times a week, I did *not* have the luxury. After some extensive pleading and flattery, I was let on last, sweaty and exhausted just in time for a twelve hour boat ride.

All this just to visit Halssel, the only one of the islands that's actually open to visitors. Which is to say: my plan B.

The original plan—scoring a meeting with Saroan Salts' owner on Saroe, the biggest of the Fakaris—fell through after a dozen unanswered emails and phone calls. Which felt okay when I had the luxury of time; after all, you can wear anybody down if you try hard enough. But now...

I swallow as the memory from two nights ago comes back to me. Let's just say there's a reason I needed to get as far away from my real life as possible.

The ferry lurches as it meets a rough wave, and my hands clasp the side of the boat so hard my knuckles go pale. Behind me, I hear a few older women gasp as a splash of seawater sprays onto the deck. As the anxiety starts to coil in my chest, I take a deep breath and reach into my pocket for my hand cream, unscrewing the cap and squeezing some out into my palm. As I rub it over the fronts and backs of my hands, the familiar scent of lavender and witch hazel hits my nostrils.

Breathe in, two, three, four, I think, closing my eyes. *Out, two, three, four...*

I can do this, I tell myself. I'll write the story, get the job at Puur, and my life will be back on track. No one needs to know what happened in the parking lot.

My stomach is finally starting to settle when I hear another commotion from the deck. I open my eyes to see a group of tourists crowding at the front of the boat and follow their gaze. Up ahead, the first of the islands is coming into view in the distance.

Oh. *Woah.*

The shape is instantly recognizable: the mountain in the back and cliffs on either side, with a colorful harbor nestled in front. The buildings around the harbor are far away enough that they look like robin's eggs, painted in deep reds and bright blues and yellows. You can just start to make out the wooden stilts that keep some of the shops on the dock above the water.

I raise my chin, trying to catch a glimpse of the other islands. In the mist of the morning you can only clearly see Halssel, but I make out the shadows of a few of the others—Westel, Oester, and Saroe—in the far distance, hovering like ghosts in the mist. Just then, the ferry lurches again, and an older woman appears beside me, grasping for the boat's edge.

"Sea sick?" I ask.

She nods grimly. "I'm not much of a boat person."

"Me, either." I laugh uneasily as we hit another wave. "How long are you on Halssel for?"

"Just a few days. My wife has wanted to visit the Fakaris for years, and I finally arranged it for our anniversary. You?"

I glance down at the lilac carry-on suitcase I've brought with me, with my giant purse resting on top.

"A week. Maybe eight or nine days, max."

"A *week?*" Her eyebrows shoot up. "There's not much to do, is there? What do you have planned?"

"I'm traveling for work," I say. *Sort of. Basically.*

"I see."

"Actually, between you and me, I'm hoping to be let onto Saroe."

She makes a face like Robert DeNiro—eyebrows raised, mouth downturned, nodding slowly like I'm an idiot.

"Well," she says diplomatically. "Good luck. I don't think anyone's been to the other islands since the nineties."

"Yep! I'm hoping they'll make an exception."

I jump as we hear a loud grinding sound coming from the floor below us, and look up to see the ferry driver pulling on the brake as we near the harbor. As the boat slows towards the dock, my eye catches a sign off of the main entrance to the harbor: *Welkommitet Fakarieilat.* Welcome to the Fakari Islands.

I feel my heartbeat quicken to a patter. This is real. It's actually happening.

The ferry comes to a complete halt, and the gate in front lowers onto the dock so we can disembark. As the older couples around me begin to get off, I hoist my heavy brown purse over one shoulder.

"Happy anniversary!" I call to the woman, who's grabbed the hand of another lady wearing a matching knit cap. She waves politely and mutters something to her wife, probably along the lines of *that girl is gonna need a miracle.*

She's not wrong. But luckily, I'm used to having to make my own miracles.

I turn to the docks and take a deep breath. I try to take note of all of it: the iron waves crashing against the rocks of the shore. The early May sun catching the spray. The smell of salt in the air. Pulling the little suitcase behind me, I step onto the dock and start to worm my way through the other tourists. Although we're the only ferry of the morning, the market is already humming with energy. Shopkeepers are preparing their stalls for the new visitors, and I can see a woman setting up tables outside of a small cafe. To the left is a gravel road leading up to the cliffs, with little red cabins nestled alongside.

I follow the main street forward, looking for the storefront I've all but memorized. Around me, a handful of tourists are admiring traditional Fakari goods—hand-knit sweaters with intricate patterns, thick wool blankets, and hand-thrown pottery being sold out of wooden stalls parked before traditional brick-and-mortar stores. I see a man selling dried fish, and a woman my mom's age organizing jars and sachets of herbs under a sign for Moon Lake Apothecary. And there, at the end of the market street, I finally see what I've come here to find: Saroan Salts.

The stall is smaller and a little less elaborate than the ones around it. Splayed across its tables are jars upon jars of different kinds of sea salt in different shades. An older couple in matching yellow raincoats is admiring the goods, the woman examining jars one by one as her husband takes a moment to sample some salt with bread and olive oil.

Behind the booth are two young men, both tall and broad-shouldered. They share the same olive-toned skin and broad, blunt features that I recognize as uniquely Fakari:; features which the addition of my mom's genes have rounded out in my own face. The one in front seems slightly older, sporting dark stubble and thick black hair. The other one has curly, wind-tousled hair and an open, friendly face. He disappears into the brick-and-mortar store behind the stall as I get closer.

I shove my nerves down as far as they can go, and walk towards the stall with my shoulders back, doing my best to project confidence.

"Morlaa'kut," I say to the tall one. The words feel awkward and foreign in my mouth, but I give what I hope is a winning smile.

He looks up at me, his eyes critical.

"Good morning," he says dryly—in English. "Welcome to the Halssel."

"Thanks so much! It's my first time here. Do you work for Saroan Salts?"

He looks pointedly at the glass jars he's leaning over to put on display, and I follow his gaze. Each jar sports the same teal-and-cream label, with the Saroan Salt logo displayed in the middle above the product name: *Traditional sea salt. Smoked salt. Samphire salt.*

"Oh, of course you do, sorry! I've been up most of the night on the ferry." I laugh, but he doesn't crack a smile. Instead he stands up straight, crossing his arms in front of him.

"How can I help you?"

"I'm looking for Mr. Greenleaf, the company's owner. We've been emailing for months."

"Have you?" His tone is challenging, and I instinctively feel my smile tighten.

"Yes. I'm here about a meeting for Puur, the wellness brand."

"Did he agree to see you?"

"Well—"

"Hey, Seb?" the other man asks, stepping out from the storefront. "We're low on the rosemary salt. Do you remember if Finn packed any this morning?"

"Gimme a second."

"Wait. You're—*you're* Seb Greenleaf?" My eyes slide over him again, taking in his broad frame and the faded leather jacket he's wearing over a flannel shirt. He can't be much older than 30. Based on my research on the company, I'd been expecting someone closer to my mom's age.

I feel my cheeks grow warm. I hate being unprepared. What I hate more? Being caught in a half-lie.

"Mr. Greenleaf, I've been trying to reach you for months," I say quickly, tumbling into my sales pitch. "My name is Maren Holt, and I work for Elspeth Waters at Puur. Well, sort of, but I'm here on behalf of Puur. They're—*we're*—really interested in selling traditional Fakari salt through the online store and pop-up locations. Puur is a thriving wellness brand—"

"Not interested," he says, turning away to lift a box of salts from the shelves behind him. He hands it to the other man and gives a nod towards the storefront, where the worker disappears with the box.

"I... but Mr. Greenleaf."

"It's Seb."

"...*Seb*, this would bring Fakari salt to a whole new demographic. The magazine is ready to dedicate an entire cover story to this, and set up a generous arrangement."

"I saw your emails. We're not interested."

"I…" I stop, flustered. "Has someone else already reached out to you? Someone from Goop? Or Naturi?" If that's true, my one shot is over. Elspeth was clear: she needs the exclusive on the next big thing. If another brand has gotten here first, she'll have to scrap the story—and my job opportunity with it.

"No, I'm just not interested."

"Well, why not?"

"We don't do business with mainlanders."

The irritation in his voice catches me off-guard, and I feel the edge of anger rising in my gut. Before I can suppress it, I snap, "What do you call this then?" and gesture at the market around us.

Seb looks up. I can see his face a little better now. Strong jaw, the edges of his facial hair just a little messy. Broad, strong features and big, dark eyes, where I can see the pupils are ringed with amber.

For a moment, I feel something in me still. He feels familiar somehow, as though I've met him before. The world around me goes soft as I try to figure out what it is. And then in a flash it's over, and the sounds of the market come back to hit me in full force.

"This is a *market*… for *tourists*," he says slowly, like I'm stupid. He starts arranging the glass jars before him again. "We focus on small trading and hospitality. Not selling out to magazines that peddle vagina candles and jade eggs to bored, rich housewives. Now, if you want to buy some salt, let me know. Otherwise, get out of my way."

My indignation hits me so hard that it takes everything in my body not to snap, *Okay, well fuck you!* I bring my fingers to the bridge of my nose, and the smell of my hand cream gives me just enough calm to make myself intelligible.

"*Please*," I say. "Think about this for a moment. This deal could be life-changing for everyone at Saroan Salts. Elspeth is ready to make a generous offer for exclusive trading rights. It's a massive influx of money that could do a lot for your company."

He turns to grab a crate from the table behind him, and I start to talk faster.

"I've read about you. I know you're trying to bring back the old Fakari way of harvesting salt. That's *exactly* why this deal could be so good for you. The money could fund a change that would impact your business for generations."

"Look, I'm *not interested*," he says, setting a crate of soaps down with force. As he crosses the stall to pick up another box, I notice he steps with a limp. I bring my eyes back up to his face.

"So tell me why not," I say.

"I don't need to explain myself to you."

"Well, I'm not leaving until I get a satisfactory answer, so it might be in your best interest to try."

He rolls his eyes. "Typical," he mutters under his breath.

"What's that supposed to mean?"

"Your behavior. It's typical. A great example of why we don't make agreements with mainlanders."

"And what if I'm not a mainlander?"

He gives me a sardonic look, his eyes meeting mine and then very deliberately dropping down. I suddenly become hyper-aware of my appearance—cute outfit obscured by my oversized green coat, cheeks flushed with the fresh morning air, curls probably having crossed the line from 'adorably windswept' to 'tumble-weed' on the ferry ride over. His gaze is deliberately mocking as he rakes it over my body, and for a moment I'm reminded of the way I felt in middle school gym, when the popular guys jeered at me as I ran by and my thighs jiggled. That was back when I still saw my generous curves and soft, rounded body as a weakness. I've fought long and hard to love myself—my big legs, wide hips, and soft stomach—and I'll be damned if some dumb salt trader tries to make me feel less-than.

Defiant, I cross my arms and raise my chin, daring him to mock me as he finally meets my eyes.

"And what if I'm a horse?" he asks.

"Ex*cuse* me?"

"Nothing. Just that you couldn't reek more of the mainland if you'd tried."

"Excuse *you!*" I snap. "You don't even know me."

"You're right, I don't. But I know the islands, and you're not from here." He turns from me as though our conversation was over. *The hell it is.*

"My last name's Winterwood," I say, so loudly that I see the heads of the elderly couple snap up from the corner of her eye.

Seb turns around to face me.

"What?"

"Maren Holt *Winterwood*. My dad was from Saroe, the big island."

I've surprised him now, I can tell. His eyes take me in again, but this time I see no trace of mockery—just genuine confusion. I watch him register my features, taking stock of my full lips, strong brow, and the wide cheekbones hidden beneath my round cheeks. Finally, he brings his gaze to my eyes with intensity, as though searching for something.

"You're David's kid," he says finally.

"Yeah, I am." It's weird hearing my dad's name on his lips, and my voice betrays my surprise. "Wait, did you know him?"

"Gabe?" Seb calls over his shoulder, ignoring the question.

The other stall worker ducks his head out from the door to the store behind them. "Yeah? What's up?"

Seb turns around and jerks his thumb to me.

"Your cousin's here."

ACKNOWLEDGMENTS

From the bottom of my heart, I want to thank the people who supported me in bringing this book to life. Thank you to Adelaide, Boo, Arnica, and Linda for reading this book and discussing these characters and plot beats with me in greater depth than any friend could be expected to do. Thank you also to A and E for being some of the first readers of this book. Em and Kieran's story is better for your input.

Special thanks to Sean Simmons (Vimesart) and Grace (Zaeyos) for bringing these characters to life through your artistic gifts, as well as to Rachael Ward (Cartography Bird) for your beautiful map skills. And thank you especially to Heather Guerre, whose book *Cold Hearted* introduced me to shifter romance that is community-centered and spotlights characters with mental health struggles. Your work has inspired me, and I will continue to recommend it to literally everyone I know (or, at least the people who are allowed to know I read wolf smut).

Finally, thanks to readers of romance for being so freaking funny, smart, creative, and passionate. I love how much you love this genre, and I hope you enjoyed this book.

ABOUT THE AUTHOR

Rowan writes romance novels featuring kick-ass heroines and couples who find wholeness and healing on the path to love. As you may have already guessed, her favorite things include found family, gorgeous artisanal and homemade goods, and really good sea salt.

She lives with her husband on two continents, and is mentally camping out on a fictional set of islands between them. If you want to hear more from her, listen to her wildly unprofessional romance book podcast, *Weak Knees*, at your own risk.

www.rowanwilder.com

Instagram: @rowanwilderromance
Spotify: **Weak Knees**